Book 2
of
The Dimension Guardian Series

Dimension Guardian
The Realm of Darkness
Blind Ambitions

K.J. Amidon

THE
AMIVERSE
www.the-amiverse.com

Website: www.kjamidon.com

Published by K.J. Amidon

ISBN: 978-0-9832280-1-1

1st Edition © 2014
2nd Edition © 2021

Cover art by K.J. Amidon

Printed in the United States of America

Dedicated to:

My 14-year-old self

J & R

Table of Contents

Chapter One

Even before the abandoned palace could be spotted among the trees, the dark energy emanating from its ruins was overpowering. Acurala Kage's horse tossed his head, snorting at the foreboding aura. When his horse gave a high whinny and reared in protest of advancing further, Acurala dismounted. His temporary valet, Tauren, had a far more difficult time calming and dismounting his own horse, not as skilled an equestrian as the demon lord.

Acurala left his horse at a tree and walked the remaining distance to the palace, following the pulsing blue light emanating from a dilapidated tower window.

Tauren steeled his resolve and trailed Acurala up the spiraling staircase. The magic grew darker the closer they drew to the door. The heaviness of the air mixed with the stench of blood was enough to turn Tauren's stomach while Acurala appeared unfazed.

He easily opened the door, though he did not enter immediately, knowing there was a very precise ritual taking place within that could not be interrupted.

A figure sat in the middle of the bare, circular room, shrouded in a black robe that was far too large. Lining the walls were buckets of various sizes, the thick, red contents having dripped over the sides as rivulets crept toward the figure, disappearing under the oversized robe. The perfectly-spaced trails of stained stone glistened with the last droplets of blood, the ritual nearing completion.

"Be sure not to step on anyone," the powerful voice warned. Even though the back of the figure was facing the door, the voice emanated directly from the walls, causing the rock and mortar to shudder.

Acurala smirked.

"I don't believe it's possible," he said, scanning the trails of blood. "Did you get enough?"

"No. I'm missing something."

"Missing something?" Acurala repeated, surprised. He saw the streams of blood drying, leading from the figure to each container where painted sigils pulsed with magic, thrumming like a steady heartbeat. He could not immediately determine what had gone amiss with the ritual.

"You may approach."

Acurala stepped forward, though Tauren refused to enter the room, trembling in the doorway as the sickening magic overwhelmed him.

"I am sure I read the ritual correctly," Acurala mused, walking around the room to face the seated figure.

"I'm sure you did as well," the hooded man said. "Yet, I am still missing most of my powers. It's everything I can do to be sitting here for this ritual. I'm weaker than I was two weeks ago."

Acurala understood the level of irritation based on the way the figure gripped and rolled the smooth black stone, the flares of green and red in the rock facets barely visible in the dim pulsing magic of the sigils. The hand was skinned, the red muscles soaked with blood and the bone visible beneath the ligaments as they shifted around the stone in a near-frantic motion.

"How is the ritual this stunted?" Acurala grumbled, once again casting his gaze around the room.

"I should think that would be obvious," the figure sneered. "The imbecile I have my soul trapped in has extra power limiters to bind me. My magic remains locked away in that pathetic excuse for a vessel. I may have all the sacrifices and the correct ritual for manifesting my own form, but that is pointless if I do not have the power to accurately perform it."

"Seems that you have the muscles and joints," Acurala noted, nodding to the hand rhythmically gripping and moving the stone, testing muscle control and coordination.

The other flayed hand brushed back the hood, revealing the figure's face. His nose and ears were mere hallows and his teeth were exposed, clenched tight. His golden eyes were large orbs in their sockets, unblinking for lack of eyelids. Under the eyes, the muscles of his cheeks were marked with three dark lines and his neck had a solid band of black markings over the sinews.

"The muscles and joints mean nothing if I bleed out because I have no *skin*," he snarled. His teeth did not open or close, as he could not yet speak through the new form—only through the magic circling the room. "I need more magic from my vessel."

"Can you just take it?" Acurala asked.

"No, I need you to take it for me," Yokouro said. "I cannot leave this place, yet."

"That's what you get for getting yourself killed," Acurala jeered. "There is no rush, you know. The Guardians you're so interested in aren't going to be competing in the tournament for another two months."

"Two months is no time at all," he said. "There is much we must prepare for in that time. But I can't do anything until I can walk without bleeding out."

"Having a physical form will be a hindrance," Acurala warned. "While this spell will animate a new flesh-and-blood body, it will require a lot of magic to keep it from falling apart. You might not have the power or concentration for your draining bewitchments."

"I will if you remove a power limiter from my vessel," Yokouro grumbled. "Besides, I'm going to need more than hex beasts and draining bewitchments. Why do you think I brought you back?"

"My brother would be a better choice," Acurala reminded him. "I'm still quite limited myself."

"I've already sent word to your brother. I'd prefer to keep him in the shadows as much as possible, though. I'm sure you understand."

Acurala chuckled knowingly. "I do."

At the door, Tauren let out a shaky breath, his wide eyes leaving no question about his reaction to the conversation. Acurala eyed the valet suspiciously, realizing the young demon was not fit to be near Yokouro and his plans if the mere mention of his older brother was enough to frighten him.

"Also, I doubt that your brother would approve of burning down a stadium like I did forty years ago," Yokouro added, drawing Acurala's attention again.

"It's not really his style."

"Therefore, I don't want you to be surprised if I ask *you* to do some of the things that he would not approve."

Acurala bowed his head shallowly. "You brought me back, Yokouro. It would be my pleasure to serve however I am able."

"I want to make myself known to Team Dalton."

"So soon?"

"Yes," he insisted. "But, before I can do that, I must find a way to manifest some skin." He lifted his hand to prove his point. "Do you think you can discreetly remove a power limiter from my vessel? If he knows what you've done, he'll run to Vestera for help and we can't afford either of them to know what we're doing this early in the game."

"I'm sure I can manage."

With another bow of his head, Acurala left the room, his flustered and worried valet following.

"Shall I join you, my lord?"

"No," Acurala said, knowing that if Tauren could not stomach the conversation with Yokouro, he certainly could not handle what Acurala planned to do to his vessel. "I will do this alone."

As Acurala rode in one direction, Tauren turned his horse and went another, using well-worn routes through the forests of the Demon Realm to another palace, far more grand and alive with activity. As night descended in the land, he could see a small gathering of lords and ladies through the illuminated ballroom windows. Tauren dismounted, nodding to the valets that rushed to take his horse as he walked along the side of the palace, searching among the richly-clad nobles in the ballroom for the demon he sought. He had to duck out of sight as the socializing Demon Realm nobility moved, waiting a few breaths before peering up again trying to catch the attention of a specific demon.

Finally, piercing hazel eyes met his.

As the demon within excused himself, Tauren slipped into the shadows of the meticulously manicured palace gardens, trying not to fidget nervously or jump at every out-of-place noise. More than his nervousness about the conversation he had overheard, Tauren was worried the news he was about to deliver would be ill-received.

When the Old Blood Lord rounded the corner of the palace, Tauren instinctively dropped his head, wringing his hands in front of him.

"What have you learned?"

"Lord Yokouro is very close to manifesting a full physical form," Tauren relayed. "He seemed...frustrated. He could not yet create skin." He nearly choked on the words, the horrifying image of the tower room burned into his mind.

The lord closed his eyes and let out a disappointed sigh.

"I knew he would get too impatient."

"He sent Lord Acurala out to remove a power limiter from Lord Yokouro's vessel so he may have more access to his magic," Tauren continued, his eyes still averted. "Because he wishes to reveal himself to the Guardians. He...he said he wants Lord Acurala to do the things that Lord Juki would likely protest."

"Did Acurala agree?"

Tauren nodded solemnly. "Yes, my lord. He agreed."

The demon lord did not show a reaction, but Tauren knew that he was displeased. He could feel it with the way static sparked over his skin and the air around them became oppressively hot.

"Very well," he finally said, turning his bright hazel eyes onto Tauren, ignoring the valet's obvious flinch. "You are dismissed from trailing Acurala, Tauren. We'll start watching over the

Guardians personally." The lord turned away from the relieved valet, grumbling under his breath, "we can't have Yokouro killing them too soon."

Chapter Two

Dalton Teban walked up the path to his house after paying the taxi driver, feeling a sense of relief flood through him at finally returning home.

As he approached the front porch step, the door flung open and his daughter scrambled out to greet him, causing the smile on Dalton's face to widen. Frieda, Dalton's wife, stood on the porch, grinning as she watched their daughter throw herself into her father's arms.

"Dad!!!" Theresa squealed. Dalton scooped her up, hugging her tightly as she squirmed and giggled. It took him several long moments before he found the strength to pull away, feeling his heart soar at being with his family again, his prior anxiety and stress forgotten. Carrying Theresa, he climbed the stairs toward his wife, leaning over to kiss her tenderly.

"Welcome home," Frieda murmured, her own shoulders relaxing in relief at his return. "Come in out of this chill and tell us all about the tournament."

She pulled her husband and daughter inside, closing the door securely behind them, throwing a quick look outside before she locked the door.

"I saw you win, Dad!" Theresa announced loudly, clinging to Dalton. "You totally beat them!" Dalton laughed and turned to his wife.

"Did you really let her watch it?" he asked, worried, but far too happy at seeing his family again to be upset. Frieda chuckled brokenly.

"She insisted on watching the post-tournament coverage with me. She didn't see the full fights."

"Did you?" he asked.

Frieda nodded, her eyes conflicted. Dalton gently rubbed her shoulder and kissed her again. While he knew they would have to talk about how Frieda felt watching the tournament, Theresa's excited reenactment of one of the fights diverted his attention.

"Theresa, come here," he said gently, sitting on the couch and pulling her into a hug. "Sweetie, the tournament is too scary for you to be watching, okay? I don't want you to get nightmares."

"I know what you do, Dad. I learn about it in school," she defended. "Mom said you wouldn't want me seeing you get hurt, but I knew that you would win. No matter how hurt you got, I knew that you would kick their butts!"

Dalton heaved a sigh, not wanting to argue with his daughter, glancing at his wife as he wrapped his arms around Theresa. Frieda shared a knowing look with her husband. Their daughter may have learned what most of the public knew about the Guardians, but she did not yet know the darker side of Dalton's job. Frieda had thought that she knew what being a Guardian meant when she had first started dating Dalton, but she came to realize that the job was far darker and more violent than she had originally heard. They both knew Theresa would eventually learn about the violent reputation of Guardians but they had done their best to ensure she did not learn of it too soon.

Dalton took another deep breath and pulled away from his daughter, smiling.

"What do you say we all go out for dinner tonight to celebrate me coming home?"

The Teban family went to a restaurant they frequented and talked about what Dalton had missed while training and competing in the Guardian Tournament. He told a few of his own stories, but there was little he could tell them without upsetting or scaring his family. He was also still processing everything that had occurred around the tournament and how much more dangerous his mission had become with the powerful demon lurking in the shadows. Even as he tried to fascinate Theresa with the tamer stories, Frieda could hear the strain in her husband's voice that he only ever had on particularly difficult cases.

Theresa was the biggest fan of Team Dalton and was already explaining how her father would win the entire tournament. Frieda joked along, but whenever she caught Dalton's eyes, she could see his worry. She was wary about the assignment, and her husband's obvious apprehension was doing nothing to ease her concern.

After dinner, Theresa begged her parents to stay up late and watch a movie but, with the excitement of the day, she was only able to stay awake for the first fifteen minutes before Dalton carried her upstairs and tucked her into bed.

Frieda was filing the movie away on the shelf and tidying up the living room when he returned downstairs.

"Just leave it for now," he said.

"It will only take a moment," she assured, reaching for the water glasses on the coffee table.

Dalton wrapped his arms around her waist before she could reach the cups, tipping them both sideways until they were sprawled on the couch. Frieda let out a yelp before laughing and wrapping her arms around Dalton, resting her head against his shoulder as they settled into a more comfortable position.

"I really missed you."

"I missed you, too," he whispered, kissing her temple.

"I was worried about you," Frieda admitted, closing her eyes.

Dalton's body tensed.

"I didn't know they had opened the tournament to the public, or that they would be broadcasting it," he said. "I'm sorry you had to see all that."

"What do you mean you didn't know?"

"No one told me," he said. "Grandfather was worried I would try to stop the tournament."

"*He* should stop it," she huffed, tightening her arms around Dalton.

They fell into comfortable silence, holding one another, reveling in the closeness. Despite the gentle embrace, Dalton did not completely relax.

"...what did you think?" he finally murmured. "About the tournament?"

"...it was...scary," she said. "But exhilarating. I won't lie, I was certainly cheering at the television when you won."

He laughed, pressing another kiss to her head. She turned, propping herself up to face him.

"A lot happened outside the tournament, didn't it?" she asked. He averted his eyes. "Dalton," she placed a hand against the side of his face, "something is bothering you. You only get that look on your face during big missions. What is it?"

He traced the edge of her jaw with his finger, smiling tiredly.

"I don't want you to worry."

"Well, it's too late for *that*," she teased. She pecked a kiss on his lips. "I can see the stress on your face. And if the DPC needs to call in two of the best Guardians in history to help you, something is really wrong."

"There seems to be a lot the DPC is reluctant to tell me," he admitted. "Keito and Hanyi say that this is the same man— demon—who caused the Tournament Slaughter forty years ago."

Frieda froze.

"The same demon?" she whispered. "Does that mean—"

"I've gone after demons before," he assured. "And I'm being very careful."

"Have you seen him?"

"No...not exactly," Dalton admitted. "Just a shaky video. He's..." He hesitated, unsure if he wanted to tell his wife about the incorporeal demon or the bone beast they had fought. "He's a bit of a mystery," he finally said. "But this is also the demon that broke the seal on the realms. He's powerful and those who know about him are being suspiciously secretive." He closed his eyes for a second before shaking his head. "I'm just worried that this is even bigger. That there's some conspiracy to keep me in the dark. This demon...seems his network is deeply rooted."

"What are you going to do?"

Dalton took a deep breath, his eyes distant as he thought.

"Do what I've always done," he finally said. "I've dealt with major criminals in the past. I know that this is bigger than anything I've dealt with before but I think that, if I stay with the team and keep doing my research, I should be able to handle it." His arms settled securely around his wife. "And then the tournament can be halted and we can go back to our normal lives."

Frieda smiled and kissed him once more.

"I think our normal might be vastly different from other people."

"Well, who wants to be like *those* boring people?"

~/\~

Mitoki's head was foggy when he woke the first morning after returning home. After parting ways with the others of Team Dalton, he had detoured to the Dimension Protection Council complex and gone into the archive office, searching for anything related to what little information he had been given about the demon they were pursuing. He had had every intention to look over the files he had checked out when he got home, but exhaustion had overtaken him. He was soon collapsed in bed, dead to the world.

He glanced at his bedside clock, blinking at the numbers, surprised that he was awake so early. Knowing that the other members of his house were not yet awake, he carefully extracted himself from the sheets and slipped into the bathroom for a shower.

Refreshed after a shower and some clean clothes, he went to his desk to confront the stack of files he had checked out of the archives.

The first file he read was related to the attack at the Mount of Marconian. He had found many files explaining the mark that had been left on the tourists' faces, but most of the files were locked in Deep Archives and he would have to petition to research in the restricted area, so he took the only file that was not restricted.

Another string of murders had occurred forty-three years previous and the perpetrators painted the same mark on their own faces with blood when they went out to kill. The group was caught and tried, and each member was sentenced to death. Their reason for killing was to perform a ritual in an attempt to awaken the demon who would cleanse the human race.

Kyan's words about demons being gods meant to pass judgment on humans echoed in his mind. Even though Keito had assured them it was an extremist group of thought, Mitoki was surprised the group had believed it enough to hunt down victims for sacrifice. Figuring the mark was just a design the criminals had adopted to emulate the mass-murdering demon they were after, Mitoki was about to brush the old case aside, rather than consider it a connection to the mass-murdering demon.

However, when he looked at the Guardians who had been assigned to the murderous cult, he saw two extremely familiar names—Keito DeVero and Hanyi Treneke.

With a heavy sigh, Mitoki looked at another stack of files he had brought home, hesitant to read through them. It felt intrusive to be looking up the cases filed by the members of Team Keito a month before the Tournament Slaughter, but he wanted to know what the Guardians had been doing on the case before the massacre.

He started at the earliest date he could, leafing through two unrelated files before opening the third, a case that had been reported by Hector, Hanyi's older brother.

The frustrated language in the case report irked him.

"The suspect evaded capture yet again…"

"DeVero pursued the suspect but did not return. He was found the following day with a shattered arm and multiple lacerations to his back and neck…"

"The kidnapped child in question was found skinned and hanging by her feet in the back of the butcher shop…"

Mitoki barely had the stomach to look at the pictures of the crime scene. He was surprised to see that, on the wall next to where the child was hanging, there was a message scrawled in blood.

Start counting.

Mitoki quickly found the follow-up file, which had been submitted by Sadee, the female member of Team Keito, with Keito's name as the advisor on the case.

"The butcher shop where the child in case #2565366 was found has been repeatedly vandalized and one pig has been removed each day for the past five days…"

"Security detail with DeVero did not provide any information. Upon hearing a noise at the back of the building, DeVero and I were distracted and the suspect removed the pig before we returned…"

The note on the file was that, at the time the girl was found, there were twenty-seven pigs in the butcher shop and of those, seven were stolen.

Mitoki grabbed another file written by Keito.

"My team has now been directly threatened. Kent woke to find one of the stolen pigs in her bed with the number eighteen carved into the meat. Her two dogs and cat were also slaughtered in her living room..."

"I am submitting immediate requests to the Elders to suspend the Guardian Tournament that is to occur in eighteen days. The connection between the numbers and the days to the tournament is too precise..."

Mitoki's wide eyes scanned the words in the report multiple times, the weight of their meaning settling heavily in his chest. The members of Team Keito knew that the massacre was going to take place. It was obvious that they did not know to what extent they would be attacked, but they had made the connection with the clues the demon was leaving.

Mitoki reached for the next file, which was submitted by all members of Team Keito.

The lavish Dimension Protection Council letterhead on the first page startled him.

"Requests for the suspension of the Guardian Tournament have been denied due to Code 9952 of the Dimension Protection Council Book of Inter-Realmal Relations: Dimension of Demons. No further requests for such suspension will be acknowledged."

Mitoki stared at the code for several moments before scrambling to his bookshelf, scanning his copies of the Dimension Protection Council books for the one he wanted. Flipping through the pages as he walked back to his desk, he continued to mutter the code number, anxious to find it.

"Code 9952..." he murmured one last time as he ran his finger down the page, sitting at his desk.

"9952: Old Blood Lords of the Dimension of Demons hold power to overthrow any requests processed through the Dimension Protection Council that are submitted by Guardians of the Demon Dimension and/or requests that could impact the dealings of the social hierarchy of the Dimension of Demons, or threaten the political power of the ruling Old Blood Lords of the Dimension of Demons."

Mitoki stared at the code, reading it over and over again, trying to figure out exactly what the text meant and how the code had been able to deny Keito's request to suspend the tournament. Mitoki wished he had asked Keito more about Old Blood Lords when they were in the Beast Realm. Apart from knowing they were the highest rung on the Demon Realm's social ladder, he had no idea how they could wield enough power to overrun decisions in the Dimension Protection Council.

A creak in his room told him that someone was walking on his hardwood floor. He whirled around, startled. When his eyes rested on the woman with blonde hair and green eyes standing by the foot of his bed, trying not to sneak up on him, he relaxed and a smile spread over his face. He closed the file and book, not wanting her to accidentally see what he had been researching.

"I'm sorry, I didn't hear you come in," he said, turning his chair.

She leapt forward with a smile and threw her arms around his neck, sitting on his lap.

"When I came home last night you were already sound asleep," she said into his neck.

"Why didn't you just climb into bed?" he asked. "You didn't have to sleep in the other room. I doubt you would have woken me," he laughed, pulling away from the hug to look at his fiancée, tenderly tucking her bed-mussed hair behind her ear.

"I knew you would be exhausted. I didn't want to bother you," Rebecca said. "I saw the coverage of the tournament. I knew that had to be draining."

"You shouldn't have watched that," he muttered.

"Why not?"

"Because...it's embarrassing."

"How is it embarrassing?"

"It sorta felt like a frenzy. We didn't know what the hell we were getting ourselves into. Plus, I'm the weakest of the team. I don't really want people, especially you, seeing me struggle."

"You looked like you were holding your own pretty damn well to me," Rebecca said. "Just because you think you're not the strongest on Team Dalton doesn't mean you're weak. You're still the top-ranked Guardian in the realm."

"I still had my ass handed to me a bit," he chuckled brokenly.

"No, you didn't," she said. He smiled and leaned forward, pecking a kiss on her lips before taking her hand in his, running their fingers together.

~/\~

The Treneke Wolf Tribe was slowly making the trek to their autumn hunting grounds, taking their time to bask in the warm sun as the day passed lazily. The wolves were still on alert after their alpha had been attacked and abducted. While they trusted Hanyi when he told them that the bone beast was no longer a threat, most still felt ill at ease, knowing that the case Hanyi had taken was exceptionally dangerous.

Hanyi was desperate to sleep in the heat of the midday sun alongside the others, but he could sense how uneasily the other wolves were resting. Despite appearing asleep, he was carefully sensing how the others of his pack felt. He could feel their apprehension and unease, and though he wanted to attribute the feelings to the residual worry after his capture, he knew the fears ran far deeper. The Treneke Tribe had already lost an alpha to Yokouro and they were worried they were about to lose another.

But he also understood that the fear in the pack was due to how secretive and silent he had been since his rescue. Even Xana was struggling to figure out what was bothering her mate, despite how many times she tried to get the answer out of him.

When dusk caused the temperature to drop and the wolves to rouse from their rested positions, they continued on their path. Xana took up the lead, but continued to throw looks back at her mate, who was walking slowly, his eyes down though he never let his head drop.

Haru trotted up to Hanyi, Hari coming to his other side.

"*Brother, your sons will meet us at the autumn hunting grounds. Maybe once there, it would be best for the pack if you were to go elsewhere. Just until things settle down.*"

Hanyi stopped walking immediately and the tension among the brothers rose. Several of the wolves nearby turned, startled by the sudden change in Hanyi's demeanor.

"*What does that mean?*"

"*We all know you have a lot to worry about with this mission,*" Hari added. "*We just thought it would be best if you did not also have to worry about the pack.*"

"*I'm fine,*" Hanyi growled. "*And walking away from the pack now would make it seem as though I don't care about our family as much as I care about the mission. You know that is not the case.*"

"*We didn't mean it like that,*" Hari assured.

"*We merely thought it would be better for you. Give you time to collect yourself.*"

Hanyi began growling, causing the other wolves around them to shy away. Xana ran to her mate, standing by his side and dropping her head to join the confrontation. Haru and Hari both lowered themselves to the ground, trying to show their submission.

"*You know how dangerous this mission is,*" Hari insisted. "*We're just worried about you.*"

"*Thank you for your concern, but the good of the pack is also something I decide, not you.*"

He curled his lips in a snarl at his brothers as he continued walking forward, shooting a sharp glare at any wolf who looked at him in concern. Xana walked near Hanyi, discreetly scanning the rest of the pack to gauge their reaction to the confrontation.

She could see that Hanyi was barely holding control over the nervous wolves of the Treneke Tribe.

Several more hours of moving and a satisfying hunt later, the tension in Hanyi's body had eased, but not vanished. Xana came over to clean the residual blood from Hanyi's snout but he shied away from her attention.

"*Tell me what you're hiding, Hanyi,*" she whispered.

"*I'm not hiding anything.*"

"*Yes, you are,*" she insisted. "*What is it? Did something else happen with that weird magical creature that you haven't told us?*"

"*No,*" he assured. "*It was destroyed. We're not in danger.*"

"*And we've tracked down the last remnants of the Opalon Pack. So what else is worrying you?*"

Hanyi looked around the other wolves cleaning the last of the deer before he turned and walked away, putting some distance between him and the others. Xana followed obediently, though her own worry began to build.

Staying close enough to the pack to watch when one would draw close, Hanyi turned to Xana.

"*I do not want any of the others to know,*" he whispered. "*But I have heard whispers through other packs that there have been sightings of two demons in the realm.*"

"*Two demons? Not Yokouro specifically?*"

"*No, two more demons. Not Guardians.*"

"*Who, then?*"

"*One said that they made the air so heavy it was impossible to breathe…that their eyes stared through them…that they could feel death all around these demons.*"

Xana's body shuddered.

"*But…doesn't that mean—*"

Hanyi turned quickly to the other wolves, reminding Xana how close they were to the rest of the pack. She hesitated, the apprehension in her belly turning into icy fingers of fear that coiled around her entire body.

"*That's…it can't be.*"

"*I saw one of them when I was captured,*" he whispered. "*They're already involved.*"

"*What are we supposed to do? No one can touch them!*" A worried whine escaped her lips and Hanyi quickly pushed his head to hers, trying to keep her silent so as not to worry the others of the Treneke Tribe.

"*We can't do anything,*" he agreed. "*I suspected they would show up, but it seems as though they're more heavily involved than they were forty years ago. And if that's the case...*" He hesitated. "*I'm just trying to figure out how to prepare our son.*"

"*What do you mean?*"

"*If they get more involved with Yokouro, this mission is going to get far more dangerous. It's possible he'll have to take the position of alpha before we anticipated.*"

Xana's whine was quieter and she pushed her body into Hanyi's, her heart breaking at the thought of what her mate was implying. She wanted to encourage him. She wanted to tell him that he would be able to stand up to the two terrifying demons, but she knew better. She had heard all the stories from forty years previous, and she knew the true terror of the Trade Masters.

She could do nothing more than push her bodyweight into Hanyi and silently share in his fear.

~∧~

"What are you doing awake at this early hour?" Master Genbuki asked when he came across Eclipse sitting in the living room.

"Just working on a case, trying to get it done," Eclipse sighed. He pushed one of the files away on the coffee table, grabbing a few pictures of a crime scene. "I don't know how the hell the Elders expect me to finish thirty-seven cases while competing in the tournament, working this other case, and completing all my work as top-ranked Guardian of the Darkness Realm."

"Maybe if you had applied yourself earlier this year, you wouldn't have to rush," Master Genbuki teased.

"What is *that* supposed to mean?" Eclipse growled. "I've been training for two months. I had just finished up Guardian Testing, then I had to go find those Guardians that went AWOL and then the tournament happened," Eclipse snapped.

"There is no need to be testy. I'm just teasing you," Master Genbuki said, sitting in his chair with his tea, sipping at it quietly as Eclipse set down the pictures and rubbed his forehead.

"I know, I'm sorry."

"Still thinking about what Erik said last night?" Master Genbuki asked. Eclipse nodded slowly.

"I haven't been paying attention to anything happening in Antiqua-Kel, but still, if Erik's meters were picking up those sorts of readings, I should have sensed it." He rubbed his eyes roughly. "It's bothersome that I didn't."

"Do you think it could be that demon you and your team are chasing?" Master Genbuki asked.

"That's what I'm afraid of."

"You should ask Keito about this demon."

Eclipse scoffed. "Believe me, we've tried. He's cryptic as hell."

"Sounds familiar," Master Genbuki jibed.

"I know that this team is supposed to be made of the best of the best, but I feel like we're fighting blind and if the best Guardians in the branch can't figure out what to do about this demon, then we're really in trouble. It's like they're just throwing us at him *hoping* we figure out some way to stop him." Eclipse took a breath and stared distantly at the case files in front of him.

"I've never seen you so unnerved by a demon before," Master Genbuki murmured.

"You should have seen the creature he created," he whispered. "It was not like anything I've seen before. And the draining bewitchments. I looked up how those work and the amount of power this demon would need to accomplish all this would have to be extraordinary...greater than any demon I've ever faced before."

"Has the council spoken to the dragons, yet?"

"They say that the dragons have been silent," Eclipse sighed. "I just find it hard to believe Vestera himself would do nothing against this threat."

"That does seem really strange," Master Genbuki agreed. "Maybe the politics are too complicated. Perhaps there is more political stake in this than you thought."

"All I know is that this demon has some social standing," Eclipse said. "And hell if Keito will go into any further detail."

"Surely he wouldn't keep information from you."

"Oh, yes, he would," Eclipse said adamantly. "I don't know...maybe Dalton can get into archives or something."

"How is it working with Dalton?"

"Fine," Eclipse said. "He's strong. Much stronger than I thought. But he's also pretty down to earth. He's a good team leader."

"Then you're getting along well with your teammates?"

"Yes, I suppose," he said suspiciously, worried what his master would ask next.

"And Mitoki?"

"What about him?"

"What did you tell him?"

"The truth," Eclipse snarled. "I told him I knew what happened to his family. Talked about the serial killer and that I didn't know he didn't know the information."

"Eclipse…"

"Don't," Eclipse growled, standing to leave the room.

"Do you really think you can keep the truth from him?" Master Genbuki asked. "Do you think that's fair to him?"

"Yes," Eclipse snapped. "He's happy now. He has a life and a fiancée in the Realm of Light. I'm going to let him live his life and enjoy it. No reason for me to tell him anything more than I already have."

Eclipse stepped out the front door, walking down the steps of the deck to the street, digging his hands in his pockets as he headed toward downtown, trying to clear his mind. The air was warm and the mugginess had not yet set in, so many people were walking in the early morning hour, enjoying the start of the weekend.

But even as Eclipse tried to clear his head, he was surrounded by conversations and news broadcasts about the Guardian Tournament. All the realms seemed excited to see the tournament in practice again, eager for the next round, debating various predictions about the outcome of the tournament.

Eclipse's anxiety grew.

He normally reveled in getting a challenging case. It allowed him to flex the power that he kept carefully hidden. But there was something foul in the air surrounding this case.

He had never felt so uneasy.

Lost in his worries, he jumped when he felt a sudden jolt of energy, as though he had walked into a cloud of someone's aura. He recognized the energy. He stopped in his tracks, ignoring the indignant snort from the woman who almost ran into his back.

He scanned his surroundings, trying to spot the familiar face.

Glancing across the street, he saw a member of his team, golden eyes focused forward, purposeful as he walked, obviously tailing someone.

Not bothering to wonder what his demon teammate was doing in the Darkness Realm, Eclipse darted across the street to fall into pace behind Keito, trying to mix in with the crowd of people walking behind the demon Guardian. Keito stopped and stared at a window where televisions were showing reports of the Guardian Tournament. Eclipse halted abruptly, trying to loom around a newspaper stand just out of Keito's sight, not wanting to let the demon know he was tailing him.

A man stepped out of the shop where Keito stood, walking down the sidewalk. Keito followed him, his head bent as he fell into step behind the man.

Eclipse also followed.

When the crowd had thinned, Keito quickened his pace. Eclipse was close behind, trying to keep up, nervous about the almost-predatory way Keito followed the man.

Before Eclipse could realize what Keito was doing, the demon Guardian leapt forward, grabbing the man and wrapping one hand around his mouth, yanking him into the nearby alleyway and pinning him against the wall, a small knife in the man's belly. Eclipse hid around the corner, peering over the dumpsters blocking his view.

He did not see Keito's knife, but he saw the man flinch in pain and almost ran into the alley to stop the demon Guardian.

"Don't scream," Keito snarled. He began patting the man's jacket, releasing his mouth.

"K-Keito?"

"Shut up."

"What...what are you—"

"Where is it?" Keito snapped.

"Where is what?" the man groaned, flinching as Keito twisted the blade.

"I really don't want to kill you, Baren," the demon Guardian snarled. "But no one told me I had to keep you alive. Cooperate and I won't put this knife through your heart."

"What do you want?"

"I want to know where the gem is," he snapped. That was when Eclipse understood—much to his relief—that Keito was working a case. "You've pulled some stupid stunts before, but breaking into the DPC vaults, that's a new level of stupid."

"I'm sorry." Baren cringed. "Damn, Keito, what do you care?"

"In case you didn't hear, I'm no longer retired," Keito said. "I took one look at the scene and knew immediately it was you." He leaned forward, digging the knife deeper into Baren's flesh. "So, you're going to answer a few questions for me. What the hell are you doing in the Darkness Realm?"

"Look, I-I tried to straighten out. I really did!" Baren said quickly.

"Doesn't look like that's working out too well for you."

"I wanted to start again, so I left home and came to live here. I know it's not safe with all the lynching, but I keep my limiters on and no one knows."

"Then why are you stealing again, Baren?"

"I got conned into it!" Baren cried, wincing again. "I'm going to bleed out if you keep twisting that knife…"

"Why should I care?" Keito snapped. "Who conned you into it?"

"Some demon."

"Give me a *name*," Keito growled, showing his teeth.

"It doesn't matter!" Baren said, reaching into his pocket and pulling out a pouch. "See? Here's the gem."

"Who were you going to give it to?" Keito asked sharply, plucking the pouch out of the other demon's hand.

"I…I don't remember his name…"

"Think harder," Keito hissed. "Or this knife is going to find a piece of your body that you care about more than your kidney."

"Okay, okay, okay," Baren said rapidly. "I didn't see his face, but he said his name was Dywen."

"Dywen," Keito repeated. "That's all he told you?"

"I swear, that's all he told me," Baren said, his eyes closing tight, shying away from Keito.

"He's the one who conned you into it?"

"N-no…some woman, I think her name was…Geniele?" Baren said, his voice shaking.

"*Geniele*?" Keito snapped. "Don't you know she's under *DeVastes* influence, you moron?!"

"No, I didn't know! I swear!" Baren shook his head almost violently. "You know me, Keito. I run Kage through and through."

"That does not ease my mind *at all*."

"Okay, look. I don't get mixed up with the Old Bloods, you know that," Baren said. "I honestly stole that because she said she would sleep with me if I did. I swear."

"Damn, Baren, is that really all it takes to persuade you?" Keito groaned, rolling his eyes.

"Hey, I have poor character," Baren admitted, gritting his teeth in pain.

Keito was quiet, staring at the other demon before he pulled the knife out of his flesh, raising the dagger between their faces.

"If I find out that you're working with Geniele again, I will come back and kill you. Do I make myself clear?"

"Crystal."

Keito nodded once and backed away.

"Go."

The other demon stumbled into the shadows of the alley and out of sight while Keito pulled the large blue gem out of the pouch, sighing heavily.

"It's already starting..." he whispered.

Chapter Three

Dalton wanted to review the files he had submitted regarding the murder of the tourists in the Beast Realm, but had been denied access to the files every time he requested them. The archive staff claimed it was because the Elders had temporarily locked it before assigning the case to a Guardian, but Dalton knew it was already his case. He was convinced the denial of his requests was a conspiracy to keep him from seeing the video of the cloaked demon again. But he did not stop trying.

"Sorry, Dalton, there's nothing I can do." Paul shook his head, typing away at his computer before turning to the top-ranked Guardian.

"Alright." Dalton let out a defeated sigh, drumming his fingers along the counter. "Guess I'll try again next week."

"Anything else I can do for you?"

"Yeah, actually…" Dalton thought for a moment. "Are the files from Keito DeVero locked in Deep Archives?"

"Not all of them," Paul said. "We have about ten years of his work still accessible."

"Could I have the last month before his retirement?" Dalton asked, trying to make the request sound casual. Paul raised a suspicious eyebrow.

"Wouldn't it be easier to just *ask* him?" he teased, typing once again. "He's your teammate."

"I doubt that would be easier," Dalton laughed brokenly.

"Is he as moody as everyone says?" Paul asked, glancing at Dalton out of the corner of his eye.

"No, he's not that bad," Dalton said. "Especially if you consider everything he went through…"

"Sorry, Dalton, but it looks like those files have been signed out," Paul said, looking over the information on his screen. "Guardian Ecaep has them."

"Mitoki?" Dalton said, surprised that the youngest member of his team would check out the same files. "Okay, I guess he and I had the same idea."

"Hey, when you see him, tell him to bring those back, he's had them for a month already," Paul chuckled.

"So…even if I wanted to just borrow them from him, I would have to sign them out again, huh?"

"Yes," Paul said. "I can't make exceptions for you, even if you are the badass Guardian Dalton Teban."

"Who called me a badass?" he asked with a disbelieving laugh.

"Everyone." He turned to Dalton with a knowing smile. "Of course, most people don't see how much your wife and daughter have you wrapped around their little fingers."

"Oh, leave me alone."

"How is Theresa doing?"

"She's doing great," Dalton said, beaming. "She's really enjoying school and she has even made some friends. I was a little worried she wouldn't."

"Kids are more forgiving than you realize," Paul assured.

"Parents aren't," Dalton said. "Most parents hear her last name and tell their children to stay away from her." He heaved a sigh. "It's tough being the family of a Guardian. Everyone is afraid of you unless you're saving their lives."

"I guess that's the price you pay," Paul said with a nod. "I'm just an office grunt."

"You're one hell of an office grunt, though."

"I'm the best," Paul declared proudly. "Anything else I can help you with? I'm sure you're swamped trying to get all your work done around the tournament."

"You have no idea…" Dalton groaned, rolling his eyes.

"Let me know when you have time and we'll go have a drink."

"Thanks, I'll probably need it," he admitted, looking thoughtful, his tone suggesting his thoughts were elsewhere.

"Dalton? What is it?"

"Hey, do you know who did the reports on the Tournament Slaughter forty years ago?" Dalton asked, his eyes focusing on the computer on his friend's desk.

"…wasn't it Keito?" Paul asked, also hesitant as he turned to his computer.

"It couldn't have been. He quit two days after the slaughter. He didn't stick around to do the report."

Paul's fingers were fast across the keyboard, his eyes scanning the lists on his computer.

"Whoa…"

"What?" Dalton asked, trying to lean over the counter to see the screen, though he knew it was pointless.

"Um…there are only seven files on the Tournament Slaughter."

"*Seven*?"

"And three of them are locked. Not for anyone below a Level Two access," Paul read, scrolling through the small amount of files. "Don't Yellow Priority cases get seven reports and filings? That's the minimum requirement, right? And the most severe, the Blue Priority, get…somewhere around thirty to forty?"

"Yeah," Dalton said, confused. "Blue Pricrity is demon slaughters, dimensional fabric ripping, mass murders…the high level things." He stared at Paul in surprise. "You're telling me the massacre at the Guardian Tournament that killed thousands of people got *Yellow* Priority?"

"That's what it looks like." Paul seemed just as surprised. "I don't know. I can't access the full file. Maybe they're all lumped into seven different investigations."

"I have Level Two clearance. I want to sign those files out," Dalton said, quickly reaching for his wallet to extract his Guardian ID, placing it on the counter.

Paul stood and grabbed the card, scanning it as he typed. Dalton's mind was swimming with confusion and concern. The Tournament Slaughter had been monumental in the history of the Guardian Branch, but the files indicated it had been given the lowest level of priority when it came to investigations. Dalton tried to tell himself that it was due to the shock and disorganization following the massacre, but he was worried it was because Council was trying to cover up Keito's case around the tournament.

The door to the archives office opened and Mitoki stepped inside, surprised to see Dalton standing at the counter.

"Mitoki."

"Dalton," Mitoki greeted, setting several files on the counter as he stood next to his team leader.

"Good morning, Guardian Ecaep," Lydia, another archives office worker, said, stepping forward to help the younger Guardian. "How can I help you?"

"I'm returning these files," he said, placing his hand on the stack.

"Are those the files you signed out of Keito's work before the Tournament Slaughter?" Dalton asked. Mitoki quirked an eyebrow.

"How do you know that?"

"I wanted to sign them out, but they were already gone," the leader of the team said with a grin. Mitoki gave Dalton a playful glare.

"Now, Dalton, don't you think it's wrong to research your teammate like that?"

"Look at the pot calling the kettle black." Dalton turned to Lydia as she returned with her clipboard. "Lydia, I would like to sign those out now that they're back."

"Sure thing, Guardian Teban," she said, placing the clipboard in front of Mitoki. Mitoki, already very familiar with what to do, began to sign and date the appropriate boxes mechanically.

"What are you doing in archives besides researching your teammate?" Mitoki asked.

"I had to file one of my minor cases and I thought I would check to see if the Mount of Marconian report was unlocked, but no luck."

"Why is it locked at all? Hasn't that case been assigned to you?"

"Not yet. I'll try again next week, but I'm not holding my breath." Dalton sighed and reached for the files Mitoki had brought, pulling them closer and opening the top one. "We'll be back with Jikia in two weeks, so I guess I'll just have to ask Keito and Hanyi more about...all that stuff," he said, casting a wary eye at the archives staff.

Everyone in the Guardian Branch knew that Team Dalton was working on finding who had fractured Vestera's Dimensional Holding Seal, but he also knew he needed to be discreet about the details of their investigations. The secretive way their demon enemy was discussed told Dalton the importance of his discretion. He had no way of knowing who was listening and leaking information.

"Hopefully they'll be feeling a little more talkative," Mitoki agreed, placing the pen back on the clipboard. Dalton continued to flip through the files stacked on the counter.

"Find anything interesting in here?" the top-ranked Guardian asked.

"Quite a bit, actually."

Dalton opened another file and his eyes shot wide.

"Is...is that a picture of—"

"Yeah." Mitoki placed his hand on the top of the files, closing them as Dalton turned to him, horrified. "There are some really graphic photos in there."

"I was about to ask if you wanted to go get lunch and talk about the files but...I take that back." Dalton shuddered, trying to get the image of the child hanging from the hook in the butcher shop out of his mind.

"Dalton," Paul called, stepping back into the room with a locked box where the Level Two files were being kept. Dalton groaned when he saw the box. "Yeah," Paul sighed, understanding why the Guardian was annoyed. "Have to keep them in the building."

Lydia came to the counter and grabbed Mitoki's clipboard, duplicating the file numbers on Dalton's sheet as Dalton signed another form for his classified files.

"Level Two?" Mitoki asked, curiously studying the box. "What's that?"

"The Tournament Slaughter," Dalton said quietly, signing his name and taking his ID back as Paul went to file the form.

Mitoki's expression became dumbfounded.

"That's it?"

"I know. Only seven files."

"What? *Yellow*?" Mitoki hissed. "That can't be right."

"That's why I'm signing it out," Dalton said, signing the clipboard Lydia handed him for the other files. "Want to look them over with me?"

"Sure," Mitoki said. "Oh, Paul," he called, motioning to the man, who turned quickly when he heard his name. "Was my petition for research in Deep Archives approved?"

"Let me check."

"Well, aren't you studious," Dalton teased. "Do you think the others are studying as hard as we are?"

Mitoki snorted. "I doubt it. Eclipse and Keito don't really seem like the research type, and I'm sure Hanyi is just taking it easy for now."

"That's probably very true." Dalton returned the clipboard to Lydia, gathering the files together as Paul looked up.

"Mitoki, I'm sorry, but the petition has been overturned."

"On what grounds?"

"Um...Code 9952. DPC Book of Inter-Realmal Relations: Dimension of Demons," Paul read from the screen.

"What the hell are you petitioning to search for?" Dalton asked, surprised even though he did not know which code had been cited.

"I'll tell you later," Mitoki said. "I've been seeing this code a lot. Thank you, Paul."

With another goodbye to the staff of the archives office, the two Guardians stepped out into the halls of the Guardian Building.

"How have you been?" Dalton asked casually, striking up simple conversation as they made their way to the back of the building, where the offices of the top-ranked Guardians were located. Dalton's office was at the back of the collection, and though their doors were very close to one another, Mitoki had only been into Dalton's office briefly in the past during Annual Guardian Testing. Dalton's office was larger than Mitoki's but otherwise, the large desk, bookshelves stuffed with code books, filing cabinets and computers were identical to those in the other offices.

"Do you think Keito had the same office, or do you think he was in Sanyai's office?"

"They told me this was his office," Dalton said with a shrug, setting the files he had taken from archives on his desk and sitting heavily in his chair. Mitoki glanced over the family photos on Dalton's desk as he sat down, unable to stop the smile that came to his face at the sight of Dalton's daughter laughing joyously while hanging upside down from a swing.

Dalton did not notice Mitoki's scrutiny, his eyes locked on the stack of files on top of the locked security box. He immediately wanted to grab the files and scrutinize every detail of Keito's case, but stopped with this hand on top of the first file.

"Yeah, I know the feeling," Mitoki whispered, seeing his hesitation.

"Was it weird to look through these? Like you were spying on Keito?"

"A bit."

"What did you find?"

Mitoki let out a heavy sigh, his eyebrows going high.

"A lot," he said. "And yet, absolutely nothing. There were dozens of accounts of them chasing after this demon, but every time the team would get close and request that action be taken by the DPC, it was always denied with Code 9952."

"What's that code?"

"Old Blood Lords of the Dimension of Demons hold power to overthrow any requests processed through the DPC that are submitted by demon Guardians and-or requests that could impact the social hierarchy, or threaten the political power of the ruling Old Blood Lords," Mitoki quoted. Dalton raised a quizzical eyebrow as Mitoki shrugged. "I told you, I saw that code a lot. And yet any time I tried to research Old Blood Lords in more detail," he lifted his hands in defeat. "It started to feel like that code was just an excuse they put in the files."

"They who?"

"I don't know, the leak? Someone who sympathizes with this demon? After a certain point, it really felt like this code was just being thrown around." Mitoki slumped back. "I tried to contact Keito to ask him more about the Old Blood Lords but he never picked up his phone."

"Sanyai told me about them once when I was working a case in the Demon Realm," Dalton murmured. "She basically said the same thing. That they're the rulers of the realm, but I do remember she said there weren't many of them."

"That might help us narrow down this demon's name."

"Even that wasn't mentioned in the files?"

26

"No, they had a code for the files," Mitoki answered. "I assume to help keep it secret what they were investigating. There were twelve separate cases of murder and mutilation the members of Team Keito submitted and they were all linked to the same demon."

"In one month?" Dalton asked incredulously.

"There's something else." Mitoki turned behind him to see the door to Dalton's office open. With a soft motion of his fingers, his magic closed the door as he turned to his team leader. "If you look at the picture of that child in the top case, you'll see the demon left a message on the wall."

Hesitantly, Dalton flipped open the top file and extracted the picture. He forced his eyes to look away from the horrific mutilation of the hanging body to the blood-scrawled message on the wall.

"Start counting?"

"After that case, all through that month, the demon would use different methods to count down days. He would murder a certain number of people, steal pig carcasses and leave them for Team Keito to find...just...all sorts of strange clues he gave them."

"Counting down to?"

"The Tournament Slaughter."

The silence that gripped the office was heavy. Dalton stared at the message, his eyes focusing only on the two simple words.

"Did they figure it out?" he whispered.

"Keito put in seven separate requests to stop the tournament. And they were all denied under Code 9952."

"Even with all the evidence, the Elders denied the request?"

"Not only denied it, they began to threaten Keito that if he did anything to interfere with the normal proceedings of the tournament, they would dismiss him from service as a Guardian," Mitoki said. "He put in another request after that and they gave him a citation. The massacre was three days later."

"Keito knew it was coming," Dalton murmured, setting the picture down slowly. "And the Elders of his time didn't listen."

"Just like our Elders aren't listening," Mitoki agreed. "It's a pattern, Dalton. And we're likely to play right into it."

"Keito is trying to help."

"But he couldn't get anywhere when this was his case," he reminded him. "He was hitting all the same barriers you're hitting. And Code 9952 is completely off the books. Who knows how many more cases have been halted because of it."

"So even if we were to track the code, we can't see how far this demon's influence runs." Dalton shook his head, disheartened. "There are too many policies and codes that protect this demon..."

"And he knows how to use them," Mitoki agreed.

The two were silent for several seconds before Dalton reached forward and hit the speaker button on his phone, typing in a few quick numbers.

"Dimension Protection Council Guardian Branch, this is Sarah," a female operator's voice sounded.

"Hello, Sarah, this is Guardian Dalton Teban. Can you tell me if Guardian Tyien has been in recently?"

There was a pause as the operator looked up the information.

"She has taken an assignment in the Realm of Light," she answered. Dalton glanced at Mitoki, who merely shrugged, shaking his head to tell Dalton he did not know what case she had taken.

"When did she take that case?"

"Two days ago," Sarah answered. "She's signed all the necessary paperwork and was approved for interrealm travel. Her Demon Guardian Realm Transfer was approved before she left."

"Oh, don't worry, she's not in trouble," Dalton assured. "Can you transfer me to her personal phone?"

"Of course. I'll connect you."

The phone sounded with a rhythmic beeping tone as Sanyai's phone was called.

"What are you going to ask her?" Mitoki asked.

"Just a little bit more about the Old Blood Lords," he said. "I don't know what she'll tell us, but if we can get a name, that's a start. And...I want to hear her reaction when I ask. See how hesitant she is to give up information."

"You think she'll clam up like everyone else?"

"I hope not."

"Guardian Sanyai Tyien," the female demon answered.

"Sanyai, this is Dalton Teban. How are you?"

"Oh, Dalton, I'm doing well. How are you?"

"Hanging in there," Dalton responded with a small chuckle. "I hear you're taking a case in the Realm of Light. Mitoki didn't know what case you had."

"Nothing serious," she assured. "I'm just relocating some refugee demons to the Middle Dimension. Do you need me to be reassigned?"

"No, no, it's not about the case. I was just wondering if you had a few minutes to talk. I have a few questions I'm hoping you can help me with."

"Okay," she said. "Is it about Keito? Because if it is, I'm afraid I have no more insight into his behavior than you."

"No," Dalton laughed. "Actually, I wanted to ask you about the Demon Realm. I've been doing some research for a case and I keep coming across the title of a demon Old Blood Lord. I remember you said something about them being the most powerful social class in the realm. Is that right?"

She hesitated. "Yes. They are essentially our rulers."

"How many of them are there?"

"There are three ruling families and four active lords."

"Only four? For the entire Demon Realm?"

"At the moment, only four."

"What are their names?" Dalton pressed, reaching across his desk for a pen and notepad. But when he pressed the pen to the paper, Sanyai still had not spoken. "Sanyai? Are you still there?"

"I'm here," she murmured. "Dalton, I know it's not my place to ask this of you, but if you're researching Old Blood Lords for a case, you need to turn the case over to a demon Guardian. Give the case to Keito, if you can."

"Keito's working with me on this," Dalton half-lied.

"Then leave the Old Blood Lords to him," she said strongly. "Trust me, Dalton. You do not want to get mixed up with them if you can help it."

"Keito said that the politics were complicated with them," Dalton said. "It seems like I'm going to be coming across them a lot in research and I just need to be able to put a name to them. Can you tell me their names?"

She sighed heavily.

"Well, Lord Vestera Hizoku is one."

"Vestera Hizoku?" Dalton repeated, startled. "He's not a demon, he's a dragon."

"The Demon Realm needs a little more hands-on surveillance than the human realms," Sanyai elaborated. "He lives in the Demon Realm as an Old Blood Lord to keep everyone in line as much as he can." She took a deep breath. "Then there is Lord Juki Kage and Lord Rutu Kaneaka-Kage. Then Lord Kakuri DeVastes."

Dalton hurriedly jotted down the names, merely guessing on how to spell them.

"And these are the only four currently active?"

"Yes," Sanyai confirmed. "Dalton, I mean it. These are extremely powerful demons. You do not want to get mixed up with them."

"Do they take an interest in DPC affairs?"

"They are not the type to sit on a throne and order others to do things in their name. These are hardworking, active rulers. If their names show up in files and archives that is not an immediate red flag."

"If that's the case, why are you so hesitant to bring them up?" Dalton pressed.

"It's really complicated, Dalton. There are a lot of secrets about demons that humans are not supposed to know. The Old Blood Lords are one of those secrets." She sighed. "I'm sorry, I have to go. If you want to know more about them, you need to ask Keito."

"You know he won't tell me anything," Dalton grumbled.

"Keito's more informed than I am. He'll know what's safe to tell you. I'm sorry, Dalton, I have to go."

With a hurried goodbye, she hung up the phone, leaving Dalton's office in worried silence once again.

"...that wasn't a good reaction," Mitoki muttered.

"Part of me would like to think that demons just underestimate what humans are capable of tolerating, but a bigger part of me believes that they know we can't handle a lot of what goes on in the Demon Realm," Dalton said.

"I guess since Vestera Hizoku himself, the most powerful dragon alive, needs to *live* in the Demon Realm to keep everything in line, that's possible."

Dalton tapped his pen next to the last name he had written, studying each letter as though entranced.

"DeVastes...I know this name."

"How?"

"I don't remember," Dalton said. "I remember hearing the name recently." He closed his eyes, trying to remember the scene around the mention of the name. "After we took this case. While we were..." His eyes shot open and turned to Mitoki. "Jikia."

"What about her?"

"DeVastes. That was the last name of the demon who killed her village. The one who was murdered in his home a few months later by all those assassins. Elder Ari said that Council made the decision he was too dangerous to be alive and they killed him."

"But he heard about the plan and performed some sort of spell to preserve his soul," Mitoki filled in. "That matches up. But it wasn't Kakuri..."

"No, it was a different first name," Dalton agreed. "And Keito also told Elder Ari that he had friends in high places." He tapped his pen back and forth between the two Kage names. "Since I'm fairly certain Vestera is not helping the demon who fractured his seal, it's probably these other two."

"I've never heard the names before," Mitoki said with a shake of his head.

"Neither have I."

Dalton turned to his computer and typed in his access code before searching the name Kage. He received multiple errors as he typed in different spellings, getting more creative as the searches came up empty.

When he finally spelled the name correctly, he knew because the error he received was entirely different. He stared at the short message in disbelief, leaning back in his chair and shaking his head slowly.

"What is it?"

"It's restricted."

"You have Level Two access," Mitoki said. "Just override it."

"Mitoki."

Dalton turned the screen to his younger teammate.

"Level *Zero* restriction?" he choked. "That means...only the Elders..."

"I've never actually *seen* a Level Zero restriction."

"We need to ask Keito about these guys. We need to know if they have some alliance with the demon we're after," Mitoki insisted.

"I agree, but I don't know if I want to know the answer," Dalton said. He pushed the files off the top of the hard box locked on his desk, drumming his fingers along the top. "Because what if it's not even the council that's inhibiting these sorts of investigations? What if Council is completely under the control of two insanely powerful demons? What if these Kage Lords also believe that demons are meant to pass judgment on humanity and are helping this demon? How do we go up against that kind of power?"

"But if that was the case, then as horrible as the event was the Tournament Slaughter was not enough to further their plans. And if this demon truly wanted all the Guardians out of his way, why let Keito live? And *how* did Keito and Hanyi live? They said it was chaotic in the stadium, but I find it hard to believe they would just leave people in there to die to this demon."

"I don't know," Dalton said. "This case is clearly more nuanced than simply tracking down a demon and ending him. This is bigger."

"We're fighting blind here, Dalton," Mitoki said. "We don't know what we're up against."

"And if that bone beast thing is just the beginning," Dalton said, "we're in way over our heads."

Chapter Four

Keito was the first to appear at Jikia's home on the day Team Dalton was to come together for the next round of the tournament. He arrived early in the morning and found the two dragons tending to their livestock, so he stepped in to help as they waited for the other Guardians to arrive. Jikia was grateful for the help, but she could also see that Keito looked pale, and he seemed to strain when lifting the heavier items, despite his demon strength. As she was about to inquire about his health, Hanyi showed up with a bright smile and long hugs for both dragons.

Dalton arrived just as the final chores were being finished and Eclipse and Mitoki arrived shortly after to be greeted with fresh cups of coffee.

Comfortably sitting around Jikia's dining table as they enjoyed their coffee, they chatted lightly about what they had managed to accomplish during the two-month break. As expected, all members of Team Dalton were scrambling to finish their required number of cases around the tournament, but Dalton also admitted to his research.

"It's also tough to focus on new cases when I'm trying to find everything I can on this demon we're hunting down," he grumbled, finishing his coffee.

"Did you manage to find anything?" Jikia asked.

Dalton and Mitoki shared a knowing glance before turning their eyes to the wooden table top.

"That was a suspicious look..." Hanyi noted warily.

"Okay," Dalton started, "since I do feel a little guilty about doing this without talking to you two first, both Mitoki and I looked over the case files you submitted the month before you retired," he told the older Guardians.

Keito's face remained impassive, but his shoulders stiffened slightly. Hanyi also flinched, his eyes going distant as if rapidly trying to recall all the things they had been investigating just before the massacre at the Guardian Tournament forty years previous.

"...I do wish you had told me you were going to do that," Keito muttered.

"I'm sorry," Dalton said sincerely.

"I started it," Mitoki interjected. "I just...we're going in blind here, and you two didn't seem willing to tell us what we're up against. I thought that the case files would give us some insight into what we might be in for."

"And did it help?"

"It actually just led to more questions," Mitoki grumbled. "Like why the Elders didn't stop the tournament when you warned them that this demon would attack the stadium."

"What?" Eclipse said quickly, focusing his gaze on the two older Guardians. "Wait, you *knew* the Tournament Slaughter would happen?"

"No," Hanyi said, raising his hands peacefully. "We knew *something* would happen at the tournament. Believe me, we did *everything* we could to try and stop it. The Elders of our time… they wouldn't hear of it."

"How did you know he would attack?"

"He left us a lot of clues," the wolf said. "He did these sick little countdowns. And once we figured out the day he was counting down to, we knew we were in danger. But we truly had no idea he would take it as far as he did."

"And Council didn't think the evidence was sufficient?" Jikia pressed, mortified.

"No," Keito hissed darkly.

Dalton opened his mouth to speak but hesitated. When Keito caught the action, his eyes narrowed.

"What else did you find?"

"That Council denied your requests because of the Old Blood Lords of the Demon Realm," he said carefully. "…then we tried to do some research on Old Blood Lords."

"Files on the Old Blood Lords should be in Deep Archives," Keito said.

"They are," Mitoki agreed. "And my petition to research was overturned for the same reason your request for the tournament suspension was denied. Because of the Old Blood Lords. So…we called Sanyai."

Keito let out a defeated sigh, rubbing his forehead in exasperation.

"Let me guess," he said. "She told you to ask me about them."

"She did."

"Did she tell you anything?" Eclipse asked.

"She gave us some names," Dalton answered. "There are only four Old Blood Lords in the realm. And apparently one of them is Vestera Hizoku himself."

"Oh, we could have told you that," Tarrena interjected. "He's been living in the Demon Realm for…well, even before the five realms were connected he was living there."

"He has called it his home for a very, *very* long time," Jikia seconded.

"Has he said anything about the other Old Blood Lords?" Mitoki asked.

"Not much that I can recall," she said. "He keeps the demon and dragon politics separate. I can't recall him saying much about demon lords."

Keito opened his mouth to speak, but hesitated a moment. "You...already know one of the Old Blood Lords."

"I do?"

"DeVastes..." Mitoki murmured, trying not to speak too loudly, worried about upsetting their trainer with talk of the demon that killed her family. Jikia's head snapped toward Keito.

"Yokouro DeVastes was an Old Blood Lord?" she demanded.

"...*is* an Old Blood Lord," the demon corrected.

A heavy silence fell over the table. Mitoki and Dalton, having already deduced that the demon who killed Jikia's family was also the demon they were chasing, were merely digesting the confirmation their demon teammate had given. Eclipse, Tarrena, and Jikia, on the other hand, were dumbstruck.

"Wait, wait," Eclipse said, raising his hands. "This is the same demon? The one that killed all those dragons is the one who broke Vestera's seal and then was killed, and now is learning how to manifest his own body again so he can come after us and try to recreate the Tournament Slaughter? Or take over the realms? Or whatever the hell his plan is?"

"In broad strokes, yeah," Hanyi said.

"Why didn't you say anything before?" Jikia demanded, leaning on crossed arms on the table as she glared at Keito. "You could have given us a name already."

"I'm sorry," Keito groaned, pressing his fingers roughly into his eyes. "Really, I am. I should have told you, but...demons are forbidden from speaking about the Old Blood Lords outside of the Demon Realm. We can actually be imprisoned or forcefully removed from service as a Guardian if we mention them."

"*Why?*"

"The council sees it as trying to instill terror in the human realms," he said. "And like I said before, politics in the Demon Realm are very complicated. Our Old Blood Lords hold an enormous amount of power, more than you can even imagine."

"Like making a hex beast out of bone," Eclipse grumbled.

Keito and Hanyi stilled, sharing a quick glance with one another before Keito rolled his head back and sighed.

"They're capable of so much more," he said. "There are four Old Blood Lords, but really, there are only two *demon* clans that hold the title of Old Blood—the Kages and the DeVastes—since Vestera is a dragon and he doesn't have a bloodline to pass his title to. The DeVastes Clan is considered less powerful than the Kage Clan, but they have the leaders that tend to make the most noise. Yokouro was one such leader when he was in power."

"So, from what I remember, you said he was a mass-murderer. Just created destruction and mayhem wherever he went," Eclipse recalled. "Was he ever organized enough to really be a threat to the human realms? To take them over?"

Again, the demon hesitated.

"He doesn't have to be," Hanyi finally answered, his tone dark. He turned to Keito. "They're going to find out eventually."

Keito closed his eyes as though fighting with himself about how to respond, but he nodded reluctantly.

"Yokouro doesn't have to be organized to be a threat," Keito agreed. "He's extremely powerful on his own, more powerful than any demon you've ever come across before."

"How much more powerful than you?" Mitoki inquired.

"*Me*? I would be *lucky* to survive two minutes in the presence of his unbridled power. I'm talking about an aura powerful enough to burn and scar people just by being too close." Keito shook his head. "Now, I'm not a powerful demon, despite what you seem to think. I may be more powerful than the other demon Guardians, but there are others in the realm who are far more powerful than me...who are far more powerful than *Yokouro*."

"How much more powerful?" Jikia asked worriedly, able to better understand the scope of Yokouro's power than the human Guardians.

"...powerful enough to rival Vestera."

Dalton's jaw dropped.

"There's no way," he said. "Vestera is the single most powerful creature in existence."

"Yes, and there are two demons who can rival him in power when they work together," Keito elaborated.

"I don't believe you," Jikia said shortly. "Surely you understand just how *powerful* Vestera is. He's the Overseer. He can quite literally change the balance of the universe."

"I know," Keito said. "And still, these two demons can match him."

"That's why they're on Level Zero restriction," Mitoki mused, leaning back in his seat and crossing his arms over his chest. He turned to Dalton. "It's the two Kage Lords. They must rival Vestera in power which is why you couldn't look them up."

"And that's the reason demons are forbidden from talking about Old Blood Lords outside the realm," Keito added. "It's a terrifying prospect to think that the Kage Lords are *that* powerful." He lowered his gaze to the table. "And they are known to help Yokouro on occasion."

"*What*?" Eclipse said.

"The politics are complicated."

"Yeah, you keep saying that," Eclipse growled. "But that doesn't actually tell us anything. Are you saying it's not just Yokouro we're up against, but these Kage Lords, too?"

"I don't know for sure," Keito said. "There are rumors that the Kages are starting to stir again. But I hope that they look at Yokouro's little games with us as beneath them and they just...stay away from us."

"But," Hanyi started, "even our old team had run-ins with them. So you need to prepare yourselves for that...in case they do take a deeper interest in what Yokouro is doing."

"All the more reason for us to find Yokouro and kill him quickly," Eclipse declared. "Before two insanely powerful demons get involved."

"I don't know that I can even fathom that amount of power," Mitoki whispered. "Are you *sure* they're that powerful? And that they don't just talk a good game?"

"Trust me, they *are* that powerful," Keito muttered. He turned his head away and coughed into his arm, shivering as he tried to pass off the cough as casual. "And I agree, Eclipse. If we can keep them from getting involved, it will be better for everyone. I would really rather you don't get involved with the Kage Lords."

"Are you alright?" Tarrena asked.

"I'm fine," Keito assured, waving the question away. "A little sick. Nothing serious."

"Do you have something you can take?" Jikia asked mechanically, her mind still chewing over the information Keito had just told her.

Keito nodded, tapping his pocket so the others could hear the rattling of pills.

"Do you think it's safe to go back to the tournament?" Dalton asked after a few long seconds of silence. "We know this demon's name. We can find him and put him down quickly so we can halt the tournament."

"You can't just kill him," Hanyi said. "First of all, he's been killed once before. Even when he manifests a full physical form, killing that body won't kill him. His soul is somewhere else, safely hidden from us. And second of all—" Hanyi glanced at Keito as if silently asking permission. Rubbing his temple in frustration, Keito shrugged and motioned with his hand that Hanyi could continue, "—the Kage Lords don't just help Yokouro on occasion. They've been his trainers since he was a kid. They protect him. If we go after Yokouro without a solid plan, we're more likely to get killed than we are to kill Yokouro for good."

"Maybe, but three extremely powerful demons going into any of the human realms will be noticed," Dalton said. "We take the fight to him in the Demon Realm."

"That's an even faster way to get killed," Keito groaned.

"Well we can't just go through the tournament as though nothing is going on," Mitoki protested.

"Actually," Tarrena said slowly, her brow furrowing in thought, "being in a human-inhabited realm might offer you some protection."

"How do you figure that?" Dalton asked.

"Because if these demons are so powerful that even their aura is too dangerous to be around, they must all wear power limiters," she said. "And in order not to tip off *Vestera* that these super powerful demons are traveling, they'd have to keep even *more* power limiters on. Which means they're easier for you to fight "

Keito pointed at Tarrena with a strong nod.

"She's got it figured out."

"Either way we're gambling with a lot of civilian life," Eclipse muttered. "You saw how things went down in the last round. The amount of civilians around is just baiting him to try another massacre."

"Less than you might think," Keito assured, his eyes closing as he let out another long sigh, looking more tired than the others had ever seen him before. "Yokouro is all about the dramatics and about making a big splash. But if he is calling the Kage Lords to his side, they have a lot more tact, and they're a lot smarter than Yokouro."

"Which really just makes them more dangerous," Mitoki groaned.

"It honestly depends on what mood they're in when he asks them," Keito said, standing slowly, flinching. "I'm sorry, I just need to lie down for a little while."

"Are you sure you're alright?" Tarrena pressed. "Is there anything I can get you?"

"Thank you, Tarrena, but I'm fine," Keito said, slowly walking away from the table. "I just need a few days to rest and recover."

As he turned the corner out of sight of the other Guardians, Dalton slumped down in his chair, hiding his face in his hands with a quiet, exasperated groan.

"I don't like knowing about those two other demons, the Kage Lords," he grumbled. "As if this whole case didn't feel hopeless already with Yokouro as a threat."

Hanyi leaned forward.

"I know how overwhelming it is," he said. "And I'm not going to lie to you and tell you that I don't think the Kage Lords will get involved. In fact, I'm almost positive they are already involved."

"What makes you say that?" Eclipse asked suspiciously.

"Uh...I might have seen one of them in the Beast Realm," he said slowly, dropping his head, preparing for an outburst.

"You *did*?" Dalton hissed, his eyes wide.

"Yes, but you didn't. And that's a good sign," Hanyi said quickly with a weak smile. "It means that they might just stay in the shadows."

"I'm sensing a but in that statement," Mitoki grumbled.

"But," Hanyi continued, "the bone beast...that wasn't Yokouro's style of attack."

"You said that before."

"It reeked of the Kage Lords," Hanyi said. "That's exactly their style. Particularly the upgraded version you fought when you came to rescue me."

"That actually explains something," Eclipse mused. "About a week ago, I was doing some meditation, trying to find traces of the energy used to puppet the hex beast. I managed to find a little bit, and when I followed it, trying to find the demon...I actually had a seizure and spent three days in the hospital."

"*What*?" Tarrena gasped.

"I'm fine, I've been checked over numerous times," he said, avoiding eye contact with the younger dragon. "But the power was so intense...my mind could not handle the scope of it."

"So they really are involved," Dalton muttered. "Great. And we're going to bring them right to a stadium crowded with civilians." He shook his head, pinching the bridge of his nose. "Speaking of, what realm are we competing in?"

"We're going to the Realm of Darkness," Jikia answered. "And if we hold our current placements, which I'm sure we will, that means our rotation is set."

"What?" Eclipse groaned, his expression somewhere between vacant and exhausted, as though the sentence had drained the final ounces of energy from his body. She smiled.

"Don't worry, I know what that all means. More likely than not, we're going to be in the Human Realm for Round Three, the Realm of Light for Round Four, and the Demon Realm for Round Five. Round Six will be in the Middle Dimension, as usual."

"Something tells me there's going to be nothing *usual* about this tournament," Dalton said. "Or maybe it will be *too* much like usual. Or maybe these Kage Lord demons will get involved and annihilate everyone and that will just be the end of it."

Hanyi closed his eyes, flinching.

"We shouldn't have told you about them."

"No, no, I'm glad you did. We need to know, to the best of our ability, what to expect," Dalton said. Hanyi clearly wanted to say something, but fought with himself for several tense seconds before he finally spoke up again.

"I…don't think you need to worry."

"What is that supposed to mean?" Eclipse demanded.

"I just don't think you need to worry," he repeated. "Focus on Yokouro. Don't worry about the Kage Lords just yet. For all we know, they're just going to stay in the shadows and we won't even see them. Let's just focus on what we *can*, mainly, finding and killing Yokouro." He nodded once. "Agreed?"

Mitoki sighed heavily. "I suppose, though I doubt we can easily kill Yokouro."

"…but he has a physical form now," Dalton reminded them, wiggling his fingers as they had seen Yokouro do in the video from the murdered tourist's phone. "Which means that even if killing that body won't kill him completely, it will probably slow him down a bit."

"Sounds like a good place to start," Eclipse agreed, offering a small smile, trying, like the others, not to be overwhelmed by the obstacles ahead of them.

Even with all the troubled thoughts swimming in their minds, being back together at Jikia's house was a comfort to the Guardians. They spent the day discussing strategies for the tournament and catching up with Jikia and Tarrena, avoiding the subject of Yokouro and the Kage Lords as much as they were able during that first day.

The second day they spent in the Middle Dimension was meant for training and preparing Jikia's home for her absence during the second round of the Guardian Tournament. While a neighbor was tasked with feeding the animals, it was up to the Guardians to help their trainer portion out necessary supplements, stack feed, and generally prepare the property to make the neighbor's job as easy as possible.

Training was halted after lunch and the Guardians set to work around the property. They kept mostly to themselves, focused on their tasks and swimming in the nervous apprehension of the upcoming tournament. Dalton, however, spent most of the early afternoon concocting a plan.

As he was finishing his last chore—moving bales of hay into the feed shed—he straightened, as if suddenly remembering something.

"Oh, damn it," he said quickly.

"What?" Eclipse asked.

"I forgot I had to sign something yesterday before I came here," he said, pulling his sleeve back to glance at his wristwatch. "Shit. Think I have enough time to get to the compound before all the secretaries leave?"

Mitoki also glanced at his watch.

"If you leave *now*," he said with a broken chuckle. "I'd start running and catch the bus at whatever stop you can. We'll finish that up. Just go do what you need to do."

"You sure?" Dalton pressed.

"Go, go," Eclipse urged, approaching the fallen bale of hay. "You know that Jikia will be ushering us out of here first thing in the morning and you won't have time to do it then. Go."

"But with Keito still down for the day—"

"We can handle a few bales of hay and a few water troughs," Mitoki assured.

Dalton hurried into the house, blurting out his excuse to Jikia as he ran out the door. He broke into a jog until he reached the street, where he picked up into a steady run, listening carefully for the bus approaching from behind.

He felt guilty for lying to his teammates about the paperwork, but he had been unable to get the thought of Yokouro DeVastes out of his mind. He felt compelled to know more, to devour all the information he could about their enemy. But the feeling was not only one of dread and curiosity—he felt as though he already knew everything about Yokouro, but he had forgotten it somehow, like a memory he was desperately trying to recall, though no details made themselves known.

Therefore, he was determined to go to the Guardian Branch and look up anything he could find on Yokouro DeVastes.

Through the entire two-month break, despite the time he spent with his family and the cases he had taken, a bone-deep anxiety had grown within him. Even before Keito confirmed that Yokouro was their target, and that there were two extremely powerful demons ready to help Yokouro in his endeavors, Dalton could feel the edge of a cliff fast approaching. He had replayed the way his power had flexed during Hanyi's rescue in the Beast Realm over and over again, trying to understand the sudden power he had been able to instinctively command. Every dream he had, every possibility he entertained about how they would defeat Yokouro, every new morsel of information he obtained, he felt as though that magic within him was growing, pulling him toward the Old Blood Lord as though they were bound together.

He refused to let the others of his team see his frantic terror. He had to be the team leader. He had to maintain his composure. And he knew that, in order to do so, he had to learn everything he could about Yokouro as soon as possible.

He managed to catch the bus at the main road and was driven to the Dimension Protection Council compound just as the sun began to set. He walked through the side gate and crossed the main courtyard of the compound toward the Guardian Building. As he started up the large, stone steps, he stopped, startled to see a wolf sitting at the top of the stairs, his bright, playful eyes locked on Dalton.

With a chuckle of disbelief, Dalton ascended the rest of the stairs toward the wolf as the animal began to wag his tail.

"I guess you can run across fields and cut through town faster in your wolf form," Dalton noted, sitting next to Hanyi. The wolf's tail wagged enthusiastically, his head turning to nuzzle Dalton's shoulder. Dalton gently pushed Hanyi away with a laugh.

"Hanyi, that's creepy."

The wolf's body morphed into his human form, allowing him to sit next to Dalton on the top step of the Guardian Building, grinning.

"Well, I think it looks creepier trying to comfort you in my human form."

"You think I need comforting?"

"Oh yeah," Hanyi said strongly. "I think everyone does right now, since we just dumped a bunch of information on you, and none of it was particularly hopeful. I tried to comfort Eclipse and Mitoki too, but they both told me it was creepy to have me pushing my head against them as a wolf."

Dalton laughed.

"It kinda is," he agreed.

"Well, I figured I would just wait with you here until you signed whatever it was you needed to sign. Then we can chat on the way back to Jikia's," he said with a strong nod.

Dalton sighed.

"You already know I'm not signing any papers."

"Yeah, I figured," he said, his eyes scanning the courtyard as a small group of assistants walked by, laughing about something amusing that had occurred at work that day.

"You came to stop me, then?" Dalton asked.

"Yep."

"I just need to know what I'm up against, Hanyi," he murmured. "I need time to think it over, to adjust, to prepare."

"Dalton, look around the courtyard and tell me what you see," Hanyi said, ignoring Dalton's plea.

"Oh no, are you getting philosophical on me?" he tried to tease.

"Not yet. We'll get to that," Hanyi laughed. "Just tell me what you see."

Dalton turned to look at the stone courtyard in front of the Guardian Building. He looked among the structures and facades of the compound, the cobblestone pathways devoid of people and vehicles, allowing the stones to flaunt their rich colors in the glow of the sunset. He saw the group of assistants disappear through one of the far gates to walk toward the row houses beyond the walls of the compound, returning home after another day of work.

"It's the compound courtyard, Hanyi."

"Then where is everyone?"

Dalton was about to make a joke about other members of the Dimension Protection Council not being workaholics like them, but something stopped him. It was unnaturally quiet within the compound. Even as he looked around the other buildings, he could not see other workers leaving for home, or the guards patrolling the wall to be sure the perimeter was secure.

"...wait, where *is* everyone?" he asked.

"Even the streets outside were almost completely empty," Hanyi added. "It's the start of the weekend, but no one is going out. Also, there isn't a single Guardian coming to collect their monthlies."

Dalton's head whirled around to look into the large windows of the Guardian Building. Even though the panels of glass were illuminated from within, there was no activity inside the halls, even though it was the beginning of the month, when Guardians collected their monthly paychecks and checked their rankings. Not a single Guardian was in sight.

"What the hell…"

"People aren't going out anymore," Hanyi said. "No one has any rational idea why they don't want to go out, but something tells them to stay inside, to stay safe, some deep instinct that they can't name or understand. And the Guardians are working overtime because of the spike in cases." Hanyi finally turned to look at Dalton "Have you heard of the calm before the storm? This is it. Everyone can feel something dangerous on the horizon. While they may not know what it is, or even that their apprehension is due to feeling threatened, they're acting on instinct. It's not rational. It's unconscious, raw instinct."

"It's probably going to help them stay safe through all this," Dalton agreed slowly.

"And it will help you, too," Hanyi said. "I know you want to research Yokouro. But that's the logical, rational part of you. Right now, it might be best to act on instinct."

"Ignore logic?"

"Ignore the logic that will spin you in circles of fear and anxiety," he corrected. "If you go in there and you research him, you're going to learn things that he's done that are going to scare the shit out of you. And then, as soon as you're face-to-face with him, he's going to seem way bigger and scarier than he actually is."

"He seems pretty damn terrifying."

"Oh, he is, but those files aren't going to tell you what you really need to know. It will give you history and statistics, but that won't tell you how you're going to take him down. All it will do is cloud your mind with fear and what-ifs, and he'll use that to get so deep under your skin, you'll collapse under the pressure." Hanyi pressed his finger to his temple. "This can lie to you. It can exaggerate and amplify, but this," he pointed to his abdomen, "that's one-hundred percent real."

"You want me to just blindly face him?" Dalton asked skeptically.

"If you really want to research him, Dalton, I won't stop you," Hanyi said. "But I know what it's like to spin yourself into a panic over this demon. And then you become more focused on your own fear and how to conquer it than the mission and how to defeat your enemy. Yokouro uses his reputation as a weapon. Your best protection against that is to know as little about him as possible and let your gut sense what he's really capable of."

"Yeah, but with Keito in such bad shape—"

"Don't worry about Keito," Hanyi interrupted. "He's durable as hell. He'll be fine."

"And the Kage Lords—"

"Okay, Yokouro's got allies. So do we," the wolf said. "In fact we probably have even more than we realize. And do you know how you're going to know who to trust?" Hanyi poked at his belly again. "Trust your gut. You have to start trusting yourself more, Dalton. Trust in your instinct to survive and protect the ones you love."

"Yeah…" Dalton chuckled brokenly, his gaze turning to his feet. "I've never been good at believing in myself like that."

"Well, *start*," Hanyi snapped with a broad smile. "Because it will be the thing that will get you out of this alive."

Dalton sighed heavily, hanging his head even as he nodded slowly.

"…I guess we should head back then," he muttered.

Hanyi leapt to his feet with a clap of his hands.

"Well, we should get out of the compound, but I think we should get some ice cream," he declared.

"What?"

"We have to make it look like you actually signed some paperwork and I want ice cream," he said with a shrug. As he started down the stairs, Dalton stared at him in disbelief.

"With everything hanging over our heads right now, how the hell can you be so cheerful all the time?" he asked.

"Well, *someone* has to be."

Chapter Five

Eclipse gave no protestation to having the Guardians stay with him for the second round of the Guardian Tournament, though there was some debate about where Jikia and Tarrena would stay while in the Darkness Realm. Eclipse assured them that there was plenty of room at his house to accommodate them, as the hotels in his city were already booked solid with tourists rushing to see the next round of the tournament. But Jikia wanted to see some former trainees in the Realm of Darkness and would stay with them, giving Team Dalton more room in their teammate's house.

Keito was in rough shape the morning they left for the Realm of Darkness. The entire team could see the way his hands trembled and his eyes struggled to remain open as he checked over his realm transfer approval and made sure he had all the necessary documentation to travel as a demon Guardian.

"Are you sure you're okay?" Dalton asked again. "I thought you said you only needed a few days to rest and you would be feeling better."

"Didn't really sleep last night," he grumbled. "I'm fine."

"Can you handle the tournament?" Mitoki pressed.

"I'll be fine," he insisted, trying to mask a cough.

Everyone tried to ignore how difficult it was for Keito not to sway as they stood in line for the portals to the Realm of Darkness. Eclipse led the way to one of the five portals that led to his city. The lines for the Darkness Realm portals were slow and grueling as many traveled to and from the largest human-inhabited realm. Because of the security measures, the Guardians of Team Dalton were split up based on which line they were funneled into and had to wait for the others in the equally crowded portal building in the city of Kang-Dron in the Darkness Realm.

Once they had grouped together again, Eclipse led them out of the large, beautifully decorated portal building toward the parking lot, passing another security checkpoint on the way out.

"I forgot how tight security was among the human realms," Hanyi grumbled.

"Yeah, the Beast and Demon Realms seem to have no security at all," Mitoki agreed.

"Well, the Beast Realm doesn't really need it," Hanyi said with a laugh. "Humans really stand out."

"I suppose that's true," the youngest agreed. "But I am a little surprised that the Demon Realm doesn't have tighter security, or even portals to different parts of the realm."

"Most demons know better than to leave the realm, and as far as traveling within the realm, most demons just dimension hop."

Dalton whirled around to look at Keito.

"That's illegal."

"It's not illegal in the Demon Realm," Keito corrected.

"Demons just go around cutting holes in dimension fabric all the time?" he gawked.

"Those who have the power to use that for traveling, yes."

"But the DPC banned dimension hopping in all realms in order to preserve the integrity of Vestera's seal."

"Well, the seal is already beyond repair," the demon said with a shrug. "And demons don't really care about the DPC rulings. They'll listen to their Old Blood Lords and Demon Council."

"There's a Demon Council?" Tarrena asked.

"It's a collection of demons in the realm who have some social status," Keito said, trying to shrug off the question. Dalton was about to inquire further when he caught a glimpse out the front windows of the portal building and finally noticed the torrential downpour of rain.

"What the hell?"

"Yeah, it's the rainy season," Eclipse said, the automatic doors opening and the muggy air hitting them all hard as they stepped onto the covered front steps.

"Do you have your car here, Eclipse?" Tarrena asked.

"Yeah, it's just over there," he answered with a point. "Where are you two staying? I could drive you there."

"I don't think you have enough room in your car. You don't strike me as the van type," Tarrena said with a soft laugh.

"Besides, we're just going to that little cafe over there," Jikia added, pointing across the road. "They'll drive us from there, but we'll be sure to stop by tomorrow and do some training." She looked up at the gloomy sky. "Or should we meet at a Guardian Training Center?"

"I don't think that's a good idea," Keito said with a tired shake of his head. "There will be a lot of other Guardians using the training centers before the tournament. Probably not smart for the highest profile team to be so easily accessible. It's caused problems in the past."

"Good point."

"It's alright," Eclipse assured. "My master has a partially-indoor training facility in the backyard, so there's plenty of room to do some light training there."

"What do you mean *partially* indoor?" Mitoki grumbled, eyeing the heavy rain pounding on the asphalt of the parking lot.

"Do you have the directions I gave you?" Eclipse asked, ignoring Mitoki's griping.

"Yep," Tarrena said with a bright smile. "We'll see you sometime tomorrow then."

Using a circle of magic to protect their heads from the intense rain, the Guardians and the dragons left the safety of the awning and went their separate ways, Dalton following close behind Eclipse as he led them to his car, eager to get out of the storm. When Eclipse unlocked the doors to his sleek, clearly-expensive car, Dalton motioned Keito forward, offering the front seat to the ill demon.

Hanyi was stuck in the middle of the back seat, but did not complain, settling comfortably between Dalton and Mitoki as Eclipse backed out of the parking space and began driving along the rain-soaked streets.

"Do you live in the main Kang-Dron district?" Dalton asked, watching the bright lights of the bustling city fight against the heavy sheets of rain.

"No, I live in the Patkegn suburb. I'm at the south end of the city."

"Were you born here?" Hanyi asked.

"No, I was born in a town called Juptoth, which is on one of the other continents in the realm. I moved here when I was nine."

"You'll have to forgive my lack of knowledge of continents in the Darkness Realm," Dalton said with an embarrassed laugh. "This is the largest realm of the five."

"I can't say I've ever heard of Juptoth," Keito murmured, thoughtful.

"It's on the Lyndmon continent in the southern hemisphere," Eclipse elaborated. "Near the Coreb Peninsula and north of Kren-Dov, if you even know where that is."

"I do," Keito said.

"I don't," Dalton chuckled.

"You don't really have an accent, though, Eclipse," Hanyi noted.

"I moved here when I was nine. I hardly remember the Dovic language anymore."

"I really forgot how big this realm is," Mitoki muttered, looking up something on his phone. "I think the only place I've really stayed in this realm is Kapra-Lin."

"I love Kapra-Lin," Hanyi and Dalton exclaimed at the same time. Eclipse rolled his eyes.

"Everyone loves that place. It's the biggest tourist destination in the entire realm. That's why they had to limit the amount of visitors they have every year."

"Hanyi used to always beg to go to Kapra-Lin when we were in the Darkness Realm," Keito said with a smile and a playful glare at the other Guardian. Hanyi pointed at him.

"Hey, you loved it, too. Don't try to lie."

"I did love it, but somehow, I would always end up carrying your nearly-unconscious body back to the car when you ran back and forth along the beaches for *hours* and wore yourself out."

"Beaches are a luxury for me," Hanyi whined. "I live in the forested mountains of the Beast Realm. I had never even *seen* the ocean until I took cases in the human realms."

"You must have been visiting before they began capping visitor numbers," Eclipse noted.

"Actually no, that's where Sadee was born. She always kept a house there, so we always had a place to stay," Hanyi said. "Unfortunately, that also meant she was based in Pejret for work, rather than a nice city like Kang-Dron."

"Ugh," Dalton groaned. "Pejret is horrible. Overcrowded and everyone is rude."

"Everyone else in the entire realm agrees," Eclipse said with a knowing nod. "But I do take a lot of cases there because crime is a lot more rampant, so it's good for work, at least."

"Hanyi, Keito, can I ask you something?" Mitoki started. Keito turned over his shoulder. "You spent time with your teammates outside of the tournament?"

"Yeah," Hanyi said easily. "I mean, one of my teammates was also my brother, but we would spend a lot of time together away from the tournament. We were all good friends."

Keito leaned his head back on the headrest.

"I think there has been a very sad change in the Guardian Branch since the Tournament Slaughter," he mused. "Guardians don't know each other the same way they used to. It used to be a very close-knit community. Now...well, I was surprised you three didn't know each other well before the tournament."

"I was surprised, too," Hanyi seconded. "Jacob and I actually used to have lunch together before we even became a team. And I was completely in love with Sadee for years, even after we became a team."

Keito began laughing, despite how it made him cough.

"Oh, gods, I forgot about that," he gasped.

"Wait, you were in love with Sadee?" Mitoki repeated. "I would think that would make working in a team difficult."

"Not really," Hanyi said. "She sure as hell wasn't interested. Besides, I quickly learned that love means different things to humans and beasts. The infatuation quickly changed to a more familial love."

"Her kicking your ass repeatedly probably helped that transition," Keito said with a sly grin over his shoulder.

"Repeatedly?" Dalton said, smiling at the way Hanyi crossed his arms over his chest in an exaggerated pout.

"It was a yearly tradition," Keito said. Hanyi stuck out his tongue at Keito before explaining.

"It started when the team first formed," he said. "Hector and I really wanted to compete in the tournament again. We had already done it once or twice but it was early in our days as Guardians. So we both begged and begged for Keito to be our team leader, and when we finally wore him down enough to agree, there was a big rush to fill the other two spots on the team. We actually had to hold tryouts because everyone wanted to be on Keito's team. Jacob was an easy choice for all of us, I think. He was an unbelievable Guardian. A lot of raw power to him. But we were struggling to fill that last spot. So, I asked Sadee if she wanted to join. She turned me down pretty fast."

Keito laughed again. "She didn't want to be part of the testosterone-fest, as she called it."

"But again, I eventually wore her down," Hanyi said.

"Actually, *Jacob* wore her down," Keito corrected.

"I had a part in it!" the wolf defended. "She finally came to me and Keito and said that the team needed her because without her, Jacob would go insane around the trio of weirdos we were."

Dalton could not help but laugh, trying to imagine how the dynamic of Team Keito worked both during the tournament and outside the competition.

"Long story short, she challenged one of us to a fight to prove herself as a worthy member of the team. I was hot-headed and I really liked her, so of course I volunteered. And I think I lasted about fifteen seconds—"

"Try *five*," Keito corrected with a bark of laughter.

"—and she had my ass on the ground with one of her daggers at my throat actually *drawing blood*," Hanyi concluded, glaring playfully at Keito. "So it became a tradition. Every year, before the start of the tournament, I would test my strength against her and see if I could win."

"And did you ever win?" Eclipse leered in the rearview mirror.

"A few times," he said. "But…a majority of the time, I had my ass handed to me."

"She really was incredible," Keito agreed, a soft edge of sadness lining his tone.

Eclipse exited the highway and entered a residential neighborhood, following the sweeping streets to the far end, where the houses stood further apart with larger backyards that often acted as small family farms. Eclipse pulled into the garage of a large, single-story house that appeared older than some in the neighborhood, but well maintained.

Retrieving their bags from the trunk, they followed Eclipse into the narrow hallway leading off the garage, toeing off their shoes and setting them next to Eclipse's before walking further in.

"Hello? Anyone home?" Eclipse called into the house, setting his keys in the tray near the garage door.

"Eclipse? Are you here?" a man's voice responded from deeper within the house.

"We're all here."

"I'm in the kitchen."

"Be there in a minute." He motioned for the others to follow him. "Well, since Jikia and Tarrena aren't staying here, you all get your own rooms." He led them to the other side of the house where smaller guest rooms sat next to one another in the same hallway as Eclipse's room. When they had each placed their bags in their appointed rooms, they followed their teammate toward the kitchen.

The spacious kitchen was clearly the newest upgrade to the house and had a substantial, sturdy dining table near a large window looking out on the neighborhood that somehow matched the aesthetic of the new appliances in the kitchen. Standing by the sink, his back turned to the door, was a tall, broad man slowly cutting carrots on a cutting board. His dark attire nearly mirrored Eclipse's style, but was interrupted by the bright, lace-trimmed straps of a pink apron.

"Master?" Eclipse started. "Why are you wearing Saki's apron?"

"Am I?" the man said, setting the knife down on the counter and turning slowly to reveal the embroidered cupcake on the front of the apron.

Eclipse groaned, hanging his head.

"You know that's not a good joke," he grumbled.

Dalton was unsure how to react. The apron was clearly too small for the broad, muscular man and stood in hilarious contrast to the rest of his appearance, but the glassy grey color of the man's eyes made Dalton turn to his teammates quizzically, unsure how to respond.

Master Genbuki pressed a hand over his chest, his fingers tracing around the embroidery before he smiled.

"Well, I wanted to make a good first impression for Team Dalton. At least they won't forget me."

Eclipse rolled his eyes.

"And don't roll your eyes at me," Master Genbuki scolded with a grin, untying the apron and pulling it over his head.

"It puts them in a position where they're not sure if they should laugh or not," Eclipse grumbled. "Didn't you think they might be a little confused on how to react to the blind man wearing a bright pink apron?"

"Actually, no," Master Genbuki said, stepping forward easily and reaching a hand forward. "Please, there is no need to feel awkward. I am not self-conscious about being blind." He stopped in front of Dalton, who moved to meet his hand in a handshake. "Welcome, Team Dalton. I've heard much about you."

"Never a good sign," Dalton joked. "It's very nice to meet you."

"Master Feburn Genbuki," he introduced as Eclipse moved across the kitchen to the carrots, picking up a few and eating them as he watched the introductions. "I'm sorry about the apron joke. Perhaps it was in bad taste for the first meeting."

"It's fine," Dalton assured.

"I was a little more concerned about you chopping carrots with a sharp knife," Hanyi noted nervously.

"Oh, I've learned to get by just fine without my sight," he assured with a chuckle, turning toward Hanyi's voice and reaching a hand out. "Hanyi, I assume. I am confident I could sword fight any of you and probably win. Well, maybe except for the demon. My old body doesn't move as fast as it used to."

"Neither does mine," Keito agreed with a laugh, extending a hand to take Master Genbuki's when the other man turned. "It's a pleasure to meet you, Master Genbuki. Thank you for welcoming us into your home."

"Of course, of course," he said, shaking Keito's hand, grinning. "*The* Keito DeVero," he mused. "Truly an honor."

Keito just smiled nervously, not sure how to respond.

"My apologies. You probably get that a lot," he said, breaking the handshake.

"I get a lot of varied responses."

"Well, you do have quite the reputation," he agreed. "And, by the way, you may be older than me, but there is no attitude in my house."

"Yes, sir," Keito said with a smile.

"Now, where is Mitoki?" he asked, turning slowly.

"Right here," the youngest member of the team called, stepping forward to meet Master Genbuki in a handshake. "It's very nice to meet you."

Master Genbuki smiled warmly, placing his other hand on Mitoki's as he shook his hand.

"Very nice to finally meet you, Mitoki."

"Okay, that's enough awkward introductions," Eclipse declared, standing straight and grabbing another carrot. "Do you guys want anything? Coffee? Water?"

"I'll make you some tea," Master Genbuki offered. "You can make yourselves comfortable in the living room. And Eclipse, stop eating those carrots. They're for dinner."

Eclipse made a face at the older man, reaching for another carrot when he lifted a finger in warning.

"Not another inch."

Eclipse sighed, his hand dropping back to his side as he lifted his eyebrows at his teammates.

"Hopefully he doesn't give you the same attitude he gives me," Master Genbuki teased, turning back to the others of Team Dalton. "I've been trying to adjust that attitude for nearly twenty years, now."

Dalton laughed at the exasperated look on Eclipse's face.

"Eclipse has been a great asset to the team," he said sincerely.

"Good to hear. Now, please, make yourselves comfortable in the living room. I'll bring out some tea."

"Would you like any help?" Dalton asked.

"No, no, I can manage."

Eclipse nodded in response to the questioning glances from his teammates and led them out of the kitchen to the living room.

"Are you sure we can't help?" Dalton whispered to Eclipse. "He's okay to do that alone?"

"Been doing it the entire time I've lived with him," Eclipse assured, sitting heavily on one of the plush couches in the large living room. "He's perfectly capable of doing everything but driving."

"Was he born blind?" Mitoki asked in a hushed voice as he sat opposite Eclipse.

"No, it was a tumor!" a voice called from the kitchen. Mitoki straightened, his eyes wide in horror at being heard. "I've been blind since I was fifteen!"

Eclipse laughed at Mitoki's mortified expression.

"He may not be able to see but his hearing is excellent." He raised his voice "Which means he hears *everything*, the old bat!"

"Taught you how to sneak around, didn't it?" the older man laughed from the kitchen. "I'm sure that saved your ass on some cases."

Eclipse rolled his eyes, leaning his head back on the couch.

"And you really need to break that habit of rolling your eyes," Master Genbuki taunted, still in the kitchen.

"Seriously? You drive me crazy!" Eclipse groaned, though he was smiling.

"Then move out!" the older man laughed. "Get a wife! Go make babies!"

"I'm never having children and you know that!" Eclipse quipped.

"You don't want kids?" Dalton asked.

"I've never been good with kids," Eclipse said with a shrug. "I've also never really had the desire to be a father, so I don't plan on having any."

"I always wanted kids," Dalton said. "I think more so than my wife did."

"I didn't want kids either, but I changed my mind after I stepped away from the Guardian Branch," Hanyi added. "It's been amazing. Children added more to my life than I thought they would."

Keito nodded slowly, drawing Dalton's attention immediately. The demon flinched from the sudden attention.

"What?"

"Do you have kids?"

"Yes," he answered. When he saw the gaping mouths and wide eyes of the humans, he laughed. "Don't look so shocked," he chuckled brokenly.

"You've never mentioned them before."

"They all have lives of their own, now. I don't really see them anymore."

"I'm sure the right woman will change Eclipse's mind," Master Genbuki said, walking into the living room with a tray of cups and a covered teapot. He gingerly set the tray on the coffee table between them. "He'll want children when he finds someone he truly cares for. I know it."

"Oh?" Dalton asked, raising his eyebrows. "He already has his eyes on someone, though, doesn't he?"

"I don't know what you're talking about," Eclipse grumbled, leaning forward to serve the tea as Master Genbuki settled into his seat.

"You have been spending a lot of time on the phone with someone at all hours of the night," Master Genbuki noted. "Is that who you've been talking to?"

Hanyi's mischievous smile grew even wider.

"Ooh, Eclipse," he leered. "Already spending hours on the phone with her?"

"Okay, first of all, shut up. Second of all, you have no idea who, if anyone, I am interested in."

"Oh, please, it's totally obvious you and Tarrena are dancing around each other," Mitoki snorted.

"*What*?" Eclipse said.

"We've seen it since training started," Dalton seconded. "It's clear with the way you two have been eyeing each other. You two seem to just *get* each other."

"You should get a girlfriend," Master Genbuki agreed. "You haven't had one since you were a teenager."

"I don't really have time for relationships," Eclipse mumbled. "Besides, a woman would have to be crazy to date a Guardian."

"Hey!" Dalton, Mitoki, and Hanyi said simultaneously.

"You dated plenty when you were training," Master Genbuki continued. "You and your brother, always trying to sneak out to meet with your girlfriends. It worries me that Erik has a girlfriend and you've been alone for so long. It's not good for you. Keeps you in a dark headspace."

Eclipse groaned. "Don't compare my relationships with Erik's. He can hardly keep their names straight."

"You weren't exactly a saint, you know," Master Genbuki leered, causing the others in the room to laugh.

"You know those movies Saki loves so much where the parents purposely say the most embarrassing thing possible in front of company? *This* is one of those moments. Don't sink to that level," Eclipse said with a glare toward his master.

"Give me some grandchildren to look over and then I can embarrass them instead."

"You're starting to sound like an old woman."

"Can you even have children with Tarrena?" Hanyi asked, his expression pensive.

"I don't think so," Keito responded, his brow also furrowed in thought. "Dragons have a very complicated way of reproducing as it is. I don't think it's possible with humans."

"Ah, so she's a dragon," Master Genbuki said, turning to Eclipse, who was sitting in his seat, arms crossed like a pouting child.

"Can demons have children with humans?" Mitoki asked, turning to Keito.

"It's not unheard of," he answered. "It's not easy, though. There are a lot of possible complications. The human male's sperm is generally not strong enough to actually fertilize the egg of a female demon, and a human female is often not physically strong enough to handle the accelerated gestation and birth of a half-demon child. But it has happened."

"Okay, okay," Eclipse said, raising his hands and shaking his head. "I don't need to know all that."

Keito laughed at his obvious discomfort. "Too weird for you?"

"A bit," Eclipse admitted. "If my brother comes over, though, he'll be very interested to hear about all of that…weird, semi-genius lunatic that he is."

"I can't tell if you and your brother are close or not," Dalton said with a confused laugh.

"They're close, they just butt heads sometimes," Master Genbuki assured. "Erik told me he tried to get tickets to see you compete in the tournament, but they were already sold out."

"Good," Eclipse said, handing the tea around to his teammates. "He would find a way to sneak into the team rooms and start asking all the demons for blood samples."

"Wouldn't be the first time that's happened," Keito joked, taking the offered tea.

"How long do you have before the tournament starts?"

"Three days," Dalton answered.

"Are you planning to do any training in that time, or are you just going to go in there and fight?"

"I'm sure Jikia will run us through some exercises to get our heads back into the tournament," Mitoki said.

"I might be misreading your energy, Keito, but you actually feel like you might be injured," Master Genbuki said. "Are you okay to fight in the tournament?"

"I'll be fine. I should be mostly healed by the time the tournament comes around."

"Wait, I thought you said you were sick," Dalton said quickly.

"I am. From a wound infection."

"What wound?" he demanded.

"It's nothing big. It's already been mostly treated. I just got careless on a case. It happens frequently," Keito said, lifting his teacup to take a sip. "That's why I never understood why everyone thought I was some great Guardian. I was hurt more often than not."

"Well, were you going after humans or other demons?" Master Genbuki pressed.

"Demons."

"Then that's understandable. If it had been humans, then I would have thought that was just sad."

"Me, too," Keito laughed.

The front door creaked open and a bustle was heard in the foyer as shoes were kicked off and a heavy backpack was dropped to the floor.

"I'm home!"

"Welcome home," Master Genbuki responded. "We're all in the living room."

"Oh, are they here?!" the teenage girl asked excitedly, rushing around the corner as she struggled to kick her other shoe off, causing it to hit the wall with a clunk as she caught her balance in the doorway to the living room. "You're all here!"

"Saki," Eclipse groaned.

"What? I can't be excited?" she defended. "These are the best Guardians in the entire Guardian Branch!" Her bright brown eyes scanned the Guardians, a smile growing over her face as she studied them.

"You *live* with one of the best Guardians in the branch. It's not that special," Eclipse reminded her.

"You're still not as good as three of the people in this room," she said, motioning to Dalton, Hanyi, and Keito.

Mitoki tried to stifle his laughter into his hand but Master Genbuki laughed loudly. Dalton let out a small chuckle in disbelief while Eclipse fixed Saki with an incredulous look.

"I see where I stand, now," he grumbled.

She smiled, walking around the back of the couch and wrapping her arms around the playfully-sulking Eclipse, hugging him tight. "Don't worry. You're still the best to me, *kan-na*," she said, using the cute word for older brother in Eclipse's birth language—one of the few words Erik had taught her as she had grown up. Eclipse sighed heavily.

"Yeah, yeah, stop kissing up to me," he teased. "Everyone, this is my brat of a little sister, Saki."

"I actually blame you for giving her that attitude," Master Genbuki said to Eclipse. "This is my daughter," he told the other Guardians.

"It's nice to meet you," she said, walking back around the couch to shake hands with them. Dalton smiled as he took her hand. "Wow, you are way more handsome in person than on TV," she complimented. Startled, Dalton blinked and let out an uncomfortable chuckle.

"Saki! Don't hit on my colleagues!" Eclipse scolded, horrified.

"What? He's good looking!"

"He's *married* And you're *sixteen*!"

"Almost seventeen."

"That's not any better."

"Would it be so bad if I married a top-ranked Guardian?" she challenged. "Someone who could protect me and provide for me?"

"Yes, it would," Eclipse said strongly. "I've already told you, *no* Guardians. And everyone here is already taken."

Saki's eyes settled on Keito and her expression became wonderstruck. Keito laughed.

"I'm *way* too old for you."

"*The* Keito DeVero..." she gasped, her hands covering her nose and mouth as she stared at him, wide-eyed. "I can't believe I'm meeting you. I've learned all about you in school."

"Okay," Eclipse declared, more uncomfortable than any of his teammates. "I think that's enough fawning over the celebrity Guardians."

"Sorry, I'm sorry, it's just...I've never been this close to a demon before. And it's not just a demon, it's the most famous Guardian in history." She shook her head. "Can I hug you?"

Eclipse groaned loudly in embarrassment, leaning his head back on the couch.

Keito stood, smiling as he walked over to hug her. As he pulled away, she grabbed his hand, turning it to look at the longer, slightly-sharper nails.

"Do all demons have nails like this?"

"Yes."

"What about your eyes? They're so bright. Can I tell a demon out of a crowd of humans by their eye color? What about your teeth? Are they sharper—"

"Saki!" Eclipse gasped. "You've been spending way too much time with Erik. Don't interrogate him like he's some test subject."

"Oh, sorry, I'm so sorry," she said quickly, releasing Keito's hand and backing away. "That was insensitive. I'm just so curious about demons. I didn't mean to offend you or make you uncomfortable." She lowered her eyes to the ground, also embarrassed. Keito smiled gently, placing a hand on her shoulder.

"It's alright," he assured. "I know demons are a little elusive. If you have questions, you can ask them. But maybe when I'm not the center of attention in the entire room. It does make me a little uncomfortable."

"Right, of course. I'm really sorry," she said, her cheeks burning bright with embarrassment.

"Well, while you were fawning over our guests, I noticed you completely forgot your old man over here," Master Genbuki said after clearing his throat. Saki grinned brightly, bouncing over to sit next to her father, kissing him on the cheek.

"Thank you," Master Genbuki said with a nod. "How was school today?"

"Ugh," she groaned, rolling her eyes.

"You also taught her that eye-rolling thing," Master Genbuki said, pointing to Eclipse.

"It was fine," she grumbled. "Some asshole boys were being assholes in science class."

"Watch your language," Master Genbuki scolded gently.

"Well, they *were*," she defended. "They were passing notes and throwing things at me all through class. I finally got fed up with it."

"Oh no, what did you do?" Eclipse asked.

"I wasn't just going to sit there and take it!" she defended. "So, when one of them threw his eraser at me, I punched him."

"*What*?!"

"In the *shoulder*, not in the face!"

"You can't just punch people."

"Yes, I can. They were *throwing* things at me. And they started this rumor about me that I'm not even human, and that I was so dangerous they kicked me out of Guardian training, which is why I'm at school rather than training to be a Guardian like you."

"Wait, they're harassing you because Eclipse is a Guardian?" Dalton interjected.

"No, they're harassing me because they're *dicks*."

"Saki, language, please," Master Genbuki said.

"I understand that you're frustrated, but you can't just punch people," Eclipse said. "I'll go talk to the teachers. Maybe we can find a new seat for you away from those boys."

"You, uh…don't really have a choice," Saki said, reaching into her pocket with a sheepish smile. Eclipse raised an eyebrow at her, reaching for the paper.

"And why is that?"

She did not answer, wringing her hands in her lap nervously as Eclipse opened the letter and read it over. When he reached the end of the letter, he let out a long sigh and turned to her slowly.

"Saki…"

"I know! I know!" she said quickly. "I'm sorry! I really didn't mean to say it, *kan-na*. I was pissed off."

Eclipse folded the letter and stood, motioning for Saki to follow him. She shuffled her feet across the floor, following Eclipse around the corner. The other Guardians looked away, uncomfortable witnessing the personal troubles of their teammate. Only Hanyi, Keito, and Master Genbuki could hear the words Eclipse whispered to Saki around the corner.

"I don't want you to be hurt because of me," he said. "And if you continue to let them provoke you to violence, you will get into trouble, and these boys are going to keep pushing you. They want to get a rise out of you. And then you might say things you regret."

"I'm really sorry, *kan-na*," she said, her voice becoming choked.

"I know you are," he said. "But very, *very* few people know this about me," he said, lifting the letter. "Okay? I'm trusting you to keep this a secret. I'll go sort things out with your school, but *please* be more careful."

"I will."

"I just want you to be safe," Eclipse said. "I couldn't bear it if I put you in any danger. Alright, squirt?" He placed a hand on her head, causing her to laugh and squirm away.

"Don't mess up my hair."

He opened his arms and she hugged him tight.

Chapter Six

When Eclipse wandered into the kitchen the following morning, he was still mostly asleep. But his drowsiness was immediately eliminated when he nearly ran into Mitoki as he walked into the kitchen.

"Shit, you startled me," he grumbled, pushing past the youngest member of the team. "What are you doing up so early lurking in my kitchen?"

"Didn't really sleep," Mitoki mumbled. "I was going to make coffee, but I can't find it."

Eclipse sighed, trudging to a cabinet and pulling down the coffee, taking it toward the coffee machine as Mitoki quietly thanked him and leaned against the counter, falling into awkward silence. The older Guardian shot a concerned glance at Mitoki when he saw the way the younger man's head was drooped and his eyes were half-closed in exhaustion.

"You look like crap," he noted. "Did you sleep *at all*?"

Mitoki groaned, squeezing his eyes shut tight for a moment before standing straight.

"Not really."

"Why not?"

"I was researching."

Eclipse continued to busy himself making coffee, letting out an exasperated laugh.

"I thought you learned your lesson that it's dangerous to research this case," he noted. "Next we're going to learn that the entire dragon clan is helping this demon take over humanity."

Mitoki snorted. "I wasn't researching the case," he corrected. "Actually, I was looking up things about Juptoth."

Eclipse froze, turning to Mitoki.

"Why?"

"It's your hometown, right?" The younger Guardian shrugged one shoulder, turning away from Eclipse's suspicious gaze. "Which means it's also where I was born."

As Eclipse waited for the coffee to brew, he leaned against the counter next to Mitoki, crossing his arms over his chest, looking everywhere but at his younger teammate.

"Does it bother you that I told you about that?" he murmured.

"No, no, I just...I want to know." Mitoki sighed, also looking away from Eclipse. "I guess...you didn't really tell me about the man who murdered my parents, and your parents, so I wanted to see if there were any news reports about a serial killer in Juptoth. I wanted to see if I could learn their names."

"Then it does bother you."

"Come on, Eclipse, you can't blame me for wanting to know where I came from."

"No, I understand that. I just don't want you feeling conflicted about the life you have now because you're chasing down ghosts from the past. I mean, don't you like your life in the Realm of Light? You have a fiancée You became top-ranked Guardian in your realm. What does it matter where you were born?"

"Nevermind, you wouldn't understand."

A heavy silence fell over them once again, the awkward atmosphere in the kitchen becoming heavier and heavier until Eclipse sighed, closing his eyes.

"What did you manage to find?"

"It's fine, Eclipse I don't want to bring up painful memories for you."

"Like I don't already think about my parents every day," Eclipse grumbled. "I guess it makes sense that you think about them, too. Trying to guess what they were like."

"What were they like?" Mitoki asked. "Did you ever meet them?"

"Yeah, I met them," Eclipse said, his eyes distant on the tile of the kitchen floor. "Unfortunately, I can't remember them very well. I was just a kid, too." He sighed. "But I do remember that every kid in the neighborhood was told that if there was ever a problem, and we needed help, we were to go to your parents' house. So, clearly, they were really good people."

Mitoki smiled. Eclipse drummed his fingers along the counter behind him, turning to see how long the coffee would take, uncomfortable.

"There wasn't a lot of information about who killed them," Mitoki said. "You said he was dealt with. So, I can only assume some sort of small-town justice occurred."

Eclipse laughed quietly.

"Yeah, that's pretty much what happened."

"I'm sorry, I shouldn't be bringing up these painful memories," Mitoki said.

"No, I'm sorry I told you about what happened. I knew it was a bad idea and it would send you down a rabbit hole."

"How much do you know about what happened? You were pretty young when the killings happened. Did you go down the rabbit hole as well when you were older?"

Eclipse drew in a deep breath.

"No," he said. "I...remember a lot of it. I was...I was the one who found my parents, so..."

"Oh, no, Eclipse, I'm so sorry. I—"

"I told you, it's alright," the older man assured. "Unfortunately, there was a lot of anticipation around the town. Families were being attacked, ominous letters were being delivered. I think everyone knew it was only a matter of time before he struck again. And let's just say that when I heard the glass of the back door breaking...I knew what was coming."

"You were *there*?"

Eclipse nodded slowly.

"Erik was at school, but I was home with my parents. I heard the glass break and I just knew I had to hide." He hesitated. "Actually, I haven't told many people this, but...I had a younger brother, too. He passed away when he was about a year old. He was just a baby when this happened so I knew I had to protect him. I grabbed him from his crib and then we both hid in the crawlspace in my closet. He woke up when my parents started screaming. I tried to keep him quiet, but..." Eclipse closed his eyes. "Anyway, obviously, he found us."

"Shit..."

"I just left my brother in the closet and jumped at him," Eclipse said with a disbelieving laugh. "I don't remember a lot before a family friend named Austin showed up. Even after that, some of it is a blur, but I do remember finding my parents in the living room. Let's just say that that was the thing that screwed me up the most, and more-or-less solidified my path to being a Guardian, trying to prevent anyone from having to experience what I did."

"I'm so sorry, Eclipse."

The older Guardian turned to the coffee, taking down two mugs from the cabinet and filling them mechanically.

"You asked why I didn't tell you sooner that I knew what happened to your parents, and truthfully, I did not know how much you knew," he said. "But I would never want you to think about your parents the way I can't help but think about mine. I try to imagine all the good times, the laughs, and the family trips, but inevitably, it comes back to seeing my parents mutilated in the middle of the living room. And I didn't want you to think about death when you thought of your family."

Mitoki nodded slowly. "Thank you, Eclipse. I appreciate that."

Eclipse handed the coffee over to Mitoki.

"You know, if you have a chance, you should go see Juptoth," he suggested. "It's a beautiful small town."

"Maybe someday," Mitoki agreed.

Eclipse began to leave the kitchen, drinking his coffee as he walked. Mitoki followed him absentmindedly. As Eclipse sat down in the living room, briefly glancing at his phone, Mitoki sat opposite him.

"Wait."

Eclipse looked up

"You said that the death of your family solidified your path to being a Guardian, but if it was just a human serial killer, that would have been something law enforcement would handle," he mused. "Was the killer not human?"

The hesitation in Eclipse's face was enough to answer Mitoki's question, but Eclipse's answer was not what he expected.

"He wasn't a demon, I do know that," he answered. "And I had to become a Guardian because no law enforcement office would accept me. And I knew that."

"Why not?"

"Doesn't matter." He pushed the question away. "Not like I could change careers now. Or would even want to."

Mitoki wanted to press Eclipse for more information about why he chose the path of a Guardian, but he could tell that he was already on thin ice. He drank his coffee slowly, falling, once again, into uncomfortable silence.

The silence was broken by Dalton walking into the living room, surprised to see both of them awake.

"You two are awake already?"

"There's coffee in the kitchen, if you want some."

Dalton turned away from his path to the couch and went to the kitchen to retrieve coffee. When he returned, he sat heavily next to Eclipse and sighed.

"I'm worried you guys aren't comfortable in your rooms with how early everyone is waking up," Eclipse grumbled.

"Oh, no, I was comfortable," Dalton assured. "My brain, on the other hand, refused to let me get much sleep."

"Yeah, definitely a lot to think about right now."

Dalton took another sip of his coffee. "Eclipse, about the stuff going on at Saki's school. There are programs to protect the families of Guardians if they are struggling with their environment."

"Oh, she's not struggling. If anything, she'll get kicked out because she's so hard-headed," Eclipse said. "And I've looked into having her transferred before, but she wouldn't hear of it. She says she refuses to be bullied away."

"Well, if you need any help, let me know. I've looked up everything I can in preparation for Theresa going through her schooling." He laughed. "Though I fear for anyone who crosses her path in the future, too. She'll probably do the same thing as Saki."

"Is she already that strong-willed?" Mitoki asked with a smile.

"She's very bright for her age," Dalton said, chuckling. "When we tell her to do something, you can see the gears turning in her head wondering if she actually *needs* to, and if we have the authority to tell her what to do."

"Probably doesn't help that you're wrapped around her finger," Mitoki noted.

"Are those rumors really that widespread?"

Both Eclipse and Mitoki nodded quickly.

"I suppose there are worse rumors to have linked to me."

The click of a door opening down the hall caught their attention. Saki stumbled down the hall, half-asleep. She groaned as she went to the couch and flopped down next to Eclipse, leaning against his shoulder with her eyes closed.

"Don't go back to sleep," Eclipse laughed, pushing her upright. "You have to go to school."

"I'm so tired," she whined. She perked up a bit when she saw Eclipse's mug and quickly snatched it away, drinking some.

"Hey! That's mine!"

"I need it more than you," she pouted.

"No, I've seen you on caffeine," he insisted, retrieving his mug. "Drink some water and do some jumping jacks. That will wake you up."

"That's the cruelest thing you have ever said to me," she grumbled. "Can you drive me to school?"

"Your bus will be here any minute," Eclipse told her, glancing at his watch.

"You're so mean…"

"I know. Now, go get your shoes on and get your bag. Remember, I'll be at your school at the end of the day, so meet me out front."

"Yeah, yeah…" She moved sleepily to the foyer.

"Have a good day," Eclipse called, smiling at her mumbled reply as she shuffled to the front door.

"My daughter is like that in the morning, too."

"Yeah, but your daughter is, what, six?" Eclipse chuckled.

They both heard the front door open and Saki said a quiet, "good morning, Keito," as she closed the door.

"Keito's awake?" Dalton asked.

"I guess so."

The front door opened again and Keito stepped inside, his face still pale and eyes bloodshot, though he did look better than the previous day.

"I didn't realize you were all up already," he said.

"We didn't know you were up, either."

"Did no one sleep?" Eclipse grumbled, standing to refill his coffee. "Maybe except for Hanyi."

As if called, Hanyi rounded the corner, surprised.

"Oh, good morning," he greeted.

"Well, now that everyone is up, we should think about breakfast," Eclipse said. "Any requests?"

"Are you cooking?" Hanyi asked, surprised.

"Why? Do you want to cook?"

"You just don't seem like the cooking type," the wolf noted.

Eclipse just sighed and stepped into the kitchen, telling the others that there was more coffee if they wanted it. As he opened the refrigerator to grab some eggs for breakfast, Master Genbuki knocked his fist against the door jamb, catching their attention.

"Good morning," the Guardians greeted.

"Good morning," he replied. "Eclipse, put those back. No breakfast, yet."

Eclipse groaned, begrudgingly obeying. "I know what that means."

"What *does* that mean?" Hanyi asked.

"It means you need to work up more of an appetite," Master Genbuki said. "I know you said your trainer would likely come over and have you run some exercises, but I would like to see for myself, so to speak, what you all are made of."

"You're really going to train us, first thing in the morning, on their second day here?"

"Of course," Master Genbuki said. "You wouldn't deny me this, would you, Eclipse? I can't watch the tournament like everyone else. I have to gain my knowledge first-hand." He turned. "Come on."

Following the broad, tall trainer out the back door, the Guardians caught sight of the partially-indoor training area Eclipse had mentioned. Using the backyard fences and the back of the garage to make up three walls, the covered area of dirt was clearly well-used, if the scorch marks along the fence were anything to judge.

"Unique way to have an at-home training center."

"It used to be fully enclosed as my home gym," Master Genbuki explained. "I was a personal trainer before I got my training license for Guardians in order to train Eclipse. Little did I know that when you practice magic in a small space, you can pass out if it becomes too potent. Learned pretty quickly that this area had to be modified to avoid long-term complications."

Dalton laughed, nodding slowly as he stepped over the damp grass and onto the dirt.

"That is why most of the training arenas are so big," he agreed.

"I barely got this one to pass the requirements for obtaining my training license," Master Genbuki continued. "They wanted me to make it twice as big, but let it slide when I told them I would only have one student."

"I just told them I would train out of the nearest training center," Dalton laughed. "Even though I train my apprentice in the backyard a lot."

"You have an apprentice?" Eclipse asked. "I didn't even know you had your training license."

"I got it just for Andrew," Dalton explained. "He's the only one I would ever consider training. He actually should be taking the oath within the year. After that, I'm going to let the license lapse. It's really hard to get a training license."

"Yes, it is," Master Genbuki agreed with a tired laugh.

"You could have just sent him to a Guardian Training Center," Hanyi noted.

"They didn't want him," Master Genbuki quipped, grinning as he hit Eclipse's shoulder a little harder than necessary. "But being a Guardian was the only thing he took seriously, so it was worth it to keep this punk from going rogue. Thankfully, I already knew how to fight because I grew up in an area where you needed to defend yourself. And being a blind teen, I had to learn that lesson quite well. And then my work as a personal trainer allowed me to sneak by on the qualifications for training Eclipse."

"Well, he is one of the top-ranked Guardians in the branch, so you did something right," Eclipse said sarcastically.

"You still can't beat me, though," Master Genbuki leered.

"Wanna bet, old man?"

"You can be my warm up," the older man declared, reaching into his pocket and pulling out what the others quickly figured was a blindfold. Eclipse took it without question, but the other Guardians became worried. "The rest of you better stretch. I'm going to have you do a few laps around the neighborhood before we spar," Master Genbuki told them.

"Um…" Hanyi started worriedly. "Is that a blindfold?"

"You Guardians depend too much on your sight," Master Genbuki said. "So yes, you will be blindfolded."

"You know, I already finished this kind of training decades ago," Hanyi said quickly. "I'm fine without a refresher course."

"Worried you'll be beaten by a blind man?" Master Genbuki laughed.

"No, I'm already certain you would beat me."

"Then what's the problem?"

"He has a phobia about being unable to see," Keito grumbled. "You'll be fine. Your hearing is better than anyone else here."

Hanyi huffed. "Do you have to do that in front of everyone? Just expose me like that?" he whined. "You just like to make me look bad in front of others. Just completely ignore my feelings…" he lamented dramatically.

"Oh, quit dramatizing," Keito laughed.

"I have never been good at the blind training stuff. I am a predator animal. I live on my sight," he huffed.

"All the more reason to spar blindfolded today," Master Genbuki declared. "But before you can do any of that, you're doing laps. Eclipse, four laps along the usual route. The rest of you, follow him."

"From one master right to another, I swear…" Mitoki grumbled.

"Before we go," Dalton said quickly, turning to Keito, "are you up for training?"

"*Training*, no." Keito admitted. "But light exercise should be fine. With the tournament in a few days, I need to build my strength up a little."

"Don't overdo it," Master Genbuki warned. "You don't want to open the wound again."

"The wound is fully closed, it's the fever I'm still fighting," Keito explained.

"I suppose it might be difficult to push yourself to your limit around humans," Master Genbuki said. "Alright, Eclipse, show them the route."

Jogging around Eclipse's neighborhood was both invigorating and relaxing, the sparse neighborhood giving the area a quaint, calm feeling to their workout. Once Keito and Hanyi knew the route, they took off at their own pace to properly warm up and Keito passed them twice, arriving at the house twenty minutes before everyone else.

"Good," Master Genbuki said approvingly, replacing the weights he had picked up for his own warm up. "Eclipse, you're up first."

Master Genbuki and Eclipse sparred easily with one another, knowing the other's style well enough to truly challenge the other man. The others leaned against the back of the garage to watch the quick, precise movements. It was obvious with the way Eclipse evaded Master Genbuki's attacks, even while blindfolded, that he was very accustomed to the exercise.

Dalton knew that all Guardians had similar training. Jikia had only trained them in the dark a few times at the beginning of their team training, but he also recalled practicing attacks in a dark room when he was at the Guardian Training Center as a kid. He had never used the training in the field, so he was concerned that the exercise would prove more difficult than he anticipated.

Eclipse was finally knocked down with a hard punch to his jaw that had everyone cringing at the sound it made. As Eclipse struggled to regain his bearings and get to his feet again, Master Genbuki dug his heel into Eclipse's chest.

"And you're dead," he said simply. Eclipse's head fell back to the ground and he gasped for breath, roughly yanking off the blindfold and blinking to readjust his eyes.

"You *always* leave that right side open," Master Genbuki scolded, moving his foot off the Guardian's chest and tapping it against Eclipse's right side. "Your enemies will notice that if you fight them long enough. Either learn to cover that right side properly, or don't drag the fight out so long."

"Fine, just let me up, already," Eclipse grumbled, turning over and getting to his feet. He rubbed his jaw. "You're supposed to be my mentor and teach me, not break my jaw to get your point across."

"If I recall, you have picked up that punching technique yourself," Dalton joked, remembering the sheer strength of Eclipse's punch.

"Well, Dalton, care to try your hand, now?" Master Genbuki asked.

"Are you going to hit me that hard?"

"Only if you pose a challenge and I actually have to put my heart into this."

Dalton stepped forward slowly.

"I think that's a roundabout way of insulting me," he laughed, taking the blindfold from Eclipse as he walked forward to meet the older man.

"Don't worry, I'll go easy on you at first. I'm not sure how much training like this you've done in the past."

"It has been a long time," Dalton admitted, surveying his surroundings quickly before tying the blindfold over his eyes, hoping he could keep his spacial awareness during the spar.

Hanyi turned to the other Guardians and gesticulated wildly, mouthing for them to sneak away and leave while Dalton was blindfolded, though Mitoki shot him a playful glare, ignoring the wolf's further silent pleading as Keito chuckled and Eclipse tried not to smile.

Dalton was surprised at how easily his training returned to him. He used his abilities in magic to heighten his awareness of his surroundings, feeling where he was in relation to everything and everyone around him. While it made it more difficult to concentrate on the fast-moving master and know exactly how to counterattack, Dalton only stumbled and missed Master Genbuki a few times.

The other Guardians, as soon as they managed to get Hanyi off the idea of leaving their blindfolded team leader as a joke, were very quiet and respectful, even when they saw Dalton miss Master Genbuki completely a few times, swinging wildly at the air.

However, a noise did break Dalton's concentration.

"Hello? Is anyone here?" a familiar voice called near the backyard gate.

"Jikia?" Dalton said, forgetting about the quickly-approaching Master Genbuki, who landed a hard punch to Dalton's abdomen. He doubled over, gasping for breath, completely disoriented.

"I'm sorry!" Master Genbuki gasped, taking hold of Dalton's shoulders and trying to keep him from falling over. "That was a cheap shot. I'm sorry. That startled me, too."

"I'm...o-okay..." Dalton gasped, trying desperately to take in air as his body radiated with pain.

"We're in the backyard," Eclipse called over his shoulder as the others of the team rushed forward to Dalton. "Just reach over and unhook the latch."

The dragons entered the backyard and caught sight of the Guardians crowded around Dalton, asking if he was alright while he laughed breathlessly.

"What happened?" Tarrena asked.

The Guardians hesitated, unsure if they should tell her the truth—that her sudden appearance had broken Dalton's concentration and resulted in him taking a harsh punch to his gut.

"Just...doing some training exercises...and I lost my focus," Dalton assured, slowly standing straight, feeling around his abdomen with wide eyes. "Wow, you weren't lying, Eclipse. That felt like a battering ram to my stomach."

"Again, I am really sorry about that," Master Genbuki said sincerely, keeping a hand on Dalton's shoulder.

"It's alright," Dalton said. "But if you don't mind, I am going to call it a day here."

"Yes, of course, you should," Master Genbuki agreed strongly. He turned in the direction of the new voices he heard. "I've been having them do some training exercises. Hope you don't mind."

"Not at all," Jikia said. "I'm Jikia Topesca, and this is my daughter, Tarrena."

A smirk crossed Master Genbuki's face, but he quickly covered it with a broad smile as he reached forward for a handshake.

"It's very nice to meet you," he said. "Eclipse has told me so much about you."

"If it's bad, it's all lies," Jikia laughed. "What sort of training are you having them do?"

"Spar with me blindfolded," he said. "Speaking of, who is next?"

"I vote Mitoki!" Hanyi said quickly. Dalton laughed.

"You really don't want to do this, do you?"

"I saw that punch. I do *not* want to experience that," the wolf laughed.

"What makes you think *I* do?" Mitoki whined.

"You're younger! You recover faster!" Hanyi insisted. "I was always really bad at this kind of training. I probably will last about thirty seconds, and then I'll get punched, and I just…I don't want that."

"It's really not that bad, Hanyi," Dalton assured. "Just use a heightened awareness, and you'll do fine."

"I also don't fight so well in my human form. Haven't you noticed that?"

"No," Dalton groaned. "You are an amazing Guardian, Hanyi."

"All I'm hearing is whining over there!" Master Genbuki taunted. "Hanyi, you're up! Let's go!"

"I don't wanna…"

"Go on," Keito said, pushing Hanyi's shoulder and forcing him to step closer to Master Genbuki.

"And Hanyi, don't pout for the rest of the day because of this," Eclipse called.

"I'm not going to pout!" Hanyi snapped, though he played up the tone to make it seem as though he was already pouting.

Hanyi did much better than he thought he would—and better than the others of his team expected. But they could see with the tensing of his jaw and his constantly-crouched position that every muscle in his body was flexed in concentration. Everyone was sure to remain as silent as possible, allowing the wolf to hear Master Genbuki's movements.

Finally, Hanyi, out of breath from running, fell to his side dramatically and called that he surrendered.

"Are you really that out of breath?" Master Genbuki asked, though he was also breathing hard from chasing the wolf.

"Hey, I'm a helluva lot older than those human kids. I'm probably double your age!" Hanyi laughed, removing the blindfold. "That, and I just faced one of my biggest fears."

"One of?" Master Genbuki chuckled, reaching out a hand to help the Guardian to his feet, though Hanyi had to almost get up as it was to take the offered hand. "What are the others?"

"Fire," Hanyi answered. "I don't like fire, and I don't like being unable to see."

The understanding silence that fell over the others was thick and uncomfortable. It was apparent everyone, even Master Genbuki, understood where Hanyi's fear of fire likely started.

"And men with beards," Hanyi added quickly.

The tension broke immediately.

"*What*?" Dalton laughed.

"Men with the big, bushy beards that cover up practically their whole face," Hanyi elaborated, his eyes wide. "Have you seen that? It's terrifying!"

Even though Mitoki was hesitant to take his turn, mostly because he had never had training of that manner before, he knew that Keito likely would not spar, so he took the blindfold from Hanyi when the wolf declared strongly that it was his turn.

Master Genbuki told Mitoki to relax and that he would go easy on him until Mitoki got the hang of the exercise. He struggled to understand how to move in his surroundings, constantly dropping his head and shoulders in preparation for bumping into something, unable to keep a strong posture. Master Genbuki got close to him a few times, forcing him to move. He then began coaching Mitoki, telling him to straighten his back and bring his arms away from his face. Those watching the spar shared impressed looks, amazed that the blind master was able to tell Mitoki what he was doing, despite being unable to see Mitoki's posture.

Mitoki was a quick study and soon was trying counterattacks, though Master Genbuki was able to easily dodge.

When the youngest Guardian was sweating and his legs were growing tired, Master Genbuki called a stop to the spar, worried about Mitoki hurting himself.

As the others congratulated Mitoki, Master Genbuki pursed his lips.

"I don't want to push you, but I am very curious to spar with you, Keito," he said.

"You also have me curious," Keito said, motioning for Mitoki to give him the blindfold. "But I've been watching your style this whole time, so I think I know how to evade the sheer strength of your punches."

"Interesting," Master Genbuki said, grinning. "But I won't force you to spar if you don't feel up to it."

"Keito," Jikia started, her tone strong, "please don't spar if it's going to make you feel worse."

"I'm sure I'll be fine," Keito said. "I know how much my body can handle. I've been living in it for over three hundred years."

"Just don't push too hard," Jikia warned. "I know you're the type to ignore injuries. I don't know if that's because you have a problem appearing weak, or if you have just learned how to deal with pain differently—"

"Wow, hit that nail on the head," Hanyi chuckled.

"—but you need to understand that we worry about you. If you won't think of yourself, please remember that we want you to be healthy, even if that means sitting on the sidelines until you're better."

"You're making it sound like I'm going up against an army of demons," Keito jeered. "It's one spar. As long as I take it easy the rest of the day, I'll be fine. But I need to keep my strength up."

"Are you certain?" Master Genbuki pressed.

"Yes," Keito said, tying the blindfold over his eyes. "Don't hold back on me. Trust me, I can take your full strength."

"I want to test that theory."

The blind man did not hesitate in going after Keito, who easily dodged the first attack and rounded to defend himself against the second. While Dalton and the others knew that Keito was not using his full speed and strength, they were still startled by how fast he had to move to get out of the way.

For the first time, Dalton spotted the exact moment Keito became fully invested in the spar. His entire body language changed. He lowered his stance and his mouth turned upward slightly at the corners. Not only was he now serious about the match, he was also enjoying it. He moved about the space as if he could see everything around him, and he countered attacks from the blind man so easily, it was as though neither of them were fighting with a handicap.

Keito was beginning to sweat when he dodged another attack and leaned forward, raising his hands in front of him.

"Let's see what you've got."

Master Genbuki threw his fist at Keito's hands. The demon caught the fist and his arms jolted. Dalton, remembering the pain that radiated through his abdomen, cringed. But his expression quickly turned to one of amazement when he saw Keito's feet slide backward from the force of the punch. The demon did not lose his balance, even though he was surprised by Master Genbuki's strength.

When the man stepped away, breathing hard, he smiled.

"Well?"

"Are you entirely human?" Keito asked, standing straight and removing the blindfold. "I don't know that I've ever come across someone like you."

"I'll take that as a complement," Master Genbuki laughed.

"You really had me running around there," Keito said.

"Oh, come on, I know you were taking it easy on me."

"I tried to spar with you like I spar with humans, but that was not enough." He shook his hands out, wiggling his fingers. "I've even got pins and needles in my hands. Dalton, Eclipse, I'm impressed you were able to recover so quickly from those attacks."

They both laughed hollowly, though they did feel better knowing even the demon had struggled with Master Genbuki's brute strength.

Chapter Seven

The Guardians were ravenous after their training exercises with Master Genbuki, so everyone worked together to nearly clear out the contents of Eclipse's kitchen. Once their hunger had been sated, the heaviness of the overcast sky, as well as the increasingly technical conversation between Master Genbuki and Jikia about the tournament, had the Guardians lounging quietly in the living room.

In the early afternoon, Eclipse disappeared into his room and returned with a stack of folded papers he put in his pocket.

"I'm going to head to the school," he announced.

"Do you want me to come with you?" Master Genbuki asked.

"No," Eclipse assured. "I can handle this."

"Eclipse," Dalton called, standing and motioning for his teammate to follow him. They stepped further into the hallway, away from any eavesdroppers, and Dalton lowered his voice. "I know it's not my place to say, but I am technically your superior. I can come and speak on your behalf if this is something you need my help on."

Eclipse glanced over his shoulder, as if to be sure no one was peering around the corner to listen to them.

"Uh, actually, it would be better if you were to come with me, but..." He lowered his gaze. "There's something you don't know about me."

"About your special classification?" Dalton asked knowingly. "I actually do know."

"You do?"

"Well, not the specifics," Dalton admitted. "I do your evaluation paperwork every year. I know that you're classified as a non-human-human Guardian, which is one of the most confusing names I've ever heard, by the way."

Eclipse laughed. "Yeah, it's pretty stupid," he agreed. "I'm human physically. Just not...magically, I guess."

"You don't need to explain anything you're not comfortable with," Dalton assured. "It also explains why you're the most magically gifted human I've ever met."

"I'm surprised you didn't bring it up sooner."

"You've passed all your evaluations and it does not seem to harm your ability as a Guardian," Dalton said. "Therefore, it's none of my business."

Eclipse let out a long breath, relaxing slightly.

"You have a very different philosophy than Guardian Jordan."

Dalton rolled his eyes at the thought of his predecessor as top-ranked Guardian in the branch.

"Yeah, well, his nosiness is what got him killed," he grumbled. "If you want to tell me, just know I won't judge, but I won't push you to do so. Since you haven't told me yet, I'm assuming it's something you want to keep secret."

"That's actually what this whole thing is about," Eclipse said, tapping the papers he had folded in his pocket. "In anger, Saki eluded to the fact that I'm...a non-human human, I guess. So now her teacher is concerned that Saki might be a danger to other students if *she's* not entirely human. I'm going to have to go there, explain we're not blood related, and show all my paperwork proving I'm not a danger. If you could come and vouch for me, I would actually really appreciate it."

"Of course," he said. "We'll get it sorted out."

"Thank you, Dalton."

With a hand on Eclipse's shoulder, Dalton turned his teammate around to return to the living room, ready to tell the others he was going to go with Eclipse. But once he reached the living room he was confronted with a large wolf sitting in his path, looking up at him, his eyes bright and his tongue hanging out of his mouth as his tail beat the floor rhythmically.

Dalton just stared at Hanyi, confused and worried that the wolf had overheard the conversation.

"What?"

Hanyi's tail picked up speed, hitting the hardwood floor with a louder thumping sound.

"What does he want?" Dalton asked with a laugh, turning to Keito for a translation.

"He wants to go to the school with you," the demon chuckled.

"Why?"

"He's never been to a human school. He's curious."

Dalton turned to Eclipse, who sighed heavily, his skeptical gaze turning onto Hanyi.

"Are you going to take no for an answer?"

Hanyi barked twice and whined, standing straight.

"You can take that as a no," Keito translated.

"Alright, fine," Eclipse groaned.

Hanyi yipped happily, jumping and running toward the garage, his feet struggling for purchase on the hardwood floor. Mitoki also stood.

"Hold on, can I come?"

"Why?" Eclipse asked.

"Because he doesn't want to be stuck here with us," Master Genbuki called over his shoulder. Eclipse closed his eyes, resigning himself to his entire team joining him.

"You can say no," Dalton assured.

"No, it's fine." Eclipse turned to Keito. "Are you coming, too?"

Keito stood. "Someone has to keep all of you in line."

Eclipse struggled to find a spot in the crowded parking lot, so the Guardians had to walk against the flow of hundreds of teenagers filing out of the school to head home for the day. Hanyi watched them in fascination, as though experiencing an entirely new culture he was desperate to understand.

"You've really never seen a normal, human school?" Dalton asked skeptically.

"No," he said excitedly. "I mean, I've *seen* the buildings from a distance, but I never had a reason to go near one."

"It's just a building full of teenagers," Eclipse said. "Really not that exciting."

"What was it like? I've seen movies about school. Was it really full of antics like that? Because I would have *loved* to go to school if it was."

The humans all hesitated.

"I actually never went to high school," Dalton admitted slowly, also turning his eyes to watch the few teenagers who had taken notice of the Guardians walking toward their school. "A part of me wanted to go, but…it just wasn't practical."

"I didn't go, either," Eclipse seconded. "I had some friends who attended this school. I would wait for them out front when I wasn't on a case and we would spend some time together once they were out of class. They would always talk about what happened at school that day and it seemed like their lives were so much simpler than mine…it did make me a little jealous, honestly."

"I did my first year," Mitoki said. "I didn't have a big case load when I first joined the branch, so I had time to enroll once I took the oath and got out of Guardian training."

"Did you like it?" Dalton asked.

"I was beat up a lot," he laughed. "And because of my classification as a Guardian, I was forbidden from fighting back." He smiled, shrugging. "Yeah, I loved it," he said sincerely. "But after my first kill case, I wasn't right in the head to be around people my own age. I dropped out and just got my educational certificate through the branch, but I remember enjoying a lot about high school."

"I forgot how young humans take the oath as Guardians," Keito said quietly.

The Guardians stood near a large tree planter at the front of the school, watching the teenagers leave as they waited for Saki to find them. When she stepped out of the doors, she smiled guiltily at them as she approached.

"Hey," she greeted, hugging Eclipse.

"Hey. Did you get into trouble again? What's with the guilty expression?" he responded.

"No, I didn't get into trouble," she said. "I mean…the teacher didn't *see*, but there might be an incident report if the kid decides to squeal on me."

"Saki!"

"I couldn't let that asshole get away with what he said," she snapped. "He said that it was lucky I hadn't found you dead in the house already because all Guardians commit suicide. And that it meant that you would snap and kill everyone in the house soon. I couldn't let that slide!"

Eclipse placed a hand on each of her shoulders, forcing her to look at him.

"You *have* to learn to let that stuff go," he said. "Do you know how many times I hear that? You know that people are uncomfortable with Guardians, and you know that there are a lot of statistics about us that scare people."

"That doesn't mean he has a right to *say* that!" she burst.

Eclipse closed his eyes. "No, it doesn't," he agreed. "But you have a choice how to respond."

"Saki," Dalton said, "if someone says something like that to you, just ask them if they would ever say that to a Guardian's face. And then tell them that they shouldn't say it to the face of someone who lives with one of the top-ranked Guardians in the branch. And then walk away."

She sighed, nodding slowly. "Yeah, that sounds like a more diplomatic approach," she grumbled.

"Plus it will actually scare them away if you add some flourish about training alongside your brother," Hanyi added with a wink.

She smiled, looking among the faces of Team Dalton.

"What are you all doing here, anyway?" she asked. "Trying to intimidate my teacher?"

"Damn straight," Hanyi said. "We're your big brothers, too, now. We have to make sure they're treating you right."

Grinning and rolling her eyes, she motioned for them to follow her into the school. The halls were mostly-deserted, some straggling students packing books into their backpacks before rushing to catch the bus, or just to escape the confines of the school. One boy shuffled toward the Guardians, his head down, forcing the group to part for him as he passed. He bumped into Dalton, but did not bother apologizing.

Keito caught the young man's arm and yanked him back.

"What the hell?!" the boy snapped, struggling against Keito. "Let me go, you freak!"

"Gladly," Keito snarled, reaching into the teenager's baggy sleeve and extracting a very familiar wallet before pushing the kid back. He flipped Dalton's wallet open, showing him the Guardian badge and ID. "Next time, kid, don't try to pickpocket a Guardian."

The boy's eyes shot comically wide and he turned, stumbling as quickly out of the building as possible.

Dalton looked between Keito and the teen in confusion.

"I didn't even notice," he muttered. "Normally, I notice that."

"Younger thieves are better than most give them credit for," Keito said, passing the wallet back to Dalton. "I just saw him push the wallet into his sleeve."

"Damn, they're starting younger and younger," Dalton groaned.

They finally reached one of the back hallways of the school, spotting a well-dressed woman standing outside an open classroom door. She crossed her arms over her chest when she caught sight of Saki, her tight, curly black hair bouncing around her face as she shook her head.

"Saki, you're late."

"I'm sorry, Mrs. Berkeley."

"Better late than never I suppose," she said. She turned to Eclipse, her expression becoming momentarily confused before she shook herself out of her stupor. "Sorry, are you her legal guardian?"

"No, not exactly," Eclipse said. "I am the Guardian in question, though. Eclipse Retani," he reached a hand out in introduction. "I apologize for being late, but I have brought all the necessary paperwork, and I hope we...can..." He trailed off when he saw the teacher's eyes widen. She had not moved to shake his hand and her wide, unblinking eyes had become unnerving. "Mrs. Berkeley, are you alright?"

"You're..." she stuttered, "*E-Eclipse Retani*?" She looked at the other four men standing behind him. "You're...Saki's older brother?"

"In a manner of speaking."

Mrs. Berkeley let out a shuddered breath, her eyes settling on Dalton. "Oh my...you're Dalton Teban!"

"Yes," he said with a nervous laugh, reaching forward in an attempt to shake her hand. "I'm here as Eclipse's superior to work out this misunderstanding."

The excited, quiet cry that escaped the teacher's mouth startled all of them. Saki, however, was pursing her lips against laughing uncontrollably.

"Then...tha-that's the rest of the team?" she half-whimpered. One of her hands covered her mouth in awe as she pointed nervously behind Dalton.

"Yes, we're in Kang-Dron for the next round of the tournament, so we're more-or-less travelling as a collective right now," Dalton said. He was both amused and concerned at the teacher's awe-filled reaction to their appearance. He was concerned that having all members of Team Dalton present would make the meeting with Saki's teacher difficult.

Mrs. Berkeley took a hesitant step closer, looking around Eclipse to Mitoki, who smiled and introduced himself. When she caught sight of Hanyi and Keito, she let out a soft shriek, both hands going to her face in surprise.

"Hanyi Treneke and Keito DeVero..." she breathed. "Oh my god...this can't be happening. You're really...*right here*."

"I never get this kind of reaction," Eclipse noted, smiling.

"I'm sorry, I'm sorry," Mrs. Berkeley said, her eyes never leaving Keito. "It's just...I'm a history teacher and I know so much about the two of you. I mean, as much as the textbooks say, which I guess isn't much, if you really think about it. But I did my thesis on your role in changing the stereotypes of demon Guardians," she said to Keito.

"Did I?"

"Oh, *yes*," she said enthusiastically. "Before you, there were *no* demon Guardians who had been raised in the Demon Dimension because those demons weren't trusted enough to take the oath." She continued to shake her head, mystified. "You changed the entire Guardian Branch. You wrote so many rules and regulations for, not just demon Guardians, but human and beast Guardians as well. You basically *made* the modern-day Guardian Branch."

"Does anyone wonder why I always felt so overshadowed?" Hanyi teased.

"I'm so sorry, I know I'm just..." She waved her hands nonsensically. "You're practically my hero! I never thought in a million years I would get to meet you in person. Is there any chance you could come and speak to my class? They would be so thrilled to meet such famous Guardians."

The human Guardians smiled at her enthusiasm, but also understood it well. Even though they had spent so much time with Keito already, there were moments where they would be struck with the realization that they were working alongside one of their heroes.

Keito smiled nervously.

"I would have to check with my team leader," he said, nodding to Dalton.

"Right, yes, of course," Mrs. Berkeley said. "We're actually covering the Guardian Tournament and its significance in honor of the next round. It would be amazing if you could come and talk to my classes and tell them your experiences within the tournament."

Dalton knew there was no way they would be able to talk about *their* experiences, but he could not help but be swayed by her enthusiasm.

"Maybe when the round is over we might have a little bit of time to come and talk to your class," Dalton said. "But we would have to take some precautions of course, so it doesn't get out of hand having us here during normal school hours."

"I'm sure my principal will love the idea," she insisted. "Actually, I need to call her for this meeting. Oh, but before I do. Would it be too much to ask you all for an autograph and a picture?"

Saki was more than happy to take multiple pictures of her teacher with the Guardians of Team Dalton. She had no idea if they knew that coming to the school as a team would put her teacher in such a good mood, but she was secretly thrilled to see the normally-stern history teacher giggling bashfully around the five Guardians.

Dalton managed to pull Mrs. Berkeley back on track to discuss the matter they were there to settle. While she called the principal to her class to commence the meeting, Dalton told Hanyi, Keito, and Mitoki to stay outside the classroom, wanting to give Eclipse as much discretion about his classification as possible. Honoring the agreement, Keito, Mitoki, and Hanyi sat outside the closed classroom door against the lockers, nodding silent greetings to the confused principal as she passed them to enter the classroom.

Of course, once she realized exactly who she had passed, she darted back out into the hallway to meet them properly, asking for pictures. Smiling broadly as she proudly looked over the pictures on her phone, she returned to the classroom while the three Guardians in the hallway resumed their seats, laughing.

"You certainly are popular," Mitoki told Keito.

"I thought most people would have forgotten me after decades of seclusion," the demon muttered. "Apparently, not much has changed."

"He used to get fan-mail," Hanyi said with a chuckle. "He was basically a celebrity. Women would actually ask him to be the father of their children."

"That only happened a few times with the really crazy ones," Keito corrected. "And don't act like that never happened to you. I know it did."

"Not nearly as often as it happened to you."

"It must be weird to be fawned over like that, though," Mitoki noted.

Keito paused, pensive. "There is a part of me that is actually really happy about it," he admitted. "I don't have a good reputation back home. I've done a lot of horrible things that I'm not proud of in my life. Having people see me as a hero, as someone who has done *good* for the world, it makes me feel a bit better about how I've turned out despite my mistakes."

"You really have changed a lot of lives," Mitoki agreed. "I hope that one day I can say I've done as much good for the realms as you have."

Keito smiled. "Don't worry, Mitoki. After this assignment, when Yokouro is finally dead and gone, you can be sure you've done the most good anyone could do for the realms."

The school was quiet as the final students left for the day, the buzzing of the overhead lights becoming a constant ring in the Guardians' ears as they waited for the meeting with Eclipse and Dalton to conclude. After twenty minutes of silent waiting, Mitoki drew his legs closer to his chest, hugging them as he shuddered.

"It's cold in here, isn't it?"

"Yeah, a little," Hanyi agreed, as if just noticing the chill.

"I don't think it should be so cold we can see our breaths," Keito muttered, watching the gentle dispelling of fog in front of his face.

"Yeah, that's not normal," Mitoki said, moving to stand.

The entire building gave a jolt, as if the cold air in the halls had snapped like cracking ice. They leapt to their feet, scanning every inch of the hallway.

"Was that some kind of earthquake?" Hanyi hissed, looking up and down the halls, waiting for the building to start shuddering. Everything remained eerily still.

With the speed of a runaway train, clacking sounds began to skitter over their heads, starting at one end of the school and quickly reverberating to the other. Lights flickered, a few bulbs bursting with a crunch of shattered glass. The air became even colder, encasing the Guardians in a freezing chill that had them shivering almost violently. Frost crept over the edges of nearby windows as another wave of clicking sounds tore through the hallway.

The door to the classroom flung open. Dalton and Eclipse rushed into the hall, looking around as the clicking noise passed over them and began to fade.

"What is that?" Dalton asked.

"No idea," Hanyi said.

"Can you guys feel that displacement?" Mitoki asked, wincing as he placed a hand on the lockers to steady himself. "The energies in here are fluctuating. It's killing my inner ear…"

"Is this something we need to attack?" Eclipse asked as another round of hurried clicking scurried over the ceiling. "What the hell *is it*?"

Keito followed the direction of the clicking noise again, his eyes sharp and his body tensed. When another wave of admittedly-quieter clacking sounds passed over them, he ran to the nearest window, studying the overcast sky through the distending glass fighting to bear up to the strange fluctuations.

"It's a ripple…" he whispered.

"What kind of ripple?"

"A big one," he answered, returning to his team. "Which means either there is a hole that has ripped in the dimensional fabric, or one of the Kage Lords is flexing his power."

"You mean one of them is here in the Darkness Realm?" Mitoki hissed.

"He wouldn't have to be," the demon corrected. "They're powerful enough to be felt across realms."

Dalton's mouth dropped open, his mind trying to wrap around the amount of power a demon would need to create such a disturbance from an entirely different realm.

"Seems to be weakening," Keito noted, the clacking above them much softer and slower on the next pass. "If it was a dimensional tear, we'll hear about it soon."

"I don't think I should be hoping for news of a dimensional tear, but I am," Mitoki noted worriedly.

Dalton and Eclipse were quick to finish the meeting with Saki's teacher, but Keito told them he was going to run back to the house and check on the others. When Eclipse arrived back home with Saki and the other Guardians, they rushed into the living room where everyone was watching the news.

"Everyone okay?" Dalton asked. "Did you feel the ripple?"

"It was *powerful*," Jikia said, muting the news as the Guardians dispersed among the living room. Eclipse stopped next to Tarrera, placing a hand on her shoulder.

"Are you alright?" he asked, noting the way she was cradling her head in her shaking hand.

"Hit me a little harder, for some reason," she said. "I'll be alright."

"Keito?" Dalton prompted.

"According to the news coverage, the Realm of Light and the Middle Dimension all reported disturbances. But the Middle Dimension has declared a state of emergency because of a massive power outage. Reports are slow coming in. They're still gathering information."

"Erik also called, wanted to see how you were," Master Genbuki added. "He said his facility was hit really hard."

"Like it was last week?"

"He didn't specify."

"What do you mean last week?" Dalton asked.

"When I was doing that meditation I told you about, where I was trying to find more about the hex beast, the power I touched was strong enough to melt the internal mechanisms of some of my brother's research meters," Eclipse elaborated.

"You didn't mention *that* part," Mitoki said.

"No mention of a dimensional tear, though?" Hanyi asked Keito. The demon shook his head slowly. "So it *was* one of the Kage Lords."

"Who?" Master Genbuki asked.

"If it was one of them, the bigger question is *why*," Dalton said. "Was it something that just happened? Something in the Demon Realm? Was it an attack?"

"It's hard to say," the demon said.

"Do you think we're in immediate danger?"

"Again, hard to say," he repeated.

Eclipse sighed, leaned back in his seat.

"I could always try and meditate on the energy, see if I can trace it back."

"Eclipse, *no*," Master Genbuki snapped. "You had a seizure last time. Like hell I'm going to let you put yourself in danger like that again."

"We can't very well *sit around* and wait to hear the consequences of whatever happened," he retorted.

"That's like saying you need to walk into a typhoon to try and stop the damage. This is beyond you. You need to be *smart* about this, not barrel into it and put yourself in unnecessary danger," Master Genbuki growled.

"He's right," Hanyi said. "As anxiety-inducing as it is, we need to be patient. Whatever the result of this ripple, we'll just have to deal—"

He stopped, turning to Dalton when he heard the other Guardian's phone ring. Extracting the phone from his pocket, Dalton looked at the screen and tensed.

"I think this is our answer," he mumbled, accepting the call and putting it on speaker. "Grandfather. What is it? Are you alright?"

"Dalton, where are you?" Elder Teban demanded sharply.

"Kang-Dron in the Darkness Realm at Guardian Retani's house. Why? Are you in danger?"

"Just stay put. The Elder convoy is coming to you."

"No, Grandfather, if there is something wrong you should remain where you are. We can come to you."

"The compound is being evacuated. Elder Renard has been abducted."

Everyone in the room turned to one another in terror, their mouths open and their eyes wide.

"Stay where you are. Lock the doors. We're coming to you," Elder Teban ordered. "We need to come up with a plan on how to handle this."

Chapter Eight

Three anxiety-ridden hours later, the Elder's convoy arrived in front of Eclipse's home. Everyone at the house was forced to remain in the living room under close surveillance while the security team secured the house, thoroughly searching every room before the four remaining Elders were able to join the Guardians.

The Guardians stood, offering their seats on the couches to the Dimension Protection Council Elders while they paced nervously.

"How long has Elder Renard been missing?" Dalton asked.

"A few hours," Elder Celeste answered. "It happened when the ripple knocked out power in the compound."

"Walk us through what happened."

The others turned to Elder Ari.

"Demetrius and I were preparing for a meeting when the ripple hit. It seemed to hit Demetrius harder than it hit me. He doubled over in pain. I didn't know what was going on. I was just suddenly dizzy. The lights started flickering and it became very cold. Then I was hit on the back of the head," he turned to show them the bandage taped to the back of his neck. "I blacked out. I don't remember anything after that."

"Once the worst of the ripple effects had subsided, we started gathering together. Normal protocol in emergency situations," Elder Lunar continued. "When neither Syrus nor Demetrius came to the chambers, we went to get them. We found a note."

One of the guards stretched a plastic-covered note forward. Dalton took it, reading over the impeccable penmanship on the paper as the others of his team gathered around him.

"*Nothing can remain hidden forever,*" Dalton read aloud. "*Humanity has lived in ignorance of its own frailty for too long. It's time to pull back the curtain. Lord Yokouro DeVastes.*"

Once the initial fear of seeing Yokouro's name signed at the bottom of the note had passed, Dalton read over the words multiple times in his head, trying to read between the short sentences in a desperate attempt to parse any clues from the declarations.

"Keito," Elder Teban started, "how much have you told them about your previous investigation?"

"As much as I felt I was allowed," Keito answered, his tone cold and clipped. "And I told them his name. They know who Yokouro DeVastes is."

"Why would you keep it a secret from us exactly who we were dealing with?" Eclipse asked. "If you knew his name, why didn't you tell us?"

"We assumed he had been weakened from the Tournament Slaughter and was not nearly as much of a threat," Elder Ari answered. "Hell, he's been almost silent for forty years. Two generations of Elders have passed. We were starting to think of him as a ghost story."

"A demon manages to lock down and slaughter an entire stadium while a dead, incorporeal being, and you think he's *weak*?" Mitoki asked skeptically.

"We didn't know the extent of what he had done inside that stadium. It was possible that that took nearly all his strength," Elder Teban retorted. "The reports were muddled, at best."

"Because the Elders were trying to cover up that they ignored our warnings," Hanyi grumbled, turning away from the Elders, hoping they did not hear him.

"We had no information on him," Elder Teban continued. "The Demon Realm isn't forthcoming about the goings-on within."

"Bullshit," Keito growled.

"Be very careful with your attitude, Keito," Elder Teban warned.

"You knew Yokouro would be interested the *moment* you approved the Guardian Tournament. You knew that he was the one who broke the seal. And because things are progressing further into chaos, you decided to take drastic measures rather than consult *any* demon. Any of us would have told you to leave the tournament dead and buried. But you didn't care." He laughed coldly. "And now, not only do you have Yokouro to deal with, you have the Kage Lords stirring. If you aren't careful, they will rip you to shreds."

"There is no proof of their involvement," Elder Lunar said sharply.

"The *ripple* should be proof enough for you," he sneered. "Even Yokouro can't cause that big of a disturbance."

"If that's the case, and they really are behind the ripple and the abduction, why take the demon Elder?" Dalton asked, trying to keep Keito from becoming angrier, seeing the way his shoulders tensed as he confronted the Elders. "Why take the Elder from their own realm?"

"That does seem like the weakest bargaining chip if they're looking for some kind of ransom," Mitoki agreed. "What would be the point of taking Elder Renard out of all the Elders? And why not just attack the compound and make a statement if that's what Yokouro wants?"

"It's not what he wants…" Dalton murmured, looking over the note again. "What if kidnapping the Elder isn't about doing harm to Elder Renard? What if it's about keeping him safe?"

"What do you mean?" Elder Ari pressed.

"The note says that humans are ignorant of their frailty and that it's time to pull back the curtain," he explained. "Sounds like a demon domination plan. Which means he probably was pulling Elder Renard out to protect him from further attack."

"Or try and turn him to his side," Eclipse added.

"Demetrius has no loyalties to the DeVastes Clan," Elder Teban said strongly.

"We don't know that," Keito retorted. "Elder Renard was born and raised in the Middle Dimension, which means he doesn't have an Old Blood Lord. It's important for a demon to have an Old Blood Lord."

"He's centuries old, surely he knows better than to ally himself with a mass-murderer like Yokouro," Elder Celeste scoffed.

Keito closed his eyes in frustration, grinding his teeth together.

"Did you ever bother to ask him about demon culture or did you just assume you knew everything like every other human in Council?" he growled.

"Keito, cool it," Hanyi warned.

"No, I'm sick of being treated like some kind of moron when it comes to my home," he snapped. He approached the Elders, though the security detail quickly stepped in front of him, keeping the aggravated demon at a safe distance.

"Listen to me," he growled. "Allegiance to an Old Blood Lord is probably the single most important thing to a demon. Our Old Blood Lords are our highest authority. And if a demon cannot ally themselves to one, other demons shun them. So all the demons raised in the Middle Dimension are angry and confused why they are shunned by humans *and* shunned by their own kind," he said. "In the first round of the tournament I fought a demon who wanted to oppose Yokouro's ideology, but he didn't know where else he could stand, because the humans he's sworn to protect look at him like a criminal not to be trusted. Like an attack dog they'll put down once he's no longer of any use. Do you really think that Elder Renard feels he's treated any different? No demon in the realm believes he does any *good* for us. His position is just a formality after all, isn't it?"

"He is a valued and highly-respected member of Council," Elder Ari said strongly. "And he is currently in the grasp of a very dangerous demon. So just answer the damn question Keito and stop making this an accusation of demon oppression. Do you think he could sway Demetrius to his side?"

Keito took a deep breath, his teeth clenched so tightly Dalton could see the muscles in his jaw flexing.

"I don't think Yokouro will try to sway Elder Renard," he said carefully.

"Then why take him at all?"

"I don't know."

"Don't play dumb with us now," Elder Teban sneered. "You claim to know so much. So tell us what he will do, Keito. Why take Demetrius?"

Keito dropped his head and retreated a step, closing his eyes and taking several deep breaths.

"Someone else talk to these people," he growled darkly.

"I agree, let's calm down a little," Dalton said, quickly stepping between Keito and the seated Elders, though he did not miss the triumphant smirk his grandfather shot in Keito's direction. "All we know for sure is that one of the Kage Lords caused the ripple, and that led to Elder Ari being attacked and Elder Renard being abducted."

"What do we do? Do we ignore the tournament and go after Elder Renard?" Mitoki asked.

"No, no, the tournament is the best way to keep the people distracted," Elder Teban said strongly. "We need to keep up appearances. No one even needs to know that Demetrius is missing."

"Keito," Eclipse said carefully, turning to his aggravated teammate, "if the demons were to learn that Elder Renard was missing, how do you think they would react?"

The demon shot a wary look at the other Elders before answering. "Truthfully, I doubt they would care."

"Really?" everyone in the room asked in surprise.

"Demons would ally with their Old Blood over Council in an instant," he elaborated.

"…that's it," Dalton whispered.

"What?"

"It's symbolic," he said. "Taking the Elder shows how little control Council has over the Demon Realm. In a sense, abducting Elder Renard puts Yokouro in control of the demon portion of the DPC."

It took the others a few moments to think through Dalton's logic on their own, but slowly, the other Guardians began nodding.

"You're right," Mitoki agreed. "It's him starting to pull back the curtain. Just as he said in the note."

"Then is he going to kill Demetrius?" Elder Celeste hissed, horrified.

"It's possible," Hanyi murmured.

"But if he does, it won't be a big production," Dalton said. "Showing that he killed the demon Elder won't scare the humans, who are already afraid of demons, and it probably won't spur the demons into action either way, given what Keito said."

"You seem confident about that," Elder Ari noted warily.

"I'm just trying to use the information Keito's given," he said. "Yokouro has already made it clear that his goal is to prove demon superiority over humans. Everything he does is going to be to further that goal. That's how we have to frame his actions."

"Then how do we counter this move he just made?" Eclipse asked.

"We get Elder Renard back safe and sound," Mitoki deduced. "Assuming he hasn't been killed already."

"Is there any way to trace Elder Renard's location?" Dalton asked, turning to the Elders. "Does he have a Council tracer?"

"We tried already, it's jammed."

"He might have a Demon Council magic trace on him," Keito mused.

"A what?" Elder Celeste asked.

"He would be a part of Demon Council. There might be a magical trace on him that can locate him. Most lords in Demon Council have one."

"How do we check?"

Keito paused for a few moments, thinking, his eyes distant on the floor. Finally, he pulled out his phone, dialing a few numbers before putting the call on speaker.

"Does the Demon Realm have phones?" Mitoki asked skeptically.

"I'm using this to focus telepathic communication," Keito corrected. "No, most demons do not have phones. But you should be able to hear him if I can connect with him."

"I had no idea you could do that," Dalton said, his eyes wide.

"Keito?" a deep voice answered, slightly distorted, though it was still obvious what he had said.

"Syien, I need to ask a favor."

"This isn't a good time, Keito. There was a huge earthquake here. Everyone is panicking."

"I'm sure. One of the Trade Masters had to be responsible. We all felt it in the Darkness Realm."

"That's what we're all thinking, too," Syien responded. "Is this favor urgent?"

"Yes, I'm afraid," Keito responded. "I don't know if you've heard, but Elder Renard is missing. There was a note left behind by Yokouro, suggesting that he abducted him when the ripple hit the Middle Dimension."

There was an extended silence on the other end of the call before Syien spoke again.

"That makes things more complicated."

"Yes, it does. The DPC can't track him down. Does Elder Renard have a Demon Council trace on him?"

"Yes, he does. Let me see if I can access it for you."

"Thank you, I appreciate it."

As the line went silent, Dalton furrowed his brow, confused by Syien's reaction to the news of Elder Renard.

"It's okay, you can talk. He can't hear you," Keito assured, seeing the questioning look on his team leader's face.

"He's a demon, right?"

"Yes."

"He didn't seem too frantic about Elder Renard being missing," Eclipse noted.

"I told you, it's just a formality," Keito said, shooting a cold glare at the other Elders. "But hopefully he can find a location on him and we can get him away from Yokouro. I truly don't know, other than the symbolic reason, why he would take Elder Renard, so I would rather get him back quickly before Yokouro gets any weird ideas."

"Keito?"

"Yes?" Keito answered Syien.

"He's in the Darkness Realm. I suspect in the same region you are."

"He's bait," Hanyi deduced, shaking his head. "Naturally."

"Any means of tracing Yokouro, yet?"

"No, not yet," Syien said.

"And the Kages?"

The line went silent again. Everyone was leaning forward, waiting to hear what the mysterious demon on the other end of the call said. Dalton was unsure he was ready to hear the information. He had learned of the Kage Lords so recently, he did not know if it would be better to know where they were, or remain blissfully unaware.

"You're not going to like this."

"They're also in the Darkness Realm, aren't they?" Keito groaned.

"No, actually," Syien corrected. "Rutu is at the Kage Palace here in the Demon Realm."

Two tense seconds of silence passed before Keito spoke.

"And Juki?"

"I can't find him."

"You can't find him? What does that mean?"

"It means I have no trace on him. He's blocking it."

"*You lost one of the Kage Lords*?!" Keito barked.

"It would appear," Syien said slowly, pensive. "I better go tell Vestera."

"You think?!"

"Put the DPC on alert. Until we can find Juki, all safety precautions need to be taken," Syien said. "I'll alert Vestera."

Keito lowered his phone, shaking his head. Everyone was still and silent, each having different reactions to the news about one of the extremely powerful Kage Lords.

"...what do we do, Keito?" Hanyi finally asked. "That means that Juki was the one to take Elder Renard. And he's likely in this realm already."

"You think so?" Mitoki pressed, his voice wavering though he tried to hide his anxiety.

Keito pocketed his phone and turned his attention to the Elders.

"It is my duty to inform you that one of the Kage Lords is currently unaccounted for, and until he is found, Demon Council asks that you take every safety precaution possible, considering the abduction of the Demon Realm Elder."

"Enough with the attitude, Keito," Elder Ari growled, irritated by the demon's cold, even tone.

"I *warned* you," Keito snarled. "Your best hope now is that we find Juki and you *beg* him not to help Yokouro. That's all we can do."

"Elders, if one of the Trade Master demons is at large, we must follow protocol and take you to a designated safe house," the captain of the Elders' security team announced.

"Wait, what about Elder Renard?" Mitoki pressed. "If he's bait for us, and you don't want us to ignore the tournament, do you want us to wait until we have a trace on Juki? Do you want us to go after him anyway? What are our orders?"

Elder Teban sighed as he stood, straightening his jacket casually while the security team prepared for their departure.

"It's too dangerous to play around with Juki Kage at large," he said. "Wait until we have a location on him. If he is holding the Elder, we'll take more diplomatic measures and hope we can reason with Juki. Attacking him would be suicidal."

"Do you think you can reason with him?" Eclipse asked.

"I don't know," he admitted quietly, his eyes downcast, refusing to look at the Guardians. "But if Yokouro really has called the Kage Lords to his aid, this is about to get very, very dangerous for all of us."

"You know he has," Keito hissed.

"Then perhaps it's best *you* talk to Juki then, Keito," Elder Teban growled, his sharp gaze finally turning on to the demon Guardian. "Since you seem to understand everything there is to know about Old Blood Lords."

He cast a quick glance around the Guardians before motioning for the other Elders to follow him. "Do not take any action to find Demetrius until we have a location on Juki Kage. We'll contact you when we hear something. Please do the same."

"Yes, Elder," Mitoki said with a shallow bow of his head.

The air in Eclipse's house seemed lighter once the Elders had departed. Master Genbuki, Tarrena, Jikia, and Saki were reeling from the confrontational nature of the encounter, while the Guardians were grappling with their panic over the involvement of the powerful demons they had just learned existed.

"Dalton, is your grandfather always that confrontational?" Mitoki asked.

"With demons, unfortunately," Dalton said. "Ever since my father was killed by one. I'm sorry, Keito. The way he treated you was uncalled for."

"Yes, it was," Keito agreed. "But I'm also used to it."

"Keito, how bad is this about to get?" Eclipse asked. "With one of the Kage Lords here?"

Keito closed his eyes, exasperated. "I truly do not know," he said. "I've been out of the loop with the Kages lately. They've been so damn quiet, I didn't think much of checking in with them. And once I started to poke around, it became obvious they were interested in what Yokouro was doing, but I don't know *how* interested."

"Was all that stuff you said about demons being loyal to an Old Blood Lord true?" Master Genbuki asked from his seat. "Does that mean that all the demons loyal to the Kage Lords are also loyal to Yokouro, since they're allies?"

"No, not necessarily," Keito said.

"Then Juki *could* be reasoned with," he pressed.

"Possibly," the demon admitted. "The problem is that Juki is smart. Far smarter than Yokouro could ever hope to be. And if Juki has his own agenda with all this, we have no way of predicting what he will do."

Chapter Nine

The Guardians were lost in their own distressing thoughts. Keito was clearly the most unsettled, though the others were unable to discern if his quiet, dark expression was due to the abduction of Elder Renard, or the way the other Elders had treated him. He barely spoke up other than to clarify a few details for Master Genbuki as they explained to him what they knew of Yokouro and the Kage Lords.

Saki excused herself to the kitchen but came back out shortly afterward.

"*Kan-na?*" she asked, her voice weak with concern about bringing up anything other than the demon they were discussing. "We never got to go to the grocery store…"

Eclipse straightened. "Damn it, I was going to go after the meeting with your teacher. Do you have a list?"

She nodded, darting back into the kitchen and returning with a shopping list.

"Looks like you guys ate half the contents of the kitchen earlier today," she tried to joke.

"Sorry about that," Eclipse laughed. "Alright, guys, come on," he said.

"Why do we have to go?" Hanyi asked.

"Because I said so," Eclipse said. "I hate grocery shopping and you are all eating whatever I buy, so come on."

Dalton was thankful for the distraction, even though he also hated going to the store. There was something about being in a grocery store that made him feel more out of place with civilians than anywhere else in his life. Mitoki was clearly feeling the same dread as he warily noted the others in the store as they entered.

It was difficult for Dalton to decide if having Hanyi and Keito constantly complain about the way humans had their lives catered to them and were no longer able to properly care for themselves without assistance was amusing or annoying. The two began a heated discussion about how humans were so disconnected with nature that it had become harmful for both the environment and humans themselves.

At first, Dalton found it amusing, but when Hanyi made a show of trying to read the ingredients on the back of some of the packages, he began ignoring the older Guardians.

Even though Hanyi complained about the entire ordeal, he had no problem running with the cart and riding it down the slope in the parking lot toward the car.

"What are you, *five?*" Eclipse groaned, opening the trunk of his car to load in the bags of groceries.

As they were nearing Eclipse's house, a call came through.

"Guardian Retani," Eclipse answered on speaker phone.

"Hey, Eclipse, it's Patrick."

"Hey," Eclipse said, surprised his field partner had called him so late in the afternoon. "What's going on?"

"Another place got hit," he answered. "Just after the ripple passed."

"Where?"

"Downtown. Golde's Pawn and Loan," the other Guardian elaborated. "They're estimating losses now."

"I'll be down there in a half hour," Eclipse said, hanging up.

"Who was that?" Mitoki asked.

"My field partner."

"Are you investigating thefts?" Hanyi asked.

"Yes, but according to all the security footage we've collected from each site, these thieves are demons," Eclipse said, explaining why a Guardian was assigned to a crime often handled by law enforcement. "They've hit five, now six, different locations and are stealing anything valuable they can find, though they generally go for jewelry. But despite everything we've seen, we can't track them down. They just hit a place and disappear."

"How many of them?" Keito asked.

"We don't know," he said. "They seem to rob each location as a group of five, but the five are almost always different. So far, we've been able to identify thirteen demons, some of them are pretty young."

"A demon thieving ring?" Hanyi asked, turning to Keito with a raised eyebrow. "In the *Darkness* Realm?"

"Bandit families are commonplace in the Demon Realm. One must have come here," Keito said. "How long has this been going on?"

"Started just after the shift in the dimensions two months ago, when we were stuck in the Beast Realm," he said. "I'm going to drop you off at the house and go meet Patrick. Go ahead and eat without me."

"Do you mind if I join you?" Keito asked.

"Do you want to?"

"I might be able to help," the demon said. "Particularly if this does involve demons."

"Any help you can give would be great. We're hitting dead ends."

Hanyi sat forward in his seat. "Can I come, too?"

"What is it with you wanting to go everywhere with me today?" Eclipse asked, exasperated.

"Hey, I'm a pack animal. I want to go where everyone else is going."

Yet again, the entire team tagged along with Eclipse to the pawnshop where the robbery had occurred after hurriedly unloading the groceries at the house. Patrick was startled to see the others of Team Dalton trailing behind Eclipse as he walked up to the front of the building.

"Wow, do you really think this case needs that much attention?" Patrick laughed.

"I can't get rid of them," Eclipse groaned. "First Keito wanted to tag along because this involves demons, which I understand, but the other three just have separation anxiety, I guess."

Patrick laughed, extending his hand to Dalton.

"Guardian Teban," he greeted.

"Just call me Dalton," he said with a smile, shaking Patrick's hand.

"And Keito DeVero," Patrick said, shaking the demon's hand. "It's an honor."

"Nice to meet you."

"Think you can find where these demons are?" he asked, walking through the magic white barrier that signaled a Guardian case was in progress, the others close behind.

"Maybe," the demon Guardian said, looking over the front of the pawn shop, stopping just before walking inside. "Were all the locations they hit on corners like this?"

"Yes," he affirmed. "They enter from the front," he pointed to the shattered front window and the warped iron bars that had granted the criminals access, "and then leave through the side or the back. And they're quick about it."

"Definitely demon with strength like that," Mitoki said, nodding to the distorted bars that had once protected the windows.

"Wait until you see how much they trash the place."

The interior of the pawn shop was entirely destroyed. The glass display cases were not only shattered, but the metal frames had been torn apart, thrown around the cascade of broken glass and ripped-open walls. The place looked as though it had been abandoned for years and left to rot and be vandalized for decades.

"Shit, they really destroyed this place," Dalton hissed.

"They do it every time," Eclipse said, walking carefully over the broken glass and bits of drywall that covered scattered items the demons did not see fit to steal. "It makes it that much harder to get any solid evidence, which is probably why we haven't been able to track them down."

"Always five demons?" Keito pressed.

"Always five, but not always the same demons," Patrick confirmed. "What do you make of that?"

"A bandit clan generally assigns a smaller party to carry out the jobs," Keito said, stepping to the nearest wall and running his fingers along the ripped edges of drywall. "That way, if some of them get caught, the majority of the family can stay safe."

"Which would suggest a base of operations," Dalton concluded. Keito nodded, walking away from the walls.

"How close have the sites been? Has there been a central point?" Mitoki asked.

"We've scoured the central point of all these sites, and nothing."

"Have they ever left anything behind? Anything that these shops don't recognize from their inventory? Like a calling card?" Keito asked.

"Is that common?" Patrick asked.

"Not common, but a few of the larger bandit clans like to sign their work, so to speak. At least back in the Demon Realm they do."

"Nothing left behind that we've ever found," Eclipse said.

"Any blood collected from broken glass?" Mitoki asked, gently kicking some of the scattered pieces on the ground.

"Only a few times," Patrick said. "No one on record with the DPC."

"This group would have to be a well-established bandit family," Keito said. "This level of destruction, the method of entry and escape…this group has been doing this for a while before they came here. This isn't a group of refugee demons trying to make some money. This is a bandit clan performing a job."

"So you don't think some demons were dropped in this realm because of the shift two months ago?" Hanyi asked.

"This feels too deliberate. Too practiced," the demon mused, shaking his head. Keito turned to Patrick. "Is there security footage of this crime?"

He nodded, motioning them to a tablet he had set up on what remained of a badly broken table. The first camera angle he showed them was stationed above the front door, showing the five demons climbing into the store and running almost too fast for the cameras to follow. Two of the demons immediately went to the jewelry cases and broke the glass to get to the valuables while the other three ignored the items in the shop and immediately set about destroying the property.

"Looks like the younger ones are the ones doing the stealing," Dalton noted.

"At least the shorter ones," Eclipse agreed.

"Smaller demons move faster," Keito murmured, his eyes sharp on the screen as he looked among the demons' faces.

"I'm surprised they did this in broad daylight," Mitoki said.

"After the ripple, downtown basically shut down," Patrick explained. "Businesses evacuated. People were panicking. During the mayhem was a perfect time to strike."

Dalton turned to Keito, more interested in his reaction than watching the destruction take place on screen.

"What do you think?" he finally asked.

Keito straightened, letting out a long sigh as he rubbed his face.

"I'm torn."

"About?"

Keito continued to stare at the screen, his hand pressed to his mouth as he shook his head slowly.

"Keito," Eclipse prompted.

"There is a part of me that wants to find them and another part of me that wants to turn away and leave you to deal with them."

"You know them," Hanyi said quietly.

"You *know* them?" several of the others around Keito repeated.

Keito sighed heavily.

"This is a delicate situation," he said. "Yes, I know this group, and yes, it is a big group. I also know where they're likely to set up shop."

"All from this video?" Patrick asked.

Keito nodded slowly. "I just can't understand why they're in the Darkness Realm. They really have no reason to be here."

"If you know where they are, we need to know," Eclipse said darkly. "Do you see the destruction we're standing in? These demons are a danger to this city."

"I know," Keito said. "I'm not saying don't go after them. It's just…" He pursed his lips. "They *might* be able to give us more information about some other things we're investigating."

Patrick drew in a deep breath. "That sounds like confidential information I'm not supposed to know."

"Sorry, Patrick."

"It's fine," Eclipse's field partner said, raising his hands. "I get it. You guys have something else you're working on. Just…" he shrugged, "I dunno, let me know if we need to call in backup to capture these thieves."

Patrick nodded to each of them as he walked toward the law enforcement officers talking with the infuriated owner of the pawn shop.

"Why would these demons be able to give us information?" Dalton asked when he was certain Patrick was far enough away.

"This is a big bandit clan," Keito repeated. "And their usual grounds are very close to the Kage Palace."

"So they might be able to tell us what the Kage Lords have been up to lately," Mitoki muttered.

"And if they've seen Yokouro lurking around," Hanyi added. "My question is, what is your relationship with these bandits? Are they going to attack you if you show up?" He raised a quizzical eyebrow at the demon Guardian.

"…it's possible," Keito admitted, lowering his head sheepishly.

"Is that a risk you're willing to take?" Dalton prompted. "Because if we capture them and you demand information, they might not be so keen to talk to you."

Keito hesitated. "That's why I'm torn about what to do."

"This is your case, Eclipse," Hanyi said. "How do you want to proceed?"

"This puts me in a difficult position as well," he said. "Do I focus on Yokouro or do I focus on this case I've been working on for months? Or do we go to these demons and deceive them that we're just there for information only to capture them later? Any direction we take is trouble."

"I think the main question we need to ask is how far are we willing to go to get information on Yokouro and the Kage Lords?" Dalton said. "Do we capture them and hope they talk to us? Or do we go in there only with the intention of getting information?"

"These demons will know if you go down there with an ulterior motive," Keito warned. "You need to make a decision."

Eclipse's eyes fell to the glass under his shoes, thinking through each option carefully.

"…Elder Renard is missing," he murmured. "And one of the Kage Lords likely has him." He met eyes with Keito. "We need to know what we're walking into."

Keito nodded once in understanding.

"Okay."

"So where do we find them?"

"Where's the oldest part of this city?"

Eclipse had a difficult time explaining to Patrick that they were going to do reconnaissance on where the demon bandits were hiding as the other Guardian wanted to join, but Eclipse did not want to tell him that they were going to discuss the abduction of the demon Elder. Eventually, Patrick caught on that there was another reason for Team Dalton to go to the demon thieves and he hesitantly backed down, warning Eclipse to be careful and that he was on standby if they needed help.

Eclipse drove the team to the old city center and pulled up an old city map of the water drainage system. When the demon walked down an alley and lifted a large manhole cover, Dalton hesitated.

"Really?"

"Yeah, really," Keito said. "It's Benny's style to hide underground. He's generally in the old catacombs near the Kage Palace back home."

"Benny?"

"The leader of this bandit clan," Keito clarified, carefully maneuvering himself onto the iron rungs of the ladder.

After a shared look of uncertainty, the other Guardians followed Keito down the ladder.

The smell of the large concrete pipe was thick and caused each of them to gag. The stench that radiated from the stagnant water at the bottom of the pipe was rancid and Dalton knew that the pipe had not been used in a long time.

"Is this some kind of spillover?" he asked.

"It's the old system," Eclipse said. "Probably only used in the worst of the typhoons and storms. Are you sure about this, Keito? We could get lost down here pretty easily."

"They're down here somewhere. I'm almost certain of it."

"This is nowhere near their targets, though," Mitoki said.

"Benny's been doing this a long time. He wouldn't make the mistake of pointing you right to him," Keito said. He looked up and down the tunnel. "Which way is east?"

Eclipse pointed.

"Then we go this way." Keito pointed in the opposite direction.

"I'm afraid to ask how you know that," Dalton grumbled, falling into step behind Eclipse as they walked single-file down the concrete drain following their demon teammate.

"Benny is also superstitious," Keito said with a gentle laugh over his shoulder. "You never attack west of your location. It's bad luck."

Keito led the others through the large tunnels of drainage pipes, turning corners as if following the movements of shadows. Dalton wanted to ask how the demon knew where to go, but there was something about the almost-predatory way Keito leaned forward as he crept along the pipes, being sure not to make any unnecessary noise, that made Dalton worry about breaking his concentration.

They entered a very large tunnel where rainwater was being diverted into a grate at the far end and Keito held up his hand quickly to stop the other Guardians.

It took all of Dalton's concentration, but he eventually heard the sounds of voices gently echoing over the sound of trickling water. His heart began racing, unable to stop the instinctive worry that they were about to be attacked by the demon thieves—assuming that was who they had stumbled across.

Keito motioned for them to stay put as he gingerly inched forward, his head cocked to the side as he listened to the voices.

Barely able to see in the dark tunnel as it was, Dalton had to wait for Keito to step under the light of a street grate to see how far ahead Keito had wandered.

In the same moment Keito was illuminated by the light, a woman leapt forward, holding a dagger to his throat as she turned him, yanking one of his arms behind his back. Keito faltered only momentarily before he turned his body and elbowed her, turning them both to push her to the ground, knocking the dagger out of her grasp and pinning her hands above her head.

The voices they had heard became muffled yells as other nearby demons drew closer.

"Easy, Tibbi, don't you recognize me?" Keito laughed.

The female demon immediately stopped struggling. Dalton and the others also halted their advance toward Keito, startled by the tenderness in Keito's voice.

"Keito?" she whispered in disbelief. She let out a laugh before pushing his hands away and grabbing the sides of his face, pulling him close and clashing their lips together in a passionate kiss.

When they broke apart, Keito chuckled.

"That certainly wasn't the welcome I was expecting."

"Are you complaining?"

"Not at all."

"Get off her, you low-life," a deep voice growled. Another demon appearing from the same adjoining tunnel to press a knife to Keito's back. The Guardian rolled his eyes with a huff.

"Gana, it's me."

"Who's *me?*" he snarled, his blade steady.

"Keito, you ass," he laughed, turning from Tibbi to knock the dagger aside, standing to face the other demon. "Seriously? Who else would be stupid enough to storm down here to find you?" he asked.

"Gods above!" Gana said with a bark of laughter. He grabbed Keito by the shoulders, shaking him slightly as he looked him over. "Keito DeVero in the flesh!"

The human Guardians could only stare in alarm at the warm greeting the demon thieves were sharing with Keito.

"Damn it, you shouldn't be sneaking around sticking your tongue in women's mouths. I might have killed you," Gana leered, hugging Keito briefly. When he broke the hug, he looked over the other demon again. "Damn, kid, you don't even look the same! Filled out a bit, huh?"

"Now I know that can't be Keito," another woman said, also stepping out of the tunnel, much shorter than the other demons.

"And why not?" Keito asked, smiling.

"Because he would never be so rude as to not say hello to me," she said, crossing her arms over her chest.

He placed a gentle hand on her jaw, leaning in to give her a long, lingering kiss.

"How about now?" he murmured when he pulled away.

"Better."

Dalton turned over his shoulder to Hanyi, who could only offer an apologetic shrug in response to the questioning glance.

"You grew up handsome, kid," Tibbi complimented, running her hand down Keito's arm. "Hard to believe you're the same little brat that tripped the alarm out of Lord Laria's palace," she teased.

Keito groaned. "You're never going to let me live that down, are you?"

"Not anytime soon," she laughed, leaning up to kiss him on the cheek. "Ooh, you smell like Night Play. I didn't know you partied that hard."

"I don't," Keito said. "I hate that stuff. That asshole Verej coated his knife with it and then proceeded to stab me four times when I tried to catch him. My fever still hasn't broken."

Dalton's head was swimming with information, and he could tell by the stunned looks on the others face that they were also reeling from the realization that Keito knew the demon thieves because he used to work with them. When a fourth demon emerging from the nearby pipe broke their stupor, Dalton's blood ran cold, knowing they had been spotted.

"What the hell are you doing bringing humans down here, Keito?"

The atmosphere between the demons changed immediately. Keito looked at the Guardians and then turned to the fourth demon.

"Eboren," he started carefully, "don't get upset. They aren't here to harm the family. I promise."

"Your promise means nothing," Eboren growled. "Rumor was you straightened out. Went to bow to the DPC and be their attack dog. So I'm assuming those are Guardians behind you."

"Guardians?!" the others gasped, quickly turning to the four confused figures further down the tunnel. "Keito, what were you thinking?! You can't bring Guardians down here!"

"Why? Because there might be some *illegal* demons down here?" Keito teased. "As a Guardian, I am doing my job. You are the ones that could get into trouble. How did you even get to the Darkness Realm?"

The four demons fell very still and silent, their eyes flicking to the Guardians behind Keito. When they each took a slow step back, standing behind Eboren, Keito straightened.

"What's going on?"

"Nothing. This doesn't concern you, Keito," Eboren growled.

"Yes, it does," he snarled. "Do you have any idea how lucky you are that I recognized Anaiis and Gana? They wouldn't just relocate you back to the Demon Realm if they found you. The other Guardians would kill you. Do you understand that?"

"I'd like to see them try," Eboren scoffed, turning his attention to the Guardians. "Why don't you come closer? Stop lingering like terrified rats."

The others of Team Dalton did step forward, but stopped when Keito sharply raised his hand to them, his eyes never leaving the demon thieves.

"Don't taunt me, Eboren," he warned. "We didn't come here for a fight."

"Did you expect us to just welcome you with open arms?" Eboren growled. "You think you can just waltz back in here and expect us to trust you?"

"You *can* trust me."

Eboren laughed hollowly. "You really think your word means *anything*?"

"Come on, Ren, it's Keito," Tibbi said gently.

"All the more reason *not* to trust him. He's the damn Wandering Child."

"Don't call me that," Keito said darkly. "I hated that name as a kid and I hate it even more now. I ran with you for three years. Was that really not enough to gain your trust?"

"Trust?" the other demon laughed brokenly. "*Trust*? Really? Can anyone ever really trust *you*?"

"If you didn't trust me, you could have turned me over," Keito snapped. "But you kept me around."

"Because you were Benny's little toy and he didn't want to let you go." Eboren's grin turned cold. "I guess that makes it easier to find us now, huh? He probably left quite the impression."

Keito's fist flew at Eboren's face, knocking him backward. The other thieves shuffled backward as well, holding their hands up peacefully as the Guardians surged forward to stand behind Keito, ready to defend him if needed.

Eboren rubbed his jaw, groaning as he propped himself up. Keito took a menacing step forward, glaring at the fallen demon.

"The last time you saw me, I was fourteen," Keito reminded him. "I assure you, I am much stronger now and better able to beat your ass into a bloody pulp. So if you want to know what it feels like to have someone from my bloodline beat the shit out of you, please, keep talking."

Eboren scrambled to his feet, ready for the confrontation, but Gana grabbed him and pulled him back.

"Hey, hey, calm down!" he snapped.

"Keito," Tibbi said gently, stepping between Keito and Eboren. "It's okay. He's just an asshole. He always has been." She looked over at the Guardians. "We know we're here illegally, but..." Her hands dropped to her side. "You know how it is right now, Keito."

"I actually don't," Keito murmured. "I need you to tell me what's going on, Tibbi."

She let out a pained sigh.

"I can't," she said. "All I can do is lead you to Benny and have him explain it."

Eboren laughed. "Oh, yes," he chuckled coldly. "Bring a bunch of Guardians to Benny. That will go over so well."

Keito growled. "If they are going to be harmed, I will come alone," he snapped. "And if we get to Benny and anyone tries to attack us, I will turn on all of you without a second thought. So make your decision very carefully."

"Benny knows we're going to get caught eventually," Gana said. "Better by you than anyone else. I'm sure he won't hurt them."

Eboren just laughed and Keito's fist clenched at his side.

"I mean it, Gana," he growled. "I will turn on you."

"Ignore that asshole," the other female demon said. "Let's just go to Benny and talk to him. He can answer your questions."

Keito stared her down, as though deliberating if she was being sincere. When his shoulders started to relax, he turned to look at the Guardians.

"Are you comfortable with that?"

"As much as we'll ever be," Hanyi muttered.

"You have a lot of explaining to do," Eclipse said. "You said you knew them. You didn't say you were *part* of them."

"It was a long time ago," Keito mumbled. "It was a very bad time in my life and I needed to find a way to survive. Benny taught me a lot, and this family was able to keep me safe for several years."

"You should be proud of him," Tibbi said with a smile, wrapping an arm around Keito's waist and sidling up to him. "He could have really made a name for himself in the underground of the Demon Realm, but instead, straightened himself out and pledged loyalty to the DPC so he could protect humans. I would think you would see that as noble. I would have happily kept him with me." She pouted as she turned to him. "I missed you when you left."

"Good to know I was missed," he said with a smile, wrapping his arm around her.

"Uh…you two didn't kiss like that when he was a kid, did you?" Dalton asked warily.

"No," Tibbi laughed loudly. "I made sure to wait until he was thirteen."

The other's choked, their eyes going wide. Keito quickly lifted a hand to stop their startled reactions.

"I will remind you that demons mature very quickly and while thirteen is a little early, fourteen is considered the norm," he defended quickly.

"Humans are such prudes," the second female demon grumbled.

"Shall we take the prudes to Benny?" Gana asked with a smile. "Come on, we're just through here."

Keito spared a glance back at the others of Team Dalton but Dalton did not know what expression was on his face, too overwhelmed to even voice his concern about going to meet the leader of the bandit clan.

"How did you know where to find us, anyway?" Gana asked over his shoulder as he led the five Guardians further into the side tunnels.

"Once I recognized you, I figured he would try and find a place like the catacombs. This was the next best thing."

"I bet that deductive reasoning is what made you such a great Guardian," Tibbi complimented.

"That and his connections…" Eboren grumbled.

"Will you shut up already?!" the second woman snapped, exasperated. "Now I *want* Keito to kick your ass."

It was a short walk through an old, small tunnel completely devoid of water until they spotted the glowing of light ahead. There were voices echoing quietly through the small tunnel, though their approaching footsteps masked the sounds of conversation.

The light ahead came from orbs of magic casting a warm, orange glow around the large tank meant to handle extreme flooding, though it was clear the chamber had never been used. Dalton was stunned by the sheer number of demons in the chamber, lines of hanging clothes separating pillows and blankets the demons were using as beds. There were young demons playing with some of the sports equipment they must have stolen, though they were using it entirely incorrectly. Groups of demons were clustered together, some chatting lightly, some drinking, and others sorting through piles of stolen goods at the back of the chamber.

"Benny!" Tibbi called as Dalton stepped out of the pipe, allowing Mitoki and Hanyi through to the chamber.

"What?" a deep voice snapped. "What the hell took you so long? I sent you to get rid of some cheap shit and you take forever. Where the hell did you go?" By the time he finished his question, he had turned around and caught sight of the Guardians, causing many of the other demons to turn as well.

Benny's dark eyes narrowed suspiciously once he caught sight of Dalton. The human Guardian refused to look away, staring back at the rotund demon confidently.

"Do you want to explain to me why the hell there are *humans* here?" Benny snarled at the thieves.

Keito slowly stepped away from Gana, taking two cautious steps forward.

"Hey, Benny," he greeted quietly. Dalton could feel the apprehension in Keito's voice and it made him both worried for Keito's safety, and relieved that his demon teammate was not showing an eagerness to mingle with the thief.

Benny was still when he looked Keito over, ignoring the surprised whispers of others behind him. He started toward Keito slowly, shaking his head as though he could not believe what he was seeing.

"Keito?"

"The one and only," he said, his voice remaining quiet. Benny took Keito's shoulders, a smile of disbelief growing over his face. Unsure what to make of what Eboren had said earlier, Dalton was just as nervous as Keito appeared to be.

However, Benny let out a boisterous laugh and yanked Keito closer, pulling him into a rib-crushing hug.

"Come here, you ridiculous fox!" he bellowed. Keito choked, his eyes bulging at the strength of the hug, but then he laughed, trying to move his arms against the vice grip Benny had around him. Benny released Keito, clapping him on the shoulder.

"Damn, how long has it been?"

"Three hundred years, give or take," Keito answered, seeming more at ease, but still nervous.

"He brought some Guardians with him," Eboren said, walking away from the rest of the group and throwing a triumphant look back at Keito, who glared in return.

"Guardians?" Benny repeated, turning to the rest of Team Dalton. Now that they were no longer surrounded by the four demon thieves, they felt very exposed under the suspicious gazes of the other demons in the chamber. Several demons hissed and growled, tensing to fight the Guardians, which put all of them, even Keito, on edge.

Benny turned back to Keito, chuckling as he shook his head, beaming like a proud parent.

"Gods be damned," he said. "You really *did* straighten out. I always thought that was just a rumor to put us all off our guard. Good for you, kid!"

"Of course you would say that," Eboren groaned.

Benny stormed over to where Eboren was sitting, growling at him in a language the Guardians did not understand. Keito turned his head away from the confrontation, his body shaking slightly, eyes locked on the ground at his feet. Eboren tried to defend himself, but Benny smacked the side of his head hard enough to knock the demon to the ground. Benny then proceeded to scold the other demon before casting a warning glare to the other demons in the chamber. Many shrunk away from the leader of their group, turning their eyes away from the Guardians.

Benny turned back to Keito, who flinched from the gaze.

"Don't worry," he laughed, taking the back of Keito's head and pulling him forward, leading Keito to a collection of pillows other demons quickly vacated for Benny. "You're not in my ranks anymore. And you're not the snot-nosed little shit you used to be. I have no power to scold you."

"I know that our appearance is troublesome, Benny," Keito said. "I was hoping you could answer a few questions for me."

"You're not here to arrest me, then? Or whatever it is Guardians do with out-of-realm demons?" Benny asked, sitting on the collection of pillows and blankets and motioning the Guardians to join him. Keito also sat, though his posture was stiff, showing his apprehension.

"I—*we*—hoped you could help us out, instead."

"With what?"

"How did you get into the Darkness Realm?" Eclipse started, sure to keep his voice strong, but not confrontational, as he sat across from Benny.

"We dimension hopped here," he said simply.

"Why?"

Benny's smile widened, hiding something that made Dalton's hair stand on end. "We were asked to."

"What does that mean?" Dalton pressed.

"It means that you should probably be taking a good, hard look at the amount of crime in the human realms right now," the demon said with a dark laugh. He leaned forward, eyeing Dalton. "You look familiar," he said. "What's your name?"

"Dalton Teban."

Benny's expression lit up.

"Oh...*you're* Dalton Teban."

"You know who I am?"

"A bit. Your name has been mentioned in some elite circles back home," Benny said. "Something about ways to break Dalton Teban's fighting spirit." He chuckled. "Looks like you caught the attention of a dangerous predator."

"Yokouro DeVastes, you mean?" Dalton asked simply, his voice confident.

All noise in the chamber stopped as the demon thieves turned to the Guardians. Dalton could not stop his startled reaction as he looked among the faces of the demons.

"So you already know," Benny noted. "Interesting." The thief turned to Keito, who had lowered his eyes, refusing to look at anyone. "It's starting again?"

"It's because of the tournament," Keito grumbled.

Benny let out an exasperated groan. "What a moronic decision to bring that back into practice," he said. "You have a demon as notorious as Yokouro who massacred thousands in the last tournament, so the plan is to set the trap and see if you can catch him before he does it again? That's like getting your hand bitten off by a lion and sticking your other hand in the cage to see if you can pull it out before he gets the other one."

"You don't have to convince me of how dumb the plan is," Keito mumbled.

"Keito said that you know the Kage Lords," Mitoki said, hesitating when he saw the way the other demons in the bandit clan turned to him, startled by the mention of the powerful demons. Benny's eyebrows rose slowly.

"My, my, you humans are well-informed," he noted quietly. "Now, what would you want with the Trade Masters?"

"We want to know anything you can tell us," Mitoki said simply.

Benny stared at the youngest Guardian, his face slowly breaking into a huge grin. Finally, he started laughing, his head thrown back as his body heaved with fits of laughter.

"You boys are *screwed* if you have to ask about them," he finally said, shaking his head as he looked among the group.

"Benny, we just need to know what they've been up to lately," Keito clarified.

"How the hell should I know?" he asked.

"Keito said you're close to their palace."

"That doesn't mean much," Benny said. "And yes, Lord Juk does keep an eye on me, but that does not mean I am privy to his affairs."

"He would know if you left the realm," Keito prompted. "And he's not stupid enough to ask the largest bandit gang on his territory to come cause trouble in the Darkness Realm."

"I'm sure he knows I've left," Benny agreed. "And he knows that being caught in the Darkness Realm is a death sentence for me, I'm sure. But I've fallen out of grace with the Trade Masters. They may not kill me themselves, but you can be certain they won't step in to save me from some human Guardians hungry for demon blood."

"Then the Kage Lords didn't ask you to come to the Darkness Realm?"

Benny's smile widened. "I didn't say that."

Eclipse ground his teeth together, leaning forward, glaring.

"We've had nothing but riddles and I'm sick of the cryptic bullshit," he growled. "Don't try and play with us."

Benny also leaned forward, the air between the two sparking dangerously.

"You're the ones who came to *me* for information. You'll get what I give."

Eclipse tensed, as though ready to spring forward and attack the demon. Keito immediately moved positions, holding a hand out to Benny and putting his back to Eclipse.

"Juki is missing," he said quickly. "Demon Council can't find Juki. We're pretty sure he's kidnapped Elder Renard and is in the Darkness Realm."

Benny's attention focused on Keito and a shiver of concern radiated through the chamber as the others in the thieving ring turned to one another.

"Benny, please," Keito continued slowly, lowering his hand, "do you know *anything* about what Juki and Rutu have been up to? Do you know if they've been meeting with Yokouro? Is there anything you can tell us?"

The five-second silence seemed to last for hours as Dalton's eyes flicked between Keito, Benny, and the demons around the flood chamber. When Benny finally let out a long sigh and slumped a little, Dalton's concern about a fight breaking out was eased, though seeing the resigned look on the demon's face caused a new anxiety to awaken in his gut.

"Lord Juki did not ask me to come to this realm and cause chaos for the humans," Benny finally said. "Yokouro is the one asking demons to create problems in the human-inhabited realms."

"Why?" Eclipse pressed.

"He's trying to start a war," Benny answered. "He's always been trying to start a war. Demons against humans."

"Why would you agree?" Keito whispered. "Benny, any other Guardian would kill you if they found you."

"Yes, I think that's the point," Benny said. "Get humans so afraid of demons they spark an all-out war."

"If that was the case, why kidnap Elder Renard?" Dalton asked. "To put himself at the head of Council?"

"I don't know," he said. He turned to Keito. "If the kidnap of Elder Renard was executed by the Kage Lords, it wasn't a plan I heard. Not to mention, it would be incredibly stupid of Lord Juki to do something like abduct a Council Elder...and Lord Juki is *not* stupid."

"It had to be him," Keito said. "He's unaccounted for. Rutu probably caused the ripple as a distraction. And Yokouro doesn't have a full physical form, yet."

"Oh, he does," Benny corrected darkly.

"How do you know?"

"Because I heard that he's started the process of reclaiming his title, and he can't do that without being physically present."

"What about Kakuri?" Keito asked.

"I'm sure they'll control the territory together."

"Wait, I thought Yokouro was already an Old Blood Lord," Mitoki said.

"He was," Benny agreed. "And then he was killed. Now, he's trying to get his position back so he can enjoy the protections being an Old Blood provides. No one would dare harm him with the Kage Lords looming behind him, but Yokouro is being sure to protect himself as much as possible."

"Then you've seen him?" Keito whispered. "He actually approached you and asked you to do this?"

"No," Benny said. "I was approached by a Kage."

Eclipse tried to suppress his irritated groan at the conflicting information the demon was giving. Benny laughed.

"You humans really have no idea what you're getting involved with," he said. "I almost pity you."

"Well, if Juki didn't ask you to come to this realm, there's no way in hell *Rutu* would," Keito noted.

Benny sighed, turning over his shoulder to see the apprehensive looks on the other demons' faces as they listened to the conversation.

"No, it was Acurala."

Dalton was about to show his own irritation at hearing yet another name that he had never heard before, but when he saw Keito's stunned expression, he remained quiet, waiting for his demon teammate to speak first.

"That would explain why the Kage Territory has been so quiet despite how much Yokouro's been doing," Keito finally murmured. "He called on Acurala first."

"How do I know that name, Keito?" Hanyi asked.

"Juki's younger brother," Keito answered. "He's been dead for about a century. But Yokouro must have resurrected him somehow so that he could keep Juki and Rutu in the shadows." He lowered his head. "That explains a lot actually."

"Do you mind clueing the rest of us in?" Eclipse growled.

"Later," Keito assured quickly over his shoulder. "So Acurala has been doing Yokouro's dirty work while Yokouro finished learning how to manifest a body?" Benny nodded slowly. "Then it's possible that Juki and Rutu aren't as involved as we believed?"

"Possible, but unlikely," Benny said. "If they really weren't involved, Lord Rutu would have no reason to cause that ripple, and Lord Juki would have no reason to keep himself off Demon Council's magical tether. And, something else you need to consider is that, with Yokouro now having a body, you are likely to see him."

"How do we kill him?" Dalton asked darkly.

Benny turned to the leader of the Guardian team, studying him for a moment.

"I'm sure there are ways. It's been done before," he answered. "Everything can be killed if you try hard enough." He cocked his head to the side. "My bigger concern, if I were you, would be why my name was being tossed around in the circle of the Old Blood Lords."

"Council has sent me after Yokouro to find him and kill him," Dalton said. "Is that something you want to stop me from doing?"

"I don't give a damn about the DeVastes Clan," Benny said, shaking his head. "I only run Kage."

"Even though you've said you've fallen from their good graces?"

Benny shrugged. "I should have known better than to screw with Lord Juki's property. Besides, my Old Blood Lords are more powerful than your tiny human brains can possibly comprehend. Yokouro may be powerful, but he's arrogant and thinks that just because the Kage Lords have shown him some attention, he's untouchable. But I'm sure if you were to remove his head from his shoulders, only a small collection of demons would be upset." He lifted a finger. "For now."

"You mean until the demons he's sent into the other realms cause enough panic to make humans attack demons," Hanyi deduced. "And then Yokouro will gain more loyal supporters from the demons."

Benny nodded slowly. "You boys certainly have your work cut out for you."

"How will we find him?" Mitoki pressed. "What does he look like?"

"Trust me, you won't miss him," Benny said with a smirk. "You'll know him by the markings."

"What markings?" Dalton prompted.

"The *Bewyn-Trensse* Curse," he elaborated. "The curse all those in the DeVastes bloodline share. When they end one thousand lives, a black scar-like marking will appear. If they kill others of the DeVastes bloodline, the marking will appear on their face. Yokouro has three of these markings on his face. And hundreds all over the rest of his body."

"He's killed his own family?" Mitoki hissed.

"His parents and his unborn sibling," Benny said with a slow nod. "And he was just a child at the time." The demon scanned the unsettled expressions on the humans' faces. "If he's covering the marks on his body, you will see a line over his face." Benny traced his finger under his eye, over the bridge of his nose, and under his other eye, "and then the lines on each cheek for his parents, and then the mark on his neck for his unborn sibling."

"That's the marking on the tourists' faces in the Beast Realm," Eclipse reminded Dalton.

"The line over the nose is the DeVastes family mark," Benny said. "If you see a demon with long silver hair, unbraided, and that line over his nose, you'll know you've found him." Benny's eyes fell on Dalton again. "And I have a feeling you'll find him soon."

Chapter Ten

Dalton felt as though he was in a fog when he and the other Guardians left the flood chamber. Once they had exited the small tunnel and stood in the larger pipe where they had first encountered the demon thieves, Dalton turned to Eclipse, taking a few moments to remember what he wanted to ask the other man.

"What do you want to do about them?" he whispered, jerking his head back to the pipe as Mitoki climbed out of the passage.

"I don't know," he murmured. "He said he knew they would get caught. I don't know if that means I should call Patrick and a few others to come and apprehend them. I don't know how much of a fight they're going to put up. They have to know we're not going to just leave them here. And after what he just told us about other demons purposely causing trouble…"

"What would you do, Keito?" Mitoki asked, turning to the silent demon.

He closed his eyes, heaving a sigh.

"It's up to you, Eclipse," he finally said. "Depending on what you decide to do, I'll do my best to advise you how to approach these demons. But I can't make an unbiased decision."

Eclipse took a deep breath, shaking his head.

"We have to take them in, Keito," he said. "They're breaking the law by being here and they're causing severe property damage. I can't just let them terrorize some other city."

"I understand."

"How do we do that without getting anyone killed?" Dalton pressed.

Keito turned to Eclipse.

"Call Patrick, tell them how many there are, and to bring at least five transport cars. I would call at least ten Guardians for backup in taking them in and transporting them," he started. "Dalton, call Sanyai. Tell her to be ready to take them at the portals and keep them contained. If you say it's Benny's gang, she'll know who you're talking about."

"How do we keep them from running or fighting back?" Mitoki asked.

"I can't guarantee they won't, but I don't think it's likely," Keito said. "They knew this was coming. They know that cooperation with the Guardians at this point is the best way for them to survive."

"And you're not going to hold a grudge about me having them apprehended?" Eclipse asked pointedly.

"I understand duty as a Guardian," Keito assured. "Go call Patrick. You might have to climb a ladder to get a signal, though. I'll stand here and make sure they don't try to move from the flood chamber."

Mitoki and Hanyi stood in silence with Keito while Dalton and Eclipse wandered back through the tunnels with their phones extended, looking for a strong enough signal to make their calls. Their voices echoed through the tunnels as they made the separate calls. Mitoki was sure that the demons in the chamber heard the calls being made, but with the way Keito's head was turned to the small tunnel, as if listening carefully, he knew Keito was keeping an ear on Benny's gang.

It was a tense thirty-minute wait for the transport cars to arrive and another ten minutes for enough local Guardians to have gathered around the nearest alley to extract the large demon group. Dalton watched the process carefully, noting that several of the human Guardians were much rougher with the demons than necessary. When Benny was pulled out of the pipe, he immediately met eyes with Keito, who dropped his gaze.

Benny leaned close to Keito, fighting against the Guardian holding his restraints.

"Keep your head high, kid," he said. "Like I said, I should have known better."

Keito closed his eyes, but did not raise his head. Benny chuckled quietly as he was wrestled away and attached to a wench that was hauling the demons to street level.

It was quite late by the time all demons were secured in the transport vans. Patrick offered to lead the convoy to the portals to meet with Sanyai, who was prepared to take charge of the demon thieves, telling Eclipse to go home and get some rest, knowing the next round of the Guardian Tournament was fast approaching.

The alleyway felt cold and still as the final van left, following the others through the old downtown buildings, leaving Team Dalton to stand in the dark alley. Eclipse finally started leading them onto the sidewalks and toward his car, though the exhausted, confused Guardians did not speak to one another, now turning over every piece of information they had gathered from Benny.

As Eclipse unlocked the car for everyone to get in, Keito slowed his step, finally stopping with a heavy sigh.

"I need to take a walk," he murmured. "I'll get back to the house on my own."

"Are you okay?"

"I'll be fine," the demon said, retreating a step, his eyes never leaving the pavement. "I just need to walk for a while."

"Okay…" Dalton said. "Be careful. Keep your phone on in case we need you."

Keito nodded, turned, and disappeared around the corner. The remaining Guardians shared worried looks with one another before climbing into Eclipse's car and driving back across town.

They trudged into Eclipse's house, feeling exhaustion gripping every muscle, though their minds were spinning in circles around what they had been told.

Hanyi stopped them as they quietly walked into the darkened house, worried about waking anyone sleeping in the early morning hours.

"Do we want to get some sleep and talk about this in the morning? Or do you need to talk about it now before we sleep?"

"No way I'll be able to sleep," Mitoki groaned.

"I agree," Dalton said. "I'm going to have a quick shower to wash this smell off, and then I'm going to sit in the kitchen and think. Maybe wait until Keito gets back to make sure he's alright."

Hanyi nodded slowly. "We should all eat something, too."

After quickly washing up, the four members of Team Dalton filed into the kitchen, where one light remained on, illuminating two notes on the dining table. One was from Jikia and Tarrena, telling the Guardians they would be by in the afternoon the following day to check on them. The other note was from Saki, telling them that there was dinner for them in the refrigerator.

Mitoki made tea for them while Eclipse pulled out the leftovers to heat up and set on the table.

While the Guardians sipped their tea, only Hanyi was able to eat his entire portion of dinner. The others picked at the food, managing a few small bites.

"A war between humans and demons, huh?" Mitoki finally said.

"Sadly, I don't think it would be that difficult to accomplish," Eclipse said. "I guess in a way, I'm surprised it hasn't happened already."

"That's because the other Old Blood Lords don't want a war with humans," Hanyi said. "Vestera is constantly trying to keep the peace."

"Then why hasn't *he* dealt with Yokouro, yet?" Dalton asked, exasperated. "He could probably just end his existence if he wanted to."

"In theory," Hanyi agreed. "But from what I know about Vestera, he's the type to watch from the shadows and only show up when he knows no one else can interfere." He hesitated. "And with Yokouro, I'm pretty sure the Kage Lords have stood between Vestera and Yokouro for centuries."

"I find it hard to believe that Vestera, the all-powerful dragon, would be afraid of the repercussions of two demons," Mitoki said.

"I don't think he's afraid of them," Hanyi said. "He just knows what they're capable of."

Dalton closed his eyes.

"I wish I knew what to expect from them," he whispered. "Are they involved? Are they not involved? And now there's a younger brother?"

"Acurala," Hanyi said with a slow nod. "I didn't see that coming, but like Keito said, it makes sense."

"Not to us," Eclipse growled.

"The demons understand that Yokouro's beliefs are radical. And while I think a lot of demons are not pleased with the DPC, they know it's in their interest to work *with* humans rather than try to cause a fuss. But Yokouro wants a war. And Yokouro is a very powerful demon, riling up all the angry demons in the realm. But his name will only carry him so far. If he can get the Kage supporters behind him, then he becomes a very large threat."

"But don't the Kage Lords already support him?"

"Not to the extent he would need," Hanyi said. "They're still separate territories. Separate Old Blood families. And I don't think Juki would be stupid enough to throw his lot in with Yokouro. Juki is a lot older and a lot wiser. But Acurala has always been a hothead, from what I've heard. So even though it's not Juki or Rutu, Acurala still has the Kage name, and that can sway a lot of demons."

"But he was dead, so now Yokouro's raising more than just himself from the dead?" Mitoki asked.

"Seems like it."

"Then how possible is it that Acurala was the one to abduct Elder Renard?" Dalton asked.

"Pretty likely," the wolf agreed.

"So Juki might not be in the realm at all," he said hopefully.

Hanyi took a moment to think. "It's possible. Juki and Rutu are very difficult to predict."

"Are they also on the demon domination kick?" Eclipse asked. "If they protect Yokouro from Vestera, they probably see humans as insignificant specks that should bow to demons just like he does."

Hanyi let out a choked snicker. "Humans *are* insignificant specks compared to them," he said. "But I don't think they want to see humanity destroyed. Every time I've spoken with them, they seemed more interested in preserving the peace than causing chaos."

Dalton held out a hand to stop Hanyi.

"You've spoken with the Kage Lords?"

"Yeah, multiple times."

"In a threatening situation? In an investigation? Socially? What do you mean?" Eclipse prompted, just as startled as Dalton.

"Um, all?" Hanyi said. "If I'm being honest, apart from the first time I met them, all my interactions and conversations with them have been very civil and polite."

"What happened the first time you met them?" Mitoki asked warily, unsure he even wanted to hear the answer.

"I had a very severe mental breakdown and had to take a three-month leave," he said. "I didn't know they existed. I had no idea that there were such powerful demons in existence back then. It was in my first few years as a Guardian, right when Keito and I first teamed up, and I was working a case with him about newly-turned demons. They were trying to open a permanent portal between the Demon Realm and the Human Realm."

"Newly-turned demons?"

"There's some potion that I can't remember the name of that will physiologically change humans into demons. It's really toxic and volatile and difficult to make, and it apparently makes these newly-turned demons into bloodthirsty menaces that are more-or-less rabid. It was this cult of maybe a dozen humans who thought that turning themselves into demons, and then using their blood in the rituals, would help open a permanent portal. Needless to say, this was quickly brought to the attention of the DPC, and we were assigned to find them and...well, stop them."

"Kill them," Mitoki said with a grim nod.

"By the time we found them, we would have had to kill them. They had taken the potion and were mad with this primal bloodlust I had never seen before," Hanyi explained. "They couldn't even do their ritual because they were so crazed. And they were *fast*. We were chasing them for weeks. And finally, we got a tip on where they were in the Realm of Light. So, we went off to follow the lead." Hanyi's eyes went distant. "And when we got there, *they* were there."

"The Kage Lords?" Eclipse guessed. The wolf nodded slowly.

"When I opened that door it was like someone had taken a sledgehammer to my ribs. Even their presence with all their power limiters was so intense...I couldn't breathe at all. And they were just standing in this abandoned office building surrounded by the dead bodies of the newly-turned demons. They had slaughtered them. And slaughtered is the nice way of explaining the carnage." Hanyi lifted his hands, finally raising his eyes to his teammates. "They had done it all with their bare hands. The entire cult. Ripped to shreds."

"Did they see you?" Mitoki asked.

"Of course they did," Hanyi whispered. "I just stood there and stared. There was nothing else I could do."

"What did they do? How did they react?" Eclipse pressed.

Hanyi took a deep breath. "Juki just walked up to me, covered in blood and gore, offered his hand to me, and introduced himself. Just like that. As though he wasn't standing in the same room where he had torn apart over a dozen bodies."

"And you actually sat down and had a conversation with these demons after *that*?" Eclipse gawked.

"Definitely not the same day," Hanyi said strongly. "Like I said, I had a severe breakdown and had to take a three-month leave." The wolf shrugged. "But later, yes, I did. You know, without all the blood and dead bodies everywhere."

"Yeah, that was not a good way for you to meet them," a voice said in the doorway to the kitchen. The Guardians jumped, on edge from the story, turning to see Keito leaning against the door frame. He lifted a hand, offering a tired smile. "Relax, it's just me."

"Damn it, you scared us half to death!" Mitoki gasped, lowering himself back in his seat.

"How did you even sneak in here?" Eclipse asked, his brow furrowed. "We should have heard the front door."

Keito gave him an incredulous look. "Just a few hours ago you learned that I was a thief in my youth. Sneaking around is second nature to me."

Keito stepped forward slowly, taking a seat next to Hanyi.

"Are you alright?"

"I'm fine," he assured. "Thank you for worrying, but I really am alright."

"I imagine that was very difficult for you," Dalton said.

Keito sighed, crossing his arms over his chest. "Not as much as I thought it would be," he said. "I just needed to get my head on straight again after everything wrapped up."

"Thank you, Keito," Eclipse said. "For understanding why we had to call them in."

The demon shook his head. "I was never going to stop you from calling them in. I was trying to decide if I was going to stick around for their arrest, or if I was going to try and get as far away from them as possible before they were captured."

The Guardians fell silent, throwing worried looks around the table.

"Did you think they would attack you?"

Keito shrugged. "I really had no idea what they would do. Sometimes, demons I thought of as friends turn on me, and other times, demons I've betrayed surprise me by not retaliating. At this point, I just assume I'm always going to be attacked so I can be pleasantly surprised when I'm not."

"And I guess…given what Eboren said about your past with Benny—"

Keito lifted his hand to stop Mitoki from continuing.

"I'd rather not talk about it, if that's alright with you," he said. "Things were really bad in my life back then. I mean, it's pretty screwed up now, but when I was young…" He trailed off, heaving a deep sigh. "But my screwed up childhood did allow me to get to know some powerful demons in the realm."

"Like the Kage Lords? I noticed you don't call them *Lord* Juki or *Lord* Rutu like Benny," Dalton said.

Keito cringed. "I really *should*, but when I was younger I spent so much time around their territory, I just ended up dropping the formalities."

"So you didn't meet them on that case with Hanyi," Mitoki deduced.

"No, no, I knew them long before that."

"Then, you actually do know them pretty well?"

"Better than most, unfortunately," Keito said. "Which is to say I know them well enough to know I will never be able to predict what they will do."

"Do you think Benny's right? About us meeting Yokouro soon?"

"If he really does have a physical body again, then yes," Keito agreed. "He used to do everything through his lackeys, and would appear to us as magic manifestations of his body. But with Acurala Kage's help, he has a lot more resources open to him."

"You said that Acurala was dead for over a century, and yet Yokouro was able to resurrect him?" Eclipse said. "That should be almost impossible for him to do with someone who's been dead for so long."

"Normally I would agree, but I think Yokouro learned a few tricks from the hex beast," Keito said. "You said that when you fought it, it looked completely different and moved much faster? That tells me that Rutu did something with that hex beast, and

Yokouro probably realized if he could collect the bones of Acurala Kage, he could resurrect him."

"But he would need to find the soul, as well," Eclipse said. "Assuming it wasn't reincarnated, or split."

"Souls split?" Mitcki asked, wondering how Eclipse knew that information.

"I guess he found it," Keito said with a shrug. "And Acurala is a very powerful tool for Yokouro. It basically gives him all the Kage resources and the Kage name, and allows him to keep Juki and Rutu in the shadows to keep Vestera from getting suspicious."

"Until he kidnaps an Elder and puts the entire DPC on lockdown because Juki is MIA," Dalton mused.

"You don't think they would actually get involved with the tournament, do you?" Hanyi asked Keito, his expression worried.

The demon was silent, his head slowly starting to shake as he thought.

"The only way to gauge what Juki and Rutu are likely to do is to wait and see if they show themselves to us at all. I think it's more likely we come across Acurala and Yokouro than Juki and Rutu."

"I hope so," Hanyi groaned, rubbing his eyes roughly. Keito hesitated.

"Yeah, me too."

Dalton could not help but hear the uncertainty in the demon Guardian's voice, and it made his own anxiety spike.

Chapter Eleven

The Guardians found themselves sleeping in when they finally crawled into their beds. It was midmorning when they pulled themselves out of unconsciousness and followed the smell of coffee into the kitchen. Master Genbuki was patient with them as they slowly made their way into the kitchen and sat at the dining table, drinking their coffee with sluggish movements, but eventually, he demanded to know what happened.

Recounting the story of their meeting with the demon thieves allowed them to get a better grasp on the information Benny had shared. Even though they were still nervous about the possibility of meeting Yokouro face-to-face, and the lurking threat of the Kage Lords, they felt more centered as the coffee woke them up and they recounted what they had learned.

Keito excused himself after the Guardians had eaten an early lunch to stand on the front porch, studying the overcast sky, his mind racing with his own concerns.

When a breeze passed over him, he shivered, feeling as if sparks were dancing over his skin. He wondered if his paranoia was due to his knowledge of the demons they were pursuing, or if he was accurately sensing danger in the air. There was a heaviness settling over the neighborhood, pushing down on the house to the point where Keito thought he could hear the wooden planks of the porch strain under the pressure.

Hesitantly, he returned inside and walked to the dining table, where the others were discussing something about Benny's fall from the good graces of the Kage Lords. He gently drummed his nails along the table.

"Are you alright?" Dalton asked, turning to the demon.

"How is everyone feeling today?" he asked quietly.

"...as good as can be expected with so much stress and such little sleep..." Mitoki said. "Why?"

"Come outside."

The Guardians followed their teammate, Master Genbuki remaining behind, worriedly listening to them leave.

As they gathered on the front porch, Keito drew in a deep breath, trying to pick up any unfamiliar scents.

"Do you feel the heaviness in the air?" he asked.

"It's just the approaching storm," Eclipse assured. "Atmospheric pressure."

"Are you sure?" Keito asked. "It's not just that kind of heaviness."

"The impending feeling," Hanyi agreed, looking up and down the street in front of the house. "Like something is pushing down on you, waiting for something to give way."

"Do you think we're in danger?" Mitoki asked.

"...I think something is coming," Keito said vaguely. "Like one of the Old Blood Lords is close."

"Can you sense which one?" Eclipse asked quickly.

"No, I'm not saying I know one of them is close," Keito corrected. "This electricity in the air might be the storm...I just doubt that it is."

Dalton closed his eyes and took a deep breath, trying to sense the same thing Keito was talking about. At first, he felt nothing. But when a breeze passed by the house, bringing the musky smell of rain, he felt the gentle dancing of sparks over his skin, his hair standing on end in response. In an instant, he was reminded of the magic that he had felt awaken in him in the Beast Realm. He could feel the swell of power in his chest and he knew it was in response to something his powers were sensing nearby.

He opened his eyes, trying to sound calm when he spoke.

"I guess it can't hurt to take a walk around the neighborhood. Maybe take an hour or two and see if we can sense or see anything amiss."

They started along the path they had jogged to warm up for their training with Master Genbuki before walking further into the suburban sprawl, keeping an eye on the clouds above and trying to sense danger around the corners. While nothing seemed immediately amiss, all the Guardians could feel the impending sense of dread growing within them.

"Do you think this is another ripple?" Mitoki finally asked when they were starting to jump at the sound of approaching cars.

"It's possible," Hanyi said. "With the tournament tomorrow, it would make sense that Yokouro would try something today, something to throw us off our game."

"That is his style," Keito agreed.

"Maybe it would be best to go back and get the car then," Eclipse suggested. "We can cover more ground, and that way—"

A sound resembling a whip crack split their eardrums and made them drop into a crouch, quickly scanning their surroundings for the source of the noise. The sound resonated through the neighborhood, echoing through the crevices of houses and rattling the windows of the nearby residences.

"What the hell was that?" Dalton hissed, slowly standing.

"Nothing good," Hanyi said. "That wasn't a gunshot..."

"No, it wasn't."

For nearly half a minute, Team Dalton remained where they were, scanning the houses around them worriedly, expecting the sound to happen again, ready to lock onto the noise and follow it to the source.

"Smoke," Mitoki noted, pointing to a dark plume rising into the overcast sky only a few blocks away.

"That's a big fire," Dalton said, his feet moving on their own, picking up a jog in the direction of the smoke.

"Fires don't get that big that quickly," Eclipse said.

"They do in one situation," Hanyi whispered, shifting into his wolf form and sprinting ahead of the Guardians.

"Keito, go see what's happening," Dalton called back to the demon. Keito practically disappeared, sprinting past the humans and running toward the smoke.

When the three humans caught up, they had to scramble for their Guardian IDs to show the officers keeping civilians away from the fire. They fumbled with their wallets, their eyes locked on the inferno they had come across. Every window of the large building was pouring smoke into the air, flames leaping out in a flash of orange and yellow when another pane of glass broke from the heat.

But what truly terrified Dalton was seeing the young children running from the building to join more groups of children in the parking lot.

Dalton ran to Keito and Hanyi, who were talking to one of the firefighters as others barked orders to get water on the flames engulfing the school.

"What happened?" Dalton demanded.

"No idea," the firefighter said quickly. "I don't know if this was an explosion. I don't know if there is a gas leak somewhere. We just got here."

He quickly stepped away from the Guardians as Dalton looked around frantically. Running to one side of the parking lot, he took the arm of a terrified teacher who was watching the flames devour the school.

"What happened?" he repeated, holding her arm to keep her attention on him. She glanced quickly at the Guardians and shook her head, dazed.

"I-I-I don't know," she stammered. "I was in my classroom and-and there was this *loud* noise. It was like a bomb went off, but *not*. Nothing in the room moved. The building didn't shake. It was just a loud sound and when I looked up…" she motioned to the school, "everything was on fire. I-I have no idea how. It seems impossible…"

Dalton turned to Keito.

"Sound familiar?"

The demon nodded. "Too familiar."

"Are all the kids out?" Mitoki asked.

"I don't-I don't know," she said quickly, looking at the terrified children gathered around her. "My kids are all here. I-I don't know about the others."

"Okay, we need to make sure everyone is out of that building," Dalton said, turning to his team. "Someone find the principal of the school, tell them to find every teacher."

Mitoki ducked away to complete the task.

"We need to secure a perimeter," he said, turning to Eclipse. "If this is an attack, we have to get the civilians as far away as possible."

The other Guardian nodded and turned to secure a perimeter, noting that two other local Guardians had arrived to help, accompanying other firetrucks and ambulances.

Dalton pulled Hanyi and Keito away from the teachers and students.

"What do you suggest we do? Do you think this was an attack?"

"Almost certainly," Keito said.

"That water won't put out the fire if it is the same kind of attack," Hanyi added. "It's a magic-based flame. It has to be put out with magic."

"Do you think we have enough magic between all the Guardians to do it?"

"I doubt it," Hanyi said, turning to Keito for confirmation.

"There might be some other demon Guardians nearby for the tournament. They might be able to help. The more magically-trained people we can get, the better," the demon said.

"Okay, I'll put out a call for local Guardians," Dalton said, immediately extracting his phone and going through the steps to put out an alert for all nearby Guardians to gather at the location. Keito and Hanyi turned to the fire, trying not to be reminded of the Tournament Slaughter.

"What do we do? We're in the middle of a crowded neighborhood," Hanyi hissed.

"Try to—" Keito stopped when he saw the way the water from the firehose reflected back toward the firefighters, bouncing off a powerful force field surrounding the building.

Dalton slowly lowered his phone as he stepped next to Keito and Hanyi, watching the way the water bounced away to shower the struggling firefighters, causing more confusion and panic.

"If the water can't reach the fire, then I'm assuming neither can our magic," he murmured.

"We have to break the force field first," Hanyi agreed.

Eclipse jogged toward them with four other Guardians, including Patrick.

"What's the plan?"

"We have to find a way to break the force field first," Hanyi repeated.

"Do we know if everyone is out of the building?" one female Guardian asked.

"Mitoki's checking that now."

"It might be dangerous to break the force field until we're certain everyone is out," Eclipse said. "We could accidentally bring the rest of the building down on the heads of anyone inside."

"Guardian DeVero," a voice called.

They all turned, seeing another Guardian approach slowly, dipping his head in a bow to Keito. "My name is Macendae. I am a demon Guardian."

"Are you the only other demon in the area?"

"I think so," he answered, distracted by the sight of the water deflecting from the fire. "This is a demon force field."

"Can you help me break it?" Keito asked. "Who is your Old Blood Lord?"

"None. Middle Dimension born and raised." He raised his hands peacefully when he saw Keito's wary expression. "I do not believe in Yokouro's radical beliefs. You have my word."

Deciding to put aside his suspicion in favor of help, Keito nodded quickly.

"Then this should work," he said.

"What do you want us to do?" Dalton asked.

"If we can get the force field broken, try to use all the magic you can to suppress the fire while also allowing the fire crews to get water on it," Keito said. "I don't know if I'll be able to break this completely, so if I can't, take any opening I can make."

"Dalton!" Mitoki called, running over. "There is one full class still inside."

Dalton's blood ran cold and he felt the color drain from his face. Keito turned quickly to the building and then to the Guardians.

"I can't risk neutralizing this force field with them inside. So Macendae and I will create a single opening. Protect yourself with magic, get in there, and get them out. But do it quick. I don't know how long the structure will last."

The two demon Guardians ran close to the fire, motioning for the fire crews to bring the hoses toward them as Eclipse and Dalton turned to explain the plan to the two other Guardians that had arrived at the scene.

Keito nodded to Macendae and the two demons closed their eyes, focusing on the other and merging their powers together at the force field, piercing through the powerful barrier and expanding their magic to create a break large enough for a Guardian to fit through.

"Get some water on that door!" Keito ordered, though he dared not lift his head in case he lost concentration on the barrier pushing against his magic. As the firemen rushed forward to pour water on the flames surrounding one of the smaller side doors, Macendae carefully turned his head over his shoulder.

"Go!" he barked, straining against the powerful force field threatening to overwhelm him. He flinched as he turned back, lifting his hands toward the barrier to better focus his magic. "Who the hell is this, Keito?!" he yelled.

"Just focus! Don't let the barrier reform!"

Realizing the strain it was putting on the demons, Dalton ran forward, the water from the hoses stopping long enough to allow him to push through the hot door and into the fire-engulfed hallway.

The moment he lowered his arms from protecting his face, he could feel the power radiating through the school. Despite the bright flames, it felt incredibly dark inside, and the roof felt as though it was brushing the top of his head, singeing his hair as he took careful steps forward, barely able to breathe around the smoke and the magic in the air.

Creating a magical barrier around himself brought him near-excruciating pain. The pressure on his magic felt like an oppressive weight threatening to break every bone in his body. He heard the pained groans around him as the other Guardians also fought to create a magical barrier around themselves.

The doors in the hallway were open, flames leaping out to char the carpet and the art projects that had adorned the walls. The building creaked and moaned, straining. The Guardians moved together, trying to listen around the sounds of the fire to where the class was trapped.

"If you can hear us, make some noise!" Dalton called loudly into the building.

Hanyi's head turned quickly.

"Over there!"

He turned at an intersection of halls, following the sounds only he could hear until turning one more corner and stopping at a door. Eclipse and Dalton were the next to reach the door, and from within they could hear the terrified cries of children and an older male screaming for help. As the other Guardians drew close, Eclipse pressed the back of his hand to the door, immediately recoiling from the heat.

"Get away from the door!" he bellowed.

Counting a few seconds to give anyone within time to get away, Eclipse balled his fists and lifted them, letting out a shout as he banged both of them against the door, dark purple tendrils of magic erupting from the impact to fill the frame as the door was flung into the room.

Eclipse stepped through the magically-reinforced door frame and assessed who was in the room. The class was huddled near the center, the children crouched under their desks, crying and screaming in fear, coughing as the smoke filled their lungs. Each Guardian rushed forward, pulling two children out from under the desks and holding their hands firmly to keep them within the protective barrier of magic as they rushed them out of the school, having to travel back along the same path to the opening in the force field Keito and Macendae were struggling to maintain.

The Guardians filed out with the children, moving as quickly as they safely could. Rescue crews rushed forward to take the children for treatment as spectators cheered loudly when the children began to emerge.

Dalton knew it was far too early for celebration. Keito and Macendae were struggling, their bodies shaking as they both held their hands forward, palms facing the barrier, focusing all their energy on their task. Dalton knew he did not have time to ask how they were faring. He ran back into the building, almost collapsing as the horrific pressure fell over him once again.

He rushed back to the classroom, ducking to yank two more children out from under the desks, his eyes stinging from the smoke and his head threatening to explode from the pain of the magic surrounding him.

"Dalton!" Patrick yelled, rushing forward and grabbing another two children out from under the desks. "We have to move fast! This building is about to collapse!"

Dalton had to ignore the terrified screaming of the boy he pulled into his arms as he took the hand of another student. He turned to the teacher.

"Stay close to me! Come on!" he barked.

"Not until my students are out!" the teacher yelled.

"Then grab two of them and follow close to me!" Dalton ordered. "We need to get out of here, *now*!"

Hanyi and Eclipse had returned to the classroom as Dalton led the teacher and the four students out of the burning classroom, hearing a section of the roof collapse nearby as the fire continued its attack on the structure. He pushed out of the door, nearly slipping on the wet concrete as the pressure eased and he became dizzy. He stumbled, trying to remain upright as the paramedics rushed forward to tend to those Dalton had rescued.

Hanyi leapt out of the building with a similar reaction, his eyes squeezing tight as the pain lessened and he was able to relax.

"How many more?" Dalton asked.

"Not sure," Hanyi panted. "The roof is coming down. We don't have much time."

Eclipse was the last one toward the door, the other Guardians needing time to recover before returning to the blaze. But as Eclipse saw the charred wood and warped metal that made up their escape, there was an agonized groan from the building. The two kids screamed and clung close to Eclipse as the roof began to collapse. The concussion of the burning debris hitting the magical barrier Eclipse had put around them made him see stars as the pain spiraled through his entire being. He fell to one knee, holding the kids close and keeping the barrier as strong as he could around the searing agony. With a shout of pain, he pushed the barrier away from him, flinging the burning debris free and allowing him to stumble out with the two kids. Dalton and Patrick helped pull him away from the collapsed school and the kids were brought to the ambulances immediately.

"You alright?" Patrick asked, placing a hand on Eclipse's shoulder.

"That hurt like hell," he groaned.

"Is everyone out?!" Mitoki barked, turning to the teacher.

The teacher, already counting his students, stopped and turned to the Guardians, his face pale.

"There's two missing…" he choked.

The Guardians turned to the building, but their hearts fell, seeing that every part of the building had collapsed, the flames burning brighter than before as the plume of smoke turned everything around them into a suffocating cloud. They remained still, frozen, unsure what to do.

Keito staggered, his hands dropping to his sides as he lost his focus. Macendae let out a cry of pain, his knees buckling as he tried to keep the tear in the barrier open so the firefighters could continue to douse the area with water.

"Keito, what do we do? There are still two kids inside," Hanyi said, quickly running to the demon and helping to keep him upright. The demon turned quickly, horrified, and then looked back at the building.

"Keito, I can't hold this open…" Macendae groaned, falling to his knees, his hands shaking as his magic began to wane.

With an angry growl, Keito lifted one of his arms and scraped his nails along his forearm, leaving three large gashes. Dalton was about to ask what the demon was doing when he saw a small metal circle drop from one of the wounds and a wave of magic erupted from Keito. Dalton knew that internal power limiters were more powerful than the traditional jewelry worn as a power limiter, but he did not expect the sudden surge of magic from his demon teammate.

Keito raised his hands toward the fire, his magic pouring toward the barrier with dark blue and silver sparks to collide with the force field. Static filled the air and flashes of light could be seen in the plume of smoke above their heads as Keito's magic tore through the barrier.

"*Enough!*" he bellowed, clenching his fists tight and swinging his hands down to his sides.

The flames retracted into the rubble, smothered by Keito's burst of magic, leaving the charred and blackened remnants of the building as the force field surrounding the fire ruptured like a popped balloon.

Intense silence followed as everyone stared at what remained of the school. Keito began breathing hard, falling heavily to the pavement as his teammates rushed toward him. Macendae fell back, desperately trying to catch his breath, his eyes rolling in their sockets as he fought against unconsciousness.

Hanyi turned to the school, sniffing the air before shifting into his wolf form and stepping carefully toward the rubble. With a nervous whine, he leapt onto one of the crumbled walls and over the roof, one of his paws disappearing into the weakened structure. He pulled himself carefully along the top of the fallen building, his nose low as he avoided anything metal that could still retain the heat of the fire.

"Help him…" Keito whispered, motioning weakly to Hanyi. "Find the kids."

Eclipse looked back at the spectators.

"I don't know that we should with all these people around," he whispered, certain they would be pulling out the bodies of the two students who had been trapped.

"Stay with him," Dalton told Eclipse, finding his own way onto the rubble as the firefighters tried to find a way to tell the Guardians to stay away from the dangerous pile of brick and metal that had once been the school.

Mitoki and Dalton were far more hesitant in their steps as they tested each section before transferring their weight, but they followed Hanyi's path, pausing to watch the wolf as he navigated what was left of the building.

Hanyi stopped, his nose in the rubble, his ears up and alert.

He let out a high whine and barked several times, trying to dig at the debris.

Forgetting all concerns when they saw Hanyi's behavior, Dalton and Mitoki clamored closer, helping Hanyi move the charred remnants of the roof.

"If you can hear us, make a noise!" Dalton called, his hands threatening to blister from the residual heat of the fire as he moved more away from the area Hanyi had started digging in.

A faint cough could be heard under the rubble followed by a choked whimper for help.

"We need more hands!" Mitoki ordered, motioning the other Guardians over.

Dalton began talking to the children, ignoring the pain in his hands as he told them to stay calm and that they were going to save them. He continuously told them they would be alright, helping Patrick move one of the larger beams as they tried to unbury the children.

Everyone in the parking lot that could see the frantic rescue held their breaths, watching the Guardians work around their own coughing and their own pain.

When Dalton pulled away a warped light fixture, a small face could be seen under a burnt desk. The little girl had tears streaming down her soot-covered face as she tried to cry for help, her voice weak from fear and smoke.

"It's okay," Dalton assured, reaching down to touch her face. "We're going to get you out. Where is your friend?"

She pointed at the space next to her and Eclipse immediately began to unload the rubble from the other desks.

"Can you see them? Are they alright?" Dalton prompted.

She looked again and shook her head.

"I don't know…" she said weakly. "He's not moving."

Working at a near-frantic pace, the other Guardians tried to uncover the last student as Dalton guided the girl from under the desk.

"Be careful…watch your head…" he murmured. "Grab onto me."

Her weak fingers gripped his jacket as hard as they could as he lifted her from the rubble. She wrapped her arms around his neck tightly, crying. "I've got you. You're safe." he whispered, worried about the rasp he heard in her voice.

The other Guardians were throwing debris back in a desperate attempt to get to the young boy, ignoring the cheering of the spectators who had seen the young girl rescued.

"Can you see him?" Dalton whispered, passing the coughing girl to a female Guardian that reached for her.

Eclipse pressed himself flat to the rubble and peered through the wreckage.

"Yeah. I see his eyelids fluttering."

Patrick, Mitoki, and two other Guardians were straining to lift a beam that would allow them to reach the boy.

"Can we get a demon over here?!" the female Guardian called back to Keito and Macendae.

Keito turned to the other demon, seeing that he could barely keep his eyes open. He pulled himself to his feet and picked his way across the remnants of the school, his face pale as he tried to catch his breath. When Keito reached them, he looked over the beam briefly before stabilizing his feet as best he could and wrapping his hands around the beam. Fighting the weight still resting on the long beam, he groaned as he lifted the metal, holding it at the level of his chest, gritting his teeth.

"Get him."

Mitoki slid into the opening and grabbed the boy, trying to be gentle as he pulled the student out from under the desk as fast as possible. Eclipse helped him out of the charred building, and they clamored out of the way as Keito dropped the beam, sitting heavily among the blackened building, his eyes closing.

Mitoki rubbed the student's back roughly, trying to push his head upward.

"Hey, hey, open your eyes for me," he urged.

The boy's eyes fluttered and his head rolled around on his neck.

"Let's get him to the ambulances," Patrick said quickly, helping guide Mitoki over the uneven rubble toward the waiting paramedics and the cheering crowds. Dalton and Hanyi helped Keito stumble over the rubble and return to the pavement, allowing the firefighters to spray down the area where they had been standing, cooling the destroyed building.

When they were at a distance to allow the emergency crews to work efficiently, Keito stopped, his legs giving way from under him as he fell to his knees.

"You okay?" Dalton asked, crouching next to his teammate.

Keito was practically gasping for breath, his eyes closed.

"I need that power limiter back," he whispered.

Hanyi darted to retrieve the item, smiling guiltily at the confused firefighters, who had no idea why the Guardian was so interested in the fallen item. Once Hanyi brought the power limiter back, Keito reopened the already-scabbed openings in his forearm and said a short spell to reactivate the artifact before placing it under the skin. Dalton shook his head.

"I had no idea you had that kind of power," he said with a laugh. Keito smiled weakly.

"That's me. Full of surprises."

Eclipse returned to them, letting out a relieved sigh.

"Seems like the kids are going to be okay," he said. "The ambulances are going to take them to the hospital now, but they're confident they'll be fine."

"That's a relief. Now, we just need—"

A startled cry and the crowd of onlookers letting out terrified gasps interrupted Hanyi's thoughts as Team Dalton scanned the area to see what had happened. One fireman was running to the truck to turn off the hose that had been released when the water, once again, reflected back, knocking them to the ground with enough force to nearly knock them unconscious. The water from the second team did the same, hitting a magical barrier and knocking them to the pavement while those near the trucks scrambled to turn off the water.

Once the water had been shut off, the Guardians gathering together once more to address the newest threat, the anxious silence was interrupted by a slow, off-beat clap echoing hauntingly off the pile of mangled walls and broken windows. Stepping over the charred skeleton of the school, a man walked toward the parking lot, his ornate purple robes scraping over the debris and his intricately-braided dark hair leaving the power of his chilling, violet eyes fully exposed.

He continued clapping, smiling and shaking his head slowly, until he stepped off the wreckage of the building.

"Very well done," he said, his deep voice chilling the hot smoke that still lingered in the air. "You did far better than I anticipated."

"Acurala," Keito growled, squaring off to the demon. Macendae retreated, his eyes low as he bowed his head, recognizing that the approaching demon was an Old Blood Lord. Dalton knew he should have been thinking about how to get the stunned and curious bystanders to leave the parking lot, and how to get the children as far away from the dangerous demon as possible. But his mind had gone blank and his blood had run cold as he stared at the demon.

"Keito," Acurala greeted. "I heard rumor that you were so much weaker after all your years in seclusion, but it turns out I was grossly misinformed. Even poisoned with Night Play, you were able to tear that barrier apart and suppress the fire." His smile widened. "Must hurt to realize that you probably could have done the same with that stadium, if you had the right motivation."

Keito leaned forward, snarling as he glared at Acurala.

"Oh, relax, mutt," he chuckled, taking a few steps closer. It was everything Dalton could do not to retreat, though he could tell from the motion he saw in his periphery that the teachers were quickly backing up, putting themselves between the demon and their students. "I was the one who told Varej you were coming after him and gave him the Night Play to poison you. I knew you were weaker. Why do you think I used such a pathetic barrier?"

"You wanted us to put the fire out? Then why bother with a barrier in the first place?" Patrick growled.

"Because I wasn't about to slaughter over a hundred children," Acurala said with a condescending laugh. "I wanted to make it a challenge, but I didn't need that blood on my hands. I was testing you without making it impossible."

"You asshole, you set a school on fire with the kids inside!" Hanyi snapped. "There is no way you could be sure we would be able to get them out in time!"

Acurala turned to the wolf, clicking his tongue on the roof of his mouth.

"Ah, Hanyi Treneke," he mused. "We've never met in person, but I've heard so much about you," Acurala chortled. "Well, mostly, I've heard you're a pain in the ass who has nowhere near the strength of his older brother." He nodded. "I can relate."

"Where is Juki?" Keito growled.

"First of all, it's *Lord* Juki to you, Keito," the other demon corrected. "And second of all, I don't know. It wasn't my turn to watch him."

"Cut the bullshit," Dalton snapped. "Alright, you set a school on fire and brought us here. If you wanted our attention, there were less drastic means."

"Dalton Teban..." Acurala grinned, taking another two steps forward, stopping just when Dalton tensed to retreat. "I couldn't very well just turn up at your door and have a chat," he said. "I'm sure you've been told all sorts of stories and, well, I needed to see who you really are."

"What is that supposed to mean?"

"You've invested so much of your identity into being a Guardian and I just had to see what all the fuss was about," he elaborated. "Personally, I don't see what's so special about you. Yokouro told me to put you in a situation where you had to put your own safety aside to save another. 'Wind him up and watch him go,' were his exact words. But honestly, after watching you go back in and seeing the strain my pathetic little barrier was putting on you," he shrugged one shoulder, "it was just sad. I almost put the fire out just to stop watching that pitiful display of heroism."

"You certainly went through a lot of trouble to see my pitiful display of heroism," Dalton snarled. "Or do you just want to cause more chaos and fear so you can spark a war between demons and humans?"

Acurala paused, his eyes brightening.

"You're much more fun to talk to than to watch," he murmured, looking Dalton over. "Alright, I knew that a more public display might serve a bigger agenda."

"You want to spark a war between humans and demons?" one of the female Guardians hissed, her voice filled with both anger and fear.

The demon lord shrugged. "I suppose?"

"What the hell is that supposed to mean?" Mitoki snapped

"I don't think a war is really necessary for what Yokouro wants to do, but it's his plan, not mine," Acurala said.

"And what is his plan? Demon domination?" Eclipse asked.

"As if we don't already dominate humans," Acurala laughed. "He just wants us to be seen as we are. We are far more than humans could ever hope to be, and yet we allow ourselves to be subjugated by humans. To be locked away, treated like freaks and monsters." Acurala nodded to Keito. "Keito knows exactly what I'm talking about."

"What Yokouro wants to do will not *help* demons," Keito snapped. "You could never understand, Acurala. You're a *Kage*."

"Exactly, I'm a Kage," Acurala repeated coldly. "Which means I have had to pretend that I care what the humans in the DPC say about my home, and then allow them to enforce some stupid regulations on where I can go, what I can do, and how I must behave and even *dress* in the human realms." He shook his head, his gaze turning back to Dalton. "I could annihilate everyone in this entire neighborhood in the blink of an eye and none of you could stop me. So who are *you* to tell me how to live?"

"That's what you get out of this?" Dalton asked. "To have power over us? To be treated like some kind of god? You just burned down a school full of kids! Why would anyone want to bow to someone willing to risk the lives of over a hundred children?"

"Oh, you would be surprised," Acurala said with a laugh. "Humans think they're so special. I will never understand what the dragons see as so precious in humanity that they keep giving you second chances, when all you do is destroy your environment, overpopulate, and create nothing but distress and pain for the entire universe."

"So you want to throw the balance of everything in the other direction? You want to do the same thing?" Dalton challenged. "Make it so demons are the ones overpopulating and causing distress? And your reasoning is just because humans are bad for the universe? You said so yourself. The dragons protect us. They don't protect you."

"Of course they don't. We don't need protection," Acurala laughed. "The dragons aren't stupid enough to attack the demons when there are demons that can kill their all-powerful Lord Vestera."

"And yet I notice your older brother isn't here to back Yokouro's plan," Eclipse said shortly.

"Oh, not to worry," Acurala assured. "Juki is keeping a very close eye on Yokouro so he can be sure exactly when he needs to step in. And when he does, you can be sure that you will see the true power demons possess."

"Why are you stalling, Acurala?" Keito asked slowly. "Is Juki coming here?"

"Why would he bother?" the older demon scoffed. "No, no, I'm just waiting for Yokouro to make his grand entrance. You know how he can be."

Dalton could feel the blood drain from his face.

"He's coming *here*?" he hissed.

"Should be along shortly. Now that I've gathered you all here."

Even knowing he should not take his eyes off Acurala, Dalton turned to note the sheer number of people around them. The teachers were slowly taking their students to the furthest side of the parking lot, the fire fighters helping to guide them away as they put themselves between the demon and the school staff. The large group of spectators seemed to have grown rather than diminish from the looming threat of the demon lord. Almost everyone had their phones out, recording what they could of the encounter while two news crews had also arrived to do a story on the fire, though the cameras were focused on the Guardians and the demon lord.

"He's going to reveal himself to the public as well," Dalton deduced.

"He's ready to get the ball rolling."

"If he reveals himself, we can bring him in to stand trial for his crimes," Mitoki said, though his voice was shaking, unable to make the lie sound convincing. "So let him come. We'll bring him into custody."

Acurala laughed hollowly. "My brother would be sure to put a stop to all that before it got too far."

"So where is he in all this?" Eclipse sneered. "You said he was watching, waiting to step in. Why don't we meet all of you so we can stop dancing around one another?"

"Are you that eager to die?"

"I think it's all just hype," Eclipse said. "All we've been hearing about is the Kage Lords and how terrifying they are and that they will defend Yokouro, but you're the first one we've actually *seen*. And I can't say I'm very impressed. Surely your brother is just as much of a disappointment to our expectations."

"Eclipse," Keito hissed, giving him a purposeful look to warn the other Guardian against angering the demon lord.

"Can't say I blame you for thinking that," Acurala agreed, his eyebrows raising. "After all, I am just the little brother of the great Lord Juki Kage, one of the most powerful demons in the history of our species. I can't hold a candle to him. I've never been able to measure up. Don't get me wrong, I love my older brother more than you could ever know, but it can be trying to have an older brother so powerful he could destroy the entire human race if he sneezes carelessly." He leaned forward. "You can doubt all you want, and you can puff out your chest and pretend you're not terrified," he lowered his voice, "but do not disrespect my brother in front of me."

"Acurala," Keito started, taking the other demon's attention off Eclipse, "you know that Juki would never approve of Yokouro making such a spectacle."

"Why do you think he's not here?" Acurala chuckled.

"You're going to completely destroy any rapport demons have with humans," Keito barked. "More demons will be hunted down and killed because of stunts like this! Not all demons want a war with humans. We want to live peacefully."

"Oh, Keito, you're such a child," Acurala groaned. "Do you really believe in that bedtime story? Demons and humans coexisting? No matter what, they will always look at you like a dangerous monster. You will *never* be equal to them."

"That doesn't mean I should try and assert myself as *more* than them!" Keito snapped. "Damn it, Acurala, you should listen to your subjects! There are demons fleeing to every other realm to try and escape what Yokouro's doing! He's tearing the land to shreds!"

"It's about time things change, and if it takes some tearing, so be it."

"No wonder you never gained full control of the Kage Clan," the other demon snapped. "Birth order had nothing to do with it. I'm trying to remember if you were always this stupid, or if Yokouro left your brain in the ground when he resurrected you."

Acurala's lip curled in a warning sneer.

"Watch your step, Keito. You've always walked a fine line with the Old Bloods. Don't get stupid now."

Dalton looked quickly between Keito and Acurala, worried about the sudden confrontational nature Keito had adopted. He saw Macendae jerking his head back to the growing police force that were lining up behind the Guardians, their guns prepped at their sides to shoot Acurala. Their nervous energy was causing the tension in the air to mount, and Dalton could almost taste the gunpowder on his tongue, knowing they were only moments away from a shootout with far too many innocent civilians and children nearby.

"Keito," he whispered, trying to get his teammate's attention.

"Why should I be scared of you?" Keito laughed, ignoring Dalton as he smirked at Acurala. "You got yourself murdered by some low-blood moron, and not even because you did anything. It was just to get under Juki's skin."

"Yokouro never told me I had to keep *you* alive, Keito," Acurala said. "Shut up before I remove your head from your shoulders."

"Would it hurt for you to know that it didn't work?" Keito challenged. "Sure, Juki killed the idiot who killed you, but that was just business as usual for him."

Acurala leapt forward to attack Keito, but a cold voice stopped him.

"Enough, Acurala."

Dalton's entire body froze, but it was not a stabbing, cold fear that forced him to still. The two words sent a furious fire from his ears, down his spine, and locked every muscle within him. His hair stood on end, his breath stuck in his throat, and even before he managed to turn around, he knew exactly who he would see.

The sea of gazes that had once been focused on Acurala swung to the other side of the street, where a figure stood on the roof of the temple that had faced the school. Against the dark storm clouds looming in the sky, his silvery-white hair and bright golden eyes seemed to glow. His dark blue robes were simpler than Acurala's, but he wore them open, exposing his chest where twisting patterns of black stood in sharp contrast to his skin. Three lines on each cheek and the line under his eyes and over his nose left no doubt in Dalton's mind about the demon's identity.

Even across the street, Dalton could feel the moment Yokouro DeVastes met his gaze. Everything disappeared around them, and despite the distance between them, Dalton felt as though Yokouro was directly in front of him. The golden eyes seemed so unnatural and yet familiar, as though Dalton was finally able to put an identity to the eyes that had been trailing him all his life. Understanding washed over him and his entire being reacted to Yokouro, determined to fight and defeat the demon to his very last breath, no matter the consequences.

The thought should have scared him to his senses. It should have surprised him how focused he became on destroying Yokouro. But the determination that burned through his veins felt natural, as though it had always been a part of him.

Each member of Team Dalton was staring at Yokouro, but it was the other Guardians that were able to see how profound the moment was for their five superiors. Hanyi's eyes were burning with anger and his fists were clenched so tightly his palms were bleeding. Keito was also glaring at Yokouro, but there was fear in his gaze that he was unable to mask as he stared at the Old Blood Lord.

While Dalton was transfixed by Yokouro, Eclipse and Mitoki seemed to come to their own understanding about the demon across the street. The other Guardians thought the two recognized Yokouro, but only vaguely, as though on the edges of a dream where they were not certain they remembered the demon, but innately knew exactly who was opposing them.

Everyone was transfixed by Yokouro. The bystanders were filming him, trying to zoom in on his face to get a better look. The police force that had lined up to confront Acurala had turned to Yokouro, but their guns remained by their sides, fascinated with the electric, wild aura that surrounded the demon. The area had gone very still, all eyes focused on the Old Blood Lord on the roof of the temple.

Yokouro's dark smile caused Dalton to jump, partially breaking him from his trance.

"That's enough, Acurala," Yokouro said again. "You've done what I've asked."

The other demon walked forward, scaring many out of their stares of morbid fascination as the bystanders yelped and tried to move away, unsure what Acurala would do. Dalton could not tear his eyes away from Yokouro, even as Acurala walked by him.

The police officers were torn between focusing on Yokouro and focusing on Acurala. A few turned and raised their guns to the Kage Lord, ordering the demon to get on the ground as they spouted every known rule they knew about demons being in human-inhabited realms. Acurala's stride halted and his eyes turned to the officers.

They silenced, their guns raised, their hands shaking, but they let the demon walk to the sidewalk, where he broke into a short sprint before leaping high into the air and landing next to Yokouro on the roof of the temple, the tiles cracking and falling to the ground.

"You told me to expect a fight," Acurala told him. "They didn't take the bait."

Yokouro, still staring at Dalton, smiled. "That's because they've been doing their homework."

"He's not moving," Acurala noted, studying Dalton. "You've scared him."

Minutely, Yokouro shook his head. "I've focused him."

So fast it startled everyone near him, Dalton reached into his jacket and pulled out his gun, aiming at Yokouro and firing five shots as screams and barked orders erupted around him.

"Dalton!" Hanyi yelled, leaping at his team leader and snatching the gun from his hands.

The Guardian did not see nor hear the chaos his attack had created around him. He did not notice his gun had left his hands, nor the Guardians desperately trying to calm the agitated police officers. He could not hear the screams of the students and teachers as they tried to find a safer location.

He stared at the unmoving Yokouro DeVastes.

"Dalton! Get back!"

Keito was suddenly at his side, shoving him backward and breaking Dalton's eye contact with Yokouro just as a high-pitch whistling sound came to his ears. A flash of metal near his feet caused him to look down, where five bullets were lined neatly in front of him, hovering just above the ground.

The bullets ruptured, creating an explosion that blew the Guardians backward and caused another round of terrified screaming. Dalton quickly scrambled to his feet, ignoring the hot cuts in his face from the shards of bullets. His ears were ringing and the disorder around him brought him back to the present. He was suddenly acutely aware of the sheer number of people around him and how easily he had ignored their presence when trying to provoke Yokouro into action. His eyes passed over the scattering crowds, the crying children huddled near their teachers, the frenzied police officers, the confused Guardians, and finally the roof of the temple.

The two demon lords had vanished.

Chapter Twelve

The injuries from the explosion were minimal. Once the chaos had calmed and the police were better able to contain the area, Team Dalton was seen by the paramedics, who were unconcerned with the small cuts, stating that even the minimal burns the Guardians had received when rescuing the children were not a worry.

Dalton tried to keep his composure through the hours of interviews, statements, and discussions about how best to contain and handle the incident. Elder Lunar's office was called to warn her about the media frenzy that was likely to occur. The frantic parents were finally allowed through the barrier to collect their children, and the firefighters asked the Guardians repeatedly about the demon that had attacked the school and the magical nature of the fire so they could conduct the appropriate investigation.

By the time Team Dalton was cleared to leave the premises, Dalton was barely containing his trembling. The walk back to Eclipse's house was silent, making it even more difficult for Dalton to maintain his composure. His mind was racing with thoughts and fears about Yokouro and Acurala, and his brain was trying to comprehend the scope of power he had felt radiating off the two demons.

But the harder thing for him to understand was his own reaction to Yokouro.

Eclipse opened the front door and was immediately greeted by Saki and Tarrena rushing to the door. Saki threw her arms around Eclipse as he tried to move further inside to give room for the other Guardians to enter the house.

"Are you alright?" Tarrena asked, hugging him briefly once Saki pulled away.

"More or less," he mumbled.

Jikia appeared in the entryway, face drawn and eyes dark.

"There have been a lot of conflicting news reports about what exactly happened today," she said.

"I think it would be better if we take a little time to process before we dive back into all that," Hanyi said, throwing a worried glance at Dalton and holding up his hand to stop Jikia from pressing further.

"I'm okay."

"The hell you are," Mitoki said.

"Maybe a shower will help clear your heads," Tarrena suggested, noting the soot on their faces. "Take some time to clean up, and then we'll talk about what happened if you feel up to it."

With silent nods, the Guardians did as she suggested. Keito, Hanyi, and Mitoki were the first ones out of the shower and back in the living room while Dalton and Eclipse were slower, taking longer to get their thoughts straight before returning to face the others.

Master Genbuki had made everyone tea, but the Guardians let theirs go cold, watching the fragmented news reports until finally, Eclipse muted the television.

"How are you holding up?" Tarrena asked.

"I honestly don't know," he said. "The whole thing feels a bit surreal."

"Who was the demon who burned down the school?" Jikia asked, turning to Keito.

"Acurala Kage, the younger brother of one of the Kage Lords," the demon answered. "He's not nearly as powerful as he used to be, though I couldn't tell if that was because of his power limiters or because Yokouro couldn't pull a full resurrection."

"He was still very powerful," Mitoki said. "I could feel it radiating off of him."

"I recognized Yokouro DeVastes by the markings," Jikia near-growled. "I suppose that means he really has come back."

"Looks like it," Hanyi agreed. "And of course he showed that to us with his typical flair of dramatics, having Acurala burn down the school like that."

"Probably a dig at you two," Eclipse noted.

"Oh yeah," Hanyi affirmed.

"That was a lot of trouble to go to just to stand on a roof for a few seconds," Saki mumbled.

"He got dozens of people to film him and Acurala," Tarrena said. "He got what he wanted."

"He's all about building tension," Hanyi added. "The entire time we were talking with Acurala, the anxiety was reaching a fever pitch, and when he showed up..." He shrugged. "That's what he does."

"But you guys know about him, the public doesn't," Saki said. "To them, it was just another demon."

"A very powerful demon," Mitoki amended.

"We could feel his aura from across the street as if he was standing right in front of us," Eclipse elaborated "I've never felt such intensity from a demon before."

"Dalton?" Jikia called, noting the way he sat with his head down, silent, his eyes distant on his ignored tea. He did not look up. "Dalton, are you alright?"

Still, he did not move.

"Dalton, please, say something..." Tarrena pleaded.

Rather than speak, he got to his feet and began walking out of the living room, turning toward the front door. Keito leapt up and rushed toward him, grabbing his arm.

"Dalton, it's not a good idea to be alone after—"

With strength that surprised the demon, Dalton ripped his arm from Keito's grasp, turning his attention on the older Guardian. Dalton's eyes had gone dark, his expression nearly vacant as he held eye contact with Keito for a few seconds before leaving the house.

"Do we go after him?" Eclipse asked, also on his feet.

Keito hesitated. "No, let's just...leave him to collect himself."

"What if Yokouro tries to attack him?" Mitoki hissed.

"He won't," the demon said. "He's done the damage he wanted."

Dalton had barely reached the sidewalk when he started running. He passed intersections and streets without taking note of what direction he was going or the people around him, almost being hit by two cars and upsetting several pedestrians as he ran. Each time he hit a red light or a fence, he would turn another direction.

He needed to move. He needed to run.

His body finally gave out on him in a park near the university just beyond the downtown area. His shaking legs folded under him and he tumbled onto the grass, shivering as the sweat coating his skin met with the cold dusk air. His lungs and eyes were burning. His head was spinning. He coughed and curled onto his side, his body wracked with violent shudders.

"Dalton," a voice called.

Dalton was about to snap at Keito, assuming his demon teammate had been following him, but when he lifted his head to do so, he was alone. He sat up, casting his eyes around the empty park. Cautiously, he got to his feet, wondering if he had hallucinated his name being called. His knees quivered with the effort to keep him standing, but he ignored the fatigue, turning in hesitant circles to survey his surroundings.

"Who's there?" he said.

"There is no need to be on such high alert," the voice responded, the words snaking around Dalton like vines as he tried to pinpoint their location. "I am not here to harm you."

"Wait…" Dalton whispered. "You're that entity from the Beast Realm."

"I am."

"Here to tell me more about unseen allies and how what I'm walking into is more dangerous than I can comprehend?" Dalton snapped. "Because I *really* don't want to hear it." He turned again, grinding his teeth together. "Show yourself, damn it! Who the hell am I talking to?!"

"I'm afraid I cannot show myself," the voice said. "I am not physical. I was killed by Yokouro many years ago."

"And now I'm talking to ghosts," Dalton groaned, sitting heavily on the grass and hiding his face in his hands. "Just leave me alone. I can't handle any more cryptic bullshit right now."

"I am merely watching over you to be sure you are safe," the voice said.

Dalton laughed brokenly. "How the hell can I be *safe*? I thought you understood what was going on. That you were an unseen ally, ghost of past Yokouro victim."

"I am." The voice felt closer, drawing nearer to Dalton as he curled around his knees. "It's okay to be overwhelmed by this, Dalton."

"That's just it," Dalton whispered. "I wasn't. I mean, I suppose I *was*, but…it was so simple once I saw him. I saw Yokouro and I just knew that I had to hunt him down and destroy him. That was it. That was my entire purpose." His fingers tightened around his skin as he curled tighter into himself. "And I went blind to everything around me." The tears began to sting his eyes. "I didn't care if I provoked him. I didn't care that he could have killed everyone around me. I was entirely focused on *him*." He let out a shuddered breath. "I don't understand what's happening to me…"

Dalton thought he felt a hand on his shoulder, but when his head bolted up to see who had touched him, again, he was alone.

"I understand your fear—"

"No, you don't," Dalton interrupted. "I have a family. What happens when I get so focused on Yokouro I push them away? Or worse, I *hurt* them?"

"You won't allow yourself to do that."

"How can I be sure?!" Dalton burst. "Everything is changing. My powers are growing. I'm having these nightmares I can't explain. And I just faced one of the most notorious demon mass-murderers in existence and there was a part of me that was *excited* about having to face him. Excited to join in his game..." Dalton shook his head. "That's not me..."

"You're right," the voice said. "It's not you. Not entirely. Dalton, you were not prepared for this challenge. You were meant to face Yokouro, but not this soon. Unfortunately, now that you two have met, nothing can stop what is about to happen."

"What's about to happen?" Dalton repeated incredulously. "Then, what? This is my *destiny*? Some epic battle against an insurmountable evil? I'm supposed to be the human facing off against the demon? And this mysterious voice I'm talking to in a random park is my ghostly trainer?" Dalton leaned his head back, closing his eyes against his frustrated tears. "Not only is it cliché and unrealistic, but if you are my trainer, then I am screwed, because you are *terrible* at it."

"I am an ally, Dalton," the voice said. "And I know you felt it today when you saw Yokouro for the first time. You felt the understanding you shared. This is your destiny, Dalton. And even though you're not ready, you must face it."

"Just leave me alone," Dalton said again, resting his head on his knees. "I need to be alone with my thoughts right now."

"Very well," the voice said. "But I also came to deliver something to you."

Dalton's brow furrowed, thinking the voice meant to deliver some news to him, but when he felt a sudden weight in his jacket pocket, he leapt up and turned. Still, there was no one around him. He dug his hand inside his pocket to find the cool, smooth texture of glass. He extracted the vial filled with dark liquid.

"What the hell is this?"

"It is something that will help you tomorrow in the tournament," the voice said. "Compliments of another ally you have in the shadows."

"Looks more like this ally in the shadows wants to poison me," he noted warily.

"That vial will help you, Dalton."

With the same unconscious understanding, Dalton knew the voice had left him. He stood on the grass, straining against the diminishing light in the sky to see the dark liquid in the vial. He glanced around him once more before scoffing.

"I'm not that much of an idiot," he grumbled, walking toward the curb and finding the nearest storm drain, uncorking the vial and spilling the contents down the grate. He then walked the vial to the nearest trash can and threw it in.

As he heard the thunk of the vial hitting the other contents of the garbage can, another weight dropped into his jacket pocket.

He stopped in his tracks, taking a few moments to build up the courage to check his pocket. As he feared, another vial, identical to the first and filled to the top with dark liquid, had appeared in his pocket.

Dalton glanced around him, carefully rolling the cold vial between his fingers, wondering just how many people were watching him in that moment.

~∧~

When Yokouro walked into the large-yet-cluttered master bedroom of the small house, he was surprised to see the demon inside replacing herbs, powders, and vials into a typical demon medicinal carrier.

"Are you alright?" Yokouro asked the older demon.

Vivid violet eyes turned to him briefly before the other demon nodded.

"Small headache," he said.

"You never told me what you thought of my spectacle for Team Dalton."

"Not true. I did tell you," the other demon said, latching the medicinal case. "I told you not to do it."

"You didn't watch the news coverage?" he asked. "I'm currently breaking news. People are curious about the demon on the roof of the temple."

The other demon only sighed in response, turning away from the desk and walking to one of the many boxes in the room. "Juki? Did you watch the news?"

"No, Yokouro, I was busy," Juki said, opening the box and rifling through the rolled scrolls within. Even though Juki's back was turned, he could almost see the disappointed look on Yokouro's face.

With a heavy sigh, the younger demon crossed his arms. "I've upset you."

"I'm never upset with you, Yokouro," Juki said with a scoff. "Or I'd be upset quite often."

"I'm trying *not* to upset you," he said. "Which is why I want you to join me tomorrow."

Juki's hand stilled among the scrolls and he turned over his shoulder. "You want me there?"

"Seems I may have overestimated a few of my men and what they're capable of," Yokouro said. "Keito knows too much. Knows how to provoke them. I need calm heads for tomorrow."

Juki stood. "If you think that's best."

"I do," Yokouro said. "Also, I need your help again with my teams in the tournament."

"There's the catch," Juki said with a laugh. "I've already given you an entire team. What more do you want?"

"A second team."

"The tournament is in nine hours and you have an entire team slot open? I certainly hope you plan more when you run your territory."

"I've been thinking that I can't just fill it with anyone," Yokouro mused, walking with Juki toward the desk again as the older demon grabbed a large, leather-bound book filled with handwritten ledgers. "I want someone who can fly. Someone who has perfect precision in his attacks. Someone who can follow orders, no matter how questionable."

Juki's hand slowed as he flipped through the pages of the book, his gaze shifting to Yokouro.

"Are you trying to go after Eclipse?"

"I was considering it," Yokouro said with a grin. "You're the one who's been telling me to ease up on the Guardians a little. I figure I should ease up on Dalton and let the others feel some heat. And before you groan and go on your lecture about being careful," Yokouro interrupted, lifting a hand, "I am being careful. Why do you think I'm asking for someone with such high qualifications?"

"You want one of my mercenaries, don't you?"

"Yes."

Juki turned to face Yokouro fully.

"The Trade Mercenaries are disciples of Rutu and myself. They are lethal and they don't know the meaning of holding back. There is a chance they will take things too far."

"Not a chance," Yokouro said. "They worship the ground you walk on. If you tell them exact orders, they won't fail."

"Am I understanding this correctly? You want me to illegally dimension hop to the Demon Realm, pull people from the Trade, as well as collect humans from other realms, grab one of my mercenaries, and bring all of them here with fake papers to enter the Guardian Tournament that starts in nine hours?"

"That's the gist of it."

Juki's eyebrows went high. "Rutu is going to throw a fit when he finds out about this…"

"I know none of this really bothers you. You just feel like complaining," Yokouro chortled. Juki also smirked.

"So what if I do?"

"Can you get it all done before the tournament starts?"

"Do you remember who you're talking to?"

"Always so reliable," Yokouro said. "Let me know when your mercenary gets here. I want to explain to him exactly what I expect."

"I'll keep you informed," Juki assured, watching as Yokouro walked out of the room, closing the door behind him. The older demon let out a long sigh and turned back to the leather-bound book, scanning through the names. He flinched when felt another stab in the side of his head.

"Damn it, Dalton."

He opened the drawer of the desk and extracted another vial filled with black liquid. He placed the vial into his robe pocket, feeling it vanish in his fingers, just as the previous four had. "Stop throwing these away. Don't you want to survive this?"

Chapter Thirteen

Dalton was yawning all morning, as was Eclipse.

"Did you manage to sleep at all?" Jikia asked worriedly, wanting to scold them both but knowing that sleep had been hard to come by the previous night.

"Yes," they both replied.

Dalton did not want to tell the others about calling Eclipse around one in the morning, completely lost and frozen with no idea how to get back to the house. It then took forty-five minutes for Eclipse to find the leader of Team Dalton and another half-hour to get back to the house. They both agreed it was best to remain silent about the matter to avoid worrying the team further.

"How are you holding up today, Keito?" Tarrena asked, turning to the demon sitting in the corner of the team room as they waited for the audience to file in above.

"I'm okay," he said. "I'm going to take it as slow as possible today. I'm drained."

Occasionally, Dalton would feel a stab of panic when he heard the noise of the audience above, and he would remember exactly where he was and what was about to happen. Most of their time in the team room, however, Dalton was fidgeting with the vial of dark liquid he seemed unable to throw away. Even as he got into Eclipse's car that morning, he had placed the vial under the seat with every intention of leaving it in the car. But once they pushed through the enthusiastic reporters and screaming audience members to get into the stadium, Dalton felt the weight return to his pocket.

An announcement came through the stadium speakers for the demon Guardians present to go to Hall A for a pre-tournament examination. Keito begrudgingly left, complaining about being too tired for the paranoia of the tournament.

"Do you think you are going to fight anyone under a draining bewitchment again?" Tarrena asked when the silence became uncomfortable for all of them.

"I hope not," Mitoki said. "Kyan was tough to beat last round, and we're all worn down from everything else that's been going on."

"I don't know why we're even bothering with the tournament," Eclipse said. "We know who we're after. We've got a missing Elder. And we're competing in a sporting event?"

"We have to," Dalton said. "You know if we try to do anything else, he'll attack the stadium just to pull us back."

"I know playing by his rules is akin to torture," Hanyi said. "But we can't break them. We have to play by his rules and still find a way to best him at his own game. He's too cunning to try and overpower with brute force."

Eclipse leaned his head back against the wall, sighing dejectedly. Tarrena sat next to him.

"One thing at a time. Get through the tournament today and we'll tackle the next thing after that."

Keito returned after the others of Team Dalton had fallen into dark, pensive silence once again. When he entered the team room, he looked troubled.

"What now?" Dalton prompted.

"The Board was very hasty and desperate to get us approved for competition," he mused. "And one of the demons I saw there I'm fairly positive is *not* a Guardian, which means we do have at least one of Yokouro's teams here."

"Under the draining bewitchment?"

The demon shook his head. "And I can't tell if that's better or worse. I wanted to talk to the Board and ask them about one of the demons, but they basically shoved me out the door."

"More or less confirms that they know that's Yokouro's team," Hanyi said with a sullen nod.

"And that the Tournament Board is under Yokouro's influence," Mitoki added.

"How much do we have to worry about his team?" Dalton asked.

"From what I saw, we should be worried," Keito warned. "That demon—"

"Attention all Guardian teams," a female voice rang over the speakers. "Please make your way to the ring to begin the second round of the Guardian Tournament."

Even below the stands, the Guardians could hear the cheering of the audience at the announcement.

As the Guardians were not in The Corner, they came face-to-face with three other Guardian teams as they exited their team room and walked the short, dark hallway toward the double doors leading to the ring. While some ignored Team Dalton, or gave them acknowledging nods, others glared, a few Guardians smirked confidently, and one even scoffed and rolled his eyes when he saw them.

Dalton was taken aback by the behavior and found himself scanning the other teams as they walked to the center of the ring for all teams to be introduced to the eager audience. He wondered if it was his lingering exhaustion, but he was almost certain all the other

Guardians in the ring were glaring at him, silently challenging him, which made it impossible for him to discern which team belonged to Yokouro.

After the opening announcements, the die was tossed and the number precluded Team Dalton from fighting in the first match, so they walked to their assigned team box, scanning the faces of the spirited spectators as they joined Jikia and Tarrena.

"This stadium is a lot bigger than the one in the Beast Realm," Mitoki said warily, sitting stiffly on the bench in the team box, looking around the far-more-modern stadium packed tightly with excited audience members. "It's a bit unnerving."

"Be very careful not to let paranoia get the better of you," Hanyi said.

"Much easier said than done," Eclipse grumbled, trying to ignore the hollering of the audience as the announcer called the fight to commence between the first two teams. He was easily able to ignore the match, scanning the opposing Guardian teams in the other boxes, allowing his heightened awareness to seek out those who meant them severe harm.

Across the ring, he spotted one team that did not immediately stand out, but one of their members was clearly the youngest they had seen competing in the tournament. His bright blue eyes were scanning Team Dalton excitedly, and he fidgeted in his seat, as though trying to restrain himself from leaping across the ring to attack the older Guardians.

"That has to be a violation of some kind," he said. "Jikia? Isn't there an age requirement for Guardians who want to compete? Don't they have to be at least sixteen? Because that kid is definitely *not*."

"Shit, I barely even saw him," Hanyi said, jumping a little when his eyes followed the direction Eclipse was pointing.

"He's a demon," Keito said.

"Still, he has to be fourteen, *maybe* fifteen?"

"More likely around twelve," Keito corrected.

"*Twelve*?" Dalton gawked. "It's not even legal to become a Guardian at that age."

"Doesn't matter when Yokouro's pulling the strings."

"We could call the tournament to a halt for violation of the age requirement," Eclipse suggested. "Sure, Yokouro can fake them being a Guardian, but it's painfully obvious that he's not the required age for being in the tournament."

"…technically, that's true…" Jikia mumbled, glancing at Keito, silently asking if he was going to explain or if he expected her to share the information.

"But?" Dalton prompted.

"But demons can enter by the age of fourteen and he looks about fourteen," Keito said. "Everyone figures that the younger a demon is, the more even the playing field. So they let demons compete younger."

"*Are* younger demons easier for humans to fight?"

"Both yes and no," he answered. "They're inexperienced so they make rookie mistakes and they are more hot-headed, so it's easy to spot their weaknesses. And since they haven't honed their skills yet, it's more likely that a human can defeat them. However, younger demons also aren't used to being around humans and they haven't developed the finer muscle control needed to not cause severe damage to humans." He forced a worried smile. "You humans are quite fragile."

"But he's no match for you, even if he does work for Yokouro," Hanyi said. "Seems weird to put such a young demon against you."

"That's what I was worried about during the pre-tournament check. I'm not certain, but I do think that this demon follows a very dangerous and volatile magic practice in the Demon Realm."

"What does that mean? Dangerous magical practice?" Eclipse asked.

"I guess you could call it a cult," the demon said. "I don't know for sure, but he *looks* like he's part of the Jjanye. They are known for isolating themselves from other demons and practicing nothing but blood magic. Most of the Jjanye were imprisoned or killed when they tried to start a war two hundred years ago, but I'm sure some of them survived."

"Blood magic?" Eclipse said. "That's the type of magic you don't want to play with. It's very volatile."

"Hence why I'm concerned," Keito agreed.

Dalton's hand returned to his pocket and gripped the cold glass vial.

"And the winner is Team Abacer!" the announcer called over the thunderous roars of the crowd. Her voice suddenly projected over the loudspeakers startled Team Dalton and they turned their attention to the ring, where the teams were collecting their unconscious teammates and limping away.

"Was *anyone* paying attention to the fight?" Jikia groaned, exasperated. The Guardians shared a nervous look before turning back to their disappointed trainer. "Unfortunately, I wasn't, either.

But someone needs to be paying attention so you know what you're up against."

"There will now be a fifteen-minute break before the next match," the announcer continued, though most of her words were lost in the hum of audience members excitedly discussing the match. Mitoki leaned back on the bench, trying to listen to those behind him and get a sense of how the match had progressed, despite the fact that his attention was divided to also studying the young demon across the ring.

Dalton sighed heavily, sitting on the bench, his hand still holding the dark vial in his pocket as he studied the exuberant grin on the young demon's face.

A momentary hush fell over the stadium, almost imperceptible in its briefness. The audience shuddered, glancing around before mentioning to their friends and family that it was unnaturally cold in the stadium. The Guardians around the ring were startled by the chill, but they all knew that it was not merely a cold breeze.

Dalton's hair stood on end and his entire body went on alert. His blood seemed to halt in his veins and his world narrowed around the feeling that passed over him. Vertigo overtook him and he had to lean forward and grab the bench seat to keep from falling. Hanyi also sat, stumbling slightly to find a seat under the intense pressure that had fallen over them.

Keito leaned on the team box wall and his eyes turned to the reflective windows of the VIP box.

"Is that..."

"Yokouro," Dalton said, his body shuddering. "He's here."

Within the VIP box, the Tournament Board was uneasy, watching Team Dalton scan their opponents, paying particular attention to the team with the young demon in team box five.

"Do you really think it was a good idea to let him come here?" one man said. "There are other demons here besides Keito. One might notice and try to suspend the tournament."

"We're the damn Tournament Board," one woman snapped. "All we have to do is provide the papers we were given and that will be the end of it."

"Not if he brings the damn stadium down on our heads," another woman grumbled.

"You don't need to worry about that," a calm voice assured behind the Tournament Board.

The men and women spun around to see three figures in the doorway. Yokouro strode confidently into the room while the two demons with him, both clad in similar dark robes, stepped just inside the door and closed it, as if standing guard. Even as the Tournament Board bowed their heads and backed away from Yokouro, they could not stop staring at the two unfamiliar demons, something inside them telling them to stay as far away as possible.

"We were not expecting you, Master Yokouro," one woman said, flicking her eyes among the three demons.

"We are, of course, honored that you are here in person," a man seconded, motioning to the chairs they had abandoned upon seeing the demons. "And you have brought associates."

Yokouro turned to the man, his expression bemused.

"Care to introduce yourselves?" Yokouro asked the two demons, though his eyes never left the members of the Tournament Board. "Or maybe if I just say the Kage Lords, that will be sufficient."

Yokouro always found it comical to watch the paling expression of realization wash over anyone who had heard of the two demons before.

"You…you mean the Trade Masters?" one woman stammered, retreating another two steps from the demons at the door.

"Lord Juki Kage and Lord Rutu Kaneaka-Kage," Yokouro elaborated. "They will be observing the tournament very closely today."

The Tournament Board was still and silent, struck dumb with the terror at realizing they were in such close proximity to the infamous Kage Lords. While they had heard of the demons before, they had never seen them, and the long, intricately-braided hair along with the bright colors of their eyes made them look regal and extremely intimidating, adding to the dangerous aura that already filled the room.

"We-we…" One woman tried to speak, to welcome the Kage Lords, but her mind had gone blank and her tongue refused to form any greeting. Yokouro chuckled, turning to Juki and Rutu.

"Come," he said, jerking his head toward the long desk that lined the front of the VIP Box, allowing them to look over the entire stadium. "I'm curious to see how they're doing this morning, considering everything that happened yesterday."

Juki and Rutu silently stepped forward, the humans of the Tournament Board instinctively retreating another step.

"They know you're here," Juki noted, nodding to Team Dalton, who were staring up at the windows of the VIP Box.

"So it would seem," Yokouro agreed. "They are more focused on me than the Jjanye." The younger Old Blood Lord turned to Juki. "He's very young, Juki. Are you certain he's reliable?"

"He'll do as he's been told," Juki said simply. "It wasn't worth it to bring one of the older ones."

"*Worth* it?" Yokouro repeated incredulously.

"For a test like this, it would have been a waste of my resources."

Rutu's quiet chuckle irritated Yokouro, but the Tournament Board was too nervous in the presence of the powerful demons to take note of the way Yokouro bristled.

"Watch the tone you take with me, Juki," he warned.

"You don't frighten me, Yokouro," the other demon said. "You asked me to fill your spots in the tournament, and I did so as best as I was able, considering there are strict rules that I had to bend to do all of this. Trying to sneak an adult Jjanye out of the realm would have been far more difficult, and I figured you would appreciate some discretion."

Yokouro decided to clench his teeth and turn back to the windows, knowing that arguing with Juki in front of the Tournament Board would make him look weak. He also knew that Rutu was waiting for another moment to lecture him about keeping a cool head in front of his subordinates, so he decided ignoring the attitude of the two older demons was best.

A digital timer went off in the VIP Box and the woman who sat at the head of the Darkness Realm Tournament Board took a step toward it, pausing when she realized she had to get close to Juki to reach the system that would allow her to tell the announcer to start the next match. Three sets of vibrant eyes turned on her, but the demon lords did not move, forcing her to steel herself as she cautiously stepped toward the communication system. She bowed her head low and mumbled a soft "excuse me, sir," as she approached Juki, hoping he would step back so she could comfortably approach the desk.

He did not move, watching with a bemused expression as she pressed herself as close to the desk as possible to pass him, reaching nervously in front of Yokouro to stop the soft beeping of the timer and press the blinking communication button.

"Kira? Next match," she told the announcer, unable to stop the shaking of her voice.

"May I have your attention, please?" the young announcer started, her words causing the audience to hush in anticipation. "The second match is about to begin! The next match will be Team

Macendae versus Team Dalton! Will those two teams please enter the ring?"

Yokouro smiled at the startled, slightly-lost expression that fell on Dalton's face when he turned back to the ring, remembering where he was and what was happening around him.

"I know, Dalton," Yokouro murmured. "I feel the same."

Rutu leaned closer to the glass, glancing at the team opposing Team Dalton, who had already entered the ring. He watched as Dalton stood, his hand in his jacket pocket. Dalton hesitated, his teammates filing out in front of him as he clenched something in his pocket before shaking his head, shedding his jacket, and rushing out to the ring.

Rutu glanced at Juki, who met his eyes in a brief, secret look.

"Strange," Yokouro murmured, catching Dalton's hesitation. "Rutu." He turned to the lighter-haired Kage Lord. "Is there any way for me to connect with Dalton through the Shadow Veil?"

"Yokouro," Rutu started, exasperated, "you're going to overload his system. I already told you, he's not ready to face you. Slow down."

"I'm trying to learn my enemy, Rutu," he said. "That's just good strategy. Is there a way to connect with him through the Shadow Veil?"

"Not enough to interact with him," he said. "You can be an observer. You cannot manipulate the spell if you are not the one to cast it."

"I'm assuming you can facilitate my observation inside the spell?"

Rutu hesitated a second before nodding once.

"Excellent." Yokouro pulled out one of the chairs, settling in casually to watch the match. "Let's see how these boys fight. First time I'll be seeing them with my own eyes. Should be very enlightening."

Juki and Rutu positioned themselves on either side of Yokouro's chair, standing as ever-vigilant guards as the Tournament Board remained clustered to the side of the VIP Box, refusing to return to their abandoned chairs.

Chapter Fourteen

It was clear Team Dalton had been caught unawares by the announcement of their match with Team Macendae. They had been quietly debating how to evacuate the stadium knowing that Yokouro was inside the building, but were immediately distracted as they approached the waiting team in the arena.

The familiar face of the opposing leader smiled.

"Dalton," Macendae greeted.

"Macendae," Dalton said, grinning. "It doesn't seem right fighting you now, after everything you did to help us yesterday."

"Duty as a Guardian," he said with a small bow of his head. "I was glad I could help." He turned to Keito. "How are you faring today?"

"Not great," he admitted with a tired laugh. "You?"

"About the same." He took a deep breath, offering a half-shrug. "I have a proposition for you," he started. "To be honest, I became a Guardian because of all your stories. Hearing about all your feats as a Guardian made me want to do something similar with my life. And I always hoped I would meet you and spar with you. Since we are both so injured and exhausted, I say we do exclusive fights, set a limit for ourselves, and see how we match up. Then the rest of our team can finish the match."

"If my team leader accepts the condition of exclusive fights, I agree," Keito said, turning to Dalton.

"Are you sure?" Dalton asked. When Keito nodded, Dalton turned to the waiting announcer, realizing that the audience was getting impatient with the chatter between the Guardians in the ring.

"I would like to have an exclusive fight between Keito and Macendae before the humans of the team fight," he called.

"Macendae, do you accept this condition?" Kira asked.

"I do."

"An exclusive fight between Keito of Team Dalton and Macendae of Team Macendae will take place before the remaining eight Guardians fight, a majority of wins taking the match," Kira explained for the audience. "Are there any other conditions?"

When neither team leader could think of another condition, they shook their heads. Kira asked the others to leave the ring as a shiver of exhilaration ran through the audience at seeing two demons fight with no other distractions in the ring.

Dalton leaned over to Keito before he left.

"Do we try and evacuate the stadium? Do we pretend that nothing is wrong?"

"Pretend nothing is wrong," Keito said. "If Yokouro senses we're about to make a rash decision, he might make one to try and beat us to the punch. Just keep a close eye out for anything out of the ordinary."

Dalton nodded, not thrilled with the idea of ignoring the looming danger in the stadium, but knowing that Keito understood better what Yokouro was likely to do.

"Also, take it easy on this spar," he ordered. "We're screwed without you."

Keito grinned and nodded. "Yes, sir."

Dalton left the two demon Guardians, casting his eyes over the half-standing audience members as he climbed into the team box.

"What kind of limits do you want to set for the spar?" Keito asked.

"Obviously, we don't want the other to pass out," Macendae laughed. "And I was wondering if I could indulge a dream of mine."

"I'm listening."

"My mother was the daughter of a Baron of Clans in the DeVastes territory," Macendae said. "So before I began training as a Guardian, she taught me the Lord's Spar, as a way to temper my strength for fighting with humans." His smile widened. "Any chance you know how to do a Lord's Spar?"

Keito raised an eyebrow.

"I figured it was foolish to ask, considering your background, but I wanted to be certain."

"I haven't done a Lord's Spar in a very long time," Keito said. "But I don't think either of us can keep going for two hours, so how about fifteen minutes?"

"Perfect," Macendae agreed, trying to contain his excitement.

Keito glanced around the stadium, hearing the irritated cries of the crowd that desperately wanted the match to begin. When he met eyes with Kira, she nodded.

"Remember, you are not allowed in your animal forms for this match. You may begin!"

The two demons did not immediately move, reaching their hands out to one another and grabbing the other demon's wrist. They bowed their heads deeply and then straightened, ignoring the impatient yelling surrounding them.

Three seconds seemed to crawl by before Macendae released his grip on Keito's wrist and lunged forward, starting the spar.

159

Once they began moving, energy filled the stadium, encompassing everyone as sparks danced across surfaces and the magical energies shifted and moved. The excitement in the stadium increased tenfold, the audience getting to their feet as they watched Macendae and Keito move around the ring, calling encouragement to whichever demon they wanted to win.

What startled Dalton most was that the demons were moving very slowly by demon standards. He was easily able to observe every strike and dodge as the two demons sparred. But the slower speed did nothing to diminish the lethal attacks. Every move appeared far more calculated and far more dangerous as they tried to bring each other to the ground and dominate the match. As they swiped and lunged at one another, the magical energy radiating from them would push against the other, static crackling through the air and making everyone shiver in excitement.

As the fight continued, the magic progressively filling the air, everyone became transfixed by the complexity and power shown in each move. Even the placement of their feet as they dodged seemed perfectly choreographed, reacting to their opponent in the moment, following a conversation that no one else understood. The match felt flawless and practiced, as though every attack had been planned and rehearsed in sequence for weeks before the match.

The cheering slowed, but no one returned to their seats, staring at the demons in the ring, enraptured with eyes wide and mouths agape.

The only ones seeming disinterested were the other demons in the stadium. The young demon was even leaning on the front wall of the team box, unimpressed, watching as though he were a judge scoring the fight.

But the audience was entranced, the silence in the stands unnerving as they stared at the fight, shuddering at the power emanating from the two demons in the ring. They were unaware of anything else in the stadium, including the black-clad man with braided dark hair who descended the steps from the upper hallway of the stadium and sat on the stairs just behind Team Dalton's box.

Even though the movements looked fluid and choreographed, the fight was very taxing on the two demons in the ring. Demons relied on explosive speed and strength in their fights, overpowering their opponents and taking them by surprise. The Lord's Spar was an exhausting practice because it required incredible restraint and control to move at such a slow pace.

Eight minutes into the spar, Macendae misstepped and had to roll away from Keito, but the older demon grabbed his outstretched arm and yanked him back to the ground, pinning him. Keito was about to let him up to continue the spar when Macendae shook his head.

"That's enough," he said, panting as he wiped a hand across his sweaty brow.

"Good," Keito said breathlessly. "I was starting to lose focus."

"And with a surrender from Macendae, Keito wins the exclusive match!" Kira announced. The audience erupted in noise, broken from their trance as they celebrated the spectacle they had witnessed. Keito helped Macendae up, nodding once when the younger demon fell to one knee and forfeited the spar in proper fashion. Once they had shaken hands, Kira asked the others of each team to come to the ring as Keito returned to his team box.

"What even *was* that?" Mitoki gasped, his eyes wide and a smile pulling at his lips.

"Did you enjoy the show?" Keito asked lightly.

"I've never seen anything like that. I mean, I have, but I haven't," the youngest said, shaking his head in disbelief.

"It was like a spar we would do in training, but...*not*," Dalton agreed, stunned. "It was so *precise*."

"It's very difficult to move that slow for that prolonged period of time," Keito explained, taking the rag offered to him by Tarrena, dabbing the sweat from his face. "But that was also a nice warm-up for the day."

"I'm not sure how we're going to be able to match up to that," Dalton said, seeing that Macendae's teammates were also praising their team leader. "That was the first time I've really seen your fighting style."

"Any critiques?"

"Just awe," Dalton said. "Might have to spar with you some more so you can teach me some tricks."

Keito grinned. "Anytime. But for now, I am sitting down and catching my breath."

As the demon took a seat on the bench of the team box, Dalton and the others made their way into the ring, prompting the others of Team Macendae to do the same to continue the match.

Keito greedily gulped down water and wiped the sweat from his brow as the audience turned their attention back to the ring. Before Keito could completely settle and adjust to ignoring the audience behind him, Jikia suddenly straightened, standing from her seat, her expression confused and a little distant.

"What is it?" Keito asked, startled by her abrupt movements.

"I forgot something," she said, turning and unlatching the back door of the team box to leave. Tarrena also stood, following her mother.

"What did you forget?"

"I don't remember," she said, closing the door to the team box. "But I'm sure I'll remember when I get to my bag in the team room."

Before Keito could ask why they were acting so strangely, the two dragons walked down the aisle between the audience and the team boxes, disappearing through a door into the interior stadium halls. Keito watched them leave before looking around the ring, to the young, smiling demon across from him, and finally up to the VIP Box, glaring darkly at the demon lord he was certain was watching him. He remained unaware, however, of the Kage Lord sitting on the stairs behind him.

Dalton was taken by surprise when one member of Team Macendae shifted into a large ram, charging him. Dalton had to react rapidly, somersaulting clumsily out of the way and scrambling to his feet to face the animal again, trying to determine how he was going to fight the fast beast Guardian.

The rest of his team was pulled away from helping their team leader by their own opponents. Hanyi and the leopard Guardian were locked in their own fight, scraping their claws at one another and biting whenever they found an opening. Eclipse and Mitoki, exhausted from the days leading up to the tournament, were struggling with their own opponents, trying not to let their desperation to finish the match lead to simple mistakes and hasty decisions.

As Team Dalton fought with the roaring of the crowd rattling their eardrums, Juki stood and walked to the back wall of their team box, leaning toward Keito's ear.

"Don't make a scene."

Keito's blood ran cold. He froze, unable to breathe, his body trembling as terror bolted through him. He carefully turned his head, though he did not need to confirm who had approached him. When he saw the bright violet eyes, his head snapped back to the arena, though his attention was acutely focused on the presence behind him.

Juki smiled.

"You don't seem as surprised to see me as I thought you would be."

"I...I knew you were involved...I just didn't expect to see you in the stadium," Keito said, swallowing hard in an attempt to strengthen his voice. "Security is going to tell you to get away from the team box."

"They won't. They work for me."

"Should have known," Keito groaned. "Thorough as always. That's why I was surprised you weren't at the school yesterday. I know you were in the Darkness Realm."

"Checking up on me?" Juki teased. "I had other matters to attend. Yokouro could handle you on his own."

"Then why did he call on you at all?" Keito asked. "What is going on, Juki? This is just one of his fixations. This shouldn't be enough of a challenge to him to pull *you* into this."

"This is bigger than it was before, Keito. It's not about killing you. Yokouro and Dalton are linked by fate."

"*How*?" Keito demanded. "Dalton is a human. How can he stand up to Yokouro?"

"You might be surprised," Juki said. "But it does have to go perfectly, which is why Yokouro called me in to assist."

"…but it's just you," Keito said, his voice trembling. "Rutu's still in the Demon Realm, right?"

"No, he's here, too."

Keito turned quickly to look at Juki, his eyes wide. The older demon smirked.

"Did you really think we would do something like this separately?" he asked skeptically. "Come, now, Keito. You know us better than that."

"Then Rutu causing that earthquake really was part of Yokouro's scheme."

"Of course."

"Vestera is going to wring your necks," Keito warned. "Not only did you kidnap Elder Renard—which I know you did—but Rutu caused problems across four different realms. Then, you smuggled a Jjanye here. You must be out of your mind!"

"You will find that there are some things your dragon friend cannot entirely control," Juki said simply. "You will also discover that the Jjanye is the least of your worries."

"What the hell is that supposed—" Keito stopped, his eyes going wide as realization struck him. "No…you didn't…"

"I did."

"You brought a Trade Mercenary here?!" the younger demon yelped, turning around completely to face the demon lord. Juki nodded. Keito spun again to scan the other teams, desperately trying to spot the demon personally trained by the Kage Lords.

"Did you come down here just to freak me out?" he growled.

"Not entirely," Juki said. "Is Dalton's jacket in there?" he asked, leaning further to look into the team box. Keito hesitated, confused, before he looked down the bench to see Dalton's jacket.

"Pick it up and feel around the pockets. Don't take anything out. When you're done, turn to me and shake your head," Juki ordered.

Keito remained still as his mind turned over every word, making sure he was not misreading the situation. He studied Juki, who nodded once, and then cautiously reached for Dalton's jacket. Dalton's wallet and badge were in one pocket, but in the other pocket was a small, cold vial. Keito's fingers briefly passed over the object, confused, but he released it, setting the jacket aside, turning to Juki, and shaking his head.

"Good." Juki leaned closer to Keito. "Make sure he takes it," he whispered.

"Is it going to hurt him?"

"No, it will help. You have my word."

Keito lowered his eyes, his conflict clear in his expression, his mind too overwhelmed with worry to recall that his teammates were fighting in the ring.

Juki's hand patting his shoulder focused him and he jumped to look at the demon lord.

"There is no need to be so worried, Keito. I promise."

Keito stared at Juki's back as the demon lord turned to walk up the stairs in the stadium once again, ignored by the audience members transfixed with the battle taking place in the ring.

Eclipse and Mitoki had managed to team up to help the other defeat their opponent, allowing them to go to Dalton's aid as he dodged the ram that continued to charge him, threatening to cause severe injury if his horns landed a hit, particularly with the magic radiating from them. Hanyi's fight with the leopard was dragging on, as he continued to glance over at Dalton's fight, worried about how unfocused his team leader appeared.

Dalton had tried multiple times to focus his magic enough to trap the beast Guardian, but his concentration was always broken by having to dodge another attack and the magic trailing in the other Guardian's wake. And even when Eclipse tried to confine the animal in a thick wall of sparking magical energy, the ram, not nearly as exhausted as the members of Team Dalton, was able to counteract the spell and charge the humans once again.

A painful kick to his gut forced Mitoki to the ground when he tried to push into the ram's body, and Eclipse could not act fast enough to try the same technique, so Dalton made a decision he was certain he would regret. He watched the ram charge him, head lowering in anticipation of impact. The audience began screaming at Dalton, horrified that he was not moving.

Dalton's entire body was screaming to move out of the way, but he waited until it was nearly too late before circling to the side, one hand grabbing one of the horns on the ram's head, though his other hand missed the other horn. The ram turned his head, stumbling as Dalton tried to keep stable footing, both hands latching onto the horn as the animal dragged him across the ring.

Even when he dug his heels in, Dalton did not have the strength to twist the running animal to the ground. It was when Hanyi leapt at the ram and knocked his hindquarters to the ground that Dalton managed to move one hand to the ram's snout and yank his head to the side, being sure he fell.

The ram kicked Hanyi and used a burst of magic to push Miroki and Eclipse away, but Dalton's grip on his horn remained firm, even as the wave of magic washed over him.

Disoriented and dazed, Dalton struggled to get his feet under him as the ram also tried to stand. The noise of the screaming audience filled his ears, almost drowning out the bleating of the ram as he flailed, managing to pull his forequarters up. Dalton groaned and wrapped both hands around the horn again, using what little concentration he had to collect his magic in his fingers.

His hands jolted and he fell heavily to the dirt, warmth spraying over his arms and chest. The ram bleated loudly and stumbled to the side, collapsing clumsily. Before Dalton could understand what had happened, Eclipse was pulling him away from the kicking feet of the beast Guardian, making it harder for the team leader to collect his bearings.

When he did, he saw blood on his arms and the curl of the snapped horn laying on the arena dirt.

The ram was bleating loudly, thrashing on the ground and rubbing his head back and forth along the dirt. Hanyi was by the other beast Guardian's head, teeth bared.

He reverted to a human form and turned to Dalton.

"He's done."

"Is he alright?" Dalton asked, his voice shaking.

"He's in pain, but that's not fatal," Hanyi said, crouching next to the slowly calming ram. "We'll get him to the medical team. They can treat him."

"With that final surrender, Team Dalton wins the match!" Kira announced, the declaration sparking a new round of enthusiastic cries around the stadium, the audience more invigorated by the strength Dalton showed than the injury caused to the other Guardian.

Macendae joined the approaching medical team as they helped the ram gather his bearings enough to revert to a human form, though his head was still bleeding and he could hardly walk straight. Hanyi sheepishly handed the fallen horn to Macendae, who took it hesitantly before following the medical team.

Eclipse was worried about releasing Dalton's arm, noting the way his team leader was shaking.

"Hey, you okay?"

"How…did I do that?"

"I have no idea," Mitoki said. "How much magic did you use?"

"I swear, I didn't think I was using that much," Dalton insisted, following the guide of Eclipse and Hanyi toward the team box. He glanced over his shoulder at the blood-soaked dirt. "Is he going to be okay?"

"They'll take care of him," Hanyi assured.

"Will his horn grow back?"

"Not likely," the wolf answered honestly. "But as long as infection doesn't set in, he should be fine."

Dalton shakily pulled himself into the team box, his stomach twisting sickly at the thought of him permanently maiming the other Guardian. A very familiar fear churned in his chest, reminding him of other times where his magic had surprised even him.

"Here, Dalton, drink some water and sit down," Tarrena murmured, having returned to the team box just in time to see Dalton break the horn from the ram's head. He took the water bottle clumsily, sitting where Eclipse guided him, stunned and confused.

"I have no idea how that happened…"

"Are you hurt?" Jikia asked.

He shook his head, and though she seemed hesitant, she turned her attention to the others, setting to treating Hanyi's bleeding wounds. But no matter how she, or anyone else tried to focus on wounds, they were glancing at Dalton, worried about his pale expression.

Dalton remained where he had been placed, staring at his hands, trying to rid himself of the exhilarated quiver in his fingers.

Juki had stopped at the top of the stairs to watch Team Dalton finish their fight. When he saw Dalton break the horn on the ram, he smiled secretly to himself. Even when he saw the horrified expression on the human's face, Juki was relieved that Dalton had already shown such progress.

He was unsurprised to see Rutu lurking in the open doorway at the top of the stairs when he turned, also watching Dalton. Juki stepped to Rutu's side, watching as the medical team rushed to the wounded Guardian and Team Dalton helped their stunned leader back to the team box.

He then turned to Rutu.

"You left Yokouro on his own?"

"I'm keeping an eye on him," Rutu said, turning with Juki to walk into the dimly-lit upper hallways of the stadium.

"What do you think?" Juki prompted.

Rutu sighed. "He's showing progress, but even though his magic is catching up as it should, he's struggling to accept his growing powers," the younger Kage Lord mused, his eyes distant on the floor as they made their way back to the VIP Box. "If Yokouro pushes him too hard, he really is going to break him."

"Keito should convince Dalton to take the potion. That should help enough for today," Juki said. "Did you already contact Vestera?"

Rutu nodded. "I just hope he also doesn't push Dalton too far."

"I pity that human," Juki said. "Caught between Yokouro and Vestera. And us."

The younger demon huffed. "I just wish Yokouro would listen to me and back off a bit. He's waited millennia for someone like Dalton to come along and he's doing everything in his power to kill him before this battle even starts."

"That's why we're here, to guide them. All of them," Juki said. He smirked, turning to look at Rutu. "For someone so powerful, you sure do worry a lot."

Rutu chuckled. "How do you think I've survived this long?"

"Oh," Juki laughed brokenly, "I thought it was because whenever you were in trouble, I'd be the one to save your ass."

"If you'll recall, a majority of the time you were the one to put my ass in danger in the first place," Rutu retorted with a grin.

"As if you never made reckless decisions without me."

When Juki and Rutu entered the VIP room once more, the Tournament Board stiffened instinctually. They were by no means comfortable being near Yokouro, but being around the Kage Lords made it almost impossible to breathe as instinctive fear invaded their lungs.

"What do you think?" Yokouro asked, not needing to turn to know who had entered the room. "See why I think Dalton could be pushed more? His magic is already growing."

"His human consciousness is struggling to keep up," Rutu warned. "I hope you're prepared to face the consequences if you push him too far."

"That's why I have you here, Rutu," Yokouro said, throwing him a confident smirk before turning over his other shoulder to Juki. "Did you find anything?"

"No," he said. "I watched Keito check the Dalton's pockets, but he didn't have anything other than his wallet. I think you're paranoid."

"He was fidgeting with something," Yokouro insisted.

"There was nothing there," Juki repeated. "He's quite anxious. He might be trying to hide a nervous habit of fidgeting because he knows you're watching. He's reacting to your proximity."

Yokouro sighed, clearly dissatisfied with the explanation.

The timer went off in the VIP Box once again. The woman at the head of the Tournament Board glanced at the roster, hesitating when she saw which teams were next to compete.

"Well?" Yokouro prompted when he saw she had not moved forward to tell the announcer to begin the next match.

"Master Yokouro...the young demon will fight next."

"Against Dalton?"

"No," she said. "Are...are you sure it's safe to have him here? I've heard about these demons and how dangerous their magic can be."

"You have no reason to worry," Yokouro said, waving her statement away before motioning abstractly to Juki and Rutu. "They have him under control."

She threw a wide-eyed glance at the Kage Lords.

"Are-are you certain?"

Rutu snorted. "For someone too afraid to even look at us, you seem unconvinced of our power."

She immediately dropped her gaze to the ground.

"I apologize, Lord Rutu," she mumbled, retreating despite the timer still chiming to start the next match. "I meant no offense."

Juki turned to Rutu with a smile. "Play nice."

Chapter Fifteen

"May I have your attention please?" the announcer called as Jikia finished cleaning up the medical supplies in the team box. "The next match is about to commence. Will Team Kyceth and Team Yare please come to the center of the ring?"

Team Dalton perked up, seeing the team with the young demon leave their team box to meet their opponents in the ring. Keito sat forward, watching intently, trying not to let his worry show on his face.

"Please state any conditions you have for the fight," Kira prompted once the teams were facing one another in the center of the ring.

The young demon was next to the man who appeared to be the leader of the team, bouncing on the balls of his feet, grinning with excitement. Dalton was unnerved by the childish joy on his face, as if he was waiting to be told he could go play.

"Keito," he started, "if he really is that young, then his blood magic abilities won't be too powerful, correct?"

"In theory," the demon answered. "Let's hope that he's too young to be a threat to the entire stadium."

"If there are no conditions, you may begin!"

With the declaration of the announcer and the approving cheers of the audience, the other four members of Team Kyceth stepped back, leaving the young demon to face the other Guardian team. Before Team Yare could take five steps toward them, the Jjanye demon lifted his hand and dragged his fingertips down his face, leaving four thin lines of blood from the small cuts on his fingers, and then turned his hand to his opponents.

A shockwave shook the stadium, causing the structure to rattle and the audience to let out startled screams, though it was difficult to tell if the cries were of exhilaration or terror. When the magic passed Team Dalton's team box, Dalton winced, feeling his bones strain under the power of the dark energy. His teeth grit, he could feel a warmth pool at the pit of his stomach, radiating outward as a fire spread through his veins. He remembered the feeling from fighting the bone creature in the Beast Realm, when the unfamiliar magic first appeared within him.

Jikia and Tarrena appeared to be hit just as hard by the dark magic radiating from the young demon. Jikia flinched away, reaching to her head as if trying to hold it together. Tarrena swayed in her seat, leaning against Eclipse as they both tried to recover from the initial shock.

"Hanyi," Keito said, "let's take everyone to the team room after this."

Hanyi, who had gone down into his wolf form, looked at Keito through squinted eyes, nodding as he let out a whimper, overwhelmed.

The Guardians around the ring, also struggling under the weight of the dark magic that was holding Team Yare to the ground, were looking at one another, wondering if they should interfere with what was clearly too powerful of an attack to use with so many humans present. Even with the barrier around the ring, the heaviness permeated into the stands, causing the audience to hold their bleeding noses or cover their ears.

Just when Keito was about to remove his power limiter to put up a more powerful barrier, the young demon flinched, his knees buckling. The dark magic instantly pulled back, leaving everyone shaken. Keito turned to the VIP Box and bowed his head in silent thanks to Juki.

The young demon petulantly straightened his stance as he watched the five Guardians of Team Yare unsteadily pull themselves upright.

"What the hell *are* you?!" one of them snapped.

"You could just surrender," the leader of Team Kyceth suggested with a dark smile.

"You can't use blood magic in the tournament!" a woman barked.

"There is nothing in the rule book that precludes it."

The young demon huffed, pulling up one of his long sleeves to reveal a row of scabbed-over wounds around his forearm. He pushed on the wounds, breaking the scabs as he muttered the words of whatever spell he intended to use. Seeing the young demon's lips moving, the Guardians of Team Yare tried to pull themselves together enough to attack before the spell took effect.

"How can the rules not preclude blood magic?" Eclipse asked.

"Because it should be common sense not to even *know* blood magic," Jikia growled. "I'm not saying I want Yokouro's team to win, but I don't want this demon to use any more blood magic around so many humans. Team Yare should surrender."

The young demon, his hand now streaked with his blood, clenched his fist and brought his hand sharply to his side.

Again, oppressive magic filled the stadium and the five Guardians opposing Team Kyceth were brought to the ground as though a fist had struck the back of their heads. The audience was still cheering, startled by the unusual display in the ring, but not fully understanding the danger the young demon posed.

"If the board wasn't under Yokouro's control, this would disqualify Team Kyceth," Tarrena mused. "There has to be something we can do."

Keito's heart was racing, his eyes darting between the five Guardians crumpled on the ground and the VIP Box, worried that the Guardians would be crushed under the growing intensity of the Jjanye demon's power.

"I really would just surrender if I were you," another member of Team Kyceth said with a condescending chuckle.

One member of Team Yare went limp, slipping into unconsciousness when his attempt at using magic was met with a heated weight that he had never experienced before. Another was holding her bleeding ears, her eyes clenched tight.

Yare, the team leader, nodded tightly to signal their surrender.

"And with that nod, Team Yare forfeits the match to Team Kyceth!"

The cheering from the audience was not nearly as raucous as before, the spectators confused and a little concerned by what they had seen in the ring. But even their lackluster cheering distracted them from seeing the young demon's knees buckle as he fell to the ground, cringing in pain as he was strictly punished for using too much magic on the humans opposing him.

While the other members of Team Kyceth pulled the young demon upright, the medical team rushed to Team Yare, loading all five Guardians onto stretchers and taking them away from the prying eyes of the audience.

Dalton was afraid to move. He had been locked in the same position since the first wave of dark magic fell over the stadium, terrified that, if he moved a muscle, he would lose control over the fire in his veins, his magic straining the one internal power limiter he possessed.

"Dalton," Keito said, forcing him to slowly turn his head. "We should go to the team room to regroup."

Unable to speak and steeling himself for what he was certain would be a very long walk to the team room, Dalton nodded and carefully rose to his feet.

The entire team was walking slowly, their knees shaking and their brains struggling to formulate a strategy about how to combat such powerful magic.

"What the hell even *was* that?" Jikia hissed when the door to the team room closed.

"Those spells…" Eclipse shook his head slowly. "Blood magic is already dangerous and potent, but those spells made the magic feel almost celestial. Like he was pulling power from every living thing around him, draining them to feed his own magic."

"Now that you mention it, it did feel celestial," Tarrena agreed. "I was so startled by how powerful he was I didn't even notice."

"I wish I had paid more attention when the Jjanye were a threat to the Demon Realm," Keito said. "Since they were mostly eradicated, I didn't bother to learn more about what they were capable of."

"Do you know if they use their blood to access celestial energy streams?" Eclipse asked.

"If they do it's only lower streams."

Eclipse's eyebrows went high. "That's still celestial magic. That's the kind of power only certain people should have access to."

"I'm sorry, *what*?" Mitoki snapped. "What the hell are lower celestial streams?"

"Celestial creatures, which operate on a different magical frequency, generally fall into two categories—upper and lower," Eclipse explained. "The upper celestial streams run at an extremely high frequency and intensity. Lower celestial streams run in the opposing direction. And everything in between is what the mortal planes, like ours, know as magic."

"Oh no…" Dalton groaned, rubbing his temple. "I hated this lesson when I was training. I never understood it."

"Think of it this way," Eclipse started. "Upper celestial streams are up here," he held his hand next to his face, "and lower celestial streams are at my feet. The magic we all know falls between my shoulders and knees. Anything above or below that is mostly inaccessible to humans because our bodies cannot handle the intensity of the magic. Upper celestial streams would crush us, and lower celestial would pull us apart."

"There is also the Superior Celestial magic, but even most dragons can never hope to achieve that sort of power. As far as I know, that's something only Vestera can wield," Jikia added.

"Vestera is going to have an aneurysm when he hears that a Jjanye was brought to the tournament," Keito said. He was secretly looking forward to watching Juki and Rutu get scolded at the next Demon Council meeting.

"Then how do we take down this demon if our bodies can't handle magic of that intensity?" Mitoki said. "Is there any way we can access upper celestial streams and…I dunno, cancel out the lower?"

"That's not how it works," Eclipse said.

"Forgive me if I never learned *forbidden* blood magic," Mitcki growled.

"I'm assuming dragons use upper celestial magic?" Dalton asked, turning to Jikia and Tarrena, who nodded. "Are there any spells you can think of that would keep us from…" he motioned abstractly in the direction of the ring.

"Not that I know, I'm afraid," Jikia said.

"Do you know of anything?" he pressed, turning to Eclipse.

"I only learned about blood magic from books and scrolls. I've never seen it *in use*," the younger Guardian said, shaking his head.

"Keito?" Dalton turned to the demon, desperate for some sort of plan on how to defeat the powerful magic.

Keito's eyes were on the floor, his hand to his mouth as he thought over everything he knew about the Jjanye. He slowly shook his head.

"The only thing I know about the Jjanye magic is that they use their blood in every spell. Past that, the only thing I really know is that they were killed or captured."

"Do you know how they were killed?"

"The Old Blood Lords," he said with a shrug. "And like hell we'll have that kind of power available to us."

Dalton sat heavily in one of the uncomfortable chairs in the team room, his leg bouncing nervously as he wracked his brain for any kind of strategy.

"Can we just ask in the conditions of the match that he not use blood magic?" Tarrena suggested. "State you want a simple physical fight. No magic at all."

"We can't ban all magic from the match," Hanyi said slowly. "Magic is part of the tournament. We can ban certain spells but if we just say that he can't use magic, they can counter it by saying that's against the premise of the Guardian Tournament."

"I could specify blood magic," Dalton suggested.

"I'm almost certain that if you tried, the Tournament Board would nullify the condition. Yokouro wants us to struggle against the Jjanye. He *wants* us to panic," Keito said.

Dalton closed his eyes and hung his head. Everyone in the team room fell into silence.

The announcer called Team Ander and Team Kaize to the ring, which only offered them a small break from having to face the tournament once again.

Dalton's leg was bouncing anxiously and he continued to rub his face in frustration. He could feel the walls closing in on him, the fear and stress becoming too much to handle. He tried to pass off his worried exhales as sighs even as he struggled to take in air. Everything in his mind was screaming at him to run as far away from the stadium as possible, though he knew he could not risk Yokouro attacking the stadium as a way to punish him for not playing by the rules of his sick game.

His claustrophobia was reaching an unhealthy level when he realized he did not feel like the walls were closing in on him—he felt as though he was growing too large for the room. His magic was pushing further outward, straining against the walls of the small team room.

He stood and left with the worried gazes of his teammates following him.

The hallway offered no relief as he could hear the excited cheers of the audience from what sounded to be a very exciting fight in the ring. He turned and went to the nearest bathroom, his shaking hands clumsily turning the knobs on the sink. He splashed his face with the cold water, trying to shock himself back to the moment and force his vision to expand from tunnel vision.

He leaned over the sink, water dripping from his skin as he gripped the edge of the counter.

"Calm down, calm down..." he chanted under his breath, feeling his muscles shake as he desperately tried to feel in control of his magic again.

His panicked brain was a confusing mix of fears as he tried to think of how he was going to overpower the Jjanye demon and how he was going to keep control over his growing magic so that he did not harm his teammates or anyone else in the stadium.

"Dalton."

His head snapped up to look in the mirror, seeing Keito standing in the door of the multi-stalled bathroom, his eyes full of concern.

"Damn it, don't sneak up on people like that!" he snapped.

"Sorry," the demon murmured. "I just wanted to check on you."

Dalton bent his head again, sighing heavily.

"I just need a few minutes."

Keito remained where he was, watching as Dalton tried to control his breathing, his shoulders shaking.

"Dalton, what is in the vial in your pocket?"

Dalton froze, his brow crinkled. He slowly turned over his shoulder to look at his teammate. Keito stepped out of the doorway, closing the door behind him.

"Do you know what it is?"

"…no. And how do you know I even have a vial in my pocket?" Dalton asked suspiciously.

"Can I see it?"

Dalton was slow in extracting the vial, placing it in Keito's outstretched hand. The demon lifted the vial, staring at the black liquid within.

"Where did you get it?"

"You won't believe me," Dalton huffed.

"Try me."

"I can't get rid of it." He shrugged. "I've poured it out. Thrown it away. Left it in the car, and every time I try to destroy it, it comes right back."

Keito heaved a sigh, extending it back toward Dalton.

"I think you should take it."

Dalton's jaw dropped.

"Are you serious?" he gawked. "A mysterious vial of black liquid that keeps appearing in my pocket? You want me to *drink* it?"

Keito sighed again, extending his hand further.

"Yes."

"*Why* would I do that?"

"Because clearly whoever is giving this to you has enough power to continue giving you this potion. And considering that we're going up against the Jjanye, we might need to take some chances."

"It could be poison."

"I doubt Yokouro would want to poison you if he's putting this much effort into making a spectacle at the tournament," Keito said.

"You seem very certain that this will be beneficial and not make me go on some murderous rampage." Keito was about to laugh, thinking Dalton was trying to make a joke, but he could hear the sincerity of concern in his voice.

He looked at the vial Dalton still refused to take back.

"I can understand you not trusting this," he gently shook the vial, "but do you think you can trust me?"

Dalton stared at the vial, his mind still racing with worries about the upcoming fight with the young demon, and the understanding that Yokouro was somewhere in the stadium watching him closely. Even though Keito's words about it likely not being a poison made sense, Dalton had no idea who else would want to continuously drop a potion into his pocket without telling him its purpose.

With a defeated sigh, he took the potion from Keito and uncorked it. His nose wrinkled at the stench that wafted through the air.

"If this kills me, I will come back and haunt you forever," Dalton warned Keito, trying to force a smile.

"Fair enough."

Dalton took a deep breath and lifted the glass to his lips, tilting his head back and downing the potion before he could think better of his decision. He choked at the bitter taste, but forced the liquid down, coughing as he shivered and cringed. Keito winced in solidarity.

"How bad?"

Dalton shuddered, gulping water from the sink to rinse the taste out of his mouth.

"That was the worst thing I've ever tasted," Dalton groaned, hoarse. "And I was one of those stupidly adventurous kids who would eat things on dares..."

Keito's lips quirked in a smile.

"Ready to go back to the others?"

"No," Dalton said.

"Okay, I'll leave you alone."

"Actually," Dalton said quickly as the demon backed away, "do you think you could stay with me for a while...just in case that was poison and I'm about to drop dead?"

Keito nodded, leaning against the wall by the door, giving Dalton some distance.

With the taste of the potion lingering on his tongue and his anxiety unquelled, Dalton leaned on the edge of the counter, sinking to his knees as his muscles remained tensed in an effort not to break down.

Chapter Sixteen

Dalton had hoped for another match before his fight with Team Kyceth, but once the fifteen minutes were over after Team Kaize's victory, Kira announced that the next match was Team Dalton versus Team Kyceth. Everyone on Team Dalton took a few deep breaths to prepare themselves to face the Jjanye demon, hoping that their very simple plan would give them enough edge to triumph over Yokouro's team.

Keito had not yet told them that Yokouro had a second team in the ring, and that team was armed with a demon more dangerous than the Jjanye—a disciple of Juki and Rutu. He knew overwhelming the humans would only decrease their chances of victory. That was the same reason he had not told them that Juki and Rutu were also in the stadium with Yokouro.

Dalton could feel his skin prickling at the wide smile on the young demon's face as he approached his opponents. He stopped a little further away than was customary and his team grouped tightly behind him, waiting for the conditions to be stated. The audience was bubbling with barely-contained delight, anticipating an extreme fight between the mysterious team that had so easily defeated their previous opponents, and the highly-favored Team Dalton.

"Please state any conditions you may have for the fight."

"I request that an exclusive fight between Keito and the demon from Team Kyceth take place before the rest of us fight," Dalton called.

"Dalton has asked that Keito and Datze have an exclusive fights, as there are two demons in the ring. Datze, do you accept?"

"No, I do not," he said quickly, giggling. "Really? That was the best you could come up with?"

"As Datze has declined, the condition will not be upheld. Are there any further conditions?"

"Any other pathetic attempts to avoid the inevitable?" the leader of the other team jeered. "Just accept it, Dalton. We've all gone through a lot of trouble to set this up for you."

"And what, exactly, is it that you've set up for me?" Dalton growled. "Other than show me how willing you are to risk collateral damage and piss me off?"

The other man rolled his eyes. "Ugh, do you ever get sick of being so self-righteous?"

"Ky, come on," Datze whined.

"Calm down," the older man snapped at the young demon. "I don't have any conditions, Dalton. I want you to fight completely uninhibited."

"Team Dalton? Any further requests?"

Dalton slowly shook his head.

"If there are no conditions, you may begin!"

Even though they had planned on Keito putting up a magical barrier around the entire team to negate the worst of the crushing effects of Datze's power, Dalton still jumped when he felt the energy surround him. He was expecting to feel the crushing weight, the fiery magic that radiated through his veins, but the power of the Jjanye demon did not even collide with Keito's barrier.

"You think too small, Keito," one of the women on the team laughed. "Datze has something far more intricate planned for the famous Team Dalton."

Datze stepped forward slowly, smiling, the four others on his team retreating.

"I'm excited to see how well you take to this," he said.

Movement in Dalton's periphery forced his eyes away from Datze, seeing that the other members were circling Team Dalton. The five Guardians went back-to-back by second nature, watching each member of Team Kyceth, not sure what to expect and worried that Keito's barrier would not hold once they decided to attack.

Dalton's eyes swung back on Datze, who had pushed up both sleeves, giving Dalton a clearer view of the deep gashes evenly spaced around his forearm, scabbed over and surrounded by angry red skin from being so often picked open. Dalton clenched his fists, his magic swelling as he leaned forward, ready to leap out of the safety of Keito's barrier to attack the younger demon, becoming almost panicked.

The second before Dalton was ready to spring into action, he noticed it was becoming difficult to see Datze. He blinked several times, wondering if nervous sweat had fallen into his eyes. It was when he lifted a hand to rub his face that he saw the gentle tendrils of fog rolling off his sleeves.

"Stay in the barrier," Keito ordered, stepping away from the edges of his magic as the fog crept closer to the Guardians, obscuring their view of the grinning members of Team Kyceth. They came closer together, each fighting with the urge to leap forward and attack their opponents, knowing they were safer within Keito's protective magic.

"Have you ever heard of the Shadow Veil, demon mutt?" one woman asked, quirking an eyebrow. "You probably have in the circles you've traveled."

"Keito, what do we do?" Eclipse demanded, feeling like a cornered animal as the fog around them became thicker and thicker, the magic within creating dancing sparks along the edges of Keito's magic.

"Stay in the barrier," he repeated strongly.

"But where's the fun in that?" Datze laughed, lifting his blood-soaked fingers and snapping, destroying the force field.

Keito let out a startled cry and fell to one knee, but was immediately rushed by one of the female members of Team Kyceth. She moved with the fog, the dark energy invading the area where they stood and wrapping each of them in a thick mist. Eclipse began to run to Keito's aid, but the nearest member of Team Kyceth intercepted him, Eclipse barely avoiding a hard punch to the face.

Dalton took a step toward Datze. The young demon lifted two fingers over his face and pressed them to his eyes.

"Just close your eyes," he said, his voice radiating through the fog like a whispering breeze, "and succumb."

Dalton flinched when a painful shockwave of magic passed through him, but pushed his fear aside as soon as he was able. When he straightened, he was engulfed in the fog, unable to see or hear anything around him. He froze, focusing entirely on his hearing, knowing his teammates had been close, though he could not hear the sounds of the scuffles he knew were occurring.

The fog moved around him, brushing against his body as if trying to find a weakness, but not willing to push too hard. He turned over one shoulder, then the other, refusing to move his feet for fear of turning away from the direction in which he last saw Datze and losing focus of where he had been standing in the ring.

He waited for something to happen. He waited for the sound of a shifting foot, for the taunting laugh of an opponent, for the labored breathing of one of his teammates struggling in their fights.

He heard nothing. Even the sounds of the audience that had once invaded his ears were eerily absent.

Dalton turned to look at his feet, barely able to make out the outline of his shoes under the layer of fog. He saw the direction his toes pointed and lifted a foot, being sure it remained straight as he took a step forward. He took another step, and then another, knowing that if he continued in that direction, eventually, he would step out of the spell's bounds, or he would find a wall of the ring.

Arms raised defensively, his eyes trained on the way his feet moved, Dalton slowly walked.

~/\~

Mitoki had tried to turn and help Eclipse, but was stopped when he saw the leader of Team Kyceth running toward him. He turned on his heel, ready to face him, but before the taller, broader man reached him, the fog engulfed him and he heard Datze saying: "Just close your eyes, and succumb."

He thought he felt his eyes close, but as soon as the momentary darkness washed over him, he snapped upright, eyes wide, somehow sitting rather than standing.

He refused to move, not because of fear, but out of confusion. He was in his bed at home, the sheets tangled around his legs as they often were after a vivid nightmare. Everything was the same. He could hear the sounds of his neighbor's dog outside, could smell the clean air that wafted through his open window, and hear the distant sounds of cooking in the kitchen.

His brain struggled to comprehend what to believe about his reality. He wondered if the tournament and meeting Yokouro was nothing more than a bad dream brought about by his mind tearing apart every piece of information he had managed to gather from Keito's filed reports. He turned around to retrieve his phone from the nightstand, but it was not there. Desperate to check the date and determine what had been a dream, he kicked his sheets away and got to his feet.

The floor even creaked in the exact same spot as always.

He had to be at home.

Even as he descended the stairs, intending to ask Rebecca where his phone was, he could not help feeling that something was *wrong* with the house. He had remembered so vividly days passing in the Darkness Realm, and the incredibly overwhelming information the team had gathered in those days. He had experienced premonitions before with his psychic gifts, but they had never been so physical.

"Rebecca?" he called, leaning into the kitchen where he had heard her cooking.

The kitchen was empty, the pan on the turned-off burner still sizzling with grease. He stared at the pan, at the three mugs that were filled with hot coffee, at the plates that had been pulled down for breakfast.

But Rebecca was nowhere to be seen.

Mitoki was very careful as he backed out of the kitchen.

A crunch of glass was followed by searing pain in his shoulder as something forced him to the ground. As he hit the hardwood floor, a deafening bang sounded from the front door and voices surrounded him, barking orders at him to stay on the ground, guns poised to shoot him.

His hands immediately went up, his heart thundering and pain radiating through his shoulder from what he assumed to be a bullet wound. He had been so focused on Yokouro and the Kage Lords and the abducted Elder that his brain could not comprehend how all the officers in black armor related to his mission with the Guardian Tournament. He could only stare in confusion, letting out a small cry of pain when one officer grabbed his wrist and turned him, painfully forcing his hands behind his back and securing them with cuffs that burned his skin, keeping him from using his magic.

"What are you doing?! Who are you?!"

"Guardian Mitoki Ecaep," one of the men started as Mitoki was hauled to his feet, "you are being taken into custody under charges of burglary, misconduct around civilians, endangering the lives of humans, murder, and violating every article of the Guardian Code to serve and protect the realms."

Cold fear washed over him, and though he knew he was likely to be shot for doing so, he began struggling.

"No! No, you have it wrong! It wasn't me!"

"Your fingerprints are all over the weapons and the crime scenes," the officer growled. "You've been caught multiple times on security tapes."

"No, you don't understand! I'm being framed!"

"The evidence speaks for itself," the gruff man sneered. "I hope they give you the death sentence for the sick shit you've done."

"No, please, let me talk to my family! I beg you! They can explain!"

"Your family wants nothing to do with you," he snapped "You've committed your last crime, you sad excuse for a Guardian."

"This is a mistake! I'm being framed by Yokouro DeVastes Give me a chance to explain!"

"How can this be Yokouro's doing?" the man growled, leaning closer and lifting his visor, exposing piercing golden eyes and dark lines on each of his cheeks. "You were the one who went out at night and robbed those places, not him."

Mitoki stared at the familiar countenance, his mind desperately trying to put together the information of how Yokouro could be posing as an officer there to arrest him, when he had not yet seen what Yokouro looked like, or even confirmed that Yokouro was the one they were pursuing.

He closed his eyes. "This isn't real," he whispered. "This is a spell. This is a hallucination. You are in the Guardian Tournament right now. You are fighting...This isn't real."

"Not real, huh?" Yokouro's chilling voice taunted.

He jabbed the butt of his rifle into Mitoki's abdomen, sending hot pain radiating through his body and forcing the air from his lungs.

"Is that real enough for you?"

Mitoki continued to chant under his breath.

"You are in the Guardian Tournament. You are in the middle of a match. This is not real. This is a spell..."

Eclipse had nearly fallen flat on his back when he barely dodged the punch from the man that charged at him. But as he stood to retaliate, a heavy weight passed over his eyelids, as though he were about to faint. He forced his eyes open, his fist raised.

But his opponent was not there.

Instead he was standing in front of a quaint house he had not seen in decades, but still remained seared in his memory.

"What the hell?" he breathed, lowering his fist.

He refused to move for several long moments, staring over the steps leading to the white railing of the porch, looking over each facet of the modest house until he was certain he was standing in front of his childhood home.

The longer he stood in front of the house, the harder it was for him to remember how he got there. It was as if he was being hypnotized by the lines and angles of his former home, drawing him closer until his hand found the doorknob.

He turned it slowly, his nerves humming with curiosity, memories, fear, and elation. The front door made no noise—it never had, his parents both were very fastidious about keeping the house in order. Even though it had been a very long time since he set foot in his childhood home, and his memories could be fuzzy at times, the feelings within the house were exactly the same. The house was bright and airy, the curtains flung open to let in the morning sunlight. The sun's rays reflected off the crystals and totems that decorated the house, which often unnerved those who did not understand the family's connection with magic.

But seeing the small trinkets from his childhood filled Eclipse with painful nostalgia that had him both smiling and swallowing back stubborn tears. He stepped up to the altar in the living room, running his fingers over the large, black feather that had been placed among candles and crystals, remembering fondly how his mother would use the feather in meditation practice, and also tickle his face with it when he was very young.

He knew he was not truly standing in his childhood home. He could not, however, determine if he was dreaming, or under a spell, or even what he had been doing before he found himself in the warm place of his youth.

A soft, gurgling sound reached his ears as he set the feather back down on the altar. His entire body went rigid, and all warmth seeped out of him. The sound was unmistakable. It was one he had heard often on his cases—the sound of the final breaths of the dying.

Every muscle in his body was tensed, knowing that if he turned around, he would be confronted with the scene from his nightmares. But he felt compelled. He had to turn around.

His eyes knew exactly where to look when his feet finally brought him to face the other direction. His father was on the floor, his glassy eyes staring up at the ceiling, blood painting his face in an upward splatter. His torso was tweaked at an unnatural angle, his ribs crushed and mangled, allowing his blood seep slowly into a large pool on the floor. Behind him, half-slumped on the couch, was his mother, her head draped over the side of the seat, causing her horrified expression to contort further around the blood that marred her pale skin. It was evident from her position that her spine had been broken in multiple places, her ribs also crushed and distorted.

Just as he had the day they had died, Eclipse stood and stared, unable to move his feet, his heart pounding and his body humming with too many emotions to name.

His staring was broken by another sound, one that filled him with more fear than the sight of his slaughtered parents.

The cry of a baby.

He clamored up the stairs, turning to the first room on the right by instinct, though the room holding the crib was dark and there was no baby fussing within. He backed out of the room and ran down the hall to the room that had once been his, forcing the door open with his shoulder and half-falling into the bedroom.

His old furniture was gone, the room desolate except for a figure standing near the closet, a yellow blanket bundled in his arms around a fussing baby.

"No…" Eclipse hissed. "Put him down."

The figure turned and Eclipse could feel the anger swelling in his body. He knew the face. The hard set jaw and dark eyes filled him with rage even so many years after the man's death.

"Hello, Thirteen."

"Put him down," Eclipse growled, taking a careful step forward.

"I'm done listening to you, you insolent brat."

Had Eclipse not been so disoriented, had he not been so engrossed in the memories of the day his parents had died, he would have put more thought into why the man's voice sounded strange— certainly not the voice he remembered.

"You didn't... you didn't kill him," he said. "I remember. You didn't kill him. I killed you."

The figure smiled, but the smile was off. The teeth were sharper, whiter, and they dropped the temperature of the room enough to make Eclipse shiver.

"Yes, you did." The figure clicked his tongue against the roof of his mouth, tutting as he shook his head. "That was a very, *very* foolish thing to do."

"You killed my family! You killed three other families in the neighborhood!" Eclipse burst. "Like hell I was going to let you kill my brothers!"

"Then why do you keep putting them at risk?" the man laughed brokenly.

"Why are you here? Why is this happening?"

"Because it was always meant to happen." The figure smiled, gently patting the rustling blankets as the baby began to fall silent. "Everything hinges on this moment, Eclipse. The moment you drew your allegiance to the Guardians, ready to defend the innocent against people like me." The unnatural smile widened. "Don't you understand? This is where you will always be, because this is where I made sure you would stay."

Eclipse could feel his mind beginning to cloud as he tried to understand. But before he could demand a better explanation, the figure's arms dropped and the yellow blanket began to tumble to the floor.

He dove for the baby, but landed hard on the carpet with his hands clutching the empty yellow fleece. He quickly pushed the folds of fabric aside, desperate to find his younger brother, but the baby was gone. When he looked up, he saw a very different sight. A young man, also familiar, was held tightly by the neck by a grinning Yokouro.

Eclipse leapt up, fist raised, growling as he lunged to attack.

Hanyi had known he was about to be attacked by the other female member of Team Kyceth, so he dropped to his wolf form and lowered himself, ready to take her legs out from under her and get her on the ground so he would have the advantage.

But he never heard or saw his opponent.

After a few moments of waiting, the fog began to clear and the sound of the cheering audience came to his ears. He straightened, bewildered, looking around the stands as he shifted back up to his human form.

A familiar laugh came to his ears as an arm locked around his shoulders and pulled him into a rough hug.

"Nothing to it, huh?"

Hanyi's heart stopped, turning his gaze to face Jacob, who was flashing his signature, large, toothy grin.

"Jacob?" he whispered.

"They should know better than to mess with the best Guardians in the branch, huh?"

Hanyi's heart constricted painfully in his chest as he turned to the triumphant face of his older brother. Hector was holding up a victorious hand to the audience, who cheered enthusiastically as he waved to each section in the stadium.

"No…this is…this isn't right."

"What? Are you saying we won by luck?" Sadee laughed, lightly punching him in the arm. "Tell that to the masters and they'll push us twice as hard for next season."

"If you get us extra training, I'll never forgive you," Jacob laughed, smacking Hanyi in the chest as he turned the younger Treneke wolf and began walking out of the ring.

Finally startled to his senses, Hanyi pushed himself away from Jacob's grip and backed away.

"No…no, you can't be here."

"What are you talking about?" Hector asked, a nervous laugh lining the words. He approached his younger brother, pressing a hand to his head. "Did you hit your head too hard, little brother? I don't call you hard headed because I think you can withstand any head injury, you know."

"Don't touch me." Hanyi backed away, horrified and confused about seeing the three members of his former team, looking him over worriedly.

"Hanyi, what's wrong?" Jacob asked, the elation in his voice gone.

"You're dead...you're all dead."

"What?" Hector asked, shaking his head. "Okay, we need to get you to Master Linnel. You're starting to scare me." He placed a hand on Hanyi's arm.

"No! Stop it!" Hanyi barked. "He's dead, too! You're not real. This is a hallucination...or something." He closed his eyes tight. "I am not on Team Keito. I am on Team Dalton. This isn't real. This can't be real."

"Keito!" Sadee called. "Something's up with Hanyi!"

Hanyi's eyes flung open.

"No! Keito, don't!"

"Hanyi, calm down!" Hector gripped his arms, trying to stop him from lunging forward. Hanyi looked wildly around for Keito, but the dark-haired demon was nowhere to be seen. "Hanyi! Hanyi! Get a hold of yourself!"

"Where is he?" he hissed. His eyes were frantic around the ring, unable to spot the demon. His gaze finally rested on the concerned face of his older brother in front of him. "Where is Keito?"

"He's right there," Hector said, jerking his head over his shoulder. "You're hysterical."

"Because you're dead! I watched you die!" Hanyi cried. He tried to push Hector away, but the older wolf's grip held. "Let me go!"

"What do you mean you watched me die?" Hector snapped. "What are you talking about?"

"Let me *go*, Hector!"

He pushed harder, but still his brother did not release him. He shoved once again, but that time, he felt his hand slip deeper into Hector's abdomen and become coated with a warm, wet liquid that he understood immediately to be blood.

His eyes shot down, seeing his hand had sunken completely into his brother's abdomen, blood gushing out of the wound.

Hector's hand grabbed his arm and he looked up, his brother's pale face set with a hard glare.

"You mean like this?" he growled.

Hanyi retreated, his hand coming away from his brother's gaping wound, followed by a torrent of blood.

"And you just *watched*?"

"This isn't real. This isn't real," he chanted.

"Then I'm *not* dead?" Hector challenged.

Hanyi closed his eyes tight, shaking his head.

"Pull it together. You know this isn't real."

"You should open your eyes and *look*," Jacob sneered. "You've already seen it once. What's a second time?"

"All you got was a broken leg," Sadee added. "Why didn't you die that day?"

Hanyi was determined to keep his eyes closed, trying to block out the words in the familiar voices of his fallen teammates. But two hands on his shoulders caused his eyes to snap open, meeting the face of his brother once more.

"Look at me," he growled. "Look at what you allowed to happen."

Hanyi struggled against the vice grip, shaking his head.

"No, no, it wasn't me...I...I didn't know that this would happen!"

"But you let it happen!" Jacob bellowed, storming over to Hanyi and wrapping a hand around his neck. Hanyi struggled and swung at Jacob, but was afraid to seriously strike him. He could see the large gash in Jacob's neck, blood pouring down his chest as he glared angrily at Hanyi. "You let us die, Hanyi. You should have died with us!"

Hanyi was suddenly brought to the ground by a dark figure. In a panic, he began swinging his fists, one punch landing squarely on the demon's jaw.

"Hanyi! Hanyi! Stop! It's me!"

"Get off of me!" Hanyi barked, kicking and swinging in desperation, fear and confusion swimming through his mind.

"Hanyi! This is a hallucination!" Keito snapped, pinning the wolf sharply to the ground. "You are in the Realm of Darkness in the second round of the Guardian Tournament with Team Dalton! Wherever you think you are, it's a lie! You're safe!"

Hanyi still swung at Keito, but his strength waned as the words slowly absorbed. Finally, he closed his eyes tight, trying to take several deep breaths.

"How do I break the hallucination?" he asked, his voice dark as he tried to focus only on Keito, and not the noises threatening to slip into his mind.

"Just hold on."

Keito's hands shifted and Hanyi was soon being dragged across the dirt ground. He could almost feel the hands of his former teammates dragging his legs backward, struggling with Keito to keep him in the hallucination.

But the hands disappeared and the air became cooler in an instant. Hanyi opened his eyes and saw the stadium lights above him, the crowd cheering when they saw Keito and Hanyi. He sat up, trying to see around the pounding of his head. His eyes widened at the large dome of smoke in front of him, blocking out most of the ring.

"What the hell is that?"

"A very powerful spell," Keito said, crouching as he caught his breath, rubbing his cheek where Hanyi had punched him. "Are you alright?"

"Yeah…" he said mechanically. "Yeah, I'm fine."

"You sure?"

"Where are the others?" Hanyi asked, looking around him.

"I still have to find Eclipse and Mitoki," Keito murmured. "Dalton is on the other side fighting Datze." He motioned to the large screens displaying Dalton and Datze circling one another in a defensive stance.

"And the others of Team Kyceth?"

"In there," Keito said, motioning to the fog. "I knocked out the one who attacked me and the one holding you in the hallucination."

"Do you want me to help you with Eclipse and Mitoki, or help Dalton?"

"I want you to stay put for a few minutes," Keito ordered. "If you go back in, the spell might overtake you again. And you're not in any state to be fighting a Jjanye. Just wait for me here. I'm going back in."

"Are *you* okay?"

"I'm fine," he assured. "Just stay." He glanced at the screens when he heard the audience start cheering again, seeing that Dalton and the Jjanye had started throwing punches. "Watch Dalton. Only step in if he looks like he's in danger."

Before Hanyi could protest, Keito disappeared back into the fog.

~/\~

An anxiety Dalton could not describe had invaded his body. While he had been filled with a lingering sense of panic the entire day, the feelings tickling at his nerves felt more like excited anticipation than the fear he had been experiencing. His senses felt sharper, better able to predict and counter the fast moves of the young demon, and even when he felt the energy radiating from the young demon, his response was not worry, but excitement at the challenge.

He managed to pin the Jjanye demon for a mere second before a knee found his side and forced him to the ground. Datze leapt away from Dalton, taking a defensive stance as he stared at the human Guardian.

"How did you manage to walk out of the Shadow Veil?" he demanded.

"Putting one foot in front of the other," Dalton retorted, standing as he quickly assessed if any ribs were broken from the kick.

"Smart ass, I *mean* why are you not hallucinating right now?"

"Maybe I am," Dalton said, shrugging as he watched the tension in the younger demon, waiting for him to leap forward and attack again. "I thought you would be much tougher to fight."

"You disgusting human. How dare you talk down to me?"

He lunged forward again, but Dalton was able to see the attack coming and easily avoid injury.

"Not so good at hand-to-hand, are you?" he taunted. "Seems like you rely mostly on spells and staying a safe distance from your enemy." Dalton smiled when the young demon turned and began attacking again, his plan obvious. "You need a lesson in what it's like to really fight."

The Jjanye swung his fist angrily at Dalton's face, relying on his demon speed and strength to give him the advantage, but Dalton was easily able to duck away and grab the young demon's shirt, pulling him back before punching Datze across the face with the back of his fist.

Datze fell to the ground, groaning in pain.

"Your *master* ever teach you that?"

"You know nothing, you moronic human!" Datze sneered. Still on the ground, he jerked forward, his hand wrapping around Dalton's ankle. When Dalton pulled away, he felt the burning of the demon's nails slicing into his skin. He recoiled, watching as Datze laughed, pulling himself to unsteady feet.

"Now I've got you," the young demon murmured, lifting his hand and wiggling the nails coated with Dalton's blood.

Before Dalton could formulate a plan, he felt a crushing weight in his stomach. He groaned and doubled over, holding his body tightly as Datze slowly closed his fist, as though squeezing Dalton's internal organs.

"I wonder what would happen if I made your lungs pop?" Datze laughed. "Show everyone that you're not as special as they think you are."

"It's…against…the rules…" Dalton wheezed. "You can't…kill me…"

Datze's face became contemplative. Dalton's face began to turn a deep shade of red as he struggled to breathe around the constricting magic in his body. Finally, Datze's fingers relaxed.

Dalton's body slumped, his lungs greedily gulping in air.

"I don't care about this stupid tournament's rules," Datze sneered. "But you are right. My masters would be upset if you died so early in the game." His smirk grew cold. "So how about this?"

He lifted his hand and clenched a fist, Dalton's body going rigidly straight.

"Let's find out what the Shadow Veil makes you see."

With a sharp tug backward, Dalton was sent careening into the fog, landing hard on the dirt floor of the ring. Datze lifted the hand with Dalton's blood and began chanting, trying to make the spell stronger and focus entirely on Dalton. The fog grew darker, and the curious cheers and excited sounds from the audience only served to make him try harder, determined to make the hallucinations work.

The fog began to spark with energy, static filling the entire stadium as the spell grew in intensity. He watched with an excited smile, feeling the lightning traveling through his veins.

But the cameras around the ring broadcasted the exact moment Datze's face fell.

The fog, which had been growing a dark shade of grey, began to move and billow, pulling closer to where Dalton had fallen. The fog funneled, as though sucked through a pipe, toward the human Guardian, the bright sparks turning into long streaks of light as the magic grew and grew.

The others in the ring were unveiled, allowing Hanyi to leap in and attack Kyceth as he held the confused Eclipse in a loose choke hold, keeping him still for the hallucination. Keito was struggling with the woman who had attacked Mitoki. As the fog cleared more, Mitoki was able to stand and look around, trying to understand where he was and what he needed to do to help Keito.

But the audience did not show any interest in the other Guardians.

All eyes were focused on Dalton.

Dalton was standing, his head down, as the fog from the spell was pulled into his body. His fists were clenched, his shoulders tensed as the spell finally vanished.

Datze retreated a step.

"What the hell *are* you?!" he cried.

Dalton lifted his head, his gaze locked on the young demon. However, instead of Dalton's green eyes, his gaze was entirely white, glowing as he took a step closer to the Jjanye demon.

The audience had fallen eerily silent, only a dull humming heard as they pointed and whispered to their friends about what Dalton looked like on the screen. The electricity in the stadium was threatening to flicker out, the screens distorting as the cameras tried to focus on the human Guardian.

Datze let out a loud shout, rushing forward with magic encasing his arms, ready to attack with all he could.

Dalton stepped to the side, grabbed the young demon's arm, and angrily twisted his hand, feeling the skin split around the scabs, allowing the Jjanye's blood to flow down his wrist and through Dalton's fingers.

"I figured it out," Dalton growled, his voice exactly as it had been before, though it radiated with a power that had the Jjanye demon shivering. "If you can use my blood as a weapon against me, I can use your blood as a weapon against you."

Dark, fiery magic spiraled down Dalton's arm and circled his fingers, slipping into the open wounds on the Jjanye's arm. The young demon screamed, scraping at Dalton's hand in a desperate attempt to release himself. He could feel the magic enter his blood stream, traveling up his arm like a wildfire, the heat singeing every nerve.

Dalton's hand released him, but Datze continued to claw and scrape at his arm, trying to push the magic down, terrified at the speed with which it was invading his body. The others of Team Dalton, having secured surrender from the other members of Team Kyceth, watched in confusion and fascination as the Jjanye demon writhed, finally falling to the ground.

He twisted and turned, his hands locked in a sharp, clawing position as he convulsed. He went still and Keito ran to him, pressing his fingers to the young demon's neck.

"He's alive," he said.

"And with a surrender from all members of Team Kyceth, Team Dalton wins—"

The announcer's declaration and the exhilarated cheering in the audience was interrupted by a burst of magic that radiated from the ring, knocking everyone back in their seats as a gust of electric wind moved through the stadium. The lights flickered and a few of the bulbs above shattered, causing glass to rain down on the ring. The screens broadcasting the Guardians warped and one cracked as the magic radiated outward and finally dispersed, leaving an excited static through the air that was not threatening, but seemed to both soothe and energize the audience at the same time.

Nervous laughter and excited clapping filled the stands as Dalton stumbled and slowly sank to his knees.

His team surrounded him quickly, Keito grabbing Dalton's jaw.

"Dalton, look at me."

The leader of the team slowly blinked his eyes, turning to focus his gaze on Keito.

"What happened?" he whispered, his green eyes filled with exhaustion.

"We were about to ask you that," Mitoki laughed brokenly, helping pull Dalton to his feet as the announcer declared them the winner of the match. Once the official announcement had taken place, the medical team ran out to gather Team Kyceth, and Jikia and Tarrena ran to Team Dalton.

"Are you okay?" Jikia asked, her eyes roving over Dalton, worry evident in her voice.

"I'm tired…"

"Let's go rest in the team room," Tarrena declared, her hands outstretched to help as Keito supported Dalton out of the ring.

Chapter Seventeen

While the Tournament Board was staring wide-eyed at the ring, still trying to process what they had seen, Yokouro's eyes followed Dalton out of the ring before he leaned back in his chair and snorted triumphantly.

"I certainly didn't expect *that*," he said. "Looks like Vestera is keeping a much closer eye on Dalton than I thought. I didn't think his magic would just eject us like that."

Juki turned to Rutu, who was flexing his right hand, holding his wrist tightly with an almost imperceptible wince of pain.

"Are you alright?"

"Fine," Rutu said with a tight nod. "He just caught me off guard."

"What…just happened?" one of the women asked shakily. "That energy coming from Dalton…"

"Was Dalton," Yokouro answered. "Just unleashed." He turned over his shoulder to Rutu. "What did Vestera just do?"

Rutu ground his teeth together briefly as he flexed his hand again, holding it to his chest with a grimace.

"Judging from the dragon energy that came out of Dalton, I would say he channeled the dragon magic Dalton possesses."

"Wait? Dalton's not human?" one of the men asked, his eyes wide.

"He is," Yokouro corrected. "But he's also not."

"The energy levels that Dalton just produced are far higher than we allow in the tournament," one of the women said quietly. "He's dangerous to the other humans at a level like that."

"You cannot disqualify him," Yokouro said.

"Why not? If he's not competing, you can focus on fighting him," she insisted, now worried she needed to get Dalton out of the tournament and get Yokouro away from them as quickly as possible, the blinking numbers on the power reader causing her heart to race in terror.

"Because this is damn good entertainment," Yokouro said. "And I'm using the tournament to train him, to see where he is in his development. I am constantly being told that this is a delicate process, so we must be sure to give him all the tests needed to be certain he is ready to face me."

"Is that young demon going to be okay?" one of the other women said, watching the medical team carry him away on a stretcher. Both Juki and Rutu leaned closer to the window to watch the scene.

"Maybe," Juki said with a noncommittal shrug.

Rutu's eyes continued to scan the ring, the audience, and the other teams waiting to compete. He was carefully reading the energies around the stadium, knowing that Vestera's magic could be overwhelming to ordinary humans. The audience seemed invigorated rather than agitated, while most of the Guardians wore pensive looks, trying to determine why the magic had felt so out of place in the Guardian Tournament.

The other team Yokouro had competing was the only team unconcerned with what had happened in the prior match. They sat casually in their team box, clearly bored with the waiting. Rutu spotted a familiar face among the team.

"Juki," he started, "care to explain to me why I see Ra-Jea sitting in team box nine?"

Juki remained silent, so Yokouro spoke.

"I asked for a Trade Mercenary."

"Why, in the name of all the gods, would you need a Trade Mercenary?" Rutu asked incredulously.

"I had to be sure everything went perfectly," Yokouro defended. "A Trade Mercenary is the best-trained opponent I could ask for."

"For Eclipse?"

"For the entire team."

Rutu's eyes turned back to Juki.

"Technically, Ra-Jea is mine," he said. "You should have asked my permission."

"I thought we shared everything," Juki said, his eyebrows high. "I know Ra-Jae is your new favorite prodigy, to whom I am choosing *not* to question your attachment, but he was the only one available that fit Yokouro's specifications."

"I am talking strictly about the contract you drew up to give him this job," Rutu said. "You need my signature as his trainer so that, if something goes wrong, we're not the ones dealing with the damage."

"We didn't draw a contract."

Rutu closed his eyes, shaking his head incredulously.

"He had no choice," Yokouro interjected. "We had a limited time frame. I asked him for a Trade Mercenary last night. You've been in the Demon Realm until three hours ago. I needed him to act quickly."

"It takes, maybe, five minutes to get my approval," Rutu said.

"You wouldn't have given it," Juki said.

"Because now we're in violation of our agreement with Vestera and Demon Council," Rutu reminded him. "The Trade Mercenaries are not to be used outside the Demon Realm. We were already on thin ice with the Jjanye. We're going to invite more of Vestera's scrutiny if we continue to break our agreements with him."

"Vestera is not going to care," Yokouro said, trying not to roll his eyes. "He might slap you with a fine, but you won't be in serious trouble."

"I know you don't care if we get punished by Vestera, but he's not an idiot. He'll know immediately that all this was at your request, and that might affect you taking control of your territory again."

"Vestera won't act. He doesn't like to get involved," Yokouro said.

"There are still rules, Yokouro," Rutu insisted. "You're pushing your luck more every day."

"Don't lecture me, Rutu," Yokouro groaned. "You are not my mother."

"Listen to him. He is trying to warn you how to proceed if you actually want to face Dalton," Juki said. "And Vestera being angry with us and being angry with you are two very different things."

"Indeed," Yokouro said, standing and turning to glare at Juki as he adjusted his robe casually. "One of these days you will have to explain to me how you have managed to stay in his good graces with everything you do."

He turned to the Tournament Board.

"What do you plan to do about Dalton?"

"You told us not to disqualify him, Master Yokouro," one of the men said, looking nervously among his colleagues.

"What would be normal protocol if a Guardian were to display those numbers in a fight?" He motioned to the power meter screen.

"We would have to submit the Guardian to testing. See if they were using magical enhancers, or were without the correct power limiters. In Dalton's case, we would also have to do bloodwork to be certain he is human, and not a demon trying to parade as a human." Her voice became noticeably weaker as she stated the last sentence, knowing it would likely upset Yokouro to hear about the treatment demons received.

The demon lord nodded.

"Fine, do that," he ordered. "But do not disqualify him."

"If you do not want him disqualified, Master Yokouro, then we do not need to run the tests."

"Go ahead and run them," he said. "Let him feel what it's like to be a demon."

Yokouro turned to leave the room.

"Where-where are you going?" the woman asked, her voice

growing weak as she realized she had just spoken out of turn. Yokouro glanced over his shoulder with a cold smile.

"To get a better view."

~/\~

Jikia was constantly tapping Dalton's cheek and head, telling him to stay awake and not fall asleep as she looked him over. His eyelids were threatening to close as sleep beckoned him, not even disturbed by the announcement of the next match as it came and went. Dalton's wounds were minimal and she had long since healed them, but she felt compelled to search him magically, trying to determine if any other damage had been caused by the blood magic.

Tarrena was tending to the others on the team, but everyone in the room was mostly focused on Dalton.

"How are you feeling?" Jikia finally asked.

"Tired."

"Besides tired."

"...normal, I guess?" Dalton shrugged. "I can't even really remember the end of the fight."

"And that's worrisome," the older dragon said. "That energy that was coming out of you, that was dragon energy. *Celestial* energy."

Dalton raised his hands, half-shrugging, half-admitting defeat.

"I don't know what to tell you."

"That spell the Jjanye used was extremely powerful," Eclipse mused. "Maybe you had some kind of...reaction to it?"

"What did I *do*?" Dalton said.

"What do you remember?" Tarrena asked.

He let out a long breath, shaking his head slowly as his eyes went distant on the floor, trying to recall everything he could.

"There was a pain in my stomach," he said. "Like my ribs were trying to break and puncture it. And then it was impossible to breathe..." He closed his eyes. "I fell back. There was heat all around me. It was almost unbearably hot. And then...I don't know, I felt like I was half-floating. Like I was seeing everything through water. Then all the heat vanished and you guys came over and asked if I was okay. And the Jjanye was on the ground."

"You seemed to absorb the fog that made up the Shadow Veil," Hanyi explained. "I don't know how you did it, but you absorbed the magic."

"What even was that spell?" Mitoki groaned. "I've never heard of a Shadow Veil."

All eyes turned to Keito, who was near the door, his face pale and covered in a light sheen of sweat.

"It's a hallucinatory spell," he answered, his stance slightly shaky. "Everyone sees something different, but it's supposed to confront you with some kind of fear you harbor. It can feel so real, you truly believe it's happening in the moment."

"So how did Dalton get out of it?" Hanyi asked. "You didn't have any hallucinations, Dalton?"

He shook his head. "No, I didn't see anything." His face brightened in realization. "That's what that was for."

"What what was for?" Mitoki asked.

Dalton hesitated, looking to Keito to see if the demon would explain about the magically-reappearing vial in his pocket, but the demon just nodded, as if telling Dalton to explain to the others what had happened.

He started from the beginning, explaining the strange voice he had heard in the woods in the Beast Realm, and how the same entity had spoken to him after their first confrontation with Yokouro. As he was going into detail about how the vial continued to reappear in his pocket, even when he tried to get rid of it, he refused to meet eyes with the others in the team room, seeing their horrified expressions.

"So, before the match...I drank it," he concluded.

"You *what*?" Jikia snapped.

Eclipse punched him in the shoulder.

"You moron!" he barked. "A voice that is likely in your head tells you about a vial from some mysterious ally, and the vial *won't be destroyed*, you're not supposed to drink it!"

"I wasn't going to, but Keito convinced me!"

"Don't blame this on me," the demon said.

"How did you know it wasn't poison and it wouldn't kill him?" Mitoki asked, glaring at Keito.

"That's...difficult to explain." Keito stumbled over the answer.

"But that vial probably is what stopped him from hallucinating," Tarrena mused. "So someone knew that there was a Jjanye demon here who would likely use the Shadow Veil, and wanted you to have some protection."

"Someone from Yokouro's inner circle," Hanyi agreed.

"That doesn't change the fact that you should not be drinking mysterious substances that follow you around like a curse," Eclipse growled.

"We were going up against a very powerful demon who uses blood magic," Dalton protested. "I had to take the chance."

"Perhaps that was also the reason for the dragon energy," Tarrena said, turning to her mother. "Do you think that Vestera could have brewed a potion to help Dalton? Perhaps it allowed him to absorb the magic of the Shadow Veil and then redirect it back to the Jjanye demon."

Jikia's face scrunched in thought as she pensively shook her head. "It doesn't really sound like him," she said. "And the aura around Dalton didn't feel like Vestera."

"I'm sure, considering everything else going on, Vestera is watching out for them," the younger dragon insisted. "But he probably can't show up in person. What if—"

There was a knock on the door of the team room. Keito opened the door. He hesitated, but before he could greet the people on the other side, they pushed past him and into the room. Seven strangers stepped in, crowding the already small space. The woman wearing a tight pantsuit crossed her arms as she turned to Dalton.

"Guardian Teban," she greeted curtly. "My name is Anne. I am head of the Tournament Board for this stadium."

He shifted uncomfortably, not sure what he should say about what had happened in the ring.

"Is there a problem?" Jikia prompted.

"I should think so," Anne said with a scoff. "The power you displayed, Guardian Teban, is far beyond what we deem safe and acceptable for the competitors in this tournament. Naturally, seeing what you did today raised many concerns about the safety of the audience and your fellow Guardians."

"The magic being used in the ring—"

Anne raised her hand to stop Keito from speaking.

"Dalton Teban, your power level peaked at over twenty-eight thousand NRM at the end of that match."

Dalton felt his jaw drop, seeing his teammates respond in the same fashion. Even on some of Dalton's best days, the highest he had ever been measured was eleven thousand.

"This far exceeds what we deem safe for tournament participation," Anne continued.

A wave of confusion washed over Dalton. There was a part of him that was worried about disqualification from the Guardian Tournament. But when he realized that disqualification would free his time and energy so he could focus on finding Yokouro, relief spread through him. Until he recalled that the only reason he had faced the Jjanye demon in the first place was because the Tournament Board was working under Yokouro's influence.

"What are you saying?" Jikia asked. "Are you disqualifying

him?"

"Not yet," Anne said. "We need to run a few tests."

"What kind of tests?" Tarrena asked worriedly.

"Standard protocol with powerful combatants," she answered. She turned and nodded to two men who wore nametags and carried with them a box that rattled whenever it moved.

"Wait," Keito said, his brow creased, "you think he's a demon?" He pointed to the box. "I can promise you that he's not."

"We can never be too sure."

"What are you doing?" Dalton asked, trying to peer into the box as the man opened it.

"We're going to run some basic tests," he said. He pulled out a portable aura reader, extending it to Dalton. With a reluctant and worried huff, Dalton placed the reader in the palm of his hand and waited, watching the small needle encased in plastic spin rapidly, to the point where it was nearly vibrating against his skin.

For one minute, the device sat in his palm before numbers flashed across the screen at the bottom.

"Nine-thousand, nine-hundred and four," the man read.

"See?" Jikia said. "That's a normal level for him."

"They certainly weren't normal earlier," Anne said sharply. "Keep going."

The man pulled out a needle, unwrapping it as his associate removed three pieces of paper, placing them on a tray.

"Wait, what are you doing?" Dalton asked worriedly.

"Just a little blood draw."

He drew some of Dalton's blood, placing several drops over designated divets in the three papers on the tray. Once he had wrapped the needle and safely placed it aside, he motioned for Dalton to stand.

"Is this really necessary?" Keito groaned.

"This doesn't concern you, Keito," Anne warned.

"I need you to strip down," the man said to Dalton.

"Excuse me?" Dalton's eyes had shot wide, and Eclipse and Mitoki were taken aback by the request.

"Just to underwear."

"*Why?*"

"Protocol," was the only answer given.

"I can assure you that Dalton is human," Jikia said. "The energy coming from Dalton was dragon energy, not demon energy. There is no need to subject him to this."

"We must be thorough to ensure the safety of everyone in the stadium," Anne said. "After the tragedy of the Tournament

Slaughter, we cannot afford to leave things to chance. Dalton will submit to the qualification check if he wishes to remain a participant."

"As if you would disqualify us," Keito grumbled. "This is just petty entertainment for Yokouro, isn't it?"'

"Who?" Anne asked.

"Don't play coy," the demon sneered. "What is this, really? Some way for Dalton to feel humiliated? Uncomfortable? So he knows what a demon experiences?"' Keito rolled his eyes. "That sounds like something he would do. Well, as the demon of Team Dalton, I will only warn you once more. Back off. Go crawl back to his feet and wait for his next orders."

"How dare you speak to us that way?" Anne said, her tone rising in anger. "I would think you, of all Guardians, would appreciate safety measures being taken to prevent a massacre like before."

"A massacre perpetrated by the very demon you're allowing to sit in the VIP Box this round?" Keito challenged. "Don't play this game with me. You don't know it well enough."

"None of that changes the fact that Dalton's power level spiked to twenty-eight thousand NRM, which is well above what is acceptable," one man said sharply, pointing at Dalton. "And the magic he was using wasn't even human."

"Of course not," Keito said. "Because the Tournament Board was so corrupt as to let an underage Jjanye demon compete, which meant that Vestera Hizoku himself had to interfere with the match to keep Dalton from being killed."

Dalton turned to Keito in confusion, wondering if his teammate was bluffing to get Dalton out of the invasive examination.

"Is that what happened, Keito?" Anne asked.

"Yes, it was," he said. "Because Vestera's interference was also how I was broken out of the Shadow Veil, which is only cast with forbidden blood magic. Not that the rules actually mean anything to you."

Anne smirked. "Oh, they don't?" she challenged. "How about this, then? No outside entity or person is allowed to enter the ring during a match, even in the form of magic attack or summoning. Rule 27B. You're still in violation."

"That might be true," Hanyi started, stepping between Dalton and the Tournament Board, "but you're forgetting the crossing rules set by the Middle and Demon Realms," he said. "The Dimension Protection Council has granted any Demon Council demons within the classifications of 001 to 023 free access to any matters concerning the safety of the participants and bystanders of the

Guardian Tournament. Oh, and an underage demon is strictly forbidden in the rules, as well. It violates Section D, Rule Four, Sub Thirteen in Qualification for Participation."

The humans of Team Dalton were staring at Hanyi in surprise, having never seen him quite so confrontational or articulate before.

"Then why did you not call for a suspension in the tournament?" one man challenged behind Anne.

"Because we knew it would fall on deaf ears," Hanyi said. "Considering that you also allowed the team with forged papers to compete. You even saw him compete against another team where he used blood magic, but you still allowed him to remain in the tournament. No going to their team room and asking him to strip down for your examination. Would you like me to state all the rules that that violates? I can give you the numbers, if you need them," the wolf said with a smirk. "But, to me, it seems that all these reasons were cause enough for Vestera to consider the safety of the audience and participants, and be allowed into the ring in spite of Rule 27B. Wouldn't you agree?"

The members of the Tournament Board were glaring darkly at the wolf. One man's angry expression grew even darker as he responded.

"Rules have changed over the last forty years, you insolent wolf."

Hanyi barked a dark laugh.

"I thought you were just touting how you were trying to be proactive about safety in light of the Tournament Slaughter," he jeered. "Are you telling me the rules have changed to allow for more dangerous demons and magical practices?"

The members of the Tournament Board had fallen very silent. The quickly-mounting tension in the room was interrupted by a soft beeping on one man's wristwatch.

"Sounds like the next match is about to start," Hanyi said. "You better go make sure everything is going according to your master's plan."

Anne's jaw clenched tightly, her eyes turning colder the longer she glared at Hanyi.

She finally broke eye contact with him and jerked her head to the door. The members of the Tournament Board began to file out as the two examiners hurriedly packed their kit again. The one who had drawn blood turned to Anne, motioning to the tray of tests.

"He's fully human and shows no signs of using magical enhancers," he relayed.

"As if that matters, you moron!" she snapped, pointing out the door.

He gathered his case in his arms and scurried away as Anne left the team room, slamming the door behind her.

"What the hell was all that?" Mitoki asked, his eyebrows going high.

"I agree," Jikia said with a broken laugh. "Hanyi, I didn't know you could talk like that."

"Like what?"

"You knew the rulebook like you had just read it," Tarrena said. "And I've never seen you square up to someone like that."

"Oh, yeah," Hanyi said with an embarrassed chuckle. "When I first competed in the tournament, I got a ruling against me and wanted to find a loophole, so I memorized the entire rulebook. I doubt it really has changed much since the last tournament."

"It was a very different look for you," Tarrena said with a grin.

He placed his hands on his hips, huffing. "Are you saying it's hard to take me seriously?"

Tarrena lifted her fingers to indicate it *was* a little difficult to take him seriously.

"What was that examination they wanted to do?" Eclipse asked as Dalton sat back on the medical table in the center of the team room. "Why would they need him to undress?"

"It's something they do for demons sometimes," Keito explained. "They would have done a quick physical examination to be sure you weren't hiding any weapons or talismans, then they would ask you to point out your internal power limiters, then they would test those power limiters, and then they would scan you for any power limiters that you didn't disclose."

"That sounds horrible," Dalton grumbled.

"It's not pleasant," the demon agreed.

"May I have your attention please?" the announcer's voice said through the speakers. "The next match will be Team Kaize versus Team Francis. Will those teams please step into the ring?"

"Are you ready to go back out there and watch?" Jikia asked Dalton.

The leader of the team shook his head.

"I need a little more time." He sighed heavily. "Hey, Keito? That thing you said about Vestera interfering with the match. Did he really interfere, or were you just trying to stop the examination?"

"No, he really did interfere," Keito said.

"But that dragon energy didn't feel like him," Jikia insisted.

"I noticed that as well," Keito agreed. "But he definitely interfered. I was in the middle of a hallucination when his voice came through with the counter spell. Then, he told me to get the others out of the perimeter of the Shadow Veil, and he would help Dalton."

"Okay, but why?" Dalton asked. "Why not just suspend the tournament?"

"It does seem strange that he would just step in and do something like this but would remain completely silent to the council. Why interfere now?"

"Who's to say he has been completely silent to the council?" Keito challenged.

"You think someone is blocking his attempts at contacting Council? Or that his advice is not being heeded?" Mitoki asked.

"You've said it before. It's strange that Vestera isn't more active about the investigation surrounding the break in *his* seal."

Dalton wanted to discuss things with his teammates. He wanted to join in on the conversation and hypothesize what was preventing Vestera from interfering further. But his mind was stubbornly stuck on the thought that Vestera Hizoku, the most powerful creature in the universe, had interfered with the tournament to help *him*.

The end of the match with Datze was a blur, but the feelings coursing through his body at the time were still sharp in his mind. The fire that seemed to ravage his veins felt like the magic he had used in the Beast Realm against the hex beast, and once again, the thought terrified him. He wanted to convince himself that both instances were because of Vestera's interference.

But he knew, as both Keito and Jikia had stated, the magic did not feel like Vestera's.

There was a dark understanding sitting in the pit of his stomach.

As the match was called to Team Kaize, the members of Team Dalton were in intermittent discussions about what had happened in the ring and what they were going to do against their final opponent—Team Kaize. Worried about Dalton's evident exhaustion and the pensive look on his face, they attempted to strategize how to handle the final fight without asking his opinion.

Dalton did not try to join.

He felt separated from his team, as though he was watching them from behind a glass wall. He could feel something jabbing at the side of his head, as though something was calling to him, trying to get his attention. It was not like when the entity had called to him, or even a feeling of premonition. It was a nagging, cold feeling that he was desperately trying to remember something.

Dalton felt it drawing closer. And closer.

Without understanding his own actions, Dalton leapt off the table and ran to the door of the team room, startling the other Guardians. They called after him, dashing into the hall as well. Dalton ran to one of the service doors and yanked it open, ascending the staircases to get to the main halls snaking under the audience stands.

Even though he knew his teammates were calling after him, telling him to stop, he could not hear their voices. His feet moved of their own volition, his senses keenly in tune with which turns he needed to take next. He shoved open the door to the largest hallway within the stadium, running past concession stands and souvenir desks as some of the loitering audience members called out to him, thrilled at seeing one of the high-profile teams up close. Security tried many times to call to Dalton and his team, asking what was happening, but Dalton ignored everyone.

He made a sharp right and climbed another set of stairs, turning to the right again and running down the narrower hallway where there were no audience members, though three medical team officials were walking casually, eating their sandwiches, when Dalton pushed through them.

"Wait! You're not supposed to be up here!" one bellowed, only to be silenced when the other four members of Team Dalton ran past them to catch up with their sprinting leader.

Dalton's eyes locked on another door and he used his magic to open it before he drew close enough to touch it. He leapt the stairs two at a time, the narrower hall echoing with his labored breaths as he reached the top of the stairs to see another narrow hall ahead, leading to a larger hallway near the edge of the stadium.

He could feel it. Yokouro was in that hallway.

Unable to feel how tired his legs were or how his lungs burned, Dalton leapt forward again, his magic surrounding his hands and arms, ready to attack the demon, every sense sharply focused on the Old Blood Lord.

He could feel Yokouro's approaching step. His fists balled, ready to attack.

He surged into the hallway beyond, lifted his fist, and punched at the figure he somehow knew would be there.

A hand closed around his fist, so he ducked low and tried to use his other hand to punch at the figure's side. But another hand stopped him.

With speed and strength Dalton struggled to comprehend, his arms were crossed and pulled, one of his shoulders threatening to dislocate with the force of the tug. He grit his teeth, muttering a basic magic spell under his breath as he circled away, the magic that had surrounded his arms launching into the hallway to attack the demon.

But the light died away quickly from his magic and Dalton was left staring, not at Yokouro, but at a demon he had never seen before. The violet color of his eyes bore into the deepest parts of Dalton's soul, ripping secrets out of him that he had long buried. The power that radiated off the dark-haired demon had Dalton both desperate to run to safety, and eager to stare at the demon in awe.

It seemed like an eternity he was staring at the demon, his heart threatening to break his ribs with its rapid beats, but when he did turn away, he saw that the dark-haired demon was not alone. Yokouro was nearby, watching with a slight smirk, his silver hair nearly glowing against the black robes he donned. Just behind Yokouro was another demon Dalton had never seen before, but the mere sight of the bright, powerful hazel eyes caused his muscles to go weak in defeat.

As Dalton returned his gaze to the dark-haired demon that had intercepted his attack, his teammates stumbled into the hallway, stopping dead when they saw the three demons in front of their leader. Eclipse and Mitoki flanked Dalton while Hanyi and Keito remained in the hallway junction, unable to move for several long moments.

"Juki," Yokouro said, as if giving him permission.

Upon hearing the name, the fear in the human Guardians' stomachs turned to lead and their blood ran cold with terrifying understanding.

Juki did not move, but Dalton crumpled to the floor with an agonized groan of pain.

He felt as though the entire building had collapsed on top of him, pushing on his head and shoulders until he was flat on the floor, his bones straining under the weight. Eclipse tried to take a step forward to protect Dalton, but his feet were stuck to the floor. His arms flailed as he tried to maintain his balance, glancing down to see that his feet did not look different, but his shadow appeared somehow darker, and seemed to come off the floor to hold the bottom of his shoes tight. Mitoki was struggling with the same predicament.

"What are you doing to him?!" Eclipse demanded.

"Would you like to find out?" Juki's cold voice challenged.

"Stop!" Keito said, finally stepping forward and standing as far away from the three demon lords as he could while still remaining between them and the humans.

Before he could interfere or protest further, an invisible force yanked him to the side, sending him careening into the wall as Yokouro lowered his hand and shook his head in irritation. Hanyi went to Keito's side to help him up, but kept his eyes locked on Dalton.

The human Guardian was grinding his teeth against screaming, his breathing coming in labored pants as he pressed his forehead to the ground, the pressure on his body becoming almost unbearable. Eventually, the screams of pain erupted from his mouth, echoing in the hallway as the other Guardians watched on in stunned terror, unsure what to do to retaliate.

Mitoki tried to ignore Dalton's pained cries, studying Juki, taking in everything he could about the demon lord around the terror that refused to abate from his own chest. Juki's features were sharper than Acurala's, and Juki carried himself with more poise than his younger brother, but he seemed imposing, as though he took up the entire hallway, choking the air out of the space and blocking the lights from the ceiling. He was the tallest of the demons in the hallway, but he was not the one with the most visible power limiters—the demon with the piercing hazel eyes wore the most. The ear piercings seemed to swell and vibrate with the strain of holding back the magic the demon possessed.

Mitoki looked between Juki and Dalton, seeing the way his team leader's body bowed and strained against a pressure none of them could see. What startled Mitoki was not that Dalton was being pushed under the weight of the demon's magic, but that even though the pain appeared immense and overwhelming, Mitoki could not sense the magic being used. There was no static in the air, no heaviness in his lungs. The only way Mitoki knew that Juki was using his magic was due to Dalton's reaction. Otherwise, Juki's control was too precise to be noticed by those not directly under attack.

The panic coiled around Mitoki's chest tightened further.

"That's enough, Juki," Yokouro's calm voice said, barely audible over Dalton's gasping cries.

Juki did not move, but Dalton's body went slack, raspy breaths being drawn into his lungs greedily as he trembled on the floor. Both Mitoki and Eclipse felt their feet grow lighter and they were able to rush to Dalton's side, trying to pull him off the floor.

Without another word, Juki walked past the Guardians, Yokouro chuckling as he studied the shaking Guardian, following Juki. The third demon trailed Yokouro, casting a quick glance over the Guardians and causing all of them to shrink away, an understanding falling over them that they were standing next to impending disaster.

Once the third demon had passed, he turned around to face them, his hazel eyes meeting each of theirs.

"Good luck in the finals," he said gently. "You will need it."

He turned to follow the other demons as they silently continued down the hallway.

None of the Guardians dared to follow.

They watched as the three demons disappeared out of sight around a corner, their footsteps barely echoing as they walked. No one dared to move until the hall was silent apart from Dalton's labored breathing.

Hanyi and Keito rushed to help Eclipse and Mitoki as they tried to straighten the shivering Dalton.

"Dalton," Hanyi said, placing a hand on Dalton's back. There was no response. "Dalton!"

Still, he said nothing, not even flinching to acknowledge he could feel Hanyi's hand on his back.

"May I have your attention please?" the announcer's voice called over the speakers. "We are about to begin the finals of the first set of Round Two of the Guardian Tournament!" The stadium rumbled with the thunderous applause from the excited audience. "At this time we ask that Team Dalton and Team Kaize report to the ring to commence the match."

The cheering rattled the roof of the hallway, but Dalton appeared not to hear the announcement.

"Dalton!"

Still, there was no response.

Chapter Eighteen

"What the hell happened?" Jikia snapped, waving a hand in front of Dalton's face as he was sat heavily in the team box. She held up her hand to the announcer, asking for a few more moments before the start of the match, much to the irritation of the eager audience.

"Honestly, I'm not sure," Eclipse said.

"Why did he go running off like that?" Tarrena asked.

"Seems he sensed Yokouro and just took off," Hanyi said.

"You saw Yokouro?"

"Yokouro and Juki Kage," Mitoki said. He turned to Keito. "And the third one?"

"That was Rutu, the other Kage Lord."

Eclipse rolled his shoulder absentmindedly, staring at Dalton as Jikia rifled for something under the bench. Dalton had been shaking and incoherent even as they had forced him to his feet and dragged him down to the ring, which unnerved Eclipse more than the lingering thought of the eyes of the Kage Lords.

"What the hell did they do to him?" he asked, turning to Keito and Hanyi. "I could sense that they were dangerous, but I couldn't sense their power."

"I didn't, either," Mitoki seconded. "The amount of control he had...I didn't know that kind of precision was possible with magic."

They jumped and turned when they heard a crunch and a gasp, followed by spluttering as Dalton jumped to his feet, blinking the water from his eyes.

"What the hell?!" Dalton snapped, angrily trying to rid his face of the clinging droplets.

"Pull yourself together and finish the tournament," Jikia growled. "You can panic later. We don't have time for a breakdown right now."

Dalton blinked his eyes repeatedly, his heart starting to slow as he realized he was out of the hallway and under the scrutiny of the impatient audience in the stadium. He looked over his shoulder to see Team Kaize waiting in the arena with expectant expressions.

Letting out a long breath, he turned to his teammates.

"We need to have some kind of team meeting after this," he grumbled.

The five Guardians stepped out of their team box, trying to get their heads back into the tournament and forget that they had just confronted the demon responsible for the previous massacre, and the two demons who were said to be as powerful as Vestera Hizoku himself. The screaming audience and rotating cameras displaying their faces around the ring did nothing to focus them on the match. They were more worried about what Yokouro was doing lurking in the hallways of the stadium.

Team Kaize straightened as the others stopped across from them.

"You look a little shaken," Kaize said, raising an eyebrow. "Did you see something you weren't supposed to?"

"Do you work for Yokouro?" Dalton growled.

Kaize made a face. "Not so much *Yokouro*."

"The Kage Lords, then?"

His opponent nodded, pointing at Dalton. "Now you've got it."

"Hanyi," Mitoka whispered, leaning over to the older Guardian. "If this is Yokouro's team, and Yokouro is focused on Dalton, why are they all glaring at Eclipse?"

Hanyi turned to study the other members of Team Kaize and was startled to see the four members behind Kaize staring at Eclipse with dark fire in their eyes.

"Please state any conditions for the fight," the announcer called. "Now that there are two demons in the ring, exclusive fights between the demons are possible."

Dalton's heart stopped. He glanced among the five members, startled to hear there was a demon on the team. Keito was also studying the members, unable to discern which of them was a demon.

"Sure," Keito said, knowing that the demon on the opposing team was one of Juki and Rutu's elite disciples, making them a near-impossible opponent for his human teammates.

"No," the man on the far side of Team Kaize said. "I do not accept."

Keito leaned toward him.

"You're not even supposed to be outside of the Demon Realm," he snarled.

The other demon leaned forward in turn. "Well, I *am* here. If you have a problem with that, take it up with management."

"Are there any other conditions for the fight?" the announcer asked again, worried about the audience turning violent with how impatiently they were waiting for the fight to commence.

"I have one," Kaize said with a grin. "Eclipse Retani will be allowed to remove his limiters and fight in his truest capacity."

The others of Team Dalton turned to Eclipse, confused. Dalton's face was sympathetic, but also confused as he did not know what the condition meant to his teammate. Eclipse hesitated before turning to Kaize.

"I can refuse," he said.

"No, you can't." Kaize raised a finger to point back to the VIP Box as the announcer's voice rang through the ring.

"The Tournament Board has approved the condition!" she called. "Are there any other conditions?"

"That my demon teammate be allowed to use his wings. Not his full animal form. Just his wings."

"Is there anything we can do to counter the condition about Eclipse?" Keito asked Hanyi urgently.

The wolf hesitated, his eyes frantically darting back and forth along the ground as he thought.

"I don't think so. Not once the board approves the condition."

"What is he asking of you?" Dalton asked Eclipse.

"I...I wear limiters that you don't know about. I don't like to take them off because I tend to lose myself a little. If I truly have to fight like that, I might be dangerous to you and the audience." He turned to Hanyi. "Does that change our ability to fight the condition?"

"If it were any other Tournament Board, yes," he said. "But I'm sure Yokouro already knows what to expect."

"The condition has been approved by the Tournament Board," the announcer said. "Team Dalton? Do you have any conditions?"

Dalton turned to Eclipse once more. His teammate slowly shook his head, looking defeated and worried.

"If there are no further conditions, you may begin!"

The audience roared to life again, but neither team moved. Eclipse remained stubbornly still, looking among the faces of the opposing team, trying not to let his fear and anxiety swell to an unhealthy level.

"All eyes are on you," Kaize said with a wicked grin.

The demon on the opposing team slipped the coat from his shoulders and tossed it aside. He arched his back forward, his shoulders twisting as he gave a small cringe and two leathery wings tore through his flesh, stretching back to showcase his enormous wingspan as he waited for Eclipse to follow through with the other condition for the fight. The audience was practically vibrating with anticipation, many staring and pointing at the wings extending from the demon's back as the cameras panned around the ring. Everyone could feel that it would be an intense match and they were almost unwilling to blink, should they miss anything.

Eclipse shared a nervous look with his teammates and then began rolling up his right sleeve.

"Listen," he started, "should anything happen and I'm unconscious, or you need to knock me unconscious, I have a personal doctor that Master Genbuki can call for me." He pushed his sleeve past his elbow, revealing a band of leather strapped tightly to his arm just below the joint. He undid the buckle and eased it away, two metal barbs leaving bleeding pinprick wounds on each side of his arm. "And if I become a danger to the audience..." he turned to Keito, his gaze dark with the unspoken question.

Keito nodded once, even without knowing what kind of danger Eclipse would pose.

Eclipse pocketed the leather band, a noticeable tremor in his hand as he rolled up his other sleeve to remove the other limiter. His breathing was labored and heavy, each exhale ending in a soft growl that sounded inhuman. Before the second limiter had been removed, the magical energy around Eclipse had grown to encompass everyone in the ring. Dalton's hair stood on end, his nerves humming in response.

Eclipse barely managed to put the second limiter in his pocket, his teeth bared as he turned his eyes on the opposing team.

Dalton had to step back, startled at the sheer power radiating from Eclipse, and admittedly worried about the way his eyes had changed from their normal hazel to a deep burgundy color.

Eclipse's frame shuddered, magic radiating to dance in sparks along the barrier that protected the audience. The cameras focused on Eclipse, and though the members of the audience could see the crazed look on his face, it only served to excite them further with the promise of an unforgettable match.

Eclipse growled, his shoulders arching as his back began to contort. In similar fashion to the demon on the other team, two large wings ripped through the fabric of his shirt, stretching high above Eclipse. They were unlike any wings Dalton had seen before, with four joints giving them a jagged appearance and feathers only lining the far edge of the black appendages, with scaled, leathery skin stretched over the rest of the wingspan.

The crowd was on their feet in excitement, while the others of Team Dalton backed away.

"Eclipse?" Mitoki asked worriedly.

"I don't think he can understand you," Hanyi said.

"He's an Antiquan Angel," Keito murmured, his eyes wide in shock.

Dalton could hardly recognize his teammate, his brain trying to adapt to seeing Eclipse with longer fingers, longer teeth, large wings, and flat horns that pressed against the side of his head, somewhat hidden by his hair as they dipped behind his ears. He had heard of Antiqua-Kel, a realm attached to the Realm of Darkness and classified as a sub-realm, but since all sub-realms were out of jurisdiction for the Dimension Protection Council, he had not bothered to learn much about the various sub-realms attached to the five realms he knew.

He wanted to ask Keito more, but when he heard Kaize chuckle darkly behind him, he was reminded that they were in the middle of a match.

"He's all yours, Ra-Jea," Kaize said.

Ra-Jea took a step forward, his wings spreading to grab Eclipse's attention as he locked onto the movement.

"Follow me, Little Antiquan Angel," Ra-Jea crooned, stepping backward as Eclipse stalked toward him.

"Eclipse can't take that guy, he's a demon," Dalton urgently said to Keito. Keito was about to speak when Ra-Jea lunged at Eclipse, arms outstretched. Eclipse grabbed both of the demon's outstretched arms, flipped him over his head, and twisted his body to land heavily on the demon, his wings extending to press into the demon's neck.

Ra-Jea smiled and turned over, getting to his feet and spreading his wings wide, taking to the air. Eclipse was instantly after him, the multiple joints on the wings allowing him greater dexterity as he shifted to follow the demon's quick movements.

An arm wrapped around Dalton's neck as another figure tackled Keito to the ground, the others of Team Kaize surging forward to start the fight once their teammate was in the air with Eclipse.

"I'd say he's doing just fine," Kaize laughed in Dalton's ear.

Hanyi immediately interfered with the panther that had leapt at Keito, tackling him and rolling him away from the demon. But as Keito was standing to help, another member of Team Kaize stepped in front of him, raising his fists. The demon looked over the new opponent, wondering if he was also a demon. It had unnerved him when he had not immediately spotted Ra-Jea as a demon, which made him wonder if Juki and Rutu were disguising others on Team Kaize.

Mitoki had his dagger brandished, waiting for the woman stalking around him to make the first move. She continued to circle, only occasionally lunging forward for a quick punch before backing away. The strange pattern allowed Mitoki too much time to throw worried glances up at Eclipse, who was rapidly flying around the ring with Ra-Jea, their midair battle gaining the most attention from the audience.

The others of Team Kaize were not the only danger Team Dalton had to navigate. Ra-Jea was throwing small, handleless blades at Eclipse, and though he could easily dodge the attacks, the blades were falling to the ring and striking the barrier that protected the audience. Once the crowd realized they were not in immediate danger from the knives, their cheering became even louder, ignoring those fighting on the ground as even the cameras focused on the flying combatants.

When Ra-Jea swooped low and collected two blades off the ground, the force of his wings pushed both Dalton and Kaize to the ground, creating another obstacle in what was already proving to be a difficult match for the overwhelmed Team Dalton.

Dalton was not as quick in getting to his feet as Kaize. He tried to throw a fist at Kaize's abdomen, but the frantic attack was poorly executed. Kaize turned, looped his knee around Dalton's arm, and fell into a crouch, grabbing Dalton's wrist and pulling, straining his bones.

"Looks like my master was correct." Kaize's voice was filled with condescension. "You boys just aren't ready for a mission of this magnitude."

"Really?" Dalton groaned, straining his arm a little further as he swung his legs to kick Kaize in the back of the head. The other man released his arm and Dalton scrambled to his feet. "What else did your master tell you about us?"

"Oh, all kinds of things," Kaize said. "They said that these poor humans were too weak and too ignorant to grasp the full scope of what is happening. Judging from how pitiful your fighting techniques are right now, clearly they were right. You're too overwhelmed."

"Then why show so much interest in us?" Dalton challenged. "Clearly there must be something they want from us."

"Of course. That power that you refuse to use without having it forced out of you." Kaize's cold grin widened at the worried look on Dalton's face. "I know that's weighing heavily on your mind. What you did to Datze."

"You don't know how I feel."

"Then you're not overwhelmed?" Kaize asked, his eyebrows going high. "You're not distracted? You're not obsessing over the powerless feeling that overcame you when you caught sight of my masters?" He tutted gently. "You don't need to lie to me, Dalton. I felt the same way the first time I stood in their presence. The best way to cope with that is to just submit."

"They're trying to destroy the human realms," Dalton snapped. "They want to see all humans dead."

Kaize dropped his head back and let out a boisterous laugh, finally unsheathing the dagger strapped to his thigh.

"You truly are ignorant, aren't you, Dalton Teban?"

On another side of the ring, Mitoki's opponent had taken advantage of the young Guardian's distraction and leapt forward to wrestle Mitoki's dagger from him. Mitoki hardly realized what had happened, more focused on Eclipse as his teammate circled away, a large gash in his side evidence of one of the blades making contact. When Mitoki got to his feet again, he saw the woman waving the dagger in front of her, grinning triumphantly.

"How have you managed to stay alive as a Guardian all this time?" she taunted.

Mitoki fell into a defensive stance, but turned when he heard the audience scream in terror. The strength of Eclipse's magic attacks had grown. One of the attacks had missed Ra-Jea completely, colliding with the barrier with enough force to create a small fissure. The heat and sparks from Eclipse's magic washed over the audience, though the barrier reformed before serious damage was dealt to the bystanders.

The woman across from Mitoki groaned.

"Pay attention!" she sang, lunging forward and almost landing a very painful gash to Mitoki's shoulder. He circled away, trying to focus on defeating his opponent. Unlike before, she continued her attacks, swiping his dagger at him with more precision than he expected, considering her prior tactics. He had to block out another pained screech from Eclipse, desperate to finish his fight quickly.

Keito spared another glance at the rest of the team, worry clear across his features. In most respects, the people they were fighting—with the exception of Ra-Jea—were not difficult opponents. But Team Dalton was struggling. Keito knew it was due to the accumulation of stress over the previous days, and being thrown off-balance by seeing Juki and Rutu for the first time.

They were also heavily focused on Eclipse's fight above them.

His brief observation period was interrupted by his opponent. The man moved far too fast to be a human, but Keito could also feel by the limited magic he was emitting that the other man was human. His opponent leapt forward, raising a fist to punch Keito's gut, but the demon was easily able to drop his stance and catch the fist before it made contact.

The power behind the punch caused Keito's eyes to go wide and his joints to lock as his body buckled. He felt some of the ground fold under him as his feet were pushed backward, despite the slower punch. Keito grit his teeth, pushing the other man back before defensively circling him.

"What the hell are you?" he whispered, knowing he could never be sure what resources Juki and Rutu had at their disposal.

The man laughed, blinking once, his eyes changing from bright blue to piercing hazel.

"Possession," Keito said. "I see your fighting style now, Rutu."

"Still astute," Rutu laughed through the man's body. "But it did take you much longer than it should have to figure me out."

"I know you're not attacking me seriously," Keito said. "So I have to wonder about your motives. What are you trying to do here, Rutu?"

"Flexing my muscles a bit," Rutu said, shifting the human body around as though he was stretching. "I'm out of practice."

Rutu lunged forward, resuming the fight in the limited human body.

The audience's attention had remained locked on the thrilling mid-air battle taking place between Eclipse and Ra-Jea. Once, Eclipse had managed to catch the retreating Ra-Jea by the ankle and bring the demon to the ground. But Ra-Jea had recovered, seeming unfazed as he took to the air again, scooping up some of the daggers that had fallen to the ground. His lowered presence had caused another distraction for the other members of Team Dalton, allowing Ra-Jea's associates to continue pestering them. After all, they had been ordered to mentally push Team Dalton while Ra-Jea focused on Eclipse.

In truth, the demon was bored with the match. He had long since pinpointed every weakness in Eclipse's style, and knew he could end the match in an instant. He had hoped that an Antiquan Angel would provide a small challenge for him, but he could see that Eclipse was far beyond any rational thought. His powerful magic had taken over his mind, causing him to fight based only on movement and perceived threat. He was unable to create a strategy. He was unable to read Ra-Jea's moves. He was acting entirely on instinct.

Ra-Jea was beginning to think that the match was a waste of the skills had honed under Rutu's brutal training.

"Now, Ra-Jea," Juki's voice told him.

Trying to suppress the relieved roll of his eyes, Ra-Jea pushed forward with a powerful stroke of his wings. He reached back to the four small daggers he had tucked into his waistband. They were small and circular, fitting perfectly between his fingers as he tilted his wings, veering from chasing the Guardian. Eclipse caught the movement and immediately turned to follow, surging forward to chase Ra-Jea.

On the ground, Keito watched in confusion as the possessed human began stumbling, his eyes rolling, his limbs limp at his sides. Taking Rutu's apparent distraction as an opportunity, Keito looked up to Eclipse's fight. He could both see and feel the difference in Ra-Jea, and saw their positions far too late to stop the attack he could see coming.

Ra-Jea fell back, allowing Eclipse to close the distance between them and grab Ra-Jea's ankle as he had before.

The demon turned in the air, ducking Eclipse's arm before slashing at his chest with the four small daggers between his fingers. Shallow gashes were sliced across his chest, causing him to retreat from the pain. His screech had caught the attention of everyone in the ring, and they watched as Ra-Jea removed one of the daggers from his fingers and drove it deep into Eclipse's shoulder. In the same movement, he turned his body, his wing colliding with Eclipse and causing him to lose concentration as he dropped several feet in the air, before catching himself instinctually.

Ra-Jea surged after him, diving like a bird of prey to rake the three remaining daggers across one of his wings, ripping long gashes in the leathery skin and causing Eclipse to falter, struggling to remain airborne.

Eclipse's hand grabbed onto Ra-Jea's ankle again, pulling himself into the air with the demon's momentum. Ra-Jea turned, smiling at the predictability. With one dagger in his right hand, his left grabbed Eclipse's shirt and hauled him closer. His right hand raised and connected with Eclipse's face.

No one had seen the small dagger in his fingers, but everyone was on their feet screaming as Eclipse screeched, pulled away from Ra-Jea, and plummeted to the ground, colliding with an audible thud. He curled on the ground, holding his face as he growled, one of his wings broken and the other flapping weakly in response to the pain.

"Oh my god!" the announcer screamed into the microphone, mimicking the response of the audience. "Eclipse just received a very violent attack to the face…um…he does not look good. Do we call the medical team? Do we…"

She trailed off, surprised by the sudden amount of movement in the ring.

The audience had also gone silent, watching as Team Dalton swiftly began defeating their opponents.

Mitoki launched at the woman, grabbing the back of her neck and forcing her to double over as he kneed her in the gut. When she was stunned, he grabbed his dagger from her hand and struck her across the face, holding the hilt. She fell to the ground, unconscious.

Hanyi ignored the long gashes on his side as he wriggled away from the panther, ducking his head and clamping his teeth on the underside of the panther's neck. He resisted the urge to shake and kill the flailing animal, managing to withstand the claws that found him and tried to push him away as the panther became more desperate. But when his struggling slowed, Hanyi released the panther and straightened to stand on two legs.

He rushed to Mitoki, who was looking between the groaning and shivering Eclipse, and the gloating Ra-Jea still flying in the air above.

"Have a plan?" he asked the youngest member.

Mitoki watched Ra-Jea fly around the ring, looking over the stunned and terrified faces of the audience, grinning to himself. Mitoki knew that getting Ra-Jea out of the air would be crucial to securing a defeat from the demon.

With a glance around the ring, something reflecting the lights caught his attention. He ran to the handleless dagger, picking it up clumsily with no regard to the cuts it left on his fingers. He focused on the lingering aura on the blade, tracing it back to the demon as he circled the ring. Placing his other hand over the blade, he poured his own magic into the weak aura connection between the blade and the demon, strengthening it, building the connection until even the audience could see the glowing strings of magic reaching from Mitoki's hand toward the flying demon.

When Mitoki knew he could make a hit, he drew his arm back and threw the knife back at Ra-Jea, using the magical tether he had built to give it enough power to reach the flying demon.

Ra-Jea turned and caught the blade, clicking his tongue on the roof of his mouth in disappointment. He was about to turn the blade and throw it back at the young Guardian when a sharp band of magic wrapped around his wrist, chaining him to Mitoki.

Hanyi wrapped his hand around the magical tether and poured his own magic into it, strengthening it further and causing it to slice into Ra-Jea's wrist. Once Dalton had knocked out his opponent, he, too, joined Mitoki and Hanyi, the three Guardians pulling on the flying demon, trying to bring him closer to the ground.

Ra-Jea's powerful wings pulled them forward as the demon struggled.

"Boys, you have no idea who you're screwing with!" Ra-Jea warned, ready to remove one of his extra power limiters when Juki's sharp voice warned him against it.

Mitoki grit his teeth and added even more magic to the tether, causing it to glow brightly, slicing open the hands of the three Guardians trying to keep it attached to the demon. With strained bellows, the Guardians pulled sharply, bringing Ra-Jea closer to the ground and reviving the roaring of the audience.

Ra-Jea's wings flapped in struggle, trying to keep him at a distance from the Guardians. But when he heard no further orders from Juki, he assumed that his job was done and it was time to surrender to the Guardians. His struggles became slower, and though his pride and the rigorous training he had endured told him to fight the Guardians until he was victorious, he allowed them to pull him roughly to the ground.

Before he could get back to his feet and say he surrendered, the three Guardians were on top of him, beating him back to the dirt with angry fists.

Keito was still struggling with the possessed man on the other side of the ring when Ra-Jea was taken out of the air. The man Rutu possessed had pinned him, his hands secured around Keito's neck.

"What...was the point of that?" Keito growled, trying to fight the altered strength of the hands choking him.

"You do not need to worry, Keito," Rutu assured. "This is a very delicate process. We were careful in our decision."

"Enough screwing around!" Keito finally pulled the hands from his neck far enough to sit up sharply, his head colliding with the possessed man's. Keito flipped them both, pinning Rutu to the ground.

"You're so adorably predictable," Rutu chuckled. "You fall to pieces when someone around you gets hurt. You'd much rather take the punishment, wouldn't you? Old habits die hard, I suppose."

"Shut up," Keito snarled, punching the man across the face. "You sick bastard. What do you gain from all this?"

"Do I need to gain something?" Rutu asked. The man's eyes were rolling in their sockets. It was obvious that he would have been unconscious if the demon lord's magic was not coursing through his veins, and Keito became worried that he would do permanent damage to the human if the match continued much longer. "You should trust me more, Keito."

"Trust *you*?" Keito snapped, yanking him closer by the front of his shirt. "This is some kind of lesson, isn't it? Some sort of metaphorical bullshit to put us on a certain track. Just *tell* me what is going on, Rutu!"

The man went limp as Rutu's consciousness left him and Keito was left staring at the unconscious, bruised face of the man that had once been possessed, his anger and fear churning coldly in his stomach.

Hearing the announcer call that Team Dalton had won the match with the final surrender of Ra-Jea had him leaving the unconscious man on the ground and rushing to the other side of the ring. Ra-Jea was angrily pushing the Guardians aside as he walked away, meeting eyes with Keito once before walking toward the nearest door, leaving his unconscious teammates to be collected by the medical team.

Once Keito was certain that Ra-Jea was no longer a threat he rushed to his teammates, who had gathered near Eclipse, though were approaching cautiously. The medical teams had stormed into the ring, ready to assist, but they were also hesitant to approach the growling, shaking Eclipse. Most of the audience was on their feet, their cheering about the final match abating as they watched curiously.

Dalton took another nervous step forward, seeing crimson pooling around Eclipse's head, blood pouring from between his elongated fingers.

"Eclipse."

"Be careful, Dalton," Hanyi warned.

"I…don't sense him," Mitoki said slowly. "I don't think he's in control of himself. It's just the Antiquan Angel side of him."

Jikia and Tarrena joined the Guardians, motioning for the medical team to remain at a distance, worried about their safety.

"What should we do?" Dalton asked, turning to his teammates, at a loss.

"He said that he has a doctor we can call," Hanyi said. "We should call Master Genbuki and ask him what to do."

Jikia immediately pulled out her phone, dialing for Eclipse's godfather.

One of the medical staff took a nervous step forward, crouching to look at the blood pouring from Eclipse's covered face.

"Broken wing, lacerations to the face, shoulder, and chest," he listed back to the others. "We need to get him treated quickly and stop that bleeding. I'm worried that there's damage to the eyes."

Dalton's heart fell at the words.

"Dagger still embedded," the man continued, motioning his hand toward Eclipse's shoulder.

He had drawn too close. Eclipse leapt forward, perceiving the closeness as another attack. With a shrieking roar, he tackled the medical staff, but as he lifted his hand to strike the terrified man, Keito's arms locked around Eclipse's torso, hauling him backward. Hanyi acted fast to pull the man away from the struggling Guardians.

Eclipse thrashed against Keito's hold, his unbroken wing striking the demon several times as Keito maneuvered him to wrap a hand around Eclipse's neck, being very careful as he squeezed.

"You're safe, Eclipse," he said, straining against the frantic strength Eclipse possessed. Eclipse contorted and struggled, growling and gnashing his teeth, blood littering the ground as the movement aggravated his wounds.

Straining to keep his teammate still, Keito's magic began to surround Eclipse, wrapping around his body before coiling over his face. As the spell took effect, Eclipse slowed in his struggles and his head dropped. The medical team rushed to lay Eclipse flat, checking his breathing and heart rate as Keito stepped away, pressing a hand to his temple.

"Shit," he groaned. "Those wings are strong."

"He's unconscious now," Jikia relayed to Master Genbuki, lowering her hand from blocking her other ear as she continued the conversation. "Are you sure? The injuries look severe. Do we need an ambulance?"

Dalton stepped closer to Eclipse, catching glimpses of his teammate as the medical team moved around him. The gashes along his shoulder and chest were shallow and were quickly glossed over. But the blood pouring from his face made it difficult to see how severely he had been wounded. He turned to Jikia, wishing he could hear what Master Genbuki was saying.

"Okay, thank you. We'll be back soon." Jikia hung up the phone and turned to the medical team. "Since he's an Antiquan Angel, he has a specialty physician being called to care for him. I'll sign his release from the tournament," she told them.

"We'll stop the worst of the bleeding in his face for now," the head of the medical team said. "Do you need a medical transport?"

"Yes," she said. "My daughter and I will accompany you."

The medical team began calling in the codes for Eclipse's transportation as Jikia turned to the other Guardians.

"Master Genbuki is calling Eclipse's doctor. They are going to treat him at the house. This is something that has happened before, so they know what to do. One of the medical transport vans for the tournament will take him there. Tarrena and I will go with the medical van back to the house and meet you there."

"What about the post-fight briefing?" Tarrena asked. Jikia hesitated.

"I forgot about that," she murmured. "Someone has to go with the medical van."

"I'll go," Keito said. "I need to get back to the house anyway. I need some of the medicine I left there."

Dalton had been worried about the pale look and sheen of sweat on Keito's face before the finals, but as the adrenaline of the fight wore down, he could see that the demon was also trembling, his face even paler and his eyes bloodshot.

"Okay," Jikia said. "Tarrena, you and Keito go with Eclipse. I'll go to the meeting for the team rankings and meet you back at the house as soon as possible. You boys drive Eclipse's car to the house."

With tired, nervous nods from everyone, Jikia turned and left the ring. Tarrena and Keito trailed the medical team as a transport stretcher was brought out to bring Eclipse to the van. Dalton, Hanyi, and Mitoki followed the group in taking Eclipse out of the ring until their teammate was loaded into the back of a large medical van. Keito and Tarrena climbed inside with the two medical team members working to stop Eclipse's bleeding, and the van drove away from the stadium.

The three remaining members of Team Dalton were silent as they trudged through the halls of the stadium back to the team room, gathering their things and searching through Eclipse's jacket for the keys to his car.

"We might have a problem," Mitoki said slowly, looking over the keys in the palm of his hand.

"What?" Dalton asked, startled by the interruption to the silence.

Mitoki lifted the keys.

"Can you drive a manual transmission?"

Dalton stared at the keys, his exhausted brain taking a few moments to comprehend what Mitoki was asking. Troubled, he turned to Hanyi, who raised his hands peacefully with a laugh.

"Hey, don't look at me."

~∧~

"Rutu, some of the tricks you come up with are truly amusing," Yokouro said, shaking his head with a smile. "Just stepping into the middle of the fight and waiting for Keito to figure it out was exceptionally entertaining."

Rutu sighed, not nearly as enthused.

"Clearly I'm out of practice," he said. "I used to be much stronger with possession. I could keep full hold on a host even when distracted." He glared at Juki upon saying the last word. The older Trade Master grinned.

"I was just testing you."

"Ra-Jea looked like he was bored through that fight," Yokouro noted. "I suppose that wasn't much of a challenge for him. But his precision was quite astounding. No wonder you favor him, Rutu."

"He still has a lot to learn," Rutu said with a shake of his head. "I'll need to talk to him about not letting his boredom break his form."

"By the way, I'm adding an extra fee for his services outside the Demon Realm," Juki added.

Yokouro waved the statement away with a scoff, turning away from the windows above Hall C where they had watched the final match. "Fine, fine," he grumbled. "I'll pay it as long as he didn't do more damage to Eclipse than previously discussed."

Yokouro began walking down the hallway, leading Juki and Rutu to the back of the stadium, where the Kage's drivers were waiting for them.

"We should go back home for a few days," he declared.

"And then come back?" Rutu asked. "Why?"

"We can't very well leave Elder Renard unattended long in this realm, and I need to be sure that everything went according to plan with Eclipse."

"Then why return at all?"

Yokouro sighed. "There are some things I need to finish up at home. And I need you both with me to be sure Vestera doesn't try to interfere." He started down one of the dark, narrow staircases. "Also, I need to kill three people."

"Who?" Juki asked, startled.

"Doesn't matter," Yokouro answered. "I'm three people away from my next marking. I need to get that out of the way so the pain doesn't catch me off guard."

Juki turned over his shoulder at Rutu with an exasperated expression. Rutu returned the irritated glance before jerking his head toward Yokouro, reminding Juki that they could not leave the ambitious Yokouro alone for long.

Chapter Nineteen

When Dalton, Hanyi, and Mitoki finally stumbled their way into Eclipse's house, they were met with confused and worried glances.

"What took you so long?" Jikia asked incredulously. "Even I made it back here before you."

"I had to figure out Eclipse's car," Dalton said sheepishly.

"Yeah, any damage to Eclipse's car was Dalton's fault," Hanyi announced.

"I would have been fine if I didn't have so many backseat drivers!" Dalton snapped.

"How could I not say something when the engine kept *dying*?"

"I'm sure it's fine, but…we had no idea what we were doing," Mitoki added. He glanced over the drawn faces filling the living room. "Is the doctor here?"

"He's with Eclipse now," Master Genbuki said.

"Dr. Grant has been with him for about forty minutes," Saki elaborated, her voice tight with barely-restrained tears. "We haven't heard anything since he closed the door."

"Where's Keito?" Dalton asked.

"He was in rough shape," Tarrena answered. "He said he was going to lie down until his medicine took effect. Hopefully, he'll start to feel better soon "

Hanyi stepped over to Saki and placed a gentle hand on her shoulder. "How are you holding up?"

Saki forced a thin smile. "I don't know," she said. "There was so much blood …"

"Some wounds bleed more depending on where they are on the body. That doesn't necessarily mean that the wound is severe," Dalton said. She shot him a skeptical glance. "I'm not just saying that to make you feel better. It's true."

"It is," Jikia seconded. "The wounds to the face probably look worse than they really are."

Even though Saki dropped her gaze and her shoulders, she did not seem at all eased. Hanyi squeezed her shoulder.

"Would it help if I changed into a wolf and let you hug me?"

She let out a quiet laugh, though her eyes began to swell with tears. Pursing her lips, she nodded tightly, the tears tumbling down her cheeks. As promised, Hanyi shifted into his wolf form and climbed onto the couch, allowing her to wrap her arms around his neck and bury her head into his fur.

Jikia raised her hands in exasperation.

"Does anyone else have injuries?" she asked. "I need to do something or I'm going to make myself sick with worry."

The others had their scrapes and bruises treated silently as everyone sat in the living room waiting for news. Saki's tears eventually abated, though Hanyi stayed next to her, allowing her to lean into his fur whenever her stress-fueled exhaustion became too much. Keito joined them in the living room once Dalton and Mitoki had been treated, though he only offered quiet nods and affirmations that he was alright before lapsing into the same worried silence.

Twenty minutes after Dalton, Hanyi, and Mitoki had arrived at the house, the front door opened suddenly, startling them. Dalton was ready to leap forward and attack the man who rounded the corner, but stopped when Saki jumped from her seat and ran to him, wrapping her arms around him tightly and burying her face in his chest.

"*Kan-na...*" she sobbed.

"It's going to be alright," Eclipse's older brother said, hugging her tightly and leaning down to kiss her head.

"Thank you for coming, Erik," Master Genbuki said, his quiet voice the only indication of his own worries about Eclipse's condition.

"I apologize for not coming sooner," he said, keeping his arm around Saki as he walked further into the living room. "I was in a seminar and only just listened to your message fifteen minutes ago."

Erik's resemblance to Eclipse was obvious, but Erik's hair was longer and shaggy about his face. Coupled with his simple suit and thin frame, he looked much older than his likely age.

"You must be the rest of the team," he said, walking toward them. "And Jikia and Tarrena. It's a pleasure to finally meet you. I'm Erik Retani, Eclipse's older brother."

"Dalton Teban," Dalton introduced himself, extending his hand.

Erik politely introduced himself to the entire team, though he seemed distracted, and even hesitated completely before shaking Mitoki's hand. He turned away from the youngest Guardian to look between Saki and Master Genbuki.

"Any word on Eclipse?"

"Dr. Grant is still with him," Master Genbuki answered indirectly.

"What happened to him? How bad are the injuries?"

Dalton opened his mouth to explain but Hanyi let out a high whine, still in his wolf form. Dalton turned to him, confused.

"What?"

Hanyi barked, jumping off the couch and going to Saki's legs, brushing them before gently biting the sleeve of her sweater.

"What?" she repeated Dalton's question.

Keito sighed. "Believe it or not, he's hungry," the demon said. "Saki, do you think you could find something for him to eat?"

"Oh...sure, I guess," she said, following Hanyi as the wolf whimpered in excitement and ran toward the kitchen. The clattering of claws on tile was followed by a loud thump and Saki worriedly asking if Hanyi was alright. Despite the gravity of the situation, the others found themselves smiling and rolling their eyes at Hanyi's antics.

"He'll keep her occupied for a while," Keito told Erik. "She's very upset. There is no reason for her to hear the details."

Erik let out a long breath and took the seat Saki had previously occupied.

"Thank you."

"The condition of the match was that he fight in his Antiquan Angel form," Dalton explained.

"He told me that he could fight a condition like that because he becomes a danger to everyone around him when he takes off those limiters," Erik said. "Why did he agree?"

"Unfortunately, he didn't have a choice. The Tournament Board is corrupt," Mitoki said. "You knew that he was..."

Erik nodded. "Of course," he said. "Hell, my parents knew before he was born that he was going to be an Antiquan Angel. It runs in the family, and when my grandmother died, we knew the next child born in the family would be the next Antiquan Angel. That's how it works."

"Then you're not an Antiquan Angel," Dalton deduced.

"Nope, as human as they come," Erik said. He leaned back in his seat. "Seems you were right, Master Genbuki."

"I wish I hadn't been," the older man murmured.

"Right about what?"

"That Eclipse needed to face his fears and learn how to control his powers," Erik clarified. "Eclipse has always had a great fear of the extent of his abilities. He used to be enthusiastic about training and learning how to do all the magic afforded to him as a sub-realmal bridge, but after the death of our parents...he changed."

"I would think he would be more motivated to master those powers," Mitoki said.

"It was more complicated than revenge against the one who killed our parents," he said. "He knew that his powers were the reason our family was targeted at all. He figured if he didn't learn them, no one would know, and he could keep those around him safe. Naturally, that means that he has no control over himself when those limiters come off. He never learned."

"We're pretty sure our enemy counted on that," Dalton said quietly. "Seems that he knows all our weaknesses."

"And who is this enemy that's been doing research on my brother?" Erik prompted.

"A notorious demon," Keito answered. "I'm sure you have questions, but it is dangerous to know the information."

"I want to know who is threatening my brother," Erik insisted.

"...then we can talk about it once we know Eclipse will be alright."

Erik dropped his head, rubbing his hands together nervously.

"Is he going to be alright?" he whispered to no one in particular.

"He's very strong, and even more stubborn," Master Genbuki said. "He'll be fine. And he'll rally back with a vengeance."

The words seemed to soothe those waiting in the living room. They fell into silence, trying to keep their breathing calm and their minds from assuming the worst about Eclipse's condition. Dalton continued to replay the moment he saw Eclipse plummet to the ground, his brain buzzing with questions about what Yokouro gained from the attack, if Eclipse was permanently damaged, and if there was anything he could have done to stop the attack on his teammate.

With the heavy silence engulfing the house, the sound of a door opening down the hall was almost deafening. Everyone in the living room was on their feet, watching the opening to the hallway as footsteps approached. Saki and Hanyi left the kitchen, also eager to hear the news on Eclipse.

Dr. Grant, a gaunt, tall man with long hair pulled into a loose ponytail walked slowly into the living room.

"How is he?" Dalton prompted.

"He'll recover quickly," Dr. Grant answered, his tone quiet and monotone. "Most of the wounds were not deep enough to cause severe damage, and his Antiquan magic will speed up his healing. However, the damage to his face, while also not as severe as I first believed, was more substantial than his other injuries."

"How bad?" Hanyi asked.

"It is very unlikely he will regain sight in his right eye."

Tarrena sat down heavily, her legs giving out from under her. Saki let out a choked sob, prompting Erik to move toward her and hug her tightly.

"Was the attack focused on the eye?" Keito asked. When Dr. Grant nodded, he continued. "But no brain damage? It did not go deep enough to puncture the skull?"

The doctor shook his head. "No. In fact, I'm a little surprised it did not go deeper. Clearly there is damage to the optic nerve, but the bones around the socket were intact, and I did not see any injuries to the brain. But even with magic healing, the eye was unresponsive. He might be able to see the difference between light and shadow in that eye, but I'll need more extensive tests on his brain function once he heals to know with any certainty the extent of damage."

"May we see him?" Mitoki asked.

Dr. Grant nodded. "He's unconscious and the room is not a pretty sight, but as long as none of you are squeamish..."

Everyone turned to Saki, who sniffed back her tears and nodded tightly.

"I want to see him."

Erik kept his arm tight around the teenage girl's shoulders as everyone walked down the hallway toward Eclipse's room.

Dalton was near the back of the group as they walked into the room, his head down. He was kicking himself for wondering about Eclipse's future as a Guardian with the extent of his injuries. Even as he walked into the bedroom and saw the bloodied rags, the open box of bandages and salves, as well as the bloodied, amputated wings that were stretched on a tarp on the floor next to the bed, Dalton could not help but be worried he would have to retire Eclipse after such a brutal attack.

Eclipse was asleep on the bed, partially covered with his sheets, his torso and face heavily bandaged, his right eye covered with a lightly-bloodied bit of gauze. His limiters were strapped tightly to his arms once again. Dalton had thought they were a training mechanism, or some sort of support band when he had seen them on Eclipse before, but the bands seemed more menacing now that he was armed with the knowledge of the power they held at bay.

Saki stepped around the amputated wings and sat on Eclipse's bed, taking his hand gently and squeezing it as fresh tears overtook her. It was difficult for everyone to find space in the room around the wings, forcing all of them to crowd around Eclipse's bed.

"Is he..." Mitoki looked between Eclipse and the wings on the floor. "Is he no longer an Antiquan Angel?"

"He is," Dr. Grant said. "He will be one until he dies. There's no way to change it. His wings are always present, but they exist on an energy level that he does not normally use. The bands keep that magic from spiking and causing them to manifest. He could eventually master how to bring his magic level down slow enough to allow the wings to retreat, but until he is able to do that on his own, the wings must be removed surgically once he returns to his normal magical pattern."

The room fell into pensive silence, everyone looking over Eclipse on the bed, lost in their own thoughts about what had happened to their teammate. When Dalton could no longer stand to stare in silence at Eclipse, he turned to Dr. Grant, trying to sound casual as he spoke.

"What does his recovery look like?"

The doctor took a deep breath, his eyebrows going high.

"Knowing him, fast," he answered. "Like I said, most of the wounds were quite shallow. Almost surprisingly minor. The biggest adjustment will be his eye." He shoved his hands into his pockets. "As for the second half of the tournament, he should be physically healed by that point thanks to his Antiquan magic. But I don't recommend he fight until he is able to properly defend himself with sight in only one eye."

"I'm not worried about the tournament right now," Dalton said.

"But it is something we're going to have to address," Jikia added.

"Not today," Dalton said, nodding to Saki, who was crying quietly while holding Eclipse's unresponsive hand.

"Juki?" Yokouro called as he walked down the main staircase of his palace. Even though he had asked the Kage Lords to return to his home and help protect him from Vestera's likely wrath, he was nervous about the two older demons wandering his palace. He figured the best way to curb his anxiety was to find them and show Juki what he had been hiding.

Despite knowing Juki for nearly his entire life, Yokouro was still apprehensive and nervous about how the older demon would react, never wanting to upset Juki too severely.

After searching the gardens and their guest rooms, Yokouro finally followed their aura to the greeting salon near the main doors of the palace. He ignored the maids and guards bowing to him as he passed, pushing open the heavy double doors and stepping into the salon.

Juki and Rutu were standing near the ornate, marble fireplace, speaking with a younger demon Yokouro was surprised to see.

"Kakuri," he greeted. The younger DeVastes demon turned and bowed his head. "Is everything alright?" Yokouro asked, noticing the tension in the youngest demon's shoulders and the nervous glancing between Kakuri and the Kage Lords, obviously interrupted from deep discussion.

"Everything is fine," Rutu assured. "Kakuri was simply worried that you would not be pleased with the way he changed the palace. I assured him that all was well."

"Kakuri," Yokouro said fondly, placing a hand on the younger demon's shoulder. "I left the palace to you. You could change it however you wished. There is no need to be concerned."

Kakuri nodded once, his eyes still averted. Yokouro pulled the younger Old Blood Lord into a hug, Kakuri returned the embrace briefly before pulling away and retreating two steps.

"I should return to Lynna and the boys," he said.

"Give them my best," Yokouro said, squeezing Kakuri's shoulder before Kakuri walked away, his head high but his eyes cast to the floor. Once Kakuri had disappeared from sight, Yokouro's brow furrowed.

"Is he really alright?"

"He's fine," Rutu assured. "It's a lot for him to process, having you here. He needs time to adjust."

"I'm sure he's not the only one. The first Open Court with the DeVastes nobility is probably going to be hell…" Yokouro let out a long sigh, shaking his head of the thought as he turned to Juki. "I was looking for you, Juki."

"Me?"

"Would you accompany me for a moment?"

Juki's brow furrowed, confused by the unusual request. He glanced at Rutu, who nodded with a mysterious smile, silently telling Juki to follow the younger lord. Juki motioned for Yokouro to lead the way, falling into pace beside him.

"Is there something you need to discuss with me privately?" he asked as they began ascending the palace stairs, stopping at the second-floor hallway and turning in the direction of the lower lords' state rooms.

"Not exactly," Yokouro said. "I want to show you something."

"Sounds ominous."

"I hope you don't see it that way," Yokouro said with a laugh that did not completely mask his concern. "I can't even begin to tell you how difficult this was to keep hidden from you for the past two months."

"Now you're making me nervous," Juki said. "Does Rutu know?"

Yokouro quirked an exasperated eyebrow. "What do you think?"

"Of course he knows," Juki groaned. "Was he upset when he found out?"

"It's difficult to tell with him," Yokouro admitted. He motioned to the door just ahead of them in the hall. "Just in there."

Juki turned his attention to the door. He was not worried about dealing with whatever Yokouro had in that room, but he was concerned that he did not know what to expect—and that Rutu had not already told him.

He stepped up to the door and pushed it open, unsurprised by the ornate furniture of the stateroom. What startled him was a familiar face sitting on the foot of the bed, fidgeting nervously. When the younger demon saw Juki, he stood, smiling.

"*Rau-ka*," he greeted, using the familiar term for the oldest son of the family.

"Acurala?"

Acurala began walking forward as Juki looked over his shoulder at Yokouro.

"What is going on?"

"I can explain myself," Yokouro assured, motioning to Acurala. "But say hello to him."

Juki let out a short breath before going into the room and hugging Acurala tightly. The younger Kage lord closed his eyes against his tears, the tension in his body easing at the realization that Juki was not angry. Despite knowing Juki extremely well, he had been worried that his brother would be upset at Yokouro pulling such a risky resurrection behind his back.

When Juki broke the hug, he shook his head in disbelief, looking over Acurala's form.

"I can't believe it…" he whispered.

"It's been an adjustment for me, as well," Acurala said.

"You've been back for two months?" Juki asked. "What have you been doing? Why didn't you come find me?"

"I was trying to strengthen my powers again. And Yokouro needed help."

Juki let out a long breath. "I am so sorry, Acurala. I—"

"No," Acurala interrupted, raising his hand. "You don't have anything to apologize for."

"I knew he was vengeful, but I really didn't—"

"Juki, stop," Acurala insisted. "You can't keep taking responsibility for everything that happens to me. I was the one who got myself killed. It wasn't your fault."

"Yes, it was," Juki said. "But not to worry. I got appropriate justice for you."

Acurala laughed darkly. "I have no doubt."

Yokouro remained in the doorway, knowing he should not intrude on the moment between the reunited brothers. Yokouro had not known Acurala had been killed until days after Juki had retaliated against his assassin, but he could never forget the way Juki had changed after that day. Of all the Kage siblings, Juki and Acurala were the closest, and when Acurala was killed just for the purposes of delivering a blow to Juki's pride, Juki had blamed himself to the point of near self-destruction. Yokouro could not let go of the image of the demon he thought to be infallible breaking apart, and it had unsettled him more than any of the horrors he had experienced in his life.

Seeing Juki with Acurala again relieved him—especially since Juki did not seem upset about Yokouro resurrecting the younger Kage without first consulting him.

But he could not stop the tension invading his muscles when Juki turned to him.

"Now, do you want to explain what the hell happened?"

He let out a sigh and stepped into the room, closing the door to keep the maids outside from eavesdropping.

"I apologize for not consulting you first. I...wasn't certain I could pull it off."

"You've never completed a resurrection on someone who had been dead for so long," Juki noted. "I'm surprised you were able to do it."

"When I saw the way Rutu reformed that bone hex beast, it gave me an idea," Yokouro explained vaguely. "I needed someone I could trust. Someone who understood what it meant to be an Old Blood Lord, but I also knew that if I started ordering you to do things out of the realm, Vestera would get nervous." Yokouro motioned to Acurala. "With Acurala working with us, you and Rutu can stay in the background more and I still have the muscle and tact I need."

"Well, not nearly as much muscle," Acurala corrected. "My powers are nothing like they used to be."

"It's still more than enough," Yokouro said.

"I cannot believe you were able to keep this from me."

"It was not easy," Yokouro groaned. "Naturally, Rutu found out the day after I raised Acurala, and I had to beg and bribe him not to tell you until I found a good way to do so."

"I'm going to have a talk with him about that," Juki groaned. Acurala snorted a laugh.

"Knowing Rutu, he'll just shrug." Acurala's face brightened. "How are your children?"

Juki's own smile grew. "They're doing well. Kree is actually set to be mated in the new year."

"Mated?" Acurala gasped with a broad grin. "I'd love to see her and give my congratulations."

"I'm sure they would all be happy to see you," Juki said.

"I'm going to leave you two to catch up," Yokouro said, taking the opportunity to slip out of the room before Juki could ask him more pointed questions about how he had obtained Acurala's bones, and how many people he had killed in order to perform the necessary blood magic to resurrect the younger Kage. He knew he could not avoid the conversation forever, but he wanted more time to prepare how he wanted to respond.

When Yokouro rounded the corner, he barely contained his startled jump at seeing Rutu leaning against the banister, waiting for him.

"Why don't you go see Acurala?" he asked.

"I'll see him later. I want to give Juki some time with him."

"Were you coming up here to see if Juki had torn me a new one?"

"No," Rutu said, falling into step beside Yokouro as they returned to the main halls of the DeVastes Palace. "But I did want to hear his reaction."

"You understand why I raised Acurala, yes?"

"I do. And in many ways, it was a very tactful move," Rutu said. "But I don't particularly approve of you using the Kage name and reputation the way you have been."

"I'm sure I don't need to remind you that you *told* me I could use your resources," Yokouro said, his shoulders straightening. He did not like that his own name was limited by the fear demons held of the DeVastes Clan, and it hurt his pride that he had to resort to using the Kage's name to get what he wanted. But he was not about to let Rutu see his guilt over his actions. "You pledged yourself to me. You both did."

"Yes, we did," Rutu said. "But be cautious, Yokouro. We are only trying to help you. And there might be a time when the Kage name will hinder you more than help you."

"You've been quite heavy with your cryptic musings the last few days," Yokouro grumbled. "If you are trying to help me, then *help* me. I have three prisoners in the dungeons. I want them brought to the courtyard so I can get this damn mark over with."

~/\~

"Welcome home, my lord," a young female servant greeted, bowing her head and reaching out to take the cloak the master of the house unwrapped from his shoulders. She smiled brightly as the warm, ruby eyes turned to her and a smile came to his lips. Vestera Hizoku always had a way to make her smile.

"Thank you, Elise," he said. "It is rather late. Have you already had your supper?"

"No, my lord, not yet," she admitted, taking a step forward to take his travel cloak. He pulled it closer to his chest, grinning.

"Please, go enjoy your supper before it gets much later. I believe we can all hang our own cloaks for once."

She bowed her head. "Thank you, my lord."

As Elise walked away, Vestera walked into a small room off the salon that stored the travel cloaks for the lords and ladies of the Hizoku Palace. He placed his among the others and closed the compartment door, absentminded, straightening his red robes as he walked through the hallways, his eyes distant on the marble floor despite how high he held his head.

"Vestera?"

He raised his gaze and smiled at Syien, the second chair of Demon Council and one of his most trusted friends and advisors. Syien was a special class of demon that was nearly extinct, with a serpentine lower body that allowed him to stand over Vestera—one of the few demons taller than the dragon.

"Good evening, Syien," he said tiredly.

"Ooh, sounds like you had a good day," Syien noted worriedly, waiting for Vestera to pass him before coiling his body around to keep pace with the dragon. "You left quite suddenly. Has something happened?"

Vestera sighed heavily.

"There is much we need to discuss."

"Did you find the energy disturbance?"

"Unfortunately."

233

Vestera turned down one of the smaller hallways that led toward the dining hall. Syien's eyes went wide as he lifted his hands in exasperation.

"Are you going to elaborate?" he prompted. "You can't just say something like that and walk away."

"I am not walking away. I am—"

He stopped when he entered the large, domed room that was the dining hall of his palace. At the long table sat over a dozen familiar demons, who turned to greet him when they caught sight of the dragon. He could tell from the mostly-empty plates and the stewards patiently stationed around the room that the main branch of Demon Council had just finished their supper.

"I was not expecting you to arrive for a few more days," Vestera noted, walking toward the head of the table. "I am sorry I was not here to dine with you."

"We know we're early, but with everything going on, and the energy disturbance, we figured it would be best to come early," Maqui said.

Vestera could only offer a tired smile as he sat at the head of the table, shaking his head and holding a hand out to the steward who stepped forward to ask if the dragon would care for his own plate. Seeing the action, Yamyhi narrowed her eyes.

"Have you eaten at all today?"

"No," the dragon admitted. "I am alright. I am just not hungry."

Syien nodded to the steward and motioned him forward, telling him to bring the food regardless.

"Now, where were you today?" Kanuo, another female of the main branch of Demon Council, asked curiously. "Investigating the energy disturbance?"

"It was particularly bad in the north. I haven't seen storm cells that big in centuries," Maqui noted. "And the static. There are at least five wildfires that seemed to spark from nothing but the magic in the air."

Vestera was staring distantly at the grain in the table, deep in thought. When the others noticed his distraction, their own worries grew.

"Vestera?" Syien prompted. "Where did you go?"

"Truthfully, Rutu contacted me."

"Rutu?" they all echoed. "I thought he was trying to avoid you after causing that ripple."

"Yes, the one that caused panic in four realms," Syien grumbled. "I hope you're bringing him in to stand trial for that. He knows better."

Vestera remained silent, and the continued distance in his gaze was becoming alarming to those around him.

"Vestera..." Yamyhi called his attention. The dragon closed his eyes, took a deep breath, and nodded.

"Today has been taxing," he said. "I had to interfere in the Guardian Tournament for Team Dalton. It seems that Yokouro has managed to manifest a full physical form again and he is starting to make earnest moves against Team Dalton."

"So, Juki and Rutu have been training him in secret," Syien deduced, shaking his head irritably.

"When Rutu contacted me, he admitted to everything. Training Yokouro, the ripple, breaking their agreements with Demon Council...everything."

Randinclough's brow furrowed. "That seems like an extremely foolish move from one so notoriously brilliant."

"He needed help," Vestera said.

While the statement seemed simple enough, Demon Council knew that Rutu asking for help was a very, very bad sign. Rutu Kaneaka-Kage was the one that all demons, both friend and foe, turned to for help. If he reached out to Vestera, it meant whatever had happened was beyond the scope of even his power.

"With what?" Yamyhi finally whispered.

"With Yokouro, to start," he said. "Yokouro ordered them to use a Jjanye demon *and* a Trade Mercenary against Team Dalton in the tournament."

"And they couldn't say *no*?" Syien growled, ignoring the horrified gasps and angry growls from the others at the table.

"Were any of the Guardians hurt?" Kanuo asked quickly. "Is Keito alright?"

"They're all fine. But Eclipse did sustain an injury to his face. It's unlikely he will regain sight in one of his eyes."

The outrage at the table grew, making it uncomfortable for the steward to place the plate of collected food in front of Vestera. He bowed away quickly, trying not to share worried glances with the other stewards about the conversation.

"This is too far, even for the Kages," the youngest member of Demon Council grumbled.

"They are in violation of at least a dozen rules and agreements we have with them," Kanuo seconded. "We cannot let them get away with this kind of interference. They may be powerful, but they should know better."

"Wait," Syien started, his face pinching in thought as he turned back to Vestera. "He knew that we would be upset at hearing all this. But he contacted you and *confessed*?"

Vestera closed his eyes, leaning back in his chair, his food untouched.

"What is it that he needs help with?" Maqui pressed.

"We have a very real threat on our hands, bigger than Yokouro," Vestera said. "I thought that the energy disturbance through the land right now was merely the result of Rutu causing the ripple. We were all caught so off guard because the Kages have been quiet for centuries, but what we failed to realize was that the intensity of the ripple was unexpected. Rutu lost control of his powers in the moment he created that distraction for me."

"Rutu losing control is not something we can speak so casually about," Randinclough said.

Vestera lifted a hand. "He's still in full control, but he was out of practice after centuries of quiet. And that one moment of him expending too much magic opened a door. He unintentionally pulled a resurrection."

"So *he* was the one who raised Acurala Kage," Yamyhi deduced.

"No," Vestera corrected. "Yokouro resurrected Acurala, but Rutu did open that exact same door. The residual energy from Acurala's own resurrection added fuel to the fire, so to speak. Rutu raised Kawakara Kage."

The table was immediately sent into a terrified uproar. Two of the demons stood, their eyes wide and their jaws dropping. The stewards around the room, trained in keeping a stoic face during all sorts of conversations, also recoiled from the information, turning to one another, their faces paling.

"We need to get rid of him immediately!" Kanuo declared. "He is going to tear apart the entire realm!"

"Everyone, please settle," Vestera said, his tone barely louder than his normal voice. Gradually, the noise decreased, silencing completely when Syien spoke.

"...does Juki know?"

Vestera slowly shook his head.

"Is Rutu going to tell him?" Randinclough asked.

"I think he's trying to find a way to do so," he said gently. "This is an extremely delicate matter. For everyone."

"No," Yamyhi insisted. "Vestera, you can eliminate Kawakara. I doubt Rutu will do it without first consulting Juki. You are the only one with enough power to do it before he wreaks havoc across the land."

"How could Rutu resurrect Kawakara?" Maqui said. "That's not something you can *accidentally* do."

"There is a very complex web around Yokouro's fight with Dalton, and it does include Kawakara Kage, as impossible as that may sound," Vestera said. "Add in Rutu's incredible power and it's very easy for events to take place out of order. That is what makes this situation so delicate."

"How could Yokouro's fight with a *human* create the need for the psychopath that is Kawakara Kage?" Syien grumbled.

"Believe me when I tell you you don't want to know," Vestera said.

"What do we do?" Kanuo asked. "Do we go after Kawakara?"

"No," Vestera said. "Everyone is to remain clear of Kawakara. No one try to kill him. No one try to handle it on their own."

"He's going to tear the land apart," Syien hissed. "You're going to let him run free?"

"I'm going to do something I'm sure I will regret," Vestera corrected. "I'm going to leave this to Juki."

"You know this will be too much for him," Yamyhi whispered, shaking her head.

"That's why I'm going to leave it to him. Right now, this is the best distraction we can ask for. If Juki is busy trying to deal with his resurrected father, and Rutu is left to run the Kage Territory alone, that will give Yokouro less opportunity to order them after Team Dalton, which will allow the humans time to collect their bearings." Vestera lowered his gaze. "I'm going to put my feelings for Juki and Rutu aside and use this to my advantage."

Chapter Twenty

Dalton woke more exhausted than when he went to bed. He had tossed and turned all night, trying to calm his mind, though he continued to jerk awake at the thought of Eclipse plummeting to the ground. His mind was a jumbled mess of terrifying encounters with powerful demons, but the one that always caused his panic to spike was the image of his teammate falling like a rock toward the dirt.

He angrily shut off the alarm on his phone, burying his head under the pillow in a childish attempt to rid himself of the headache knocking angrily behind his eyes.

Rather than lay in bed in pain, he pulled himself upright, dressed, and went into the kitchen in search of painkillers.

Saki and Master Genbuki were already awake, cooking breakfast together in silence, their own exhaustion evident in their slumped shoulders.

"Good morning, Dalton," Master Genbuki greeted, not turning from the stove.

"Morning."

"Are you hungry?" Saki asked. Dalton's heart broke for her when he saw the pale face and red, swollen eyes of the fiery teenager.

"No, thank you."

"You need to eat something," Master Genbuki said. "You haven't eaten since before the tournament yesterday."

"I know, but my stomach is really jumbled right now," he said. "I will take any painkillers you have to offer, though."

Saki rummaged through one of the cabinets, bringing a bottle to Dalton before going to retrieve him some orange juice.

Master Genbuki turned off the stove, scooped the scrambled eggs into a serving bowl, and brought it to the table, setting it down in front of Dalton before grabbing a stack of plates and setting them next to the food. Dalton took his painkillers and watched as Master Genbuki and Saki placed the fresh fruit, sausage, and pancakes on the table.

Master Genbuki sat next to Dalton with a sigh.

"How are you holding up today?"

Dalton shrugged, shaking his head.

"Honestly? No idea."

"There's nothing weak about being frightened, Dalton," Master Genbuki said. "If you weren't frightened right now, after everything that happened yesterday, it would mean you're stupid."

"I can rationalize all I want," Dalton muttered. "But that doesn't make this any easier to deal with." He rubbed his eyes roughly. "I just keep thinking that all this is my fault."

"Why do you think that?"

"I should have found a way to fight the condition that he fight as an Antiquan Angel. I should have just stayed put instead of running after Yokouro. I should have…"

"Dalton," Master Genbuki interrupted.

"I should have protected my teammate. That's my job as the leader of this team."

"Eclipse is a grown man. You can't take responsibility for him. If you really want to place blame, hell, place it on me. I should have pushed for him to train his Antiquan magic more so he could keep control of himself."

"No, I should have done more for him."

Master Genbuki could not stop his exasperated laugh.

"Sometimes you have to accept that things are just out of your control," he insisted. "My mother constantly blamed herself for the tumor that cost me my sight. She felt guilty that she did not have the money to seek treatment earlier. And no matter how many times the doctor told her that it was not something she could have noticed beforehand, she blamed herself until the day she died. My body decided to grow something that, in the end, left me blind. She couldn't have changed that."

"But I could have changed what happened to Eclipse…"

"No, Dalton, you couldn't have," he insisted. "And even if you could, which you could *not*, it's done now. You can't wallow in hypotheticals."

"But if this is just the beginning of what Yokouro wants to do, then I need to know how to stop him from doing worse."

"I think you're taking the wrong approach," Master Genbuki said.

"How so?"

"Yokouro was not attacking Eclipse. He was attacking *you*," he said. "Look at how torn up you are about this. He knows you feel protective and responsible for your team. Causing injury to you is not going to hurt nearly as much as causing injury to them. He wants you to tear yourself apart with guilt. He knew something about Eclipse and he used that to his advantage to strike the sharpest blow he could. He's feeling you out, Dalton."

"Well, it's working," Dalton grumbled.

"Yokouro's move was actually quite brilliant."

"How do you figure that?"

"Whoever he hired to attack you was clearly given orders not to severely damage Eclipse to the point where he would not recover."

"He's lost sight in one eye."

"And he's had a trainer who is *blind*, who has trained him how to fight blind." Master Genbuki's smile grew. "Again, he's feeling you out, Dalton. He's jabbing at you, taunting you, seeing how far he can push you. It's just like a dog or a child pushing boundaries to see when you finally explode in anger, or break down."

Dalton's brow furrowed as the words reverberated through his mind.

"So, if I may give you some advice, don't fall for it," the older man said. "Eclipse is going to be just fine. So pick yourself up and don't let Yokouro see how shaken you are."

"Morning," Mitoki said in the doorway. He trudged forward, sitting heavily in the seat next to Dalton. "Where is everyone else?"

"Keito and Hanyi went out earlier today, but they didn't say where," Master Genbuki answered. "Jikia and Tarrena went to file a follow-up report about Eclipse's injury with the Tournament Board. Erik is still asleep. I had to move him out of the chair in Eclipse's room around dawn." Eclipse's trainer motioned to the food on the table. "Are you hungry?"

"No."

"Too bad. You're both going to eat something," he grumbled. "Get a plate, get some food, and I expect you to have eaten something within the next hour. And don't try to pull any tricks on me. I *will* know."

The two smiled tiredly, reaching for the plates on the table, being sure to only put a little on their plates.

"I can make you some coffee," Saki offered.

"That would be great, Saki," Dalton said.

Mitoki reached across the table for the bottle of painkillers as Dalton passed him the glass of orange juice knowingly.

The youngest let out a long sigh and poked his fork at the eggs on his plate. "Do you think Eclipse will be okay?" he whispered.

"Dr. Grant seemed confident he would heal very quickly," Dalton answered indirectly. "I wish I knew more about Antiquan magic. I don't know how much that will speed the healing. And even then, who knows how quickly he'll adjust to only being able to see out of one eye."

"You seem to be forgetting who his trainer is," Master Genbuki said with a quiet laugh, standing from the table and moving toward the refrigerator.

"Do you think he'll be able to stay a Guardian?" Mitoki's question was so quiet Dalton barely heard it. He closed his eyes, taking a deep breath.

"I've been worrying about that all night," he whispered.

"How long do you think until he wakes up?"

"I'm awake."

Everyone in the kitchen whirled toward the doorway. Eclipse was leaning against the frame, looking almost as pale as his bandages.

"*Kan-na*," Saki choked. Abandoning her coffee mugs, she ran to him and hugged him tightly. He gripped the doorframe, trying to keep his balance while his other hand held her head gently in the hug.

"Be gentle, Saki," Master Genbuki warned, sensing Eclipse's weakness.

Saki's arms only tightened around Eclipse as he leaned his head down and kissed the top of her head.

"I'm alright," he said.

"The hell you are," she hiccupped.

"I am," he insisted. "Just a little tired. Some coffee would help."

Even though she struggled to pull away from him, she nodded and returned to preparing coffee for the Guardians. Eclipse moved away from the door, mis-stepping and causing Mitoki to leap forward and guide Eclipse to one of the chairs. Eclipse only resisted the help once before allowing Mitoki to guide him.

"Just take it slow," Dalton suggested, his hands raised to help if needed.

"I promise I'm alright," he repeated. "Master, what the hell did Dr. Grant give me? I feel drunk."

"He put you on a very heavy sedative," the older man said. "He'll be by in a few hours to check up on you."

Eclipse nodded, closing his eyes and heaving a deep breath as he gingerly rubbed his face in an attempt to wake himself. He flinched a little when his fingers grazed over the bandages, but passed off the action with a groan of frustration. He turned his eye on his teammates.

"You both look like you just saw me rise from the grave," he jeered.

"It feels a bit like we did," Dalton admitted.

"You don't need to be worried. I'll be fine."

"And you don't need to act as though you haven't been affected by what happened yesterday," Mitoki said.

"This?" Eclipse asked, motioning to the bandages. "I'll get used to it. I'm still breathing, that's what counts."

Mitoki was about to speak when they heard the front door open.

"We're home! Hope no one is sleeping!!" Hanyi's voice rang loudly through the house. Even with the grim feelings around the dining table, the Guardians could not help but laugh quietly. Master Genbuki turned, grinning broadly and pointing in the direction of the door.

"Have I mentioned that I like him?"

"We're in the kitchen, Hanyi!" Saki called.

A few moments later, Hanyi and Keito entered the kitchen, followed by Jikia and Tarrena. Hanyi put his arms around the dragons' shoulders.

"We found them wandering around outside and they followed us home. Can we keep them? *Please?*"

The dragons were about to play along with Hanyi's joke, but everyone's eyes fell on Eclipse.

Tarrena quickly stepped forward, placing a tentative hand on his shoulder as she approached.

"You're already up and about," she noted in surprise.

"Can't very well stay in bed all day," Eclipse said with a shrug. "I need to get up and get moving. That's how I'll get my strength back."

"Just make sure you allow yourself to recover before you start building strength again," Keito warned.

"Oh, right, look who's talking," Eclipse teased. "As I've already said, I promise that I'm alright."

"Are you certain?" Jikia pressed, sitting next to Dalton as Tarrena took the seat next to Eclipse. "I just came from meeting with the Tournament Board and they asked if you were going to withdraw due to your injuries."

The team went silent, looking among one another before their gazes settled on Eclipse. Dalton would have preferred Eclipse make the decision, not wanting to speak for someone who had suffered such a traumatic injury. The bandaged Guardian met eyes with everyone staring expectantly at him before his gaze settled on Dalton.

"If you're thinking of withdrawing after all this, then I've misjudged you."

"Eclipse, the tournament is not important compared to your health," Dalton insisted.

"You think I chose this job for my health?" Eclipse asked with an incredulous laugh. "The tournament is just a part of this job, now.

It's the reason we're together as a team and, at the moment, the tournament is our best link to Yokouro. If we're not there, I have no doubt Yokouro will massacre another stadium. So no, we're not withdrawing."

"Eclipse, this is a serious injury," Mitoki said. "You can't just brush it off."

"I'm not brushing it off. I'm just reminding you all of why we're doing this to begin with."

The silence that fell over the table was filled with tension. Clearly everyone wanted to tell Eclipse not to compete in the tournament after the attack, but they also understood that withdrawing from the tournament was not an option they could safely take. Eclipse chuckled brokenly, shaking his head.

"You surprise me," he said. "You're more worried about the eye than the fact that I'm an Antiquan Angel."

"Well…I figured we would discuss that a little later in the day," Hanyi said.

"How did you manage to keep that a secret?" Mitoki asked. "I mean, at least Dalton should have known."

"I did know…sort of," Dalton said. "I knew he had a special classification, but I didn't know what that meant."

"I'm surprised I didn't know," Keito said. "I've met Antiquan Angels before. But I did not pick up any sense that you were one."

"What exactly is an Antiquan Angel?" Mitoki asked. "Isn't Antiqua-Kel a sub-realm?"

"The Antiquan Angels, which is a really stupid name, act as a bridge between the sub-realm, Antiqua-Kel and the Realm of Darkness. The sub-realm was where a lot of the magic known to the Darkness Realm came from before the holding seal was put in place. When the holding seal was set, and the sub-realms were locked for all of the five realms, there were still families and connections between the Antiqua-Kel plane and the Realm of Darkness. My position is to be an intermediary between the two realms."

"What does that job entail?" Dalton asked curiously.

"A lot of magic," Eclipse said. "Because of the way the sub-realms work with the realms we know, souls and magic pass between the barriers easily, and sometimes that can cause some unbalance and lead to natural disasters, plagues, and all sorts of other problems in both the Darkness Realm and Antiqua-Kel I am basically in charge of making sure that the energy of the dominant Darkness Realm does not overwhelm and absorb or decimate the Antiqua-Kel sub-realm."

While Keito, Tarrena, and Jikia nodded in understanding, Hanyi, Mitoki, and Dalton were staring at Eclipse in confusion.

"I don't get it," Hanyi finally said.

"It makes sense why you were able to meditate on magic across realms," Keito mused. "And why your magical abilities are so strong."

"But Master Genbuki said you haven't been using your powers in years. So...have you not been monitoring the energies of Antiqua-Kel?" Hanyi asked.

"I have, but very minimally," Eclipse said. "There is an entire force of Antiquan Angels that monitor the sub-realm. The others have been keeping track of everything."

"How many are there?" Dalton asked.

"Thirteen. That's actually my name in Antiqua-Kel."

"They just call you Thirteen?"

Eclipse nodded. "It follows my family's bloodline. My grandmother was Thirteen, and after she died, I was the next one born. So I became Thirteen."

"Wait, you said you didn't want children," Hanyi said. "So what would happen after you died?"

"It would pass to my brother's child, if he had one. And past that, it would go on to cousins. Whoever has the next strongest connection to me would have a child that would be the next Thirteen." Eclipse leaned his head tiredly on his hand, propping his elbow on the table. "I guess I'm a bit of a double Guardian, both for the Darkness Realm and Antiqua-Kel. My job as Thirteen is pretty much the same as it is as a Guardian. Kill those who are a threat, manage magical disasters and imbalances, try to stop individuals from crossing into the realms illegally."

"I'm impressed you've been raised to top-ranked when you basically had double the work," Hanyi said.

"Well, I don't have as much paperwork in Antiqua-Kel. Everything is much less formal over there." He closed his eyes. "Which means I've done a lot of things I'm not proud of. And when that magic takes hold of me...well, you saw how I was."

"Don't worry, you weren't that scary," Keito said with a small smile.

"I'm sure not to *you*, considering the demons you know," Eclipse teased back.

"Eclipse, if you're worried about us being nervous about working with you, I can assure you, we're not. None of us are normal in any respect." Dalton smiled. "We're a family of miscreants. We'll accept you, murderous magical powers and all."

Eclipse scoffed. "You should probably rethink that policy."

"We'll just make an exception for you."

Despite the fact that both Dr. Grant and Erik had ordered Eclipse to take it easy in the days before the next set of matches in the tournament, Eclipse was determined to be a difficult patient.

When Dalton looked up from the news reports about the chain of storms coming to Kang-Dron, he noticed Eclipse was gone.

"Where's Eclipse?" he asked quickly.

For the third time that day, everyone scoured the house, trying to find Eclipse. Mitoki finally spotted him in the outdoor training area, trying to focus his magic in his hands around the pain of his injuries.

"Eclipse!" Mitoki snapped, drawing the attention of the others, who also went to the backyard. The youngest stormed toward him. "You are supposed to be *resting*!"

"I feel fine!" Eclipse insisted, backing away from Mitoki. Dalton also went to the training area.

"Well, you're *not* fine!" Mitoki insisted, trying to grab his arm. Eclipse jerked away, his magic sparking around his fingers in preparation to fight. "Stop being so damn stubborn and just take some time to *heal*!"

Mitoki's last word came out as a startled yelp as he dodged Eclipse's magic that was thrown at him in retaliation.

"I told you, I'm fine," Eclipse said, flexing his fingers. "Want me to prove it?"

"Knock it off, Eclipse. You need to save your strength," Dalton insisted, his voice becoming firmer as he tried get Eclipse to stop using his magic. "Come on. Come inside."

"I'm going stir-crazy."

"You've been down for half a day," Dalton snapped. "You can last a few more days. Now, come inside—"

Dalton felt something sharp and hot latch onto his ankle and yank his leg upward, flipping him to his back as Eclipse chuckled, his hand lowering as the magic eased.

"Or, you could train with me."

"No, we are not training!" Dalton insisted, wincing as he stood. "Now, you will get inside right now."

"Or what?" Eclipse asked, lifting his other hand to show his magic sparking brightly.

Mitoki grabbed Eclipse's right wrist and yanked his hand behind his back, straining his wounded shoulder.

"There," he snapped. "You didn't even notice I was coming up to you. You are not ready to start training—"

Eclipse twisted, hooking his other arm under Mitoki's and turning him, tossing him to the ground heavily.

"This is a good way to learn," he insisted.

Hanyi chuckled, leaning against the house next to Keito as they watched.

"They're like little kids, aren't they?"

The demon raised an eyebrow at the wolf. "You aren't exactly the image of maturity."

Dalton and Mitoki were facing Eclipse, debating with themselves about whether or not to force Eclipse inside, or leave him outside on his own, hoping he would not drain himself of energy if he did not have an opponent. Before they could try and reason with Eclipse again, Jikia's voice sounded from the door leading to the backyard.

"Boys!" she snapped. "What the hell do you think you're doing?"

"Eclipse is saying he wants to train!" Mitoki said quickly, pointing.

"Snitch," Eclipse grumbled.

"Are you trying to be funny?" Jikia growled, walking toward the covered dirt area as Master Genbuki leaned against the doorframe, smiling. "Eclipse, you heard the doctor. You are not to train. You are to take it easy until the day of the tournament. And then, he—"

"I know, I remember. But I know my body. I feel fine. I want to start training how to fight with sight in only one eye."

"Well, you can't, yet," Jikia snapped. "You're likely to rip something open or get an infection. You can take a few days to rest."

"At least today, Eclipse," Dalton pleaded.

"I agree," Master Genbuki called. "At least take today to be quiet. In fact, I think you should go light a candle for the fallen Guardians today. It's the forty-first anniversary of the Tournament Slaughter."

Darkness seemed to settle over the backyard, intensifying the grey of the heavily-overcast sky. Eclipse's magic halted in his hands and Mitoki and Dalton turned to look at one another, startled. With almost frightening synchronicity, everyone turned their gazes to Keito and Hanyi, who had lowered their eyes to the ground.

"That's where you were this morning," Dalton said.

"We wanted to pay our respects before others showed up," Hanyi whispered. "Sadee is actually buried in Kang-Dron, so we went to see her, lit a candle, and then got out of there before anyone saw us."

Dalton looked back at Mitoki and Eclipse before speaking to his older teammates.

"I would like to pay my respects. If you two are willing to go with us, I would like to visit Sadee's grave as well."

Hanyi turned to Keito, who was looking over Dalton as though evaluating if Dalton was being genuine, or was only trying to appear thoughtful.

"I would like to go, as well," Mitoki seconded. Eclipse nodded, stepping to Dalton's side.

"We should," he added.

"Are you alright to go back, Keito?" Hanyi asked.

Even though he did not speak, the muscles in his jaw clenched tightly, he nodded and turned to walk back into the house.

Grabbing their jackets and umbrellas in case of rain, the Guardians piled into Eclipse's car to go to the Guardian Cemetery of Kang-Dron. Dalton had to drive once again, much to his dismay. Eclipse instructed him, surprised that no one else in the team felt comfortable driving his car. Dalton was better able to drive with Eclipse teaching him, but he still stalled the engine several times as they made their way through the city.

When they arrived, the heavy downpour made the cemetery feel even drearier than usual. There were many people entering the cemetery, and while most were family members of fallen Guardians, Dalton was sure there were some Guardians coming to light a candle at the temple and pray for those lives lost in the massacre—perhaps in a desperate attempt to ward off a similar tragedy with the new Guardian Tournament.

Most Guardian cemeteries were expansive, but the one in Kang-Dron felt enormous, sprawling around the large temple in the middle of the grounds.

"Is there a section for Guardians that were victims of the massacre?" Dalton asked Hanyi. The wolf nodded silently, leading them through the aisles of tombstones to a collection of simple headstones. Under the engraved seal of the Guardian Branch was the name of each Guardian, the years of their birth and death, their achievements and honors as a Guardian, and at the very bottom, in smaller print, it read: Killed in the Line of Duty. Massacre at the Guardian Tournament.

They moved slowly among the graves. Dalton knew that Guardians often avoided Guardian cemeteries out of superstition. All Guardians had come to terms with the reality that the job would likely kill them, but when confronted with the reality of what that meant—particularly with so many untended graves of Guardians who had no family members—the gravity of their job fell heavier on their shoulders.

Dalton looked at Hanyi and Keito, who were walking slowly among the headstones, eyes cast to the graves, dark. Dalton had never lost another Guardian that he was close to—at least, not yet. Seeing the pain in their features, and remembering the way Eclipse looked as he fell to the ground the previous day, made Dalton's chest ache with deep pain, an agony tearing into his ribs that he could not describe. Even though Yokouro had clearly not meant to kill Eclipse, the reality was far closer than Dalton was comfortable with, and he began to grasp the scope of grieving Keito and Hanyi had endured.

The two older Guardians slowed as the smaller graves gave way to larger, more elaborate headstones, finally stopping in front of one that depicted a woman resting her head over the tomb, face hidden by her arms as she mourned the dead. The name etched above the long list of achievements was familiar.

Sadee Kent.

Hanyi retreated a step, allowing Keito closer to the grave, his eyes lost in the carvings of the name of his former teammate. Dalton read over the impressive list of achievements under Sadee's name, trying to get a sense for who the woman was before her murder. It was clear she had been an impressive Guardian, but the drawn expressions on his older teammates' faces told him more about who she had been than what was listed on her headstone.

Keito remained still a few moments before lowering his umbrella and abandoning it to one side. He stepped closer to the grave, finally kneeling before it and pressing his fists together, pushing his knuckles against his forehead as he bent his head in prayer, his eyes shut tightly.

Dalton's chest ached. His mind wandered to questions about what Keito and Hanyi had seen that day in the stadium. He wondered if Keito had come across her fallen body when trying to escape, or if her body had been found after the fire had been put out...or if he had watched her death happen before his eyes. It became harder to breathe and Dalton could feel hot tears burning at his eyes as he thought of how painful it would be to see anyone on his own team be slaughtered so mercilessly.

"It was much worse this morning," Hanyi whispered to the humans, his eyes still on Keito. "He really believes he could have saved them. That it was *his* fault the massacre happened at all."

"Hanyi…"

"*I* told him to wait. I told him that there had to be another way…and I finally convinced him…"

"Hanyi," Dalton said, placing a hand on his shoulder, "you cannot blame yourself for what Yokouro did."

"I don't," Hanyi said. "I blame myself for my arrogance. For thinking that I could outsmart Yokouro." He finally turned his eyes to look at the three humans. "I never want you to feel the way we do."

The humans understood the weight of the statement. They had been frustrated with the older Guardians for not sharing more information, but seeing the pain in their faces, they understood that they were afraid of losing more people—or of inflicting the same pain on the humans of Team Dalton if the same mistakes were repeated.

"He might be a while here," Hanyi whispered. "It was hardest for him to lose Sadee."

"That's fine," Mitoki assured. "We're in no rush."

Dalton stepped to Keito's fallen umbrella and held it over Keito's head, trying to shield the already-drenched demon from more rain. Keito turned slightly to glance at Dalton before returning to his deep prayer over Sadee's grave.

The others were patient with the demon, saying their own prayers for Sadee's peaceful rest while they waited for Keito. When Keito did stand, he did not speak, nor raise his eyes from the ground as the team walked toward the temple. Inside the structure was the stone statue of a dragon, wings spread wide and low to the ground, symbolizing the dragon's protection over the souls of the Guardians. Many candles on the stands in front of the dragon were already lit, and a few people sat in the pews, praying quietly for deceased loved ones. Others were lighting more candles, and even though a few stared at Team Dalton as they entered, they did not say anything, merely bowing their heads in acknowledgement before returning to their tasks.

Slipping coins into the box, they each took a candle, set it on the stands in front of the statue, and lit it, watching the flames become steady, and then dropping their heads in prayer.

Dalton wanted to say a prayer for the Guardians who had lost their lives. He wanted to honor their sacrifices and bravery, but he found himself pleading for their help. He wanted their strength and guidance to get him through what he knew would be a very difficult battle against Yokouro DeVastes.

When Team Dalton slowly filed out of the temple, Hanyi and Keito stepped back into the rain first, Mitoki following close behind to be sure the older Guardians were alright. Eclipse started down the steps in front of Dalton. Dalton stopped abruptly when Eclipse did, the younger man turning to stare back into the temple.

"Eclipse? Are you alright?"

"Dalton," Eclipse started slowly, "can I still be a Guardian?"

Dalton tried to hide the way his entire body tensed at the question. Eclipse turned his unbandaged eye on his team leader, his expression hard. "I'm blind in one eye, and looking at the graves today, I realize that it's another step closer to getting me killed. All someone would have to do is attack me from the right, and that would be that. I don't know that training will ever truly make up for the loss of sight." He hesitated, his voice becoming choked. "Can I still be a Guardian?"

"Do you still want to be a Guardian?"

"I think it's the only thing I *can* do," Eclipse murmured. "If I stop, I'll have to sit by and *watch* as everything happens and...I think that is worse than death. But, in the end, it will be up to you whether or not I can still function as a Guardian. So, I'm asking you, can I still be a Guardian?"

"Protocol states that I would have to submit you to an evaluation," Dalton started. "But, of course, I can't do that until you're completely healed." He smiled at Eclipse. "And who knows how long that will be..."

A smile crept across Eclipse's face. "I think my doctor and trainer said about two months should do it."

Dalton nodded. "Then, I guess we'll have to see how you're doing in two months. Until then, you're still a Guardian."

Chapter Twenty-One

When they returned to the house, Erik opened the door to the garage before they finished climbing out of the car. Dalton was worried something horrific had happened, but the older Retani brother quickly went to Eclipse and grabbed his shoulders.

"You can't just disappear like that on me."

"What are you talking about?" Eclipse groaned, lightly pushing Erik away.

"You're supposed to be resting."

"For the last time, I *know*!" Eclipse snapped. As soon as the words left his mouth and he saw the startled locks on the faces around him, he sighed and closed his eyes. "I have a really bad headache. Sorry."

Erik followed Eclipse into the house.

"See? You're not ready to be pushing yourself," he said.

"And as usual, you're right," Eclipse grumbled, kicking off his shoes and stepping further into the house. The others were trailing behind Eclipse and Erik, feeling both uncomfortable and amused by the brothers.

"I'm not trying to scold you. I just want to make sure you're alright."

"I'm *fine*. The headache is because of the sedative."

"How can you know? You're not a doctor." Erik said.

"Neither are you," Eclipse reminded him.

"Hey, I am a doctor. Just because I'm not a medical doctor, doesn't mean I'm not a doctor. And I actually do know what I'm talking about, Eclipse." He watched as Eclipse reached for the bottle of painkillers that had not left the dining room table before plucking the bottle out of his hands and opening it for him, offering two pills forward. "How much have you eaten today? What about water?"

"Leave me alone, Erik," Eclipse moaned, walking to the refrigerator. Erik beat him to it and pulled out a bottle of water, opening it and handing it to him.

"You need to stay hydrated."

"Erik, I swear, if you keep babying me, I'm going to kick you out of the house."

"This is my house, too," Erik said, shoving the bottle into Eclipse's hand. The younger brother took the two pills and then reached for the cap of the water bottle.

"*I* pay for this house, not you," Eclipse reminded him. "Now, kindly back the hell off."

"You could have died, Eclipse. Forgive me for being worried."

"I didn't die. I was barely hurt," Eclipse insisted. "I'm more in danger of dying on a normal case than in the ring of the tournament. So, take a deep breath and calm down. I'm fine."

"Then you'll have no problem remaining quiet for the next few days. Master told me about you trying to train earlier. You can't be doing that right now, Eclipse."

Eclipse ground his teeth together, turning his head to glare through the opening to the kitchen, catching sight of his teammates also clustering close to keep an eye on him. He lifted his hands in exasperation.

"Alright, everyone listen up. I appreciate your concern, but I *promise*, I feel alright. I'm an Antiquan Angel. I have almost the same healing abilities as a demon. I get that everything that happened yesterday was…upsetting, but there is no need to baby me."

"We're not babying you," Erik insisted.

"Yes, you are," Eclipse sneered, pointing at his older brother. "And I may be a little weaker today, but if you keep smothering me, Erik, I will punch you in the face."

"The hell you will," Erik scoffed, rolling his eyes.

"I don't suggest you try me today," Eclipse said. "Now, I'm going to go sit, *quietly*, in the living room while my headache eases. Is that alright?"

He pushed past his teammates and entered the living room. Dalton was worried that they were upsetting Eclipse, but Hanyi shook his head with a thin smile.

"I'm sure a lot of the irritation is the headache," he said, also returning to the living room while Dalton turned to Erik. The older Retani brother sighed, rubbing his face roughly in frustration.

"I'm sorry, Erik," he whispered.

He straightened. "Sorry? What for?"

"I should have protected him better. None of this should have happened."

"No, Dalton, it wasn't your fault," Erik said, walking to the Guardian. "The only one I'm truly angry at is this demon. Yokouro, was it?"

"That's him," Dalton said.

"None of this was your fault, Dalton," Erik said again, clapping him lightly on the shoulder. "Don't obsess over it. Eclipse will be fine, I know he will be. I just wish he would slow down for a *few* days."

Dalton and Erik also walked into the living room, Erik sitting in one of the single chairs at the far end of the room, as most of the seating on the couches had been occupied. The television news was on mute as the anchor prattled on about further storm preparations. Everyone appeared to be lost in their own private thoughts, barely aware of the moving images on the screen.

Erik clapped his hands together quietly.

"So, is anyone going to tell me about this demon? Yokouro?" he prompted.

"I don't know that we're allowed to," Mitoki said, giving Dalton a questioning glance.

"I might be able to help in some way," Erik insisted. "My research facility is dedicated to researching demons, magical beings, the essence of energy, pretty much everything that Guardians deal with in the job."

"Not a big leap to see how you got turned onto that line of research," Hanyi teased lightly.

"We should talk about him a bit," Tarrena agreed. "After all, Dalton, you were face-to-face with him yesterday."

"What possessed you to run off and find him?" Jikia asked sharply.

"I don't know. I can't explain it."

"I'm assuming that this is the demon who was on top of that temple when the school burned down," Erik said, trying to catch up with the conversation. "How powerful is he? Do you know his NRM rating?"

Dalton was surprised he had not thought to look up something as basic as the numerical number of Yokouro's power.

"Do you know, Keito?"

The demon was silent, his eyes scanning the others in the room.

"You're not going to like the number…"

"What else is new?" Eclipse grumbled.

"The last measure taken on Yokouro was over seven hundred, fifty thousand NRM."

Dalton was sure his heart had stopped at the number. When his power had spiked to twenty-eight thousand, he had felt the weight of that amount of power. With Yokouro's number being so high, Dalton felt even more powerless than before.

Erik also choked at the number.

"That's not possible…"

"It is very possible," Keito said somberly.

"What about the other two? The Kage Lords?" Tarrena asked quickly.

"Who are they?"

"Other extremely powerful demons," Keito answered Erik vaguely before turning back to Tarrena. "Unfortunately, they don't have an NRM rating. They're too powerful to be measured by our means. They break the machine. The only scale of power large enough for them is dragon rankings."

"A *demon* being powerful enough to be measured by *dragon* standards?" Erik gawked.

Keito lifted two fingers. "Two demons."

"How does a demon even become that powerful?" Erik asked. "I think the most powerful demon I've ever heard of on record was close to one-hundred thousand."

"Then you haven't heard of any of the Old Blood Lords," Keito said.

"Then it's a bloodline thing?"

"Bloodline is one of the most important factors, but it takes many things for a demon to get as powerful as an Old Blood Lord. The Old Bloods have a lot of power in their family, but they are also all very old, and have had a lot of time to grow and hone their powers. Yokouro is over nine-thousand years old."

"What's the average lifespan?" Erik pressed, leaning forward and focusing all his attention on Keito.

"Again, it depends," Keito said. "For a DeVastes of Yokouro's generation, I would say anywhere between two-hundred to five-hundred thousand would be about average."

Dalton's eyes bulged. "Are you serious?"

"Then, Yokouro is still very young," Erik noted.

"In many respects, yes."

"And age helps a demon become more powerful?"

"Only if they're considered pure-blooded," Keito clarified. "And, nowadays, it's quite difficult to come across pure-blood demons outside of the Old Blood Lords."

"Then you're not pure blood?" Erik guessed.

"My parents were both pure-bloods, but because I am a mix, I am not. So my lifespan would be about eighty to one hundred thousand, assuming I would die of old age and not by someone's hand."

"Fascinating," Erik said, shaking his head slowly in disbelief.

"Erik, your nerd is showing," Eclipse jeered.

"Does being pure-blooded mean inbreeding?" Erik asked, ignoring his younger brother.

"It used to," Keito answered with a nod. "But the Old Bloods now are far more diverse than they were in the feudal age of the

Demon Realm. The DeVastes Clan has several different bloodlines that make up the clan, but there is not to be any cross with another breed of demon in order to preserve the purity of the clan."

"And the others, the Kages, right?"

"Similar rules, but the Kages are far more relaxed about their bloodline than the DeVastes. The successors to the Kage Clan are mixed, but they are a mix of two of the purest bloodlines in the entire Demon Realm, so not many think of them as being hybrids or weak, like they would for a demon like myself"

"And the Kage Clan is the one that has two demons so powerful they have to be measured on dragon scales?" Erik asked. "What are they like? Can they even be in the presence of humans?"

"They can," Dalton whispered, his eyes down. "We saw them yesterday, as well."

"You *saw* them?" Erik gasped.

"What did he do to you, Dalton?" Jikia asked, pulling Dalton's attention to her. "You were almost unresponsive when they brought you to the ring."

Dalton took a moment to collect himself before speaking.

"It wasn't anything different than what I've experienced before," he mused quietly. "It was a magical pressure. I've used that on people, as well. He was just pushing me to the ground. But..." He shook his head, his eyes filled with disbelief. "It was so much *more*."

"How so?" Mitoki asked.

"Generally, you can still move and shift when you have that weight on you. It falls on you like a blanket or a block of stone, but there's room to move, you know? Not with him It was like every inch of my skin, every muscle in my body, every bone inside me was crushed by the same weight. There was no way to move. No place where that pressure wasn't crushing me."

"Did you see how many power limiters he wore?" Mitoki asked, looking at Eclipse. The other Guardian nodded. "I didn't count all of them, but there had to be over a dozen. And I could tell those power limiters were straining to hold."

"I know that you think we've exaggerated the power the Trade Masters hold," Hanyi started, "but I can assure you, we have not. And even though they have a lot of power, it's their control of that power and their limitless connections that make them truly terrifying."

"Trade Masters?" Erik asked. "What's that?"

"It's a title they have in the realm," Keito said.

"Where does it come from?" Eclipse inquired. "I've been meaning to ask."

Keito pursed his lips in thought. "The Trade is the economic hub of the Demon Realm," he said slowly. "It's difficult to explain to humans because your society is set up very differently from demon society, but...it's..." Keito trailed off, trying desperately to think of the words to explain the Trade. "It's a business that deals in manual labor."

There was something sickening that sat in the air with the words.

"That sounds a bit like slavery," Dalton said cautiously.

"Not quite slavery, more like indentured servitude," Keito corrected. "Basically, the Trade trains and distributes workers around the realm. Maids for the palaces and nobles, equestrian caretakers, cooks, blacksmiths, builders, soldiers, and many of the others who might be considered 'lower class' are trained by the Trade and then, in some cases, sold to households or nobles based on their needs."

"Slavery," Dalton said strongly.

"For some," Keito finally admitted. "Those in the Trade who are sold to households as servants or maids or caretakers are then the responsibility of the noble, and many let them work and live in the palace. If they have families there, then the families are not part of the Trade. Then, if they want to retire, once they have some money saved, the noble or demon of status that purchased them from the Trade can let them go and they live their lives." Keito rubbed his temple. "That's really the best way I can describe it, but it's difficult when your society is so different from ours."

"And this is a business Juki and Rutu run?" Eclipse asked.

"Started and have been running for eons." Keito shrugged. "It's actually where a lot of our opponents in the tournament came from. They were part of the Trade, children of Trade employees, or were human employees and allies, which was actually very beneficial for us."

"How so?"

"Juki and Rutu are called Trade *Masters* for a reason," he said. "They run a very tight ship. They would never be careless enough to let loose someone they could not completely control. We were even up against one of their specially-trained mercenaries, and he still did not take Eclipse's injury further than what I suspect he was ordered."

"A Trade Mercenary?!" Hanyi gawked, startling everyone around him. "Ra-Jae was..." He stopped, his eyes wide as Keito nodded grimly.

"I'm assuming that's bad," Erik said.

"Trade Mercenaries are the elite of the elite when it comes to internal demon disputes," Keito elaborated. "There are a few freelance mercenaries who work for the nobles, but almost all demons who want someone taken care of or something stolen will turn to a Trade Mercenary. Juki and Rutu only select a small number of demons with potential and train them themselves."

"They do the training themselves?"

Keito nodded slowly. "And that allows Juki and Rutu to keep a very close eye on the lower lords and ladies throughout the entire realm. They know who's plotting, who's scheming, and who's losing money. But the Trade Mercenaries are brutal because they've been trained by the two most powerful demons in the realm."

"But wait," Mitoki said, his voice becoming filled with anxiety. "Those weren't all demons we were fighting in the ring. You said there were *human* employees?"

Keito shifted uncomfortably, dropping his gaze. "There are some things that the Trade does in the human realms as well."

"Like what?" Dalton asked, not sure he wanted to hear the answer.

Keito hung his head, sounding pained as he spoke. "It's...not *common*, but some very wealthy and influential humans have been known to...buy demon children to keep as exotic pets."

"*What*?" Everyone else in the room straightened in disgust.

"And Juki and Rutu just sell demon children to humans?!" Mitoki barked.

"They do. Rarely, but it does happen," Keito said. "Now, knowing Juki and Rutu as I do, I'm fairly certain anyone they send home with a human is actually one of their spies, but it did give Juki and Rutu a loophole around Vestera's rules and allowed them to hire human employees of the Trade. Which, again, is where many of our opponents came from yesterday."

"Then they have spies everywhere?" Eclipse asked.

"Probably more than we will ever know."

Dalton slumped back in his seat, trying not to let his feelings of helplessness overwhelm him.

"There...is *nothing* we can do against them, is there?" he finally choked out.

Based on the silence that followed, he knew that everyone else in the room was wrestling with the same crushing realization.

When Keito spoke again, the words startled Dalton.

"We might not have to do anything."

"What do you mean?" Eclipse asked.

"I wasn't sure if I should tell you this, but I think it's important," Keito started. "You mustn't think of Juki and Rutu in the same way you think of Yokouro. It's not that we're going against Yokouro, Juki, and Rutu. We're up against Yokouro. And Juki and Rutu are…entirely different players in the game." He rubbed his hands together nervously. "They are not working for Yokouro's benefit. They have their own agenda."

"I thought they were working for Yokouro," Dalton said.

"In a way, yes, but they're too powerful to fully bow down to him," Keito explained. "While Yokouro moves us where he wants us, Juki and Rutu also move him around to serve their own needs."

"That is *not* comforting," Eclipse groaned.

"It should be," Keito said. "Because I am fairly certain that, right now, they're working in our favor."

"What makes you say that?" Master Genbuki asked, chiming in for the first time.

"Because Juki was the one who gave Dalton that vial to protect him against the Shadow Veil."

Dalton straightened, turning to Keito with wide, horrified eyes.

"And you convinced me to *drink* that?!"

"It helped you!" Keito defended. "And I knew it would. I…don't want to get into details, but I know Juki quite well. Better than I ever cared to. And I knew when he told me about the vial that he was working to thwart Yokouro's plans as much as he was able while he was under Yokouro's watch."

"You trust one of the Kage Lords that much?" Mitoki snapped. "He could have been playing *you*, as well."

"You certainly did put a lot of confidence in him not lying to you," Dalton agreed.

"It wasn't just Juki. You should be thanking Rutu as well," Keito added. "If it wasn't for Rutu, you would have been a pretzel of broken limbs from the Jjanye demon. Rutu was the one who called Vestera in to save us."

"I thought Juki and Rutu were Vestera's rivals," Eclipse said.

"No, no, far from it," Keito said quickly.

"But…they can match up to him. Maybe even kill him. And they're working for Yokouro."

"Again, they're separate pieces in the game," Keito repeated. "They're not on Yokouro's side and they're not on Vestera's side. They are working to their own benefit, whatever that is. Believe it or not, Juki and Rutu are actually close friends with Vestera."

Dalton turned to the others on his team, his expression paling as he met their confused glances.

"Now I'm worried that not even Vestera is our ally…"

"You can trust Vestera," Jikia assured with a strong nod. "He's…kinda friends with everyone. But I know he does not want to see humanity destroyed. You can trust that he is on your side."

The doorbell ringing caused the on-edge Guardians to jump. Even Erik was startled by the sudden noise, and slowly rose to answer the door.

"Anyone expecting guests?" he asked.

Dalton was confident that none of their enemies would walk up to the front door and ring the doorbell, but his body was still tensed with apprehension. He heard the gentle whine of the hinges and then Erik's warm, but surprised, greeting.

"Oh, Austin," he said. "I'm assuming you heard about what happened."

"Of course I did," a deep, serious voice responded.

The man named Austin walked around the corner and into the living room. His black hair was slicked away from his sharp, angular face, which only made his hardened expression that much more intimidating. Eclipse stood, surprised.

"One," he greeted.

"Thirteen," Austin said, approaching him and taking the younger man's chin, turning his head to look at the bandages over his eye. Eclipse pushed his hand away.

"Stop."

"A demon did this?" Austin prompted.

"It's…complicated," Eclipse said, too tired to even start explaining the nuances of the case he was working around the Guardian Tournament.

"Too complicated to call me and tell me that you were going up against an extremely dangerous demon?" the older Antiquan Angel growled. "You're my responsibility, Thirteen. You should have told me."

"I didn't think I had to check in with you for *every* case."

"Thirteen, this demon clearly knows your weaknesses. If you had told me, perhaps I could have helped you train to master your powers, since you've refused to listen to reason so far."

"Austin, it's not fair to attack him like that," Erik said shortly.

"He could have been killed," Austin snapped.

"I am aware."

"And this injury makes things more complicated for his duties on Antiqua-Kel as well," Austin insisted.

"Screw his duties," Erik snapped. "He—"

"Both of you, stop," Eclipse said. He sighed, shrugging. "I don't know what to tell you, One. I was careless. I realize that. But I'll be alright."

"Regardless, you've been summoned officially." Austin pulled an envelope out of his jacket pocket, handing it to the younger man. "I don't suggest you push your luck with this one, Eclipse. Answer the summons. Explain to our master that you will now work on perfecting control of your powers so that you can return to your duty."

"Austin," Eclipse started, shaking his head.

"Don't start with me. You have been selfish about this long enough. It's time to grow up."

"Austin," Master Genbuki said sharply, adopting a stern tone that surprised everyone, "I know I do not need to remind you that disrespecting my son in front of me will result in me forcibly removing you from my home."

The older Antiquan Angel took a deep breath, retreating a step from Eclipse as he finally glanced over the unfamiliar faces in the room.

"Quite a full house you have," he noted.

"Right, sorry," Eclipse said quickly. "Austin, this is Dalton, Hanyi, Mitoki, Keito, Jikia, and Tarrena. They're all working with me on this case and the tournament."

Austin's dark, narrow eyes scanned each of them. Dalton was unsure if he should be ready for a fight, or if he always had a sharp look in his eyes that felt threatening. When Austin's eyes fell on Keito, Dalton could barely hear a warning growl emanate from Keito's throat.

"Then I should go. Leave you to your Guardian missions."

Austin turned to leave.

"One, come on," Eclipse groaned. "What do you want me to do? I have other responsibilities. You have other Antiquan Angels to work with."

"They're not you," Austin said shortly. "Answer the summons. And then...do whatever you think is best."

Austin pushed past Erik, who stared after him in confusion as the other Antiquan Angel left the house.

"He seemed friendly," Hanyi noted.

"He's not normally like that," Erik mused.

"No, he's not," Eclipse agreed. He turned his gaze to the envelope in his hands. "Something must be wrong."

He resumed his seat before lifting the red wax seal and removing the letter, tossing the envelope on the coffee table as he read. Hanyi stared at the envelope curiously before snatching it up, studying it as Eclipse's eye moved over the words written.

"What did he mean that you've been officially summoned?" Dalton asked. "Are you in some kind of trouble?"

"I'm always in some kind of trouble over there," Eclipse said with a disinterested shrug. "I'm sure with the injury they're worried that I'll be unable to be an effective Antiquan Angel." His brow began to furrow as he continued to read the letter. "It also says that I need to explain why my brother has an illegal contract in Antiqua-Kel."

His head shot up from the letter to stare at Erik. The older Retani brother immediately raised his hands.

"I have no idea what you're talking about," he said quickly. "I don't have a deal with anyone in that plane."

"It says right here that you do," Eclipse growled.

"Eclipse," Keito started, taking the envelope from Hanyi's hand, "do not answer that summons."

"It's not a big deal," he assured. "They're not going to imprison me or anything."

"No, I'm pretty sure it's a trap," Keito said. "This wasn't sent by your master."

"I know," he said. "It's Antiquan's successor. He signed it right at the bottom."

The demon of Team Dalton went very still, holding the envelope even though his expression had gone blank. Startled by the look, Dalton leaned forward.

"Keito? Are you alright?"

The demon did not respond at first, taking a few moments before he turned his head slowly. "Do you get letters often from Antiquan's successor?"

"Yes," Eclipse answered slowly, unsure what to make of the worry on Keito's face. "Antiquan the Third himself is too busy ruling over Antiqua-Kel to fuss over every problem the angels have. His successor has taken control of managing us."

Keito slumped back in his seat.

"What is it, Keito?" Hanyi asked. "You're scaring the hell out of me."

"I don't know how to tell you this, Eclipse, but you've been receiving letters and instructions from Yokouro." He turned the envelope around to show them the red wax on the back. "This is Yokouro's seal."

Chapter Twenty-Two

Everyone in the room had different reactions to Keito's declaration, but eventually, all eyes were locked on Eclipse, their mouths slightly open as they tried to think of what to say.

"Are you certain, Keito?" Tarrena finally whispered.

"Is the handwriting the same as previous letters?" Keito asked Eclipse. When the younger Guardian nodded, Keito closed his eyes. "No one else would have access to this seal."

Eclipse leapt to his feet, the others flinching in surprise. Erik rushed forward as Eclipse began storming out of the room.

"No, take a breath," he said sharply, shoving Eclipse backward.

"Get the hell out of my way, Erik!"

"What the hell do you think you're going to do? Kill him?!"

"Of course I'm going to kill him!"

The others had also gotten to their feet, rushing to restrain Eclipse. Dalton took one of his arms while Hanyi took the other.

"We'll figure it out, Eclipse," Dalton said. "But you can't just storm after him. He'll kill you."

"I will rip that bastard to shreds!"

"He's counting on you to lose your composure," Keito said, pushing Eclipse backward when he managed to get an arm free from Dalton's grasp. "Think about it. He's riling you up. He made sure this letter was delivered to the house when we were all here, and where he knew *I* would recognize his seal. He's *baiting* you."

"I don't give a shit! You have no idea…"

"I have no idea what?"

Eclipse's nostrils were flared as his entire body shook against Dalton and Hanyi's grip. Erik's eyes fell to the ground in understanding.

"This means I've been *working* for Yokouro," Eclipse snarled. "I've been working for a demon that is set on destroying humanity."

"You didn't know," Tarrena said gently, standing by the couch, watching the struggle with sympathetic eyes. "You can't blame yourself for not knowing."

Eclipse's head drooped and he shook off the two older Guardians, his body still quivering with anger. Master Genbuki also stood, walking to Eclipse.

"She's right," he said. "You were deceived."

"How is that even possible?" Mitoki asked. "I thought you said that anyone who can bridge between Antiqua-Kel and the Dimension of Darkness had a bloodline link. Yokouro is a demon."

"Decisions about who takes over the position of Antiquan are far beyond my paygrade," Eclipse grumbled. "Sometimes, it's just about who is strongest. Antiquan the Third would have chosen his successor as soon as he ascended to power...and the timeline fits with Yokouro's age." His eyes still burning with anger, Eclipse reached into his pocket and pulled out a small, rounded stone, holding it out in his palm to show Keito. The flares of green and red shimmered under the living room lights, the colors shifting like smoke against the glossy black. "Do you know if Yokouro was born with something like this in his hand?"

Keito could not hide his surprised expression.

"Is that an omen stone?"

"I don't know if that's what they're called, but this is the one I was born with. It was how my parents confirmed I was to be the next Thirteen."

Keito let out a nervous sigh. "Yes, he was born with an omen stone."

"Did you know about all this?" Hanyi demanded.

"I only knew about the omen stone," Keito said. "The entire land knows he was born with a black stone. All demons assume it was an omen for the destruction Yokouro would create. I had no idea it had any another meaning."

"Then he's been commanding the Antiquan Angels for millennia," Erik mused. He turned to Eclipse, his face paling. "Do you think he commanded Six?"

"Of course I think that," Eclipse growled. "That damn letter is Yokouro flaunting in my face that he was the one who had our parents killed."

Dalton had not thought the air could become any heavier until the words filled the room. They fell very still. Eclipse looked at each stunned face before turning angrily away and storming toward the back door. Erik started after him, but Master Genbuki held out a hand to stop him.

"Let him go," he said. "He won't go after Yokouro. But he needs to process this."

Erik hung his head in defeat.

"This demon has been toying with Eclipse since he was kid..." he whispered. "How *can* he process that?"

"It was another Antiquan Angel that killed the families in our hometown?" Mitoki asked. "My family, too?"

Erik turned to Mitoki, horror crossing his features.

"I'm so sorry, Mitoki, I...I didn't even think about..." He trailed off, taking a moment to clear his throat and compose himself.

"Yes. Six was the Antiquan Angel who killed your parents. He terrorized our hometown."

"Why did he do it?" Tarrena asked.

"Eclipse has always been quite powerful. It runs in the bloodline. In simple terms, Six didn't like being outshone by a kid. When Eclipse said he was thinking about using his Antiquan Angel powers to become a Guardian and help the people of the other realms, Six saw it as a challenge and taunted Eclipse, killing others to prove that Eclipse couldn't actually protect anyone."

"He was just a kid, though," Dalton said. "Surely he understands that he couldn't have protected those people from a maniac like that."

"Six still threw the murders in Eclipse's face, and it ate away at him," Erik said. "But attacking another Antiquan Angel is forbidden. Eclipse's hands were tied. Until Six killed our parents and nearly killed our younger brother."

"Younger brother?" Hanyi asked.

"We had another brother. He was just a baby at the time. He died shortly afterward. Unrelated to the attack. But when Eclipse saw Six going after him…" He shrugged. "Eclipse killed him. He then threw himself into becoming a Guardian, because at least as a Guardian, he would have been able to go after Six without repercussions from Antiqua-Kel." Erik pressed his fingers into his eyes. "This is a mess…"

Master Genbuki placed a hand on Erik's shoulder.

"This must be very difficult on you as well, Erik."

"I just don't know what to do to protect him, or even help him," Erik said. "It's very unsettling to know that Yokouro's been interfering in our lives since we were both children."

"And that, in the end, it was because of Yokouro that Eclipse became a Guardian," Hanyi added. "And eventually made his way into this tournament with us." He turned to Keito, his expression dark. "Yokouro's been planning this for a very long time."

The fear in the room was stifling, choking out the air as the others quietly wondered what else Yokouro had orchestrated in their lives.

~/\~

Tarrena slipped out to the backyard once the Guardians had resumed their seats, though no one was in the mood for conversation after the revelation of Yokouro's connection to Eclipse's life. She quietly closed the door behind her, walking through the crisp dusk air to the training area, where Eclipse was angrily punching at one of the dummies by the fence. She approached slowly, her heart breaking for the pain and anger she saw displayed in his tensed shoulders.

She watched him for a few moments before intervening, worried about him aggravating his injuries.

"Eclipse," she called, knowing better than to startle him. He continued to punch at the dummy, the thick plastic underneath the padding crunching, showing he had already shattered some of the internal structure. "Eclipse," she repeated louder, placing a hand on his shoulder.

He stopped, his breath coming in short pants as he stared darkly at the dummy. Tarrena's hand tightened on his shoulder before she took his bloodied fist, tenderly placing her hand over the knuckles and healing the small wounds.

"He's been manipulating my life from the moment I was born," Eclipse growled.

Tarrena healed his other hand, remaining quiet.

"What else have I done because of his commands?"

She squeezed his now-healed hand.

"You can't obsess over that," she whispered. "He's revealed his influence, and now that you know, you need to think of ways you can use what you know to bring this son of a bitch down."

Eclipse turned away from her, leaning against one of the support posts of the roof.

"It's not that simple."

"I know," she agreed, stepping to his side. She hesitated, unsure if the action would be welcome, before she wrapped her arm around his. He turned to look at her, but did not move away. "But just because he's been manipulating your life doesn't mean he's controlling you. He's trying to lead you in a direction he wants, but in the end, it was your skills and your determination that helped you get to the position of top-ranked. You've helped hundreds if not thousands of people. And I am certain that the good you've done for the realms outweighs whatever Yokouro has tricked you into doing for him."

The slightest hint of a smile pulled at Eclipse's mouth.

"You're a good man, Eclipse. Yokouro cannot change that, no matter how much he tries to influence you."

He placed his hand over hers, squeezing gently.

"Thank you, Tarrena."

The two fell into silence. Tarrena wanted Eclipse to talk about how he was feeling, but she could feel the tension still lingering in his frame, and knew it was not the right time to push him. So they stood, her arm wrapped around his and his hand on hers, staring up at the mostly-clear sky as night fully descended and the stars began to sparkle.

Eclipse finally lowered his gaze and turned to her.

"We...really should talk about this."

"About what?"

"This." He squeezed her hand. "That we're getting to a point where we're comfortable doing this."

"I thought that was how humans courted," she said, confused.

"Courted?" Eclipse grinned. "Is that what dragons do? Court one another?"

"I suppose," she said with a shrug. "Dragons have a very different way of showing interest in other dragons."

"How so?"

"Well, the male dragon is mostly responsible for expressing his interest in female dragons, and even when the female ignores him, he's expected to flaunt for her until other females chase him off. From what I've seen in humans, the female has to be receptive for the male to continue his advances."

The tension in Eclipse's body eased as he started laughing.

"What?" she asked, also smiling. "Is that not how it works?"

"No, it's not that, it's just...you talk about it as though you studied it. Like how Erik studies his charts."

"I had to," she said with a giggle. "How else was I going to know how to best get your attention?"

He lowered his gaze.

"Do you really like me in that sense?" he asked. "I'm human. I would think I would be boring to you."

Tarrena sighed, rolling her eyes.

"*Dragons* are boring," she said. "Everything is in preparation. Everything is planned. There is nothing spontaneous or exciting about them. Humans are so unpredictable. So exciting. You feel deeper than any dragon. It's fascinating and truly beautiful to see."

"Doesn't particularly feel that way," Eclipse said with a heavy sigh.

She placed her other hand against his cheek, slowly turning his face.

"It's still beautiful."

His other hand gently wrapped around hers, pressing it harder to his face. Her fingers caressed the bandages around his eye and her expression turned sad. He shook his head.

"I'll be alright."

"Are you just saying that?"

"For now," he said with a quiet laugh. "But Keito is right. I can't let Yokouro rattle me. I'll just use this as more motivation to train so I can kill that son of a bitch."

With a tender smile, Tarrena rolled up onto her toes and gently pressed her lips to his.

Both appetites and conversations were low following the realization of Yokouro's manipulations in Eclipse's life. It was clear that Mitoki wanted to ask more about what had happened when they were children, but he could tell from the dark look on Eclipse's face that the conversation would not be well-received.

Everyone else in the house tried to leave Eclipse to his thoughts. He did not realize how much his team had avoided him until there was a knock on his bedroom door and he opened it to see Keito standing in the darkened hallway twenty minutes after everyone else had gone to bed.

"Keito? Is everything alright?"

"I'm sorry to disturb you, Eclipse, but there is something I need to discuss with you."

"If this is concern for me, I appreciate it, but I'm really not in the mood—"

"It's not," Keito interrupted.

"Does it have more to do with Yokouro? Because, again. I'm not really in the mood. Save it for tomorrow morning when you can tell the whole team."

"This is a private matter," Keito said. "I don't think it's something you want me to tell the entire team."

Eclipse stared at his demon teammate, debating if he had the mental strength to discuss anything with Keito. But when Keito did not back away at seeing the fatigue on his face, he stepped aside and motioned for Keito to come in. When he closed the bedroom door, he crossed his arms over his chest with a heavy sigh.

"Alright, what is it?"

"I was looking over the summons you received."

"Confirming it was from Yokouro?"

"It was his hand," Keito said. "But the part about your brother having made some sort of deal had me worried."

"Like you said, it's probably a trap."

"I'm not so sure of that anymore."

"Erik is fine. He's not stupid enough to make some sort of arrangement—"

"I'm not talking about Erik."

Eclipse's expression froze. He refused to show how much the declaration made his heart speed up, or the nervous tremor that ran down his spine.

"Your younger brother isn't dead, is he?"

"What makes you say that?"

"Observations I've made and how well I know Yokouro's games," he answered. "Erik said that your younger brother died after the attack on your family, but it was unrelated to the attack. If that was a lie you told to protect him from further revenge from the other Antiquan Angels, I understand, but Yokouro would know the truth. And he wouldn't have put that information in the letter just as an empty threat. He's telling you that he knows your younger brother is alive, and that he's in danger."

"He's baiting me again?"

"Yes, but this one is not something you should ignore," Keito said. "You need to make some decisions, Eclipse. Either tell Mitoki the truth, or let him hear it from Yokouro."

The silence that fell over the bedroom was thick and made it harder for Eclipse to breathe.

"Why would I tell Mitoki?"

"So he doesn't have to hear it from Yokouro."

"There's nothing to tell him."

"I already know, Eclipse," Keito said. "I've been wondering since you told Mitoki the story of how his parents died. But seeing the way Master Genbuki and Erik treat him confirmed what I already suspected."

"It doesn't matter where he came from," Eclipse said, his voice growing dark, warning Keito that he was stepping on a very sensitive topic. "He has his own life, now. He's his own man. What good would it do to tell him more than what I've already shared?"

"What if he has a child with his wife?" Keito asked. "Then your bloodline continues and one of his descendants could be Thirteen."

Eclipse turned away from the demon, his crossed arms tightening over his chest.

"I have worried about that..."

"And Yokouro likely knows that Mitoki does not know of your relation," Keito continued. "And he will use that against the both of you. I don't think that information in the summons was incorrect. Something is tying Mitoki to Antiqua-Kel...and therefore, to Yokouro."

Eclipse closed his eyes.

"What do you suggest I do?" he asked sharply. "Tear Mitoki's world apart? Accuse him of some illegal deal with Antiqua-Kel? Say he's been working for Yokouro, too?"

"You don't have to do anything at this moment," Keito said. "But you need to know the way Yokouro plays his information. He rarely tells idle lies. He knows the truth has a sharper edge. You need to take some time to consider what you want to do about Mitoki. Because you can be sure that Yokouro will use him as a weapon against you. I just want you to be prepared for that."

Eclipse clenched his jaw tightly, keeping his eyes averted from Keito.

"I apologize for upsetting you. But I thought it was best that you knew so you could prepare yourself."

Keito started toward the door, but Eclipse slammed his hand against it, glaring at Keito, keeping him in the room.

"Do not *dare* tell Mitoki what you know."

"It's not my information to tell, Eclipse," Keito said, his voice quiet and even. "I have done what I think is best for you. I'm letting you know how our enemy operates. What you decide to do with that information is entirely up to you."

Many sensations were still new to Yokouro. The vast, cold throne room of the DeVastes Palace felt so much larger around his physical form than it had when he had not been confined to a body. The gold embellishments under his arms were warming under his touch, as was the smooth, black stone he rolled between his fingers. He had been trying to focus on Eclipse, to see how his Antiquan Angel was handling learning about Yokouro's involvement with Antiqua-Kel, but his eyes continued to get lost in the flares of color that barely shone through the black stone in the flickering candlelight surrounding him.

He remembered staring into the stone for hours as a child, becoming lost in the billowing colors. He had often wanted to throw the stone away, cast it into the oceans, shed the burden the stone had brought onto his life, but the moment he had thrown it as hard as he could into the deep gorge that was Bandit's Canyon, he had felt the loss deep within his chest—a pain that forced him to scale rapidly down the sheer edges of the canyon and search for his stone for four days until he could hold it in his hand again.

The omen stone, as the demons called it, was what made him feel as though he was unwelcome, even before he had been placed in his mother's arms. Of course, he could not remember the day of his birth, but he always felt that he was out of place, as though it would have been better had he not been born at all. After all, the stone had been seen as signaling the end of the DeVastes Clan, and he had been born clutching it tightly, crying whenever it was taken from him.

It was easier for the clan to lock away both the stone and the child so attached to it than separate them.

Even when Yokouro had broken free of his confinement and killed his spiteful parents, he had been sure to take the stone with him, holding it to his chest as he was chased from the DeVastes Palace at the young age of ten.

But the pain of his family's curse caught up with him quickly, and when he had collapsed to the ground, clawing at the sting in his face from his first markings, he still kept the stone tight within his grasp. He was nearly dead from blood loss, holding tightly to the little rock that had determined so much of his life already, when Juki and Rutu first appeared. They healed his wounds and carried him to their own palace, tending to him, unconcerned with the omen stone he clutched.

Yokouro never understood why, once he was healed, those two magnificently powerful demons bent to one knee and pledged their resources and power to him.

Of course, Yokouro was not a fool. He knew that Juki and Rutu were more powerful than he could ever hope to be, and he knew that he had no way to completely control them. He always kept it in the back of his mind that Juki and Rutu had their own agenda, and he could not trust them to obey his every command. Yet, he admired and respected them, looked up to them like fathers. They had taught him everything it took to be an Old Blood Lord, but still had allowed him freedom to make poor, immature decisions. He owed them everything.

Which was why guilt was angrily clawing at his chest as he sat in the throne room, holding his stone in one hand and staring at the letter unfolded in his lap. Vestera had been certain to explain to Yokouro that he had a part in bringing about the newest threat to the Demon Realm—a threat that he knew would devastate Juki.

But he knew he had to tell him.

The sentries at the throne room doors announced the arrival of the Kage Lords and pushed open the doors, breaking Yokouro out of his trance. He slipped the stone back into his pocket and folded the letter, setting it on the arm of the throne as Juki, Rutu, and Acurala crossed the expanse of the large room.

"Yokouro," Juki greeted. "What is this about? You sounded urgent."

The youngest Old Blood Lord lifted the folded parchments. "A letter came to me from Vestera."

"Has he threatened to remove you from power?" Juki asked knowingly.

"No, not this time," Yokouro said. "This is actually something concerning you."

"I don't understand," Juki said, throwing a brief glance back at Rutu and Acurala. Yokouro stood, walking down the two steps of the dais, nodding to Acurala.

"Acurala, why are you here? I did not send for you."

"I was with my brother when you called him."

"Thank you for making the journey, but I need to speak with these two in private."

Acurala's eyes moved between the other demon lords before he shook his head.

"I am sorry to object, but there should be nothing that you cannot say in front of me."

The guards around the room tensed, sensing the change in the air as the power relations between the demons were strained.

Juki turned to the sentries by the door.

"Escort Acurala from the room," he ordered. The uniformed demons stepped forward as the younger Kage brother turned to Juki in surprise.

"*Rau-ka*!"

"Yokouro is the master of this household and if he wishes to speak with me and Rutu privately, then he has the authority to ask you to leave."

"But, Juki, I—"

"Do not fight me on this," Juki interrupted. The younger brother fell silent at the scolding, refusing to follow the guards trying to guide him from the room. He turned to Rutu, hoping the other Old Blood Lord would speak for him to remain, but Rutu shook his head before looking to the door, telling Acurala to leave.

Worried, Acurala's step was hesitant as he was taken from the throne room.

Once the doors had closed, Juki turned back to Yokouro.

"The look on your face is worrying me," Juki said.

"I...I truly do not know how to say this," Yokouro said, drumming his fingers along the folds of the letter.

"What has Vestera said? Is he ordering us to dissolve our alliance? I warned you about being too aggressive in your moves against the Guardians."

"This is more personal," Yokouro said. "As you know, I raised Acurala so that I could keep you two in the background." He pursed his lips, dropping his gaze from Juki's concerned expression. "It appears that when I pulled that resurrection, I left that door open. And now, your father has been brought back to our land, as well."

The guards around the room, having not heard the information before, were unable to stop their own gasps and terrified reactions. They turned to one another, wanting to say something but unable to speak, fear gripping their bellies at the news that the most notorious demon in the history of the land—even worse than Yokouro—was alive once again.

Through millennia of practice, Juki was able to keep his expression straight, but everyone saw the tensing of his shoulders and the way his breathing quickened. Rutu was watching Juki closely, though his eyes could not hide the flicker of pain he also felt. When Yokouro saw the expression, he gave the other Kage Lord an apologetic look, realizing too late that he should have asked Rutu to leave the room as well.

After what seemed like several minutes, Juki closed his eyes, though he refused to let his head drop. He took two deep breaths in an attempt to calm his racing mind before he turned over his shoulder to look at Rutu.

"You knew," he whispered.

Rutu averted his eyes as Yokouro turned to him in surprise.

"That's why you've been acting so strange," Juki said. "Why didn't you *say* anything?"

"How could I?" Rutu murmured. "How could I have told you something like that?"

"Juki," Yokouro said, "I can help you. I can kill him for you."

"No, you can't."

"I can. I know he's powerful, but he's been resurrected. He's nowhere near the strength he once was."

"You don't know that," Juki insisted. "He was able to claw his own way back to a living plane. Without assistance, I'm assuming, since no one in their right mind would actually *want* to bring him back."

"I won't let that bastard live a second time," Yokouro said. "Vestera told me not to get involved. To leave it to you. But I can't do that. He's going to try and rip you apart, Juki. Let me do this for you."

"I appreciate the concern, but you have to leave this to me."

"Why?" Yokouro challenged.

"There's more to this than you realize," he said. Juki briefly turned his eyes to Rutu before returning his attention to Yokouro. "I have to do this alone, Yokouro. You cannot interfere."

"At least let me help," the youngest Old Blood Lord insisted. "The three of us can track him down and end him today."

"No," Juki said, his voice firm. "I have to do this alone."

"Rutu." Yokouro turned to him, his eyes pleading. "You know how dangerous he is. You can take care of him quickly."

"Rutu is not to interfere with this," Juki said, turning once again to Rutu, his voice dark. "You are not to be involved. Understood?"

Yokouro could see how torn Rutu was by the order, but he nodded reluctantly, turning his attention to Yokouro.

"There are many more factors about your fight with Dalton that you know nothing about," Rutu explained. "You have waited a long time for someone like Dalton, and with you making such dramatic moves, things are stirring. It's best to let Juki handle this He understands how best to remove him."

"Juki, I'm begging you, let me help," Yokouro said. "This is going to be too much for you. I need your help with the Guardians. If we eliminate him—"

"This is my fight, Yokouro," Juki interrupted, his tone dark and cold, causing the youngest Old Blood Lord to retreat a step instinctually. He opened his mouth to protest once again, but a glance at Rutu warned him against pushing his luck. When Juki held out his hand for the letter, Yokouro reluctantly handed it over, acquiescing that he would not involve himself in Juki's affairs

Chapter Twenty-Three

Despite the stress and concern that had plagued them for days, Team Dalton had found the two days of little activity restful. The pensive mood was even broken by laughter when Dalton struggled to drive Eclipse's car to the stadium the morning of the tournament.

Security had to guide Team Dalton out of the parking lot and into the stadium, as the reporters and audience members surged forward to call out questions and praise to the Guardians. They were pressed tightly together, barely able to shuffle toward the door within the ring of burly security guards.

They met Jikia and Tarrena in the team room, as they had taken a taxi to the stadium and had not been mobbed at the door.

"Wait long?" Hanyi asked with a laugh.

"Big crowd today?" Tarrena asked.

"The tournament is gaining momentum," Keito noted. "The fights are going to get more exciting for the audience members as the rounds continue."

"Great..." Eclipse groaned. "Not like more attention to the tournament will cause any further problems."

Jikia walked up to Eclipse, her sharp face staring up at his.

"Are you sure you're okay for today?"

"Dr. Grant said I could compete."

"He didn't say those *exact* words," Hanyi corrected. "I think he was intimidated by how much you were glaring at him."

"Still, he said I could come to the tournament today."

She leaned closer, looking over the glassy, grey eye.

"The scabs have completely closed. I doubt you'll even have much scarring," she noted. "Your healing abilities are quite strong."

"Told you," Eclipse said.

"Regardless, I want you to take it easy today," she snapped. "The rest of the team can step in and take over for you if needed. Do not push yourself."

"I'll cover for you," Keito assured with a nod.

It was not until Dalton walked out under the bright lights to the thunderous cheering of the audience that he realized his odd reaction. He no longer felt anxious about the tournament. Scanning the other teams in the ring and listening to the booming announcer's voice no longer filled him with apprehension about how he would fair in the ring. There was still the lingering sense of danger, as the threat of Yokouro still loomed over them. But as he calmly looked over the opposing Guardians, he realized that the competition was no longer at the forefront of his mind.

Even with one team having withdrawn due to injury from the first round, the finals started off without a hitch.

"The first match will be Team Sioran versus Team Lin. Other teams, please exit the ring," the excited young announcer, Gwen, called into the microphone.

"I recognized a few more people this round," Dalton said with a smile as they sat in their team box to watch the first match. "I worry that by the time we reach the finals, it will be only faces I recognize from the higher-ranked Guardians."

"That's always a possibility," Hanyi said.

"I don't sense anyone from Yokouro's ranks here," Mitoki noted. "I don't know if I should be relieved or even more worried."

"Maybe after everything he did to Eclipse, he's going to back off a bit," Tarrena suggested hopefully.

"Maybe..." Keito said slowly. "But knowing Yokouro, I wouldn't count on it."

"Please state any conditions you have for the match," the announcer said.

"I have a few." Sioran started, raising a hand and stepping forward, a broad grin on his face. His voice was higher than Dalton expected by looking at his strong, angular face and broad frame. "First, I request that all lights in the stadium be turned off."

"What?" everyone in Team Dalton said, startled by the strange condition.

"Next, I request that only blade weapons can be used. No throwing weapons, no bludgeoning weapons. Only daggers and swords."

Even the audience was becoming confused by the list of conditions. Most Guardians did not use the conditions in their matches, so the audience did not know what to expect from Sioran's strange requests.

"Also, I shall take on all five of these Guardians alone," he continued, motioning over Team Lin with a condescending wave. "That will allow the others of my team to rest. We had a hell of a party last night, and they're not feeling well today."

"Uh..." Gwen said, unsure how else to respond.

"And my final condition," he continued. "Is that the beautiful wolf Guardian there stay in her human form." He gave her a wink and a sickening smirk that made everyone else in the stadium feel uncomfortable.

"Who is this asshole?" Eclipse growled.

"I doubt some of those conditions can be executed," Jikia said. "The lights being turned off? There's no way—"

"It appears that the Tournament Board has approved all of Sioran's conditions," Gwen said, unable to keep the incredulity out of her tone. "Team Lin, do you have any conditions?"

"I think we found Yokouro's team," Hanyi said.

"Keito, do you think we need to be worried about the lights being turned off?" Dalton asked, turning to the demon.

"I don't think so," he said, though his tone was hesitant. "He is quite powerful. I can feel that from here. But it would be too drastic, even for Yokouro, to attack an entire stadium when he's still toying with us."

"If you see anything, though, let us know," Dalton said. "We can't be too careful."

When Team Lin could not come up with any conditions to oppose the bizarre rules Sioran had placed on the fight, they shook their heads.

"If there are no further conditions, the match may begin. The lights to the stadium will be turned off in two minutes. Please be sure you are in your seats before the lights are cut."

"It won't be completely dark in here, will it?" Mitoki asked, glancing at the windows that lined the top rim of the domed structure.

"He might use a shadow spell, but if not, we should be able to see a little bit," Keito said, also turning to the windows. "But the storm clouds out there are pretty dark."

"Great, you all know how much I love being unable to see," Hanyi grumbled.

The other four members of Team Sioran took their seats in their team box, looking bored, though Dalton was only able to look them over briefly before the humming of the stadium lights began to fade, and with four large clicks, the sections of lights were shut off, plunging the stadium into murky shadow.

The storm clouds made the little light that permeated the ring become a dark blue, being swallowed by the darkness before it reached the combatants in the ring. Strips of dim, yellow lights lined the stairs of the stadium, but their faint pinpoints of light were not nearly enough to illuminate the fight.

An eerie quiet fell over the audience as everyone strained to listen to the fight they could hear starting.

Dalton, who had been standing near the front wall of the team box to study the other members of Team Sioran, gingerly stepped backward to take a seat on the bench. However, when his foot connected with someone's leg, he turned in surprise, losing his balance and falling to the floor, his elbows catching his weight as he fell onto his back.

"Are you alright?" Jikia asked with a laugh.

"I'm fine," Dalton assured. "Just thought I'd get to know the floor a little," he joked. He pressed a hand to the front wall of the team box, guiding himself upright, ducking his head even though he knew there was nothing he could hit it on as he stood. The darkness was so thick, he felt that everyone was simultaneously too far away and also directly in front of him.

"Hey, have I mentioned that I don't like being unable to see?" Hanyi said meekly.

"You're alright, Hanyi," Tarrena assured.

"Can you hold my hand until the lights come back on?" he asked.

Dalton finally managed to find the lip of the bench with his other hand and used that to guide him closer, though when he tried to sit, he quickly realized he had found someone's leg.

"Or, you know, sit on me. That works, too. As long as someone is close," Hanyi said.

"Sorry, Hanyi," Dalton said with a laugh. "I can't see a thing." He shifted carefully away from Hanyi, sitting next to him on the hard bench of the team box.

The Guardians in Team Dalton tried not to move. They were listening intently to the distant sounds of the combatants in the ring, trying to match sounds with injuries or techniques they knew, though it was already difficult to hear. They jumped when one Guardian in the ring loudly called their surrender, their voice laced with pain. Dalton desperately wanted to see what was happening in the fight, knowing that they would also be facing Yokouro's team.

As he wondered how he would be able to fight Sioran in the pitch darkness, Keito spoke next to him.

"I would duck," he said quickly.

Without questioning it, all those sitting on the bench leaned forward and ducked their heads. They barely managed to do so when a terrified yelling soared over them and collided with the audience members seated behind.

"Oh, good," Keito grumbled. "When they turned off the lights, they turned off the barrier. Brilliant."

The pained groans and confused shouts of the audience behind their team box covered the commotion within Team Dalton.

Having no spacial reasoning as they ducked, Mitoki and Eclipse collided heads when they leaned forward. Mitoki reeled backwards in pain, as Eclipse let out a colorful curse. Mitoki's elbow then connected to flesh beside him.

"I'm so sorry!" Mitoki gasped, trying to reach out to the person who had groaned. "Are you alright?"

"I'm fine..." Tarrena gasped. "Just...need to catch my breath."

"Are you sure?" Mitoki asked, trying to take her arm, though his hand accidentally brushed her chest. He let out a startled yelp and backed away. "Sorry! I'm so sorry!" His hurried apologies broke into a soft wail as he recoiled enough to collide with Eclipse again, who shoved him away. He slipped from the bench, his arms windmilling and smacking knees and shins as he fell backward to the floor.

"Shit. Sorry, Mitoki. Are you alri—where did you go?" Eclipse asked, reaching his hands out to find the younger Guardian.

"Mitoki? Are you okay?" Dalton asked, moving to help search for the youngest member of the team when Mitoki cried out as Dalton's foot trapped his fingers. "Sorry!" Reaching down, he managed to find Mitoki's shoulders and help guide him upright. "Are you alright?"

"I'm fine..." he groaned, sitting up and scooting across the floor until his back was pressed against one wall of the team box. "I'm just going to stay here for a minute."

"Who is this?" Hanyi asked, his voice shaking.

"That would be my face, and if you hit my eye, I will knock your teeth out," Eclipse growled. "Stop touching me."

"I'm just trying to find someone," Hanyi whimpered.

"Just get away from me," Eclipse grumbled, shoving Hanyi backward, but Hanyi's hand latched onto Eclipse's wrist.

"No, just let me keep track of where someone is!"

"Let go of me!"

He pushed Hanyi harder, then lifted his fist to punch at Hanyi lightly, though he connected with Dalton's shoulder, who was trying not to get hit by Hanyi's flailing arms as the wolf practically collapsed on top of him.

"What the hell was that for?!" Dalton yelped, holding his shoulder.

"Sorry, I can't see a damn thing," Eclipse defended. "I was trying to hit the idiot."

"Oh, thanks," Dalton grumbled. He pushed at Hanyi. "Hanyi, get off of me."

"No, Eclipse is going to hit me," Hanyi whined. "I just want to know where everyone is."

"Come anywhere near me, and I will throw you into the ring," Eclipse growled. "Just stay put, wolf. You're fine."

"We have just received word that the fight has been won by Team Sioran," Gwen's voice erupted through the stadium, startling everyone, even though their surprise quickly gave way to relief that the lights would come back.

Following the same four clicks, the lights began flicking on again, illuminating the stadium. The audience flinched and blinked, allowing their eyes to adjust before they studied the scene in the middle of the ring. Sioran was standing in the middle of the ring, one foot on the back of one unconscious Guardian and his hands raised in triumph.

The audience cheered, though the section behind Team Dalton was being tended to by some of the security guards, who were assessing injuries to the audience members, while also carting off the fifth, unconscious member of Team Lin.

Team Dalton was a mess, as well.

Hanyi was half-curled on Dalton's lap, his expression resembling that of a five-year-old that had just been scolded. Dalton was rubbing his shoulder, asking Eclipse if he was alright as he pressed his hand over the sensitive skin of his injured eye. Mitoki was seated against the side wall of the team box, flexing his fingers slowly and flinching at the pain he felt in them.

Keito was sitting on the front wall of the team box, his legs dangling over the edge and into the ring. He smiled back at Team Dalton.

"For Guardians you are quite danger-prone," he teased. "It's a miracle you've survived this long."

Jikia started laughing, Tarrena pursing her lips against her own giggling. Dalton turned to the others on his team and let out his own exasperated laugh. Mitoki smiled in response, standing to take a seat on the bench. Eclipse was glaring, not finding the situation funny around the pain in his head, and Hanyi was smiling sheepishly, avoiding eye contact with everyone.

"Keito!" Sioran called loudly, startling them out of laughing. The leader of the other team was stalking to the other side of the ring. The cheering that had filled the stadium turned to worried whispering when the audience saw the way he moved toward Team Dalton. "What are you doing sitting on the barrier? Trying to interfere in case I got *out of hand*?"

Keito leaned closer as Sioran approached. "The thought had crossed my mind."

"Well, why don't you get into the ring now, then? Why wait?"

"There are *rules*."

"Aw, look at what a good pup you are," Sioran mocked. "So willing to obey your master's orders."

The other four Guardians immediately stood, leaning over the edge of the team box to glare at Sioran.

"Why don't you run back to your team?" Eclipse sneered. "There's no need for you to be over here."

"Oh, I think there's plenty of reason for me to be over here."

Leaping up, Sioran grabbed the front of Eclipse's shirt, yanking him over the edge of the team box and into the ring. Eclipse landed heavily on his back, too disoriented to see how the others of his team leapt into the ring, causing an uproar to fill the air around them as the audience reacted to the sudden fight. Mitoki helped pull Eclipse to his feet as Keito snarled at Sioran.

"Stay back," the demon warned, seeing the security rushing into the ring out of the corner of his eye.

"Stay out of this, mutt demon. I actually don't give a shit about *you*." He pointed back at Eclipse. "I'm after him."

"Yokouro's done more than enough," Dalton snapped. "I'm not going to let you hurt him."

"I don't care about what Yokouro wants! This is personal."

Eclipse pushed forward, ignoring the barked orders of the security to back away from one another. As a dark smile took over Sioran's face, Eclipse could feel the energy sparking off the younger Guardian. The aura gave him pause, and the look of realization on Eclipse's face caused Sioran's grin to widen.

"What do you say, Thirteen?" he whispered. "Should we just fight now?"

"Sioran," a voice snapped beside them. The familiarity of the voice caused all of them to turn. Dalton was surprised to see Acurala standing among the security officers, dressed in a simple shirt and pants, though his long hair was still intricately braided and his power limiters were still proudly displayed.

"My lord, I am merely—"

"No excuses, Sioran," Acurala growled. "There is a certain level of decorum we must maintain. Return to your team, *now*."

Sioran turned back to Team Dalton, glaring darkly, fighting with himself about whether or not to obey the demon's orders. When Acurala took another step forward, Sioran retreated, turning away with a huff and walking back across the ring.

"You boys get back into your box, now," Acurala instructed, nodding behind them. "You'll get your chance."

The security guards followed Acurala out of the ring, and though the audience was whispering and pointing, wondering if the long-haired demon they had seen in the ring looked like the one that had been on the news earlier in the week, most were too busy excitedly discussing the near-brawl that had occurred with Team Dalton.

"Are you alright?" Tarrena asked Eclipse as they returned to their team box and the normal procedures of cleaning the ring and tending to the unconscious began again.

"I'm fine. He just knocked the wind out of me."

"What personal grudge do you think he has against you?" Dalton asked, sitting next to Eclipse.

"He's the new Six," Eclipse answered strongly. "I felt the Antiquan magic on him. No doubt he's another Antiquan Angel. Considering he's younger than me, I have no doubt that he's the new Six."

"Well, that would explain the personal grudge," Hanyi said simply.

"Yokouro certainly is picking on me in this round of the tournament, isn't he?" Eclipse noted dryly. "Dalton, can I ask a favor of you?"

"What favor?"

"If we end up going against Sioran, I want to make it a one-on-one match."

"You're in no shape to be fighting that hard," Jikia said sharply. "I don't care if Dalton allows it, I won't."

"If he requests it first, then there's nothing we can do about it, right?" Eclipse insisted. "The fact that I showed up here today is me saying I'm well enough to fight. I can't very well claim injury now to get out of a one-on-one. It's better to request it first."

"You heard his long list of conditions," Hanyi agreed. "It would be advantageous to get ahead of him in that regard."

"But I don't think you can make exclusive fights with another Guardian unless you're a demon," Tarrena said. "Other than a Martyr Match."

Eclipse turned back to Dalton.

"Do you trust me to fight him and win the match for the team?" he asked.

Dalton hesitated. "Normally, I would, but I'm worried about your injuries."

"I'm healed."

"But you're not used to only being able to see out of one eye," Dalton insisted. "Look, you know I don't care about winning the

281

tournament. It's just a means to an end. But I can't have you hurting yourself further."

"I want to do this," Eclipse insisted. "I've barely been involved with Antiqua-Kel since I was a kid. Now knowing that Yokouro has such strong ties to that plane, coupled with the fact that everyone likely knows about my injury, I need to prove that the injury has not diminished my strength. I don't need other Antiquan Angels who hold a grudge to track me down in an alley somewhere."

"We're just worried about your health," Mitoki said.

"And I appreciate that. But this is something I need to do." He turned his eyes on Dalton. "In the end, it's your call, boss. But I would appreciate it if you could grant me this favor."

Dalton felt the weight of the eyes resting on him, waiting to hear his decision. He tried not to stare at Eclipse's glassy eye, but as the bandages had only been removed the previous night, he was still getting used to seeing the mismatched color. Even though the obvious injury still caused worry to radiate through his chest, Dalton took a deep breath and nodded.

"Thank you, Dalton."

"Just know that if you get hurt, everyone is going to tear me limb from limb, so please fight intelligently."

"I'm not worried," Eclipse said, glancing across the ring to Sioran, who was sending Team Dalton a cocky smile. "He's already proven to be too hot-headed for decent strategy. I'll put that kid in his place."

Jikia huffed, standing and walking out of the back door of the team box.

"Where are you going?" Hanyi asked.

The older dragon did not respond. Tarrena offered an apologetic smile for her mother's behavior.

The next match did not interest Team Dalton. As time progressed, Dalton was given more time to second-guess his decision to allow Eclipse a one-on-one fight with Sioran. He understood that Eclipse needed to save face in front of the other Antiquan Angels, but Dalton also knew that Eclipse had no idea how to properly fight while only having sight in one eye. Dalton also could not help but smile when he thought about how Yokouro would likely react if he heard that Eclipse was able to easily defeat Sioran so soon after his injury.

But he also worried that Yokouro would see that as a sign that he was not pushing Team Dalton hard enough.

The team that won the match limped away with two unconscious members. Hanyi could hear the worried conversations from the other team about whether or not to seek the attention of the medical team, or try to stay in the fights. Hanyi knew that team would not be a threat to Team Dalton, allowing them to focus their attention on Sioran.

Once the rest period had ended, the announcer called Team Dalton and Team Sioran into the ring. Sioran practically bounded into the ring while his disinterested teammates trailed behind him. Dalton could feel his anxiety crawling into his throat as they drew closer to the other Antiquan Angel. He was about to turn and tell Eclipse he had changed his mind about letting his teammate take on Sioran alone when the announcer started speaking.

"Please state any conditions you—"

"I have one," Eclipse said, interrupting Gwen when he saw Sioran open his mouth to speak. The younger man smiled, pressing a hand to his chest.

"Ooh, Thirteen, taking charge. Makes me all tingly."

"I request a Martyr Match between myself and Sioran," Eclipse said, ignoring the taunting.

"That was going to be my condition as well," Sioran said. "Read my mind."

"If the Tournament Board approves the condition, Sioran, do you agree to the Martyr Match? This means that the loss of this fight will result in the disqualification of your entire team."

"Of course I accept."

"Dalton, do you accept the condition?"

Even though the more logical side of Dalton was screaming at him to reconsider, he nodded.

The three seconds before the Tournament Board approval came through the loudspeakers had Dalton's heart pounding angrily against his ribs. He turned to Eclipse as the audience cheered in excitement at the promise of a one-on-one match. He opened his mouth to ask Eclipse if he was certain that he could handle the match, but he knew it was already too late for his teammate to change his mind. Eclipse nodded once to Dalton, reassuring his team leader that he was confident in his ability to win.

"As the Tournament Board has approved the Martyr Match, I ask that the other members of both teams please exit the ring."

Dalton gave Eclipse an encouraging pat on the shoulder, more to reassure himself than for Eclipse's benefit. He then trailed behind the others to the team box, avoiding Jikia's sharp gaze as he had been doing since she had returned. He sat on the opposite side of the team box from his angry trainer, trying not to let his own fears about Eclipse's well-being show on his face.

"Are there any conditions for the Martyr Match?" Gwen prompted.

"What do you think, Thirteen?" Sioran asked with a cold laugh. "I'm sure you have a long list of conditions to warp this to your benefit since you're still recovering from what the Trade Mercenary did to you."

"You were the one with the conditions list a mile long," Eclipse grumbled.

"If you're worried I'll ask that you change into your Antiquan Angel form, you can rest easy," Sioran said. "I know that you can defeat me easily in that form, Thirteen. So I say we keep this simple. No angel forms. No weapons. Just hand-to-hand combat. How does that sound?"

"Sounds just fine."

"No, it doesn't," Hanyi groaned from the team box, even knowing the two in the ring could not hear him.

"What do you mean?" Mitoki asked. "He's not going into his angel form."

"No, that part is fine," the wolf said. "What isn't fine is that he has altered depth perception. He doesn't know how to appropriately compensate for his lost vision."

Dalton could feel the anger rolling off of Jikia on the other side of the team box.

"Are there any other conditions?" Gwen asked. Both combatants shook their heads. "Then you may begin!"

Before she even finished her declaration, Sioran lunged at Eclipse. He barely dodged, startled and off-balance, leaving his stance open. Sioran took advantage of the opening and grabbed Eclipse's wrist, spinning him around so he could elbow him in the gut. Eclipse wrapped his other arm around Sioran's neck and threw the younger man to the ground, circling away to regain himself.

Sioran rolled to his feet fluidly and surged forward with incredible speed to attack Eclipse again.

As Dalton watched the two move around the ring, punches and kicks flying at one another amid the booming encouragements from the audience. Dalton could see the weakness in Eclipse's moves. As Dr. Grant had told them, Eclipse was no longer at risk of reopening his wounds, but that did not mean that his body had recovered its strength after the severity of the attack. Not only did he have to learn how to fight without sight in one eye, his body was still weakened from needing to heal. The longer the fight progressed, the more concerned Dalton became.

The only thing that gave him hope about Eclipse's ability to win the fight was that he had not once hit the ground. Sioran attacked with explosive power, clearly putting all his strength behind each punch and kick, but Eclipse was able to dodge, bear up to the hit, or redirect the power of the attack elsewhere. It was clear his basic fighting reflexes were still extremely strong, despite everything.

"Sioran is so strong," Tarrena whispered.

"His movements and style are very similar to Yokouro's," Keito noted. "The explosive power, the way he holds himself...it's obvious he's either spent a lot of time learning from Yokouro, or watching the way Yokouro fights."

"I doubt Yokouro would waste his time training one young Antiquan Angel," Hanyi said.

"True," Keito agreed. "He likely just studied Yokouro. And even though he is trying to fight in the same way, he clearly doesn't have the same amount of practice. He's relying too much on his power and not enough on the techniques."

"Looks like Eclipse is taking the opportunity to learn how to fight with his new limited sight," Mitoki said. "He hasn't fallen once, and he doesn't seem worried about his ability to win the fight."

Sioran changed directions from his original attack and crouched to the ground, trying to bring Eclipse to the ground by attacking his right side. Eclipse lifted his knee directly into Sioran's face, the younger man's own momentum causing the simple attack to do even further damage, blood erupting from his broken nose.

Wasting no time, Eclipse turned and landed a hard punch to Sioran's face, forcing him to the ground. Eclipse pinned Sioran, though his waning strength trembled as he tried to keep the enraged younger man pinned. At the sight of the blood, the audience had leapt to their feet, bellowing at Eclipse to finish the fight.

Sioran grit his teeth, pushing as hard as he could against Eclipse, finally lifting his arms just enough to raise his head and connect sharply with Eclipse's cheek. The older man reeled backward, pain exploding through his skull at the aggravation to his already-wounded face. The pain blinded him temporarily, giving Sioran the opportunity to flip them, pinning Eclipse to the ground and giving another exciting turn in the fight.

Those in the audience were cheering in excitement, the tremor of their energy radiating through the stadium and causing everyone's heart to race.

"Hear that?" Sioran asked, jerking his head to the audience before leaning down to Eclipse. "That's because I'm going to be the one who disqualifies the favored Team Dalton."

"No, they're waiting for me to put you in your place," Eclipse said with a short laugh. "You know you can't win against me, Six. You're too obvious in your form."

Sioran shook his head with a disbelieving chuckle. "You are a sad excuse for an Antiquan Angel. Even though you killed my uncle, I could not help but admire everything I heard about you. About how strong you were, even as a child. And then you had to let your feelings make you go soft."

"Your uncle killed my parents," Eclipse growled. "I wasn't about to be part of a world where I could not bring him to proper justice. I didn't back away from my responsibilities. I chose to use my power where it was most useful."

"Bullshit," Sioran snapped. "You ran away and threw a tantrum." His smile turned sinister. "You know, when Master Yokouro takes over for Antiquan the Third, he will force you to answer his call. You can't disobey him, Thirteen."

"The hell I can't," Eclipse snarled. "I'm going to kill that son of a bitch for good."

Eclipse yanked his pinned arms down to his sides, causing Sioran to pitch forward as his hands followed the motion. Eclipse rotated his shoulders, catching Sioran's jaw as he flipped the younger man onto his back. He then yanked Sioran closer by the front of his shirt and landed a hard punch across his face. Sioran scrambled to get away as Eclipse went on the offensive, chasing the younger Antiquan Angel around the ring.

Dalton was both unnerved and invigorated by the thrilled cheering emanating behind him. As he watched Eclipse land punches and kicks, he began to relax, seeing that Eclipse was easily gaining ground against his opponent.

Sioran finally turned, irritated at the chasing, and tried to meet Eclipse's attack with his own surge of strength.

Eclipse dodged the fist, grabbed the back of Sioran's neck, and used their combined momentum to run Sioran into the wall surrounding the ring.

The Guardians in Team Dalton's box cringed away, turning back to see that Sioran had fallen to his back in the ring, unconscious.

"With Sioran unconscious, the winner is Eclipse, securing the win for Team Dalton!"

The audience was already on their feet, drowning out the announcement as Eclipse stepped back from his opponent, allowing the medical team to rush forward and take the unconscious man. He spared a glance at the other four members of Team Sioran as they walked out of the team box to follow the medical team, clearly thrilled to be getting away from the tournament, and unimpressed with the fight they had witnessed.

He walked toward his own team box, gingerly rubbing his bruised face as the headache began to settle into his skull.

"How are you doing?" Tarrena asked, looking him over as he stepped into the team box.

"Headache, but otherwise, fine," he said. "That also wasn't as satisfying of a fight as I thought it would be. It was too easy. If that's what the Anticuan Angels are like now, then Yokouro is not very good at leading them."

Dalton let out a soft laugh, shaking his head.

"I was worried about you the entire time," he said. "I thought you were still too injured, but here you are saying that the fight was too easy."

"Well, it was."

"Attention everyone," Gwen said, causing the chattering audience to silence, surprised by the sudden announcement. "I know you all wanted to see more fights today, but Team Devin, due to two of their members still being unconscious, have opted to drop out of the tournament, making Team Dalton the winner of the Second Round of the Guardian Tournament here in Stadium 14D!"

Even though the audience cheered for Team Dalton's victory, their disappointment at the short set was apparent.

Hanyi stood, stretching with a broad smile on his face. "That was easy. I could have stayed in bed today."

Chapter Twenty-Four

The throne room of the DeVastes palace was alive with hot arguments as the members of demon aristocracy under the influence of the DeVastes Clan patiently waited for Yokouro. Clad in rich brocades with ornamentations donning every place they could, the throne room glittered with wealth, but that did nothing to ease the dark feelings in the lavish room.

The Demon Realm was in turmoil, and it seemed to be getting worse.

The sentry announced Yokouro's arrival loudly over the chattering nobles as the doors opened. The demon lords and ladies filed to the sides of the room, clearing a path for Yokouro to walk to his throne. He was dressed in intricate, lavish robes that made his already-broad frame appear even larger. He strode easily through the gathered lords and ladies, paying them almost no mind as he approached his throne.

Behind him, Juki and Rutu walked to the dais, dressed more simply due to being on another Old Blood's territory. Their heads were high, but their eyes were low out of respect, and their stride was just as confident and practiced as Yokouro's.

However, as the lords and ladies raised their heads once the Old Blood Lords had passed, the whispering started. Everyone could see the bandage around Juki's left hand, as well as the bandages around the base of his neck. He had not bothered to cover the two scratches above his left eye, nor could he completely disguise the limp in his step.

"Who do you think brought back Kawakara?" one woman whispered. "Someone trying to sabotage Juki, probably."

"He's a fool if he thinks he can kill his father. Everyone knows he's too afraid to face him," another snickered.

"I'm surprised he showed his face, considering Kawakara is still running free," a third growled.

"My cousin saw the fight. They told me that Juki just laid down and took the abuse."

Once Juki had reached the dais, he turned around, his vivid eyes scanning those in the throne room.

"Good lords and ladies of the DeVastes Territory," Juki said loudly. They silenced and lowered their heads in a bow. "I understand that you have little else to do with your time other than idle gossip. However, if there is something you must say about the situation with my father, say it to my face, not to my back."

Yokouro sat in his throne. He did not appreciate the way his court was muttering about Juki's injuries, but he was thankful that Juki's appearance had taken attention away from Yokouro's own weakness. He was desperate to hide the pain radiating through his entire body. The DeVastes Territory was already feeling unsettled by Yokouro's return to power, and he could not afford to show any weakness.

Once the muttering had ceased, Juki and Rutu positioned themselves on each side of Yokouro's throne, sure to stand just behind the younger lord.

"My lords and ladies," Yokouro started, "I agreed to hold an Open Court next week. What is it that you were so insistent we discuss today?"

"First," one lord started with a deep bow of his head, "we wanted to welcome you back and pledge our loyalty to you, our Old Blood Lord, as you have taken over the position of Lord Kakuri."

"I have not taken over his position," Yokouro corrected. "I would never force him to leave his position. I love him dearly and would never do anything to harm him. We are running the territory together. You are still welcome to go to him with your concerns, as he is still Old Blood Lord of the DeVastes Clan."

Yokouro tried not to smile when he saw the relief on the faces of many demons in front of him. He was greatly impressed with Kakuri's ability to keep the people in line without using fear, as Yokouro did. Yokouro had long learned that, no matter how kindly he treated his subjects, they still responded best to fear, so he used his reputation to his advantage. Clearly, Kakuri had no reason to do the same.

"What other matters did you wish to discuss?" Yokouro prompted.

"We have grievances, my lord," another man said, stepping forward and bowing deeply. "We are all very proud of the DeVastes Clan, and wish to do everything we can to support you, as you have supported us. However, considering the connection with the Kage Territory, we are concerned that the problems currently facing the Kage Clan will soon threaten our territory, as well."

"I do understand the threat of Kawakara," Yokouro agreed. "But the problem is being handled."

"Respectfully, my lord, I do not agree with you," one woman said strongly. She turned her gaze to Juki. "Your father is a menace, Lord Juki. You know that better than anyone. But this is not a problem that concerns only you, as it did in the past. He is dangerous to all of us," she said. "I am not your subject, therefore I know I cannot plead for a certain course of action. But I must implore you, for the safety of every demon in the realm, let Lord Rutu help you in eliminating your father."

"You are correct," Juki said coldly. "You are not my subject and cannot make pleas to me. How I run my territory is not your concern."

She bowed her head and retreated, knowing that any further protest would be dangerous. One lord, seeing how she shied away, took a bold step forward.

"My Lord Yokouro," he said, bowing his head. "I trust that you will be able to serve as Old Blood Lord with as much glory and wisdom as before. I am, however, concerned about your sudden interest in the human realms, and why you felt the need to bring Lords Juki and Rutu to your side."

Yokouro leaned back in his throne, successfully hiding his pained cringe. He had known that his lords would become anxious with the Kages so clearly influencing their land.

"There are important matters to which I must attend outside the Demon Realm," Yokouro answered. "Matters that concern all demons, not just the ones on the DeVastes territory."

"Is there anything we can help with, my lord?" another demon asked.

"Surely you all have felt the pressure of the Dimension Protection Council and the infinite mockery of a system that keeps demons under such tight constraints. Now that their Guardians are beginning to turn on the people of the realms, and the people are turning on the Guardians and the council, the Elders wish to blame *demons* for their lack of control over their subjects. There have been talks of removing our representation from the Dimension Protection Council, though they would still want us to pay to maintain the portals, and they want certain demons to act as Guardians still, since they want our strength without having to tolerate our culture."

The lords and ladies in the room turned to one another, grumbling about how unfair the treatment was, though they had all known it was only a matter of time before the humans became skittish and tried to lock away the demons.

"I am going to be sure that we are treated with the respect we deserve," Yokouro continued. "This work, naturally, means I am spending more time in the human-inhabited realms and with the DPC to be sure that I make the appropriate changes." He motioned his hand back to Juki and Rutu. "And I have called the Kage Lords to my side because they have far more finesse in dealing with the humans than I do."

"What changes are you going to put in place, my lord?" another woman asked.

"Nothing that you need be made privy to, yet."

"What is Demon Council's position on these changes? Have you consulted Vestera?"

"No one does anything without Vestera's knowledge," Yokouro said with a bored sigh. "He knows full well what I plan to do, and he understands the changes I want to make."

No one missed how Yokouro did not disclose whether or not Vestera was in support of Yokouro's plan.

Most lords in the room knew that Vestera had made no mention of Yokouro's plans in the most recent session of Demon Council a month previous. The demons all knew that Vestera was extremely powerful and it was very difficult to plan a coup against him, but they were worried that their Old Blood Lord was about to declare war on the most powerful dragon in the known universe.

"Are there any further, urgent grievances?" Yokouro prompted. "I have an appointment to keep. Please keep in mind, also, that Open Court will be in the next week."

The lords and ladies turned to one another. There were many more things that needed to be discussed with their Old Blood Lord, but apart from the problems on the Kage Territory, and how it might affect them, little else had to be said that day. They also understood that Yokouro was telling them the emergency gathering was over unless something dire was brought to his attention.

"I will leave you now, my lords and ladies," Yokouro said.

Gathering his strength, he stood as fluidly as he could manage, ignoring the pain in his back as he moved. He stepped easily off the dais and passed through the other demons toward the doors of the throne room, ignoring the way they bowed deeply to him and turned their eyes away from Juki and Rutu in fear. The sentries opened the doors and Yokouro turned to the nearest room next to the throne room.

The study was dark, as scholars of the clan used the rooms in the evenings after they had finished giving their lectures. The coolness of the air was soothing to Yokouro as he approached one of the chairs and nearly collapsed into it, cringing and breathing hard through his nose, his teeth grit against the pain.

Rutu went to his side, helping him straighten.

"No change?" he asked.

"It's better than it was last night," Yokouro disagreed. "Still feels as though I had salt poured onto multiple stab wounds."

"Perhaps it would be best to remain here, then," Juki suggested. "Traveling in your state will only increase the pain. You should save your strength and rest until you are feeling stronger."

"No," Yokouro insisted. "I want to speak with them, to have a proper introduction. Then…we can all rest a bit." He winced, his back twitching as he tried to move away from the pain. "Rutu, will you look at it? It feels like it's still bleeding."

As gently as he could, Rutu helped Yokouro remove the layered robes until his back was exposed. Sprawling over his left shoulder blade, a dark, swirling pattern of skin was outlined with angry, swollen skin that popped and oozed, blood trickling down Yokouro's back. Rutu studied the curse mark, shaking his head slowly.

"It is still bleeding," he noted, his thumb wiping away some of the larger rivulets as Yokouro groaned in pain. "This is still very fresh, Yokouro. You should let it breathe and try not to move your arm too much."

"Is there anything you can do for the pain?"

"This is a curse, Yokouro," Rutu said. "I could give you all the drugs I have and still the pain would be overwhelming."

"Are you certain you can handle seeing Team Dalton again?" Juki pressed. "If they sense your pain, they may attack you and take advantage of the opening."

"That's why we're separating them," Yokouro said. "I can fight them if I need to, but this is just a little chat and a small test. The tournament wasn't enough for me to see how well they rallied back from Eclipse's injury. I need to see if the stress is already too much for them."

"With the amount of pain you're in, you might not be able to remain focused," Juki warned.

"I'm fine," Yokouro said. He nodded to the cuts above Juki's eye. "What about you? When I saw you last night you looked three steps away from death."

"I am just fine," Juki said. "That vile healing tonic Rutu cooks up always makes me look like a walking corpse."

"Is your shattered leg healed today?" Rutu asked. "You're welcome."

"Are you coming with me to the Darkness Realm?" Yokouro asked the older Kage Lord.

"If you are certain that you are ready to do so, then I will go with you," Juki said.

"Then call Acurala. Tell him we're ready to move forward."

~/\~

Dalton was already struggling to drive Eclipse's car, but with the torrential downpour that struck the roof like machine gun fire, not only was it difficult to drive, but Dalton could hardly see through the windshield.

"Maybe we should have taken a cab or something," Mitoki mused when the engine roared angrily and then jolted forward, water sloshing under the tires as they drove.

"I'm doing the best I can," Dalton grumbled. "I can't see shit in this storm."

"Will you shift gears already? Do you *hear* the engine?" Eclipse snapped from the passenger's seat. Dalton shifted the car to a higher gear, popping the clutch and causing the car to rock forward again.

"Dalton," Hanyi whined from the back seat. "Stop making the car do that rocking, shaking thing..."

"He's popping the clutch," Eclipse groaned.

"I'm doing the best I can!" Dalton repeated. "It's not my fault we were called back to the stadium during a damn monsoon."

"Why do you think they called us in?" Mitoki asked.

"Probably something to do with Sioran," Keito said. "He lacked a certain subtlety that the others working for Yokouro had."

"That's for sure," Eclipse grumbled. "Think we should expect a confrontation? A fight?"

"Perhaps," Hanyi said. "All three of you have your guns, right?"

"Made sure I had mine when we left the house," Mitoki said.

Dalton turned a corner, the car rocking as, once again, he struggled to drive the unfamiliar vehicle in the heavy rainfall.

"I think I'm getting whiplash," Hanyi moaned. "I hate cars."

"Yeah, you don't look so good," Mitoki noted.

"The most interaction I have with cars is chasing them," the wolf tried to joke.

"Dalton, construction!" Eclipse gasped, the reflective tape on the orange cones finally visible as they drew closer. Dalton slammed on the brakes, killing the engine and causing another round of groans from his passengers.

"Eclipse," Hanyi whined, "please drive the car and spare us from Dalton's driving."

"I can't do that safely," Eclipse said.

"Was the construction here when we left the stadium?" Keito asked, looking out the window as Dalton turned the car and began following the signs for the detour.

"Must be a flood," Mitoki said.

"Do you know where we're going?" Dalton asked, leaning closer in an attempt to see through the water rushing down the windshield.

"Just keep going straight. You'll want to take a right a few blocks up."

Dalton managed to get the car cruising at a smooth pace when the car let out a loud pop and jolted once more, spluttering as the engine slowly died. Dalton barely managed to get the car to the side of the road before it came to a complete stop, all lights on the dashboard illuminated.

"How did you manage to kill it this time?" Eclipse demanded.

"I don't know," Dalton said. He tried to turn the car on, but the engine remained stubbornly silent.

"Dalton finally broke the car," Mitoki announced.

"You better not have," Eclipse said, leaning over to look at the warning lights on the dashboard.

"I didn't do anything," Dalton defended.

"That's weird," Eclipse said, also trying to turn the car on. "What did you do to it?"

"I swear, I didn't do anything!"

With an irritated groan, Eclipse unbuckled his seatbelt and stepped out of the car, bowing his head to the pouring rain. Dalton also got out of the car as Keito went to help Eclipse. Dalton's clothes were already soaked through when he managed to lift the hood. Eclipse leaned in close before shaking his head.

"No good," he said. "I can't see anything and this rain is going to make it harder to find the problem."

"Do we call Erik to pick us up?" Keito asked.

"He's probably in a lecture or something," Eclipse said, motioning for Mitoki and Hanyi to get out of the car. "We're going to have to leave it here and walk somewhere to get out of this rain. Then we'll figure out what to do."

"Something wrong with your car?" a man under a black umbrella asked, noticing them crowded around the car from his spot on the sidewalk as Hanyi and Mitoki climbed out.

"Seems like it," Eclipse answered.

"There is a covered bus stop just down there," the man said, pointing down the sidewalk. "You better get out of the rain before you get soaked through."

Dalton dug into his pocket and pulled out his phone, hunching to follow his teammates as he ducked under the awning of a closed boutique. When he tried to click his phone to life, the screen refused to turn on.

"My phone's dead…" he mumbled.

Mitoki pulled his phone out as well, but could not get the device to light up.

"Mine, too."

Dalton lifted his head but the last thing he saw was the closed black umbrella of the passerby flying at his face before he was struck violently in the side of the head and fell unconscious amid the yelling of his teammates.

Chapter Twenty-Five

The first sensation Dalton became aware of as he surfaced to consciousness was his pounding headache. Even though he was groggy, the pain was enough to wake him and he shakily pulled himself off the floor, the chains wrapped around his wrists pinching as he tried to straighten. He had to use his shoulder to clumsily wipe the blood from his eye as the wound in his forehead obstructed his vision.

Mitoki and Hanyi were in the small, cramped room with him, their hands bound in similar fashion, still unconscious and each sporting a bleeding head wound.

Dalton pulled himself along the grit-covered floor to Mitoki, shaking him.

"Mitoki," he called. "Come on." When Mitoki did not stir, Dalton shook him harder, almost violently as the worry that Mitoki was dead gripped his gut. The youngest let out an agonized groan and turned his head in the direction of Dalton's voice.

"D-Dalton?"

"Good, you're okay," Dalton said with a sigh of relief.

"I don't...think that's the right word." Flinching at the pain of the chains binding his wrists and using Dalton as a support, he managed to pull himself into a seated position, looking around. The single lightbulb near the door did little to illuminate the room. There was nothing within the room apart from two small ventilation grates and a door with a grime-coated window.

"Where the hell are we?" Mitoki asked as Dalton shook Hanyi awake.

"Hell if I know," Dalton said, his eyes looking in each corner frantically as Hanyi began to stir. "Where are Keito and Eclipse?"

Mitoki's heart stopped as he noticed their absence.

"Hanyi, Hanyi, come on, wake up."

"What the hell is going on?" Hanyi grumbled, his partially-swollen jaw obstructing his speech. "Where are we?"

"Don't know," Dalton answered. "But Keito and Eclipse are not here with us."

Hanyi forced himself upright, looking around quickly, taking deep, deliberate breaths to catch any lingering scents.

"They must have been taken to a different room immediately. Their scents aren't nearby." He looked over Dalton and Mitoki, his eyes finally falling to the chains around their wrists. "Let me see if I can get those loose."

Dalton extended his hands to his older teammate, but just as Hanyi started running his fingers along the chains to find the end, the handle of the door rattled. The door opened to reveal Acurala, three burly, black-clad demons behind him.

"Looks like we have a little infestation here."

"What the hell are you playing at, Acurala? Hasn't Yokouro played with us enough?" Hanyi snapped. "At the rate he's going, he'll kill us before he gets what he wants."

"Or, he'll learn how to temper his behavior based on your reaction," Acurala quipped. "He doesn't want to spend all his time playing with three new humans only for them to die on him like the last group did."

Hanyi gnashed his teeth in an angry growl and tried to move toward Acurala, but one of the demons stepped into the small room and grabbed the wolf, pushing hard on his shoulder to force him to his knees.

"Where are Keito and Eclipse?" Dalton demanded.

"They're alive," Acurala said. "That's all I'll tell you."

A part of Dalton wanted to struggle and fight against the guards, thinking that they could get just enough space to get out of the store room and find someplace to hide while he formed another plan, but the pounding in his head prevented him from further developing the plan before he was sharply hauled to his feet and pushed toward the door.

Acurala easily stepped in front of the Guardians as they were led roughly out of the storage closet and down the hallway of the office building. All the doors were closed, but the empty name plates next to the doors and the lack of furniture told the Guardians that the building was abandoned. The sight of the sheer number of doors also worried Dalton that finding Keito and Eclipse would be an impossible task once they were freed from whatever game Yokouro had set up for them.

When they were led into an echoing stairwell, Hanyi tested the guards, trying to push back against the one guiding him while they were on the stairs, clearly intent on sending them both careening down the staircase. But the demon managed to grab the back of Hanyi's shirt and turn them both, staying standing despite Hanyi's efforts.

Acurala sighed, leaning over the railing on the next flight of stairs.

"If you just cooperate, this will go a lot easier for all of us."

"You expect us to just be led into some sort of trap?" Mitoki snapped.

"You already fell into the trap," Acurala laughed. "The faster you cooperate, the faster you can try and escape it."

He continued walking, the demon guiding Hanyi pushing him up the stairs roughly as Dalton and Mitoki shared a glance. Cold worry stabbed Dalton. Thinking back to the numerous closed doors and the sheer number of stairs they were climbing, he was worried that whatever test Yokouro had for them would prove too difficult.

When Acurala finally opened a door that led them to the offices on the fifth floor, Dalton could not bring himself to feel relieved to no longer be climbing stairs. He could feel his hair standing on end, his blood racing like hot needles through his veins.

He could feel Yokouro nearby.

Acurala led them down three twisting hallways before opening the door to a conference room. The guards almost violently shoved the Guardians inside, but did not follow them in. Dalton did not notice when Acurala closed the door—he was too focused on the three figures standing at the other side of the room.

Boiling anger licked the walls of his stomach and he wanted to charge at Yokouro, even with his bound hands. But Juki and Rutu standing on either side of him forced Dalton to reign in the urge to attack. Mitoki and Hanyi were more wary than Dalton, and lingered as close to the opposing wall as possible.

"I say it's about time we had a proper chat," Yokouro greeted with a thin smile.

"Where are Eclipse and Keito?" Mitoki demanded.

"Relax. They're both fine, for now." He took a careful step forward, his smile widening when he saw the way they tensed in response. "You'll get to see them soon."

"What was the point of bringing us here?" Hanyi growled. "Don't you think you've done enough damage already?"

"Yes, I've done enough damage to get the humans to realize my capabilities," the demon lord agreed. "But now, I need to test you and see just how far I can push you before you break."

"Why are you doing all this? What is the point of the tournament? Of coming after me?" Dalton asked, his voice dark enough to drop the temperature of the room. Yokouro turned his eyes on him, as if startled, but very pleased, by the tone.

"I should think that would be obvious," Yokouro said, crossing the expanse of the room. Mitoki and Hanyi retreated a step by instinct, but Dalton leaned closer, every muscle in his body tensed to attack the demon when he got close enough. "Don't you feel that, Dalton? That pull toward me? That overwhelming desire to destroy me?" Yokouro stopped just a few paces short of Dalton. "I have been waiting a very long time for you, Dalton Teban."

The words sparked something in Dalton. He lunged forward, raising both his bound wrists in a clumsy swipe at Yokouro, but before the warnings of his teammates reached his ears, a hand was on his chest, pushing him back.

Juki stared coldly at Dalton, forcing him to back two steps away from Yokouro.

"I suppose I should make formal introductions," Yokouro said. "This is Lord Juki Kage. I'm sure you've heard all sorts of things about him. And back there, is Lord Rutu Kaneaka-Kage. You have probably heard them referred to as the Kage Lords or the Trade Masters. They are also very close associates of mine."

Juki lowered his hand and returned to the other side of the room, somehow understanding that Dalton would not lunge forward and attack.

"What is it that I'm supposed to do?" Dalton demanded. "Am I supposed to join you? Help you in your quest for demon domination? You're insane."

"No, no, your job is to die by my hand," Yokouro corrected with a cold grin. "But as I have recently learned, it's not enough to just kill you." He leaned closer, as though telling Dalton a secret. "You and I have been destined to fight for centuries, Dalton. I thought I was just supposed to kill you, and your ancestors that have carried this power before you."

"You've been tracking and attacking my family for *centuries*?"

"I have," Yokouro affirmed. "Do you feel that fire raging within your chest? That anger so sharp it's like knives moving through your body? That is what I have felt every time one of your ancestors has started to tap into that power in your bloodline. In the past, I have just eliminated them." He laughed hollowly. "I even tried killing you when you were just a baby."

Dalton's heart stopped as dark realization settled over him.

"It was *you*..." he whispered.

"Yes, Dalton, it was me," Yokouro said. "But your father was a tough son of a bitch. Took weeks for that spell to finally wear off and unbind me. Truly, I should thank him. It forced me to research other ways I was supposed to end your life, and only then did I find out I've been doing this wrong for generations."

"You *murdered* my father," Dalton snarled.

"I've murdered thousands of people, Dalton," Yokouro said, his tone bored. He motioned over the visible black markings peering out from under his simple shirt. "And apart from you, the only mark your father left on the world," he pulled the collar of his shirt aside, pressing his finger into a large, swirling black design on his collarbone, "is right here."

Again, Dalton started forward, his vision tunneling, ready to fight Yokouro with everything he had when Juki, once again, crossed the room with unseen speed and pushed Dalton back.

Yokouro laughed, nodding approvingly.

"Good, Dalton. That's what I want to see."

"Yokouro, quit playing games with him," Hanyi snapped.

"But the game is to Dalton's benefit," Yokouro said. "You see, this destiny that we share means that you will face me in battle, but you and I must stand on equal ground. I cannot use underhanded tricks, nor slit your throat in your sleep. I'm building you up, Dalton. You should be grateful."

"You're a lunatic," Mitoki sneered. "Dalton's human. You're a demon. No matter what you do, he'll never be able to stand on equal ground with you."

"That's where you come in," Yokouro said with a wink, pointing at Mitoki. "You and Eclipse."

Mitoki was about to speak up again when the heaviness in the air gave him pause. Dalton also noticed the very pointed way Yokouro had not mentioned Hanyi or Keito. Despite the way Yokouro smirked at the wolf, Hanyi did not look surprised or upset, merely resigned, as though he had already understood that Yokouro planned to eliminate him before facing Dalton.

"Also, Dalton is not entirely human. Well, physically, I suppose he is. But the magic he possesses is not human." Yokouro's gaze turned back to Dalton, quirking a smile at the way Juki continued to push the human back just insistently enough to dissuade him from attacking. "There's dragon magic within you, Dalton. You got a little taste of it at the tournament. You've known for a long time that you have power within you. Do you remember the first time you let it overwhelm you?"

"I will kill you," Dalton promised, pushing against Juki's hand, even though the demon lord was far too strong to be fazed.

"Maybe, but it's far more likely I'll kill you," Yokouro said with a shrug, retreating to the other side of the room, his arms spread wide and a broad smile on his face. "Because just like the last Guardians, you will fumble at the finish line."

Hanyi growled, also taking a step forward when Juki turned, his other hand raising to the wolf, his sharp eyes warning the older Guardian to remain where he stood. Yokouro laughed triumphantly at the display.

"You know I'm right, Hanyi," he said.

"Nothing is going to stop me ending you," Dalton vowed. "We need to be on even ground? Fine. I'll do everything in my power to get there so I can kill you."

"That's the spirit, Dalton," Yokouro said. "Then this little test can be the start."

Juki pushed Dalton back another two steps and then walked to the other side of the room, resuming his position at Yokouro's side. The younger demon motioned abstractly with his hand toward the wall of frosted glass.

"Out there, somewhere in the building, you will find Eclipse and that mutt demon of yours," he explained. "If you just follow the traces of their magic, you should be able to find them easily. But there are a few things that will make this particular rescue difficult. The first being that your friends might not be themselves when you find them." The darkness in Yokouro's smile made the Guardians at the other end of the room shudder. "And secondly, you have a time limit. This building is set for demolition tomorrow. I took some time to finish connecting the charges and I will be detonating them if you are not out after a certain amount of time. Sound fair?"

The three Guardians looked to one another, their faces draining of color as they tried to understand the task Yokouro had put in front of them.

"What do you say? Thirty minutes to search the building and drag them out?" Yokouro asked, seeing their fear growing. "That should be more than enough time."

"What does this have to do with training me to become stronger?" Dalton demanded.

"It tells me how well you work under pressure after I have relentlessly toyed with you," Yokouro said with a wink. "Not to worry, I'll give you some time to regain your bearings if you survive."

"And if I die in this moronic test? Then we can't have the fight you said you've waited so long for."

Yokouro shrugged again. "It is a possibility. If that happens, then I'll just have to keep tracking your family, your daughter her children and so on, until another one with your capabilities comes along." Yokouro turned to Rutu. "So about seven hundred years?"

Rutu nodded.

"That's what will happen if you die tonight," Yokouro said, turning back to Dalton's angry expression. "But I have faith in you, Dalton. If you let that dragon energy you possess reach out and search the entire building, this task should be quite easy."

The demon could see every muscle in Dalton's body tensed for attack. His smile grew, feeling his own angry energy rising in response, causing his body to shudder with anticipation of the fight he had so meticulously planned.

"I'll leave you now, Dalton," Yokouro said, taking a step forward, allowing his magic to reach out just enough to push the Guardians back against the wall, keeping them from attacking him as he left the room. "I'll start timing you from the moment I leave the room."

Yokouro started toward the door, the Guardians half-heartedly fighting against Yokouro's magic, worried more about their teammates than immediately attacking the demon. They turned to see Juki and Rutu begin trailing Yokouro obediently, but their struggles stopped immediately when they saw that Juki and Rutu were also still standing against the far wall. Dalton quickly looked between the standing Juki and Rutu and the two identical figures that followed Yokouro out the door.

The Juki standing at the far end of the conference room lifted a finger to his mouth, warning them to stay silent.

The door was left open, and the Guardians could hear Yokouro tell Acurala to start the timer, his voice growing fainter as he approached the stairwell. When they heard the door to the stairwell close, the three jumped, their eyes still trained on Juki and Rutu, who were still and silent at the other end of the room.

The five stared at one another for what felt like an eternity before Juki leaned over to Rutu, causing the Guardians to tense, ready for an attack.

"I think they're afraid of us," he said with a soft laugh. Rutu smiled, taking a step forward.

"Be assured, we will not harm you," the younger Kage Lord said, moving his fingers in a gentle, upward motion. The chains around their wrists unwound and fell heavily to the floor, clattering loudly as they were freed.

Juki and Rutu stopped a few paces in front of the Guardians.

"If we get any closer, will you attack us?" Juki asked.

"Why *wouldn't* we attack you?" Mitoki snapped.

"Because we're trying to help," Juki said. "You're shivering from the rain and you're wounded. This task was impossible enough. Your physical state will only make it more difficult."

"Are you going to tell us where Keito and Eclipse are?" Dalton asked.

"Yes," Juki said. "We're going to tell you where they are the fastest way out of the building, and we're going to tell you where Elder Renard is so he doesn't die in the demolition."

"Elder Renard is here?" Hanyi gasped.

"How are we supposed to rescue *three* people before the explosions start?" Mitoki cried.

"By listening to us and letting us help you," Rutu said simply. "We know you're not ready for this. You will die if you don't take our assistance."

Dalton and Mitoki were still hesitant as the two demons stepped forward. Since Hanyi was more at ease, Juki stepped over to him and placed his palm against Hanyi's shoulder before pulling his hand away, droplets of water clinging to his hand as he drew the water out of Hanyi's clothes. The water orbed against Juki's palm, before evaporating easily into the air. Rutu placed one hand on both Dalton's and Mitoki's shoulder, repeating what Juki had done. Dalton could feel the water move out of his socks, pulling moisture away from his skin as the rainwater moved up his body to his shoulder, finally leaving his clothes dry.

Once Juki had healed Hanyi's swollen jaw and the cuts over his neck, he reached into his pocket and extracted three small pouches.

"Keito and Eclipse have had a spell cast on them," he explained, handing one of the pouches to Hanyi as Rutu healed the minor injuries on Dalton and Mitoki. "The counter spell takes far too long, so this is going to be the easiest way to get them to cooperate "

Juki handed one pouch to Dalton and the third to Mitoki.

"The spell makes them very violent. They will attack anything that moves. If they see you, they will attack you, and being the two physically strongest on your team, they will overwhelm you. When you find them, take a pinch of that," he nodded to the pouches, "and throw it on their faces. It will knock them out almost immediately. It's very strong, so be sure you're far enough away that you don't inhale any by accident."

"How do we know this won't kill them?" Dalton asked. "How can we trust you?"

"You don't have a choice, right now," Rutu said. "You are already short on time."

"Where are they?" Hanyi asked, pocketing the pouch.

"Elder Renard is on the ground floor in a storage closet by the elevator shafts," Juki answered. "He is tied up but otherwise unharmed. It should be easiest to get him out of the building. Keito is on the eighth floor," he pointed above them. "From the stairs, it's two lefts and a right turn before you find the office he's in. I made sure to leave a light. And Eclipse is on the third floor. One left turn, one right turn, and two lefts again. There is a light in there, also."

"You're..." Mitoki's brow knitted together in confusion, "you're really helping us?"

"I told you, this is an impossible task," Juki said.

"The fastest way out of the building is through the front doors. Hauling your teammates down the stairs is going to be the hardest part once they're unconscious. Just move as quickly as you can and get as far away from the building as possible," Rutu added. "I've already tampered a little with the trip system. That will buy you a few extra minutes, but if Yokouro gets impatient enough, he'll trigger the charges with his magic, so I cannot guarantee how long that will stall him."

"Let's split up," Dalton said, looking at the other Guardians. "Mitoki, you get Elder Renard. Hanyi—"

"I'll get Keito. I can run faster up the stairs as a wolf," Hanyi said.

"I'll find Eclipse," Dalton decided. He cast a quick glance at the Kage Lords. Juki nodded once to him, and as though that released Dalton from a different kind of binding, he darted to the open door, the other two close behind.

"It really would be easier if Demetrius died," Rutu mused as he heard the door to the stairwell swing open.

"Maybe, but at least Demetrius still has enough of his wits to tell us when things are getting out of hand," Juki agreed. "It would be difficult to convince Yokouro to put a Kage demon as the new Elder rather than a DeVastes demon."

Rutu let out a sigh. "Do you think they'll be able to get out in time?"

"We'll see," Juki said, unconcerned. "But we should get out of here, just to be safe."

Dalton and Mitoki leapt down the stairs as fast as they safely could while Hanyi shifted into a wolf and sprinted to the eighth floor, the pouch in his mouth.

Dalton threw open the door to the third floor as Mitoki continued his rapid descent. He turned immediately left, then took the first right turn he saw, sprinting past doors of offices long abandoned. He turned left once he came to the end of the hall and was confronted with another immediate left turn.

Near the middle of the hallway, a beam of light shone from under one of the doors.

Scrambling to extract the pouch from his pocket as he ran, he approached the door.

Before he could put his hand on the knob to open it, there was a loud bang against the door, and the wood started to split near the latch. Dalton opened the pouch and pinched some of the fine powder in his fingers. As he was extracting his hand, the door burst open, the doorknob flying toward Dalton. He ducked, but had no time to straighten before Eclipse was after him, snarling angrily, his eyes the deep crimson of his Antiquan Angel form. His magic was sparking angrily, choking the air and making Dalton worry that Eclipse would accidentally trip the demolition charges.

Dalton turned and began running, noticing the orb of magic that had been producing the light had faded, making it even harder to see in the dark hall.

Eclipse charged after him with thundering steps and angry growls. Dalton turned the corner and then the corner immediately after, spinning around just in time to throw the powder at Eclipse when he followed.

Dalton dropped the pouch when Eclipse tilted forward and fell heavily against him, unconscious. Stunned at how quickly the powder had worked, it took him a few moments before he could haul Eclipse over his shoulder and hurry back the way he had come.

With his teammate unconscious and heavy on his back, Dalton tried not to let panic set in. He had no way of telling how much time had passed, how slow he would move going down the stairs, or if Hanyi and Mitoki had been successful in their own rescues. He could feel something inside him pulling, begging him to reach out with his magic and find them, but he refrained, trying not to imagine how much Yokouro knew about Dalton's magical abilities.

Going down the stairs was extremely difficult. Dalton only managed not to fall purely by adrenaline. His magic was reacting to his fear, helping to steady him as he kept pace down the stairs, finally leaning against the bar on the stairwell door to stumble into the lobby. His breath heaving and sweat dripping down his face, he clumsily made his way to the glass doors he could see on the other side of the lobby. He pushed open the door, seeing Mitoki disappear behind a large tree with Elder Renard at his side.

Seeing his younger teammate, Dalton began jogging as fast as he could while still balancing Eclipse. He rounded the same tree, catching the attention of the other two.

"Dalton!" Mitoki called, running back to him. "Did you see Hanyi?"

"No," Dalton groaned, allowing Mitoki to help guide Eclipse off his shoulder. "Do we go back in there?"

"There's a chance you'll get caught by the detonation," Elder Renard said.

"We can't leave them," Mitoki insisted.

"Oh, shit," Dalton gasped, remembering the way Yokouro had omitted Hanyi's and Keito's names earlier. "I'm going back in there."

"Dalton! You can't! It's too dangerous!" Elder Renard called after him, but Dalton ignored the warning, a new surge of terror pushing his muscles to work harder, bringing him back to the front doors of the building. When he could not open the door from the outside, he used his magic to break the glass and rush inside.

As he reached the door for the stairwell, a hand beat him to the handle.

Elder Renard yanked open the door and began running up the stairs, his demon speed startling Dalton, who had never seen the Elder move so quickly.

"Hanyi?!" Dalton called, running after him.

"Up here!"

By the time Dalton found Hanyi, Elder Renard was already pulling the unconscious Keito across his back. Hanyi was gripping the railing tightly, blood running down his arm from four large gashes across his bicep.

"What happened?" Dalton asked, grabbing Hanyi's other arm to support him down the stairs, following the demon Elder.

"He got me before I could get the powder out," Hanyi explained weakly. "I think he heard me coming."

By the time they reached the front door, Hanyi was struggling to keep his feet under him, the blood loss affecting his coordination. Dalton was also feeling his own weakness trying to take hold as they stumbled around the same large tree.

"We have to get farther away from the building," Elder Renard said, nodding to Mitoki to pick up Eclipse. "We're too close."

With a few deep breaths, Dalton pushed forward, following Elder Renard as they crossed the street and stumbled through the alley between two other office buildings. Before they cleared the other side of the alley, a series of thundering booms shattered their eardrums and a shockwave radiated past them. Dalton's weak legs gave out, he and Hanyi falling heavily to the rough pavement. Mitoki also collapsed, covering his mouth from the dust cloud rapidly approaching. Elder Renard turned, but when he saw the approaching debris, he crouched to the ground and ducked his head.

Dalton lifted his hand to cover his own mouth and nose, but realized too late the clinging residue of powder on his fingers As the cloud of dust surrounded them, his head fell to the pavement and his world went dark.

Chapter Twenty-Six

It was not a groggy, confused state that greeted Dalton when he woke. He jolted upright, alert, and determined they had to get further away from the explosion. It was only when he moved his arm to cover his face that he felt a sharp pain in his elbow that startled him back to the present.

He was in a hospital room, the stark white walls stinging his eyes as he studied his surroundings. He felt weak, but relatively unharmed, which startled him considering what he could recall from the previous day.

Assuming that he had not been unconscious even longer.

He turned over his shoulder and found the nurse call button. He had been in the hospital a few times as a Guardian, and was able to find it almost by second nature. He then reclined back on the bed and waited, his mind trying to unravel his clouded memories of the explosion.

When the nurse did arrive, a familiar face was directly behind her. Erik let out a short breath of relief as he walked over.

"You're awake," he greeted.

"Erik? What are you doing here?"

"The hospital called Master Genbuki, who told me."

"How long have we been here?"

"About sixteen hours," Erik said.

"How are you feeling?" the nurse asked, walking to Dalton's other side.

"Confused, but…okay."

"Can you tell me your full name?"

"Dalton William Teban."

As the nurse ran through a list of questions to see how alert Dalton was, she nodded with an approving smile.

"Just as I thought," she said, smiling at Erik. "I told you there were no side effects."

"What side effects?" Dalton asked.

"You were found with a very illegal demon sleeping aid in your system," Erik teased. "Now, I'm sure that there is a reason why you, Keito, and Eclipse were all drugged, but we can't figure out why Mitoki had twenty doses of it in his pocket."

Dalton opened his mouth to speak before letting out a short laugh.

"It's a long story."

"Under the orders of Elder Renard, this little substance use will stay off the record," the nurse said.

"Is he alright?"

"He's doing very well," the nurse assured. "We're keeping him for one more day, but he should be good to go home tomorrow. And you should be good to leave later today."

"What about my teammates?" Dalton asked.

"Guardian Ecaep suffered a nasty bump on the head, we think from flying debris. Guardian Treneke has been patched up, but he's lost a bit of blood, so we're keeping him quiet. Guardian Retani is sedated, but should be awake once the specialist gives the okay. And Guardian DeVero is also sedated."

"But they're all okay?"

"They will be well," she said. "Just rest here for a little bit and I'll get the doctor."

As she left, Erik pulled one of the chairs closer to Dalton and sat with a tired sigh.

"Hell of a night," he muttered.

"You're telling me…" Dalton agreed. "Is everyone really okay?"

"Yes, everyone is fine," Erik assured. "There was some kind of incident with Keito. I don't know what it was, but they said he's stable now. Demons are always hard to treat since their entire physical makeup is still such a mystery." His eyes turned sympathetic. "Are *you* okay?"

"I think so…"

"What happened? When you weren't back by dinner we were all frantically trying to find you. It wasn't until we heard about the explosion and then got the call that you were in the hospital that we realized you had probably been captured."

"It was Yokouro," Dalton said quietly. "Some sort of stupid test."

"At least you passed."

"Not without help," Dalton groaned, his eyebrows going high. "So that powder was an illegal demon sleeping aid?"

Erik laughed. "It's very illegal here, I don't know if it is in the Demon Realm. But that stuff is powerful. How'd you get it?"

"The Kage Lords gave it to us as a way to subdue Eclipse and Keito," Dalton explained. "Do the doctors know they had some sort of aggression spell cast on them?"

"Elder Renard explained what he knew," Erik assured. "The healers were called to assess damage and they said they'll both be fine. I suppose the very powerful sedation was enough to counter it." Erik leaned forward. "You're saying the Kage Lords helped you?"

"They did," Dalton said, confused. "They told us where to find them in the building, gave us the powder, and told us how to get away. They even said they tampered with the trip system to give us more time."

"Why would they do that?"

"I don't know," he whispered. "They openly deceived Yokouro right in front of us. They created some sort of illusion to make Yokouro think they were following him, and then they stayed behind to help us survive." Dalton rubbed his temple with a groan. "As if this whole case wasn't confusing enough."

"What was it like to be in the same room with them?" Erik asked. "Could you feel their power? Was it overwhelming like before?"

Dalton playfully glared. "Are you asking because you're worried about me, or for the sake of your curiosity?"

"Both?"

"No, I couldn't feel their power the same way I did before," Dalton said. "Juki actually looked a little injured, so maybe he was in some sort of fight and was a little drained. Or maybe they had more power limiters on."

"I would love to be able to study demons that powerful," Erik said wistfully. "It's so difficult to find demon participants in my studies, let alone those who are extremely powerful."

"You could probably ask Keito when he's awake," Dalton suggested.

"You don't think that would be weird?"

"I think Keito has a very flexible definition of weird."

The doctor checked Dalton over and asked him to perform a few coordination tests to be sure he was able to stand before telling him he could get dressed. As Dalton pulled on the clothes Erik had brought, the doctor asked Dalton to stay at the hospital until the others of his team were awake, since he was their superior.

As the doctor left, Dalton grabbed his phone and wallet.

"I don't suppose anyone found my gun?" he asked.

"No," Erik said.

"Can we go see the others?"

"Mitoki is just down the hall," Erik explained. "The others are in different wards since they're all not human, or not *quite* human." His face brightened. "Actually, maybe you know something about this." His pace quickened as they walked down the hallway.

"Know something about what?" Dalton asked as he hurried to catch up.

"The doctors were asking me about these weird scars on Mitoki's chest. I didn't know what they were, but maybe you do."

"Scars?"

They entered the room quietly, not sure if Mitoki was awake or not. Dalton was surprised to see the amount of bandages on Mitoki's head, but otherwise, the young Guardian looked unharmed. Erik approached Mitoki's bedside, carefully pulling down the hospital gown around his neck to show Dalton the tops of several scars.

"What are those?"

"You've never seen them before?"

"Not that I can recall," Dalton said. "Mitoki said he was self-conscious about his body, but I never really thought anything of it."

"It's a little worrying that he thinks this is something he has to hide," Erik mused. He pulled the gown down a little further. "See? They're like Xs. They extend all the way down his torso. The doctors didn't know what they meant, or if there was any internal damage from them. I have no idea what they're from, so I hoped you would."

"I don't, I'm afraid," Dalton said. "But Guardians find themselves in all sorts of weird situations. This could have been from a case."

"That does seem like the most likely option," Erik agreed. "Just a little concerning. Particularly if he's trying to hide them from you."

"I can ask him when—"

Mitoki slowly blinked his eyes open, letting out a small groan as he did so. Erik quickly released the hospital gown and backed away, smiling as the younger man blinked drowsily.

"Welcome back, Mitoki," he greeted.

"Where...where am I?"

"You're in the hospital," Dalton explained as Erik hit the call button. "You were hit in the head. Do you remember anything?"

"Bits and pieces," Mitoki answered, his eyes sliding shut again.

"Just rest for a moment. The nurse is on their way."

The nurse checked over Mitoki, talking to him gently as he fought the heaviness of his eyelids. She told him that the sedatives should wear off very quickly, but she did not want him to stand until a certain amount of time had passed.

Mitoki was far more alert when there was a soft knock on the door and Hanyi walked in, smiling broadly.

"Here they are," he greeted, walking in. "Everyone alright?"

"We're fine. Are you okay?" Dalton asked.

"I'm fine," the wolf assured, walking up to the bed. "Got stitched up and got some breakfast, or I guess late lunch at this point. Little weak, slightly light-headed, but overall, I'm alright." He smiled at Mitoki. "How're you doing?"

"I have a horrific headache."

"Looks like you really took a wallop," he agreed. "Are they keeping you here?"

"No," the nurse assured. "His blood work looks fine and we've got some prescriptions for him, but the healers did most of the work. He should be good to go in just a few hours. Which will give your teammates time to wake up."

"Where are they, anyway?" Hanyi asked.

"Different wards. Keito's on the other side of the hospital. Eclipse is two floors down," Erik explained.

"The doctor will be in in just a few minutes to give you one last check and then we'll just wait for that sedative to wear off a little more," the nurse said, nodding to everyone in the room before leaving.

"You said Keito was on the other side of the hospital?" Hanyi asked.

"They've moved him a few times," Erik said. "I know there was some kind of incident with him, but no one would tell me what it was. So they had him moved. I've heard he's stable though."

"They don't have him sedated, do they?" Hanyi asked.

"Yes. They had to sedate him."

Hanyi took a deep breath, closing his eyes.

"What's wrong?" Dalton asked.

"It's just not a good idea for Keito to be asleep for long periods of time," Hanyi said vaguely.

The door to the room opened and a nurse poked her head in.

"Excuse me, is one of you Erik Retani?" she asked.

"I am."

"Your brother is awake. He's asking for you."

Erik quickly turned to the others. "I'll go check on him. Just ask the nurse for the room number when you're ready. We'll be there."

He hurried out of the room as Mitoki groaned and slowly sat up.

"Hey, the nurse said to wait for a while," Dalton said, his hands instinctively darting toward Mitoki.

"I'm fine," Mitoki said. "My head hurts, but otherwise, I feel fine."

"No need to push yourself," Hanyi said.

"I hate hospitals. I want out."

"At least wait for the nurse to come and take out the IV."

Mitoki impatiently waited for the nurse to return, and when she took out the IV and the doctor had gone over the prescriptions she assigned Mitoki, the youngest of Team Dalton was allowed to dress and leave the room.

Once they had taken the elevator to the correct floor, a nurse led them to Eclipse's room, where he was already getting dressed. Tarrena was also in the room and greeted them all with a broad smile and a gentle hug.

"Where's Jikia?" Mitoki asked.

"She stayed back, just in case something happened at the house. We had no idea what had happened to you." She looked around the group. "Where's Keito?"

"On the other side of the hospital," Erik said. "At least, I think that's where he is."

"We can go to the nurses' station and ask," Dalton said. "I'm sure I have to sign something to get us all out of here anyway."

The tired Guardians trudged to the nurses' station where Dalton was asked to fill out several forms and Erik asked for Keito's room number.

The nurse became very still when she heard the question.

"He is in an isolation unit right now," she explained carefully.

"Why?"

"There was an incident," she said, still hesitant. "We're waiting for someone from demon containment to arrive before he's moved or released."

"Did he hurt anyone?" Hanyi asked. "Keito does not do well under sedation."

"He did injure a few nurses and orderlies before he was contained again," the nurse explained, her eyes low as she spoke. "No one was severely injured. But it does mean we have to follow protocol to be sure he's not a danger to himself or others when we halt sedation again."

"He's still sedated?" Hanyi asked, his eyes wide. "The longer he's asleep, the harder it will be to get him to come back to his senses. If he's in an isolation unit, it would be best to stop sedation and then stay away until he's had ample time to wake up."

"We can't leave him unmonitored," the nurse insisted. "He's not under my care, there's nothing I can do. I can call the nurses' station down there and ask them how they want to proceed."

"Please do," Hanyi said. "I am willing to help however I can if they have questions."

As she turned away, Dalton forced his attention back onto the paperwork, though he desperately wanted to ask Hanyi more about Keito's strange behavior.

"Is it dangerous for all demons to be asleep for long periods of time?" Erik asked.

"I don't know about all demons, but I know it's not good for Keito. He…loses himself a bit. And when he's in a place he doesn't recognize with people he doesn't know, it can perpetuate the problem."

"What have you done in the past when it's been a problem?" Erik asked.

"Generally, just let him wake up and be sure you're far enough away. Once he's been awake for a few minutes he regains himself."

Dalton hurriedly finished signing the paperwork and turned to Hanyi.

"He's that dangerous?"

"Think about it this way," Hanyi said. "The last thing he likely remembers is either Yokouro, Acurala, Juki, or Rutu. If he wakes up in an unfamiliar setting after that, he's going to think he's in danger."

It took all of them pressuring the nurse for information for her to tell them what floor Keito was being treated on. They went down to the second floor and to the far west side of the building, which was mostly empty and surrounded by police officers, as that was the area where criminals were treated.

"Hello," Dalton greeted, walking up to the nurses' station. "Amy called you from the third floor about Keito DeVero."

"Are you the other Guardians?" he asked.

"Yes, Keito is our teammate."

"We're waiting for either a demon Guardian or a member of the Demon Containment Unit to arrive before we halt sedation," he said. "I'm afraid I can't follow your suggestion until another demon or demon expert shows up."

"Who have you called?" Erik asked.

"We called the local Demon Containment Unit and we put a call into the DPC for an available Guardian. We did mention that it was Keito DeVero, so I'm sure that has slowed down their responses as they find someone with the qualifications to help a demon as powerful as him."

"Sanyai," Hanyi said, snapping his fingers. "Dalton, call her. She'll know what to do."

"Are you saying that you're not going to do anything for Keito until someone else shows up?" Dalton pressed the nurse.

"That is correct," he said. "You're welcome to wait here until they arrive. Or if you have someone you can call that might be able to come sooner, we can stop sedation then."

Dalton was quick to call the operators of the Dimension Protection Council and be transferred to Sanyai's personal phone. He began to explain the situation, but the moment he said that Keito was sedated, she demanded to know the hospital and floor, saying she would be there as soon as possible.

Dalton disconnected the call and turned to Hanyi.

"So this is something a lot of people know about Keito?" he asked with a quizzical eyebrow.

"People who have known Keito long enough, yes."

"Does he not sleep?"

"He catches a few hours of sleep, but he doesn't need much to keep him going through the day."

"Does he just get disoriented?"

"Something like that," Hanyi said.

About twenty minutes later, a member of the local Demon Containment Unit arrived, leading to more conversation about what was to be done when waking the demon of Team Dalton. The young man with Demon Containment was clearly relieved when Dalton said that he had called in Sanyai to help. He then stated simply that it was not a situation he knew how to handle, since their job generally entailed sedating demons that had been caught outside of the Demon Realm without permission.

Nearly an hour after the first man had arrived, Sanyai half-ran into the waiting room. Dalton remembered being surprised when he first met her because she did not immediately look like a demon. Her short brown hair and brown eyes were set into a soft face, not giving a hint of the lethal power she held.

"Dalton," she greeted, hurrying across the waiting room toward him. "Have you seen him? What's going on?"

"They're not letting us get close," Dalton said. "They said there was an incident earlier and he injured some of the hospital staff."

"Severely?"

"No."

"Do they have him restrained?"

"I don't know."

Sanyai went to the nurses' station, and once again, Team Dalton got to their feet to join her. The exhaustion was clear on their faces, and the longer they lingered waiting for news on Keito, the heavier their steps grew.

"I'm Guardian Tyien, here to advise on Keito DeVero," she said, flashing her Guardian badge to the nurses. "How long has he been sedated?"

The nurse glanced at his watch.

"His second sedation started just under four hours ago."

"Oh shit…" Hanyi groaned, turning away from the desk. Sanyai also let out a heavy sigh.

"His sedation needs to be stopped as quickly as possible. Is he restrained in any way?"

"Yes, he has demon-warded restrains on his ankles, wrists, and neck."

"Those need to come off him immediately," Sanyai insisted. "If he wakes up disoriented *and* restrained, he will become panicked, and you can be damn sure those restraints will not hold him for long."

"It's against protocol to release dangerous demons—"

"He's not dangerous. He's confused," Sanyai interrupted. "I'll be in the room with him when he wakes to be sure he does not get out before he remembers himself. But the longer you keep him sedated, the more likely he is to hurt himself or someone else. I am top-ranked Demon Guardian, and as his superior, I am telling you that I will handle him. But those drugs need to be halted, *now.*"

"Yes, ma'am."

Sanyai let out a heavy sigh, turning to Dalton as the nurse turned to call a doctor.

"Sorry about all this," she said. "It's just not good for Keito to be sedated, especially for a long period of time."

"Is that common for demons?" Erik asked, peering around the Guardians, his curiosity getting the best of him.

"It's not *un*common," she answered. "Keito's case is particularly severe, but I have seen other demons have the same problem when waking from deep sleep. And the lingering fogginess that comes with drug sedation can certainly make it worse."

"Are you going to be alright in there with him?" Hanyi asked. "He's been out for a long time."

"I'll be alright," Sanyai said. "It's safer for me to be in there than a human. And he knows me, which will help."

"Anything we can do?" Dalton asked, feeling helpless as he tried to think around his fatigue and confusion.

"No, I would just stay outside the room at first. I don't know how long it will take him to come to himself."

"Guardian Tyien?" a voice called as a female doctor peered out of the hallway. Sanyai turned and quickly walked to the doctor.

"How bad can this get?" Eclipse asked, turning to Hanyi. "Do we need to evacuate the wing?"

"It depends on how well Sanyai can contain him," Hanyi said. "The way you acted when you were an Antiquan Angel is about the same way I've seen him act, if that helps you understand better."

Dalton tried not to let the worry show on his face. He had been worried when Eclipse had been out of control as an Antiquan Angel—he could not imagine that same level of disconnect in someone as powerful as Keito.

Without thinking too much about his actions, he started walking to the hallway he knew to hold Keito's hospital room. The others immediately followed, ignoring the way the nurses called after them.

Dalton saw the doctor step out of the room, being sure the door was latched before she began walking away. She motioned for another nurse to leave the hallway before seeing Team Dalton walking toward her.

"I don't think it's a good idea to go in there," she said. "Guardian Tyien said she had it under control."

"We're not going in. We're going to wait outside."

"Please be careful," she said. "The only reason I'm not insisting you wait out there is because you're all Guardians. You might be needed if he gets out of hand again."

"Wait," Hanyi called to her as she started to pass them. "What did he do when his sedation was last stopped?"

"He woke very quickly. His system burned through the sedation faster than we anticipated. He then attacked the two orderlies and the nurse in the room with him. They came away with some gashes, but none of them are in critical condition. I told them all to file a report with the Guardian Branch, just to have a record."

"Please do," Dalton agreed. "Thank you, Doctor."

She quickly moved out of the hall as everyone approached the door, clustering as best they could to see through the small window into the hospital room. Keito was in the bed, Sanyai moving around him quickly to remove the thick chains and cuffs that had held him down. Dalton could see her lips moving, talking to Keito. Even when she had removed his restraints and stationed herself at his bedside, she continued to talk, her eyes watching Keito's face.

Dalton could not stop his startled jump when Keito suddenly turned onto his side, curling up tightly as though in pain. Sanyai stepped back, still talking, her hands raised to the other demon. After a moment of Keito remaining curled on the bed, he leapt up and grabbed Sanyai by the neck, pushing her against the wall, his growl loud enough to be heard in the hallway. The Guardians began to step forward as Erik cursed quietly, but Hanyi stopped them.

"Don't! You'll confuse him more. Sanyai's alright. She can handle herself."

It took all of Dalton's self-control to watch as Keito began to lift Sanyai off her feet. She grabbed his wrist, trying not to struggle as she continued talking.

With a slow motion that made Dalton worry Sanyai was suffocating, Keito lowered her to her feet. As his hand gently released her neck, she lunged forward and hugged him tightly. His arms wrapped around her, his head dropping to her shoulder.

Mitoki let out a long breath of relief.

"That wasn't as bad as I thought it would be."

"It's still not a good idea to go in there," Hanyi said. "I'm sure he's still groggy and confused. We should wait for Sanyai to come out and get us."

Dalton watched as Sanyai continued to hug Keito, as though comforting him, finally backing away and smiling gently. He touched her neck again, speaking quietly. As she shook her head and took his hand, he smiled, letting out a long breath that seemed to ease the tension in his shoulders. After a few more seconds of conversation, Sanyai walked to the door, smiling when she saw them through the window.

"He was wondering where you were," she said, opening the door and motioning them in. "I'm going to get the doctor. He's a little groggy, but he's alright."

They wasted no time walking into the room as Keito sat on the bed, rubbing his elbow where the IV had been placed.

"Hey," Dalton greeted awkwardly. "How are you feeling?"

"A little drunk," he admitted. "I don't know what they had me on, but it is making me very dizzy." He looked among his teammates, smiling weakly. "You're all dressed and ready to go, I see. Is everyone alright? Mitoki, what's with the bandages?"

"I'm okay," Mitoki said, gingerly touching the gauze. "They think a piece of rubble hit me in the head when the building collapsed."

"We were around a collapsing building?" he asked, both confused and mortified.

"What is the last thing you remember?" Hanyi asked.

"I remember being in the car, and the rain, and it gets a little fuzzy after that. Next thing I know, I'm here." He took a deep breath, rubbing one of his temples as he groaned. "What did Yokouro do? Why did a building collapse?"

"We'll fill you in," Dalton said. "But maybe in ten or twenty minutes when you feel a little less groggy."

"That might be best," Keito agreed.

The doctor came in, more wary than the others, but feeling safe enough to give Keito his examination under the watchful eyes of the Guardians. Keito appeared unharmed apart from his headache from the sedatives. The doctor explained that he had been found with the illegal drug in his system, which caused him to turn to his teammates in confusion.

"We'll explain," Dalton repeated.

"Are you feeling well enough to stand?" the doctor asked.

"I think so."

With Keito on his feet, the doctor had him perform a few coordination tests before saying that he could get dressed and be signed out by Dalton or Sanyai. She told him to rest and stay hydrated, and to keep an eye on his low-grade fever.

As Keito dressed, he asked the others to explain what had happened, allowing Tarrena, Sanyai, and Erik to also hear about what had transpired in the condemned building. They asked more questions than Keito did, particularly when Mitoki explained how Juki and Rutu had told them where to find the others and had given them the sleeping powder.

"Why did they help you?" Tarrena asked in surprise.

"I honestly have no idea," Dalton groaned.

"I told you," Keito said with a small laugh, straightening the shirt Erik had brought him. "You can't think of them as working for Yokouro or Vestera. They do what they want to do. We should take advantage of that while we can."

"It was thanks to them that we survived that," Hanyi agreed. "And there were times before where they would help us. It confused the hell out of us back then, too."

The Guardians finished explaining everything to Keito as they returned to the nurses' station and Dalton signed the necessary forms for Keito's release. Even though Keito was listening to what Mitoki said, he was also noting the wary eyes of the nurses and passing doctors when they spotted him.

Sanyai put a hand on his shoulder.

"It's alright," she said. "I promise."

As they were leaving the hospital, Sanyai smiled, looking over the large group.

"Need a lift home?"

"We don't want to keep you any longer than necessary," Dalton said. "I'm sure you were busy when I called you."

"Not really. Just organizing the convoy for Elder Renard's return to the Middle Dimension," she said. "Besides, I would rather make sure you get back safe and sound. I'm sure you're all exhausted and public transportation might be just a little overwhelming right now."

"I have my car, too," Erik said. "Not everyone can fit in my car, so I would have to take two trips, anyway."

"I have my rental car right over there," Sanyai said, pointing. "Let's get you boys home."

Chapter Twenty-Seven

It was Patrick's shift to stand outside the hospital room of the demon Elder, waiting for the convoy that was to come and collect him. There had been a lot of confusion about when Elder Renard was to be discharged, as the Middle Dimension wanted him back as quickly as possible, worried about the limited security of the hospital, but the doctors wanted to be certain that he was alright to travel.

Patrick just knew that he was meant to stand guard outside the door for four hours until someone came to relieve him. Nurses would occasionally step into the room to check on Elder Renard, but they would do little more than nod at the Guardian posted outside, hurrying away to continue their rounds.

When he heard several boots coming down the hall, he stepped away from the door just in time to see a collection of black-clad guards round the corner and stride toward him. He resumed his post immediately, even though he was certain they were part of the convoy meant to take Elder Renard back to the Middle Dimension.

The two in front were dressed differently from the six behind them. While those in the back had thick body armor and visors over their eyes to protect their faces, the two in front were dressed in black shirts and pants, their eyes covered with sunglasses. One of them had short black hair while the other had longer, sandy-brown hair pulled back from his face into a braid. There was no doubt in Patrick's mind that the two in front were demons, while those who trailed behind were standard Council security guards.

"Are you Guardian Patrick Donaldson?" the demon with the short, black hair asked as they approached.

"Yes."

"We are here from the DPC," he continued, extending a mass of folded papers to the Guardian. "This will release you from your protection duty so that we can take over. Please sign at the bottom of pages one, two, nineteen, and twenty-two."

Startled by the commanding nature of the demon, Patrick quickly unfolded the papers.

"The doctors said they wanted to keep him one more night."

"We spoke to the doctor just now," the demon said. "If you like, you can call him and discuss this with him. We will wait."

"What position do you hold in the DPC?" Patrick asked, looking between the two demons. "Can I see your credentials?"

The two reached into their back pockets, pulling out a laminated card and showing them to the Guardian.

"We're part of the Middle Dimension Demon Containment Unit," the dark-haired demon said. "The other Elders called us in to escort Elder Renard in case any demons attack the Elder during his travels."

"And them?"

Understanding the deeper meaning of the question, the six guards behind the demons extracted their badges, allowing Patrick to see each one of them.

"Standard DPC protection detail," the demon continued.

"I think I should call the doctor, just to be sure," Patrick said. "If you're willing to wait a little."

"We will wait. We understand that you want to be sure the Elder is in the right hands."

Something about the statement made Patrick feel uneasy.

"I'll just go speak with the Elder briefly and call the doctor. He should be here soon and then we can get this going," he said, ducking into the hospital room to tell the demon Elder about the detail that had come to collect him.

"You know," the demon with the longer hair started, "if you had just disguised me as a human as well, he probably wouldn't be so hesitant to release him."

Juki laughed, turning to Rutu.

"But there is no guarantee they would release Demetrius to humans, even disguised as DPC employees. Demons need demon protection, particularly after his recent abduction."

"I am clearly out of place here," Rutu insisted. "Did you hear that young woman in the lobby? She clearly said, 'oh, I love her hair.'"

Juki barked a laugh. "You do have good hair."

"She thought I was a woman."

"Maybe, but it's not the first time someone has questioned your sex."

"Don't be an ass," Rutu said with a chuckle. "Long hair does not immediately mean female. The bulging biceps should at least clue some people in."

"I wouldn't say *bulging*," Juki said, casting an eye over Rutu.

"Don't make me hurt you," Rutu said, smiling thinly. "You have more than enough power to disguise me properly, but you choose to leave me looking like this."

"I did cover up your power limiters. You're not obviously an Old Blood. This is all strategic. Trust me."

322

The door to the hospital room opened and Guardian Donaldson walked out, looking perplexed. Rutu could sense that he was worried about signing over Elder Renard, but also knew that there was no reason for him to protest keeping him in the hospital.

"The doctor said he would be right up. There should be some nurses coming to get him ready and give him his treatments."

"Very good," Juki said.

Patrick was very unsettled by the eight black-clad individuals in the hallway with him. The nurses and other hospital staff also did their best to avoid them, sticking as close to the walls as possible when they had to pass, casting nervous glances at the group. Juki and Rutu stood, unconcerned and confident, waiting for the doctor.

Two nurses slipped into the room to give the Elder his prescriptions and get him ready for transfer. They had been in there for two minutes when the doctor also approached.

"Ah, yes," he said, nodding and turning to Patrick. "This is the group that the DPC sent over. Guardian Sanyai Tyien arranged for the transport. The hospital called her, confirmed everything, and they were let in."

"I thought you wanted to keep him one more night," Patrick insisted.

"Elder Renard has requested to be returned to the Middle Dimension. He is worried about being attacked again," the doctor said. "That is why the DPC also sent to demons from the Demon Containment Unit to escort him. Thank you for double-checking, Guardian Donaldson, but I assure you, this is all above board."

"...thank you, Doctor," Patrick said slowly, still uneasy despite the constant reassurances. There was something about the powerful aura that surrounded the two demons that made him uneasy. As the doctor left, Patrick jerked his head back over his shoulder at the room. "I'll go retrieve him."

"Thank you," Juki said.

The six Kage guards behind the two lords were accustomed to being assigned strange tasks by their Old Blood Lords, but even they were uncomfortable being stared at by the humans that passed through the hallways. They were becoming fidgety, though one quick glance from Juki made them go still as he silently reminded them to keep their composure.

The door opened yet again and Elder Renard was guided into the hall. When his eyes fell on Juki and Rutu, his brief hesitation was hardly noticed. He turned to Patrick and smiled.

"Thank you, Guardian Donaldson," he said.

"We just need you to sign those release papers," Juki reminded Patrick, nodding to the large stack of papers in his hand. Borrowing a pen from one of the nurses, Patrick signed the forms, watching as Elder Renard approached Rutu.

"I'm confused why you're here," he whispered, too quiet for the humans to hear.

"Not to worry. We're returning you to your post," Rutu assured in the same near-silent tone.

Juki took the papers from Patrick and thanked him once more before nodding to the guards, who fell into easy formation around the three demons, leading them toward the elevator and finally out of one of the back doors of the hospital, as was common procedure.

Three large vans stood near the door, the middle one already manned with one disguised demon guard next to the open side door. Elder Renard stepped inside, Juki climbing in after him as Rutu went to the driver's seat, the rest of the guards dispersing to the various vehicles in the convoy.

"Your return will certainly cause a stir in Council," Juki said as the door was closed and Rutu started up the engine. He removed his glasses and ran a hand through his short hair, causing it to grow rapidly in length, the intricate braids weaving together as his eyes lightened to their typical violet and his face changed to his normal shape.

"Why did you come here yourselves if you're not here to take me captive again?" Elder Renard asked. "Why not just let me die in that explosion?"

"That had been a consideration," Rutu said over his shoulder.

"We decided you were of more use to us alive than dead," Juki elaborated. "Yokouro wants you dead because you're no longer obedient. Needless to say, he is not pleased that you have survived, but we can keep him off your back for a while."

"At what cost?"

"Fall in line," Juki said. "Follow orders. Stop trying to fight them. And, when you feel you cannot follow the orders, you call me."

Elder Renard stared into Juki's eyes, trying to read the demon lord's true intentions, though Juki was too practiced to let his expression slip.

"That will not keep Yokouro from killing me," Elder Renard finally said. "And I cannot just stand by and watch—"

"You're not standing by," Juki interrupted. "You're working for Yokouro because you're working for *me*."

Elder Renard backed away in his seat, confused.

"You have never wanted eyes in the Elders before," he noted. "I remember you even saying that the Elders were just talking heads at the top of a heap of lunatics and morons."

"And they are," Juki agreed. "But even DPC demons know more about what is going on than humans, and they're likely to run their mouths. You are going to be sure that they keep their damn mouths shut."

"They just want to warn the humans. All the changes in power in the Demon Realm, your brother being resurrected, your father—"

"There is a reason we are not supposed to talk about the Old Blood Lords outside of the realm," Juki interrupted, nearly growling as he leaned closer to the Elder. "Once the information is out to the public, they can never go back to that ignorant bliss, which means we're giving Yokouro more fuel for this moronic war he wants to start. We are going to curb that the best we can, and the way to do that is to have a demon in a superior place of power telling other demons to keep quiet."

"Are you trying to help or sabotage Yokouro?" Elder Renard whispered.

"Neither," Juki said. "We outrank Yokouro. If you want me to keep you from dying in some horrifically painful way at Yokouro's hand, you'll do what I say. You work for me, now."

There were many surprises waiting for the Guardians when they returned to the Retani house, the first of which was Eclipse's car parked safely in the driveway.

"At least they returned your car," Dalton said as he stepped out of Sanyai's car. Eclipse hurried up the driveway and looked over the vehicle, being sure it was not damaged. He plucked the folded note under the wiper.

"*Filled the fuel tank. Nice car. Rutu.*" He looked over his car, shaking his head. "For some reason, it really disturbs me to think of him driving my car."

The second surprise came after they had been enthusiastically greeted by Saki, Jikia, and Master Genbuki.

"This is going to sound very strange, but someone delivered your guns early this morning," Jikia said, motioning them to the living room where the guns had been put on the coffee table. They had clearly been thoroughly cleaned. Dalton grabbed his gun, looking it over, confused by the oddly-kind gesture.

They were confined to the living room until all details of their abduction and escape had been thoroughly discussed and questioned, leaving the Guardians exhausted to the point where they hardly remembered climbing into bed that night.

The following morning, Dalton received a call from the office of the Elders saying that Elder Renard had been safely returned to the DPC compound, though they wanted the members of Team Dalton to file their own reports about the Elder's rescue.

Deciding to take one more day of rest at the Retani house, the Guardians prepared to return to the Middle Dimension for paperwork, before finally heading home for some much-needed recuperation.

Even after resting, they found it difficult to focus on the amount of paperwork and reports they had to file about the Elder's rescue. They sat at one of the round tables in the filing office, asking how they should describe the involvement of Juki and Rutu, and how they should refer to Yokouro.

Paperwork done, they sat together in the mess hall of the Guardian Building, which was mostly empty at that point in the day, and lightly chatted about what they were going to do on their two-month break between rounds.

"I'm worried that Yokouro will try to go after us individually," Eclipse noted. "He really did not give us any time to breathe during this round of the tournament."

"I think that was his plan, though," Keito said. "Push us as hard as he thought he could so that he could see where our limits were. Besides, I'm sure he needs some time to sort out other affairs. Even though he's going after us, he's a busy demon, particularly if he's going to be a full-time Old Blood Lord again."

"What about Juki and Rutu?" Mitoki asked.

"They're even busier than Yokouro," Keito said. "And considering what they did for us, I don't think they want to harm us. I think we can relax a little and take some time to catch our breath."

"Good, because I'm going to need to sleep for the entire two months," Hanyi groaned, flopping dramatically to the table next to his empty tray.

"Two months seems like such a short time now," Mitoki agreed.

"Actually, I was wondering if I could ask a favor of all of you," Dalton said, grinning. "My daughter's birthday is just before the third round of the tournament, and she has been begging me to bring all of you to celebrate her birthday. We always take a couple days and go up to my lake cabin and she really wants you to join."

"She wants a bunch of Guardians at her birthday party?" Eclipse asked skeptically.

"She's dying to meet you," Dalton laughed. "She wants to know who I'm spending so much time with. She's also watched a few highlight segments of the tournament and thinks that you four are the coolest people in all five worlds."

"Well, she's not wrong," Hanyi said with a grin.

"Would you guys be willing to meet earlier than usual to go on this vacation with my family?" Dalton asked. "It would mean the world to her."

"Oh, well, when you put it like *that*," Mitoki said. "How are we supposed to break a six-year-old's heart?"

"I don't know how much fun she's going to have with a bunch of Guardians around, but sure," Eclipse agreed.

"Of course," Hanyi said. "It would actually be nice to spend time with everyone outside of the case. We can bond better."

"Theresa will be so happy. Then we'll meet a week earlier than usual. I better call Jikia and Tarrena to tell them."

"Five Guardians and two dragons," Keito laughed. "That will be a birthday party to remember."

"I am still convinced we should kill him," Yokouro said, leaning back in his desk chair with a heavy sigh.

"None of us have time to monitor or manipulate a new demon Elder appointment," Juki said, standing in front of Yokouro's desk with Rutu. "We gave him his orders and he knows that if he wants to keep breathing, he has to fall in line."

"A lot of good that's done me so far," Yokouro grumbled.

"The order came from me this time," Juki said. "Trust me, he'll follow through."

"Ah, yes, because the great Juki Kage never has a lapse in judgment," Yokouro quipped.

"Watch it, Yokouro," Rutu warned. "We have warned you time and time again that you're stretching yourself too thin. That's why the spell is starting to crumble and why you're scrambling to get a handle on the Elders again. If you don't like the solutions we offer, don't ask for our help."

Yokouro leaned his head back on his chair, sighing.

"What's wrong with you?" Juki asked. "The mark still bothering you?"

"Yes," Yokouro said. "But my moronic family is also kicking up a fuss. Something about tradition, and honor, and all those other ideals they try to use against me."

"I did not realize your brothers were upset about your return to power," Juki said.

"They don't care so much about that, but they're warning me that if I start making too many waves, my sister is going to become a problem."

"And that worries you?" Juki asked, still confused by Yokouro's irritation.

"No, she's the weakest in the family. But if she decides to go after Dalton behind my back, it would be a problem. And what's worse is I can't eliminate her without…" He rubbed a hand over his neck, reminded immediately of the excruciating pain that came with a cursed mark for the spilled blood of a family member. "I sent Acurala out to track her down."

"You didn't ask him to kill her, did you?" Juki asked, his tone firm. "Because I cannot have anyone in my bloodline killing a royal member of the DeVastes Clan. You know that."

"I told him not to kill her. I'm not an idiot," Yokouro said. "But I need to find some way to eliminate her. Force her to break some law where I can order her execution."

"You have no proof she'll interfere," Rutu said. "Just keep a watch over her. That should be enough. Don't rush into having her killed. That could turn the rest of your clan against you."

"They won't turn against me," Yokouro said. "I scare them too much."

"Then don't make things harder for Kakuri," Rutu added. "Your time is already split too much between the Guardians and your duties as an Old Blood Lord. Not to mention your commitments on the Antiqua-Kel plane. You don't have to do everything yourself. Distribute tasks among those you trust. We've taught you this."

"Yes, but my people aren't as efficient as your people."

"Then you need to get new people," Juki said.

"Maybe you'll have better luck with this than my spy had," Yokouro said, snatching a piece of paper from his desk and extending it to Juki. "I'm trying to find this woman, but none of my people have any leads."

Juki glanced at the name and stilled.

"Shannon Marrone?"

Yokouro smirked. "Dalton's mother. Since I've already met his father, I think it's time I had a formal meeting with her."

To Be Continued...

Dimension Guardian: Realm of Humans
Fate

More Works by K.J. Amidon | Kyra Anderson

The Dimension Guardian Series:
The Realm of Beasts – The Guardian Tournament
The Realm of Darkness – Blind Ambitions
The Realm of Humans – Fate
The Realm of Light – Imbalance
The Realm of Demons – Scars in Time
The Realm of Exile – Continuum

The Roadside Paradise Series:
Into Oblivion
Wander the Lost
Until Dawn Breaks
Hiding from Sight
For Fools
Challenge Gods

Inside
(Written as Kyra Anderson)
Inside – Pt. 1
Inside – Pt. 2
Inside – Pt. 3
Inside – Alternate Pt. 3
Inside the Commission: Tales from Within
Inside Special Expanded Edition

The Significant
(Written as Kyra Anderson)

The Significant Expanded Story:
(Written as Kyra Anderson)
The Degenerates
The Deserted

The Faith Series:
(Written as Kyra Anderson)
The Faith
The Sacred

The Coalition Series:
(Written as Kyra Anderson)
Forged Under Fire
The Rising Tide
With Banners Raised

www.ingramcontent.com/pod-product-compliance
Lightning Source LLC
Chambersburg PA
CBHW030637020726
47493CB00006B/1748